PRAISE FOR MADELINE MILLER'S

CIRCE

"*Circe* is a bold and subversive retelling of the goddess's story that manages to be both epic and intimate in its scope, recasting the most infamous female figure from *The Odyssey* as a hero in her own right."
— Alexandra Alter, *New York Times*

"One of the most amazing qualities of this novel is: we know how everything here turns out — we've known it for thousands of years — and yet in Miller's lush reimagining, the story feels harrowing and unexpected. The feminist light she shines on these events never distorts their original shape; it only illuminates details we hadn't noticed before."
— Ron Charles, *Washington Post*

"An epic spanning thousands of years that's also a keep-you-up-all-night page-turner."
— Ann Patchett, author of *Commonwealth*

"Miller's spell builds slowly, but by the last page you'll be in awe. In prose of dreamlike simplicity, she reimagines the myth of Circe."
— *People*

"Miller gives voice to Circe as a multifaceted and evolving character...*Circe* is very pleasurable to read, combining lively versions of familiar tales and snippets of other, related

standards with a highly psychologized, redemptive, and ultimately exculpatory account of the protagonist herself."
— Claire Messud, *New York Times Book Review*

"The story of Circe's entanglement with Odysseus lasts far beyond the narrative of *The Odyssey*, making for compelling material to revisit. But ultimately it's as a character that Circe stands apart...Through her elegant, psychologically acute prose, Miller gives us a rich female character who inhabits the spaces in between."
— Colleen Abel, *Minneapolis Star Tribune*

"Miller, with her academic bona fides and born instinct for storytelling, seamlessly grafts modern concepts of selfhood and independence to her mystical reveries of smoke and silver, nectar and bones."
— Leah Greenblatt, *Entertainment Weekly*

"*Circe* is the utterly captivating, exquisitely written story of an ordinary, and extraordinary, woman's life."
— Eimear McBride, author of
A Girl Is a Half-Formed Thing

"Miller's lush, gold-lit novel — told from the perspective of the witch whose name in Greek has echoes of a hawk and a weaver's shuttle — paints another picture: of a fierce goddess who, yes, turns men into pigs, but only because they deserve it."
— Annalisa Quinn, NPR.org

"Spellbinding...Miller has created a daring feminist take on a classic narrative; although the setting is a mystical world of gods, monsters, and nymphs, the protagonist at its heart is like any of us."
— Tayari Jones, O, *The Oprah Magazine*

Circe is also a smart read that has much to say about the long-term consequences of war and a culture that values violence and conquest over compassion and learning... Miller mines intriguing details from the original tale to imagine a rich backstory for Circe that allows readers to revisit the world of Olympians and Titans in Greek mythology. From the court of the Titans, the reader meets Circe's parents, the god Helios and nymph Perse, and is introduced to a world of supernatural power players that is every bit as backbiting, gossip-filled, and vicious as any episode of *House of Cards*." — May-lee Chai, *Dallas Morning News*

"With lyric beauty of language and melancholy evocative of Keats's 'Ode on a Grecian Urn,' *Circe* asks all the big questions of existence while framing them in the life story of the famous goddess who had the magic of transformations. A veritable who's who of the gods of Olympus and the heroes of ancient Greece — Circe knows them all and we see them through her perceptive eyes. This is as close as you will ever come to entering the world of mythology as a participant. Stunning, touching, and unique."

— Margaret George, author of
The Confessions of Young Nero

"*Circe* bears its own transformative magic, a power enabled by Miller's keen eye for beauty, adventure, and reinvention. Through the charms of a misfit heroine, the world of gods becomes stunningly alive, and the world of our own humanity — its questions, loves, and bonds — is illuminated. This book is an immense gift to anyone who reads to find their own bravery and quest."

— Affinity Konar, author of *Mischling*

CIRCE

ALSO BY MADELINE MILLER

The Song of Achilles

CIRCE

A NOVEL

MADELINE MILLER

BACK BAY BOOKS
Little, Brown and Company
NEW YORK BOSTON LONDON

Copyright © 2018 by Madeline Miller

Back Bay Books / Little, Brown and Company
Hachette Book Group
1290 Avenue of the Americas, New York, NY 10104
littlebrown.com

The publisher is not responsible for websites (or their content) that are not owned by the publisher.

Printed in the United States of America

Originally published in hardcover by Little, Brown and Company, April 2018
First Back Bay international mass market edition, April 2019
First Back Bay paperback edition, April 2019

10 9 8 7 6 5

For Nathaniel
νόστος

CIRCE

CHAPTER ONE

WHEN I WAS BORN, the name for what I was did not exist. They called me nymph, assuming I would be like my mother and aunts and thousand cousins. Least of the lesser goddesses, our powers were so modest they could scarcely ensure our eternities. We spoke to fish and nurtured flowers, coaxed drops from the clouds or salt from the waves. That word, *nymph*, paced out the length and breadth of our futures. In our language, it means not just goddess, but *bride*.

My mother was one of them, a naiad, guardian of fountains and streams. She caught my father's eye when he came to visit the halls of her own father, Oceanos. Helios and Oceanos were often at each other's tables in those days. They were cousins, and equal in age, though they did not look it. My father glowed bright as just-forged bronze, while Oceanos had been born with rheumy eyes and a white beard to his lap. Yet they were both Titans, and preferred each other's company to those new-squeaking gods upon Olympus who had not seen the making of the world.

Oceanos' palace was a great wonder, set deep in the earth's rock. Its high-arched halls were gilded, the stone floors smoothed by centuries of divine feet. Through every room ran the faint sound of Oceanos' river, source of the world's fresh waters, so dark you could not tell where it ended and the rock-bed began. On its banks grew grass and soft gray flowers, and also the unnumbered children of Oceanos, naiads and nymphs and river-gods. Otter-sleek, laughing, their faces bright against the dusky air, they passed golden goblets among themselves and wrestled, playing games of love. In their midst, outshining all that lily beauty, sat my mother.

Her hair was a warm brown, each strand so lustrous it seemed lit from within. She would have felt my father's gaze, hot as gusts from a bonfire. I see her arrange her dress so it drapes just so over her shoulders. I see her dab her fingers, glinting, in the water. I have seen her do a thousand such tricks a thousand times. My father always fell for them. He believed the world's natural order was to please him.

"Who is that?" my father said to Oceanos.

Oceanos had many golden-eyed grandchildren from my father already, and was glad to think of more. "My daughter Perse. She is yours if you want her."

The next day, my father found her by her fountain-pool in the upper world. It was a beautiful place, crowded with fat-headed narcissus, woven over with oak branches. There was no muck, no slimy frogs, only clean, round stones giving way to grass. Even my father, who cared nothing for the subtleties of nymph arts, admired it.

My mother knew he was coming. Frail she was, but crafty, with a mind like a spike-toothed eel. She saw where the path to power lay for such as her, and it was not in bastards and riverbank tumbles. When he stood before her, arrayed in his glory, she laughed at him. *Lie with you? Why should I?*

My father, of course, might have taken what he wanted.

But Helios flattered himself that all women went eager to his bed, slave girls and divinities alike. His altars smoked with the proof, offerings from big-bellied mothers and happy by-blows.

"It is marriage," she said to him, "or nothing. And if it is marriage, be sure: you may have what girls you like in the field, but you will bring none home, for only I will hold sway in your halls."

Conditions, constrainment. These were novelties to my father, and gods love nothing more than novelty. "A bargain," he said, and gave her a necklace to seal it, one of his own making, strung with beads of rarest amber. Later, when I was born, he gave her a second strand, and another for each of my three siblings. I do not know which she treasured more: the luminous beads themselves or the envy of her sisters when she wore them. I think she would have gone right on collecting them into eternity until they hung from her neck like a yoke on an ox if the high gods had not stopped her. By then they had learned what the four of us were. You may have other children, they told her, only not with him. But other husbands did not give amber beads. It was the only time I ever saw her weep.

At my birth, an aunt — I will spare you her name because my tale is full of aunts — washed and wrapped me. Another tended to my mother, painting the red back on her lips, brushing her hair with ivory combs. A third went to the door to admit my father.

"A girl," my mother said to him, wrinkling her nose.

But my father did not mind his daughters, who were sweet-tempered and golden as the first press of olives. Men and gods paid dearly for the chance to breed from their blood, and my father's treasury was said to rival that of the king of the gods himself. He placed his hand on my head in blessing.

"She will make a fair match," he said.

"How fair?" my mother wanted to know. This might be consolation, if I could be traded for something better.

My father considered, fingering the wisps of my hair, examining my eyes and the cut of my cheeks.

"A prince, I think."

"A prince?" my mother said. "You do not mean a mortal?"

The revulsion was plain on her face. Once when I was young I asked what mortals looked like. My father said, "You may say they are shaped like us, but only as the worm is shaped like the whale."

My mother had been simpler: *like savage bags of rotten flesh.*

"Surely she will marry a son of Zeus," my mother insisted. She had already begun imagining herself at feasts upon Olympus, sitting at Queen Hera's right hand.

"No. Her hair is streaked like a lynx. And her chin. There is a sharpness to it that is less than pleasing."

My mother did not argue further. Like everyone, she knew the stories of Helios' temper when he was crossed. *However gold he shines, do not forget his fire.*

She stood. Her belly was gone, her waist reknitted, her cheeks fresh and virgin-rosy. All our kind recover quickly, but she was faster still, one of the daughters of Oceanos, who shoot their babes like roe.

"Come," she said. "Let us make a better one."

I grew quickly. My infancy was the work of hours, my toddlerhood a few moments beyond that. An aunt stayed on hoping to curry favor with my mother and named me *Hawk,* Circe, for my yellow eyes, and the strange, thin sound of my crying. But when she realized that my mother no more noticed her service than the ground at her feet, she vanished.

"Mother," I said, "Aunt is gone."

My mother didn't answer. My father had already departed for his chariot in the sky, and she was winding her hair with flowers, preparing to leave through the secret ways of water, to join her sisters on their grassy riverbanks. I might have followed, but then I would have had to sit all day at my aunts' feet while they gossiped of things I did not care for and could not understand. So I stayed.

My father's halls were dark and silent. His palace was a neighbor to Oceanos', buried in the earth's rock, and its walls were made of polished obsidian. Why not? They could have been anything in the world, blood-red marble from Egypt or balsam from Araby, my father had only to wish it so. But he liked the way the obsidian reflected his light, the way its slick surfaces caught fire as he passed. Of course, he did not consider how black it would be when he was gone. My father has never been able to imagine the world without himself in it.

I could do what I liked at those times: light a torch and run to see the dark flames follow me. Lie on the smooth earth floor and wear small holes in its surface with my fingers. There were no grubs or worms, though I didn't know to miss them. Nothing lived in those halls, except for us.

When my father returned at night, the ground rippled like the flank of a horse, and the holes I had made smoothed themselves over. A moment later my mother returned, smelling of flowers. She ran to greet him, and he let her hang from his neck, accepted wine, went to his great silver chair. I followed at his heels. *Welcome home, Father, welcome home.*

While he drank his wine, he played draughts. No one

was allowed to play with him. He placed the stone counters, spun the board, and placed them again. My mother
drenched her voice in honey. "Will you not come to bed,
my love?" She turned before him slowly, showing the lushness of her figure as if she were roasting on a spit. Most
often he would leave his game then, but sometimes he
did not, and those were my favorite times, for my mother
would go, slamming the myrrh-wood door behind her.

At my father's feet, the whole world was made of gold.
The light came from everywhere at once, his yellow skin,
his lambent eyes, the bronze flashing of his hair. His flesh
was hot as a brazier, and I pressed as close as he would let
me, like a lizard to noonday rocks. My aunt had said that
some of the lesser gods could scarcely bear to look at him,
but I was his daughter and blood, and I stared at his face so
long that when I looked away it was pressed upon my vision
still, glowing from the floors, the shining walls and inlaid
tables, even my own skin.

"What would happen," I said, "if a mortal saw you in
your fullest glory?"

"He would be burned to ash in a second."

"What if a mortal saw me?"

My father smiled. I listened to the draught pieces moving, the familiar rasp of marble against wood. "The mortal
would count himself fortunate."

"I would not burn him?"

"Of course not," he said.

"But my eyes are like yours."

"No," he said. "Look." His gaze fell upon a log at the
fireplace's side. It glowed, then flamed, then fell as ash to
the ground. "And that is the least of my powers. Can you
do as much?"

All night I stared at those logs. I could not.

* * *

My sister was born, and my brother soon after that. I cannot say how long it was exactly. Divine days fall like water from a cataract, and I had not learned yet the mortal trick of counting them. You'd think my father would have taught us better, for he, after all, knows every sunrise. But even he used to call my brother and sister twins. Certainly, from the moment of my brother's birth, they were entwined like minks. My father blessed them both with one hand. "You," he said to my luminous sister Pasiphaë. "You will marry an eternal son of Zeus." He used his prophecy voice, the one that spoke of future certainties. My mother glowed to hear it, thinking of the robes she would wear to Zeus' feasts.

"And you," he said to my brother, in his regular voice, resonant, clear as a summer's morning. "Every son reflects upon his mother." My mother was pleased with this, and took it as permission to name him. She called him Perses, for herself.

The two of them were clever and quickly saw how things stood. They loved to sneer at me behind their ermine paws. *Her eyes are yellow as piss. Her voice is screechy as an owl. She is called Hawk, but she should be called Goat for her ugliness.*

Those were their earliest attempts at barbs, still dull, but day by day they sharpened. I learned to avoid them, and they soon found better sport among the infant naiads and river-lords in Oceanos' halls. When my mother went to her sisters, they followed and established dominion over all our pliant cousins, hypnotized like minnows before the pike's mouth. They had a hundred tormenting games that they devised. *Come, Melia,* they coaxed. *It is the Olympian fashion to cut off your hair to the nape of your neck. How*

will you ever catch a husband if you don't let us do it?
When Melia saw herself shorn like a hedgehog and cried,
they would laugh till the caverns echoed.

I left them to it. I preferred my father's quiet halls and
spent every second I could at my father's feet. One day, perhaps as a reward, he offered to take me with him to visit his
sacred herd of cows. This was a great honor, for it meant I
might ride in his golden chariot and see the animals that
were the envy of all the gods, fifty pure-white heifers that
delighted his eye on his daily path over the earth. I leaned
over the chariot's jeweled side, watching in wonder at the
earth passing beneath: the rich green of forests, the jagged
mountains, and the wide out-flung blue of the ocean. I
looked for mortals, but we were too high up to see them.

The herd lived on the grassy island of Thrinakia with
two of my half-sisters as caretakers. When we arrived these
sisters ran at once to my father and hung from his neck, exclaiming. Of all my father's beautiful children, they were
among the most beautiful, with skin and hair like molten
gold. Lampetia and Phaethousa, their names were. *Radiant* and *Shining*.

"And who is this you have brought with you?"

"She must be one of Perse's children, look at her eyes."

"Of   course!"   Lampetia — I   thought   it   was
Lampetia — stroked my hair. "Darling, your eyes are nothing to worry about. Nothing at all. Your mother is very
beautiful, but she has never been strong."

"My eyes are like yours," I said.

"How sweet! No, darling, ours are bright as fire, and our
hair like sun on the water."

"You're clever to keep yours in a braid," Phaethousa
said. "The brown streaking does not look so bad then. It is
a shame you cannot hide your voice the same way."

"She could never speak again. That would work, would it not, sister?"

"So it would." They smiled. "Shall we go to see the cows?"

I had never seen a cow before, of any kind, but it did not matter: the animals were so obviously beautiful that I needed no comparison. Their coats were pure as lily petals and their eyes gentle and long-lashed. Their horns had been gilded — that was my sisters' doing — and when they bent to crop the grass, their necks dipped like dancers. In the sunset light, their backs gleamed glossy-soft.

"Oh!" I said. "May I touch one?"

"No," my father said.

"Shall we tell you their names? That is White-face, and that is Bright-eyes, and that Darling. There is Lovely Girl and Pretty and Golden-horn and Gleaming. There is Darling and there is — "

"You named Darling already," I said. "You said that one was Darling." I pointed to the first cow, peacefully chewing.

My sisters looked at each other, then at my father, a single golden glance. But he was gazing at his cows in abstracted glory.

"You must be mistaken," they said. "This one we just said is Darling. And this one is Star-bright and this one Flashing and — "

My father said, "What is this? A scab upon Pretty?"

Immediately my sisters were falling over themselves. "What scab? Oh, it cannot be! Oh, wicked Pretty, to have hurt yourself. Oh, wicked thing, that hurt you!"

I leaned close to see. It was a very small scab, smaller than my smallest fingernail, but my father was frowning. "You will fix it by tomorrow."

My sisters bobbed their heads, *of course, of course. We are so sorry.*

We stepped again into the chariot and my father took up the silver-tipped reins. My sisters pressed a last few kisses to his hands, then the horses leapt, swinging us through the sky. The first constellations were already peeping through the dimming light.

I remembered how my father had once told me that on earth there were men called astronomers whose task it was to keep track of his rising and setting. They were held in highest esteem among mortals, kept in palaces as counselors of kings, but sometimes my father lingered over one thing or another and threw their calculations into despair. Then those astronomers were hauled before the kings they served and killed as frauds. My father had smiled when he told me. It was what they deserved, he said. Helios the Sun was bound to no will but his own, and none might say what he would do.

"Father," I said that day, "are we late enough to kill astronomers?"

"We are," he answered, shaking the jingling reins. The horses surged forward, and the world blurred beneath us, the shadows of night smoking from the sea's edge. I did not look. There was a twisting feeling in my chest, like cloth being wrung dry. I was thinking of those astronomers. I imagined them, low as worms, sagging and bent. Please, they cried, on bony knees, it wasn't our fault, the sun itself was late.

The sun is never late, the kings answered from their thrones. It is blasphemy to say so, you must die! And so the axes fell and chopped those pleading men in two.

"Father," I said, "I feel strange."

"You are hungry," he said. "It is past time for the feast. Your sisters should be ashamed of themselves for delaying us."

I ate well at dinner, yet the feeling lingered. I must have had an odd look on my face, for Perses and Pasiphaë began to snicker from their couch. "Did you swallow a frog?"

"No," I said.

This only made them laugh harder, rubbing their draped limbs on each other like snakes polishing their scales. My sister said, "And how were our father's golden heifers?"

"Beautiful."

Perses laughed. "She doesn't know! Have you ever heard of anyone so stupid?"

"Never," my sister said.

I shouldn't have asked, but I was still drifting in my thoughts, seeing those severed bodies sprawled on marble floors. "What don't I know?"

My sister's perfect mink face. "That he fucks them, of course. That's how he makes new ones. He turns into a bull and sires their calves, then cooks the ones that get old. That's why everyone thinks they are immortal."

"He does not."

They howled, pointing at my reddened cheeks. The sound drew my mother. She loved my siblings' japes.

"We're telling Circe about the cows," my brother told her. "She didn't know."

My mother's laughter, silver as a fountain down its rocks. "Stupid Circe."

Such were my years then. I would like to say that all the while I waited to break out, but the truth is, I'm afraid I might have floated on, believing those dull miseries were all there was, until the end of days.

CHAPTER TWO

WORD CAME THAT ONE of my uncles was going to be punished. I had never seen him, but I had heard his name over and over in my family's doomy whispers. *Prometheus.* Long ago, when mankind was still shivering and shrinking in their caves, he had defied the will of Zeus and brought them the gift of fire. From its flames had sprung all the arts and profits of civilization that jealous Zeus had hoped to keep from their hands. For such rebellion Prometheus had been sent to live in the underworld's deepest pit until a proper torment could be devised. And now Zeus announced the time was come.

My other uncles ran to my father's palace, beards flapping, fears spilling from their mouths. They were a motley group: river-men with muscles like the trunks of trees, brine-soaked mer-gods with crabs hanging from their beards, stringy old-timers with seal meat in their teeth. Most of them were not uncles at all, but some sort of grandcousin. They were Titans like my father and grandfather, like Prometheus, the remnants of the war among the gods. Those who were not broken or in chains, who had made their peace with Zeus' thunderbolts.

There had only been Titans once, at the dawning of the world. Then my great-uncle Kronos had heard a prophecy that his child would one day overthrow him. When his wife, Rhea, birthed her first babe, he tore it damp from her arms and swallowed it whole. Four more children were born, and he ate them all the same, until at last, in desperation, Rhea swaddled a stone and gave it to him to swallow instead. Kronos was deceived, and the rescued baby, Zeus, was taken to Mount Dicte to be raised in secret. When he was grown he rose up indeed, plucking the thunderbolt from the sky and forcing poisonous herbs down his father's throat. His brothers and sisters, living in their father's stomach, were vomited forth. They sprang to their brother's side, naming themselves Olympians after the great peak where they set their thrones.

The old gods divided themselves. Many threw their strength to Kronos, but my father and grandfather joined Zeus. Some said it was because Helios had always hated Kronos' vaunting pride; others whispered that his prophetic gift gave him foreknowledge of the outcome of the war. The battles rent the skies: the air itself burned, and gods clawed the flesh from each other's bones. The land was drenched in boiling gouts of blood so potent that rare flowers sprang up where they fell. At last Zeus' strength prevailed. He clapped those who had defied him into chains, and the remaining Titans he stripped of their powers, bestowing them on his brothers and sisters and the children he had bred. My uncle Nereus, once the mighty ruler of the sea, was now lackey to its new god, Poseidon. My uncle Proteus lost his palace, and his wives were taken for bed-slaves. Only my father and grandfather suffered no diminishment, no loss of place.

The Titans sneered. Were they supposed to be grateful?

Helios and Oceanos had turned the tide of war, everyone
knew it. Zeus should have loaded them with new powers,
new appointments, but he was afraid, for their strength already matched his own. They looked to my father, waiting
for his protest, the flaring of his great fire. But Helios only
returned to his halls beneath the earth, far from Zeus' sky-
bright gaze.

Centuries had passed. The earth's wounds had healed
and the peace had held. But the grudges of gods are as
deathless as their flesh, and on feast nights my uncles gathered close at my father's side. I loved the way they lowered
their eyes when they spoke to him, the way they went silent
and attentive when he shifted in his seat. The wine-bowls
emptied and the torches waned. It has been long enough,
my uncles whispered. We are strong again. Think what
your fire might do if you set it free. You are the greatest
of the old blood, greater even than Oceanos. Greater than
Zeus himself, if only you wish it.

My father smiled. "Brothers," he said, "what talk is this?
Is there not smoke and savor for all? This Zeus does well
enough."

Zeus, if he had heard, would have been satisfied. But he
could not see what I saw, plain on my father's face. Those
unspoken, hanging words.

This Zeus does well enough, *for now.*

My uncles rubbed their hands and smiled back. They
went away, bent over their hopes, thinking what they could
not wait to do when Titans ruled again.

It was my first lesson. Beneath the smooth, familiar face
of things is another that waits to tear the world in two.

Now my uncles were crowding into my father's hall, eyes
rolling in fear. Prometheus' sudden punishment was a sign,

they said, that Zeus and his kind were moving against us at last. The Olympians would never be truly happy until they destroyed us utterly. We should stand with Prometheus, or no, we should speak against him, to ward off Zeus' thunderstroke from our own heads.

I was in my customary place at my father's feet. I lay silent so they would not notice and send me away, but I felt my chest roiling with that overwhelming possibility: the war revived. Our halls blasted wide with thunderbolts. Athena, Zeus' warrior daughter, hunting us down with her gray spear, her brother in slaughter, Ares, by her side. We would be chained and cast into fiery pits from which there was no escape.

My father spoke calm and golden at their center: "Come, brothers, if Prometheus is to be punished, it is only because he has earned it. Let us not chase after conspiracy."

But my uncles fretted on. *The punishment is to be public. It is an insult, a lesson they teach us. Look what happens to Titans who do not obey.*

My father's light had taken on a keen, white edge. "This is the chastisement of a renegade and no more. Prometheus was led astray by his foolish love for mortals. There is no lesson here for a Titan. Do you understand?"

My uncles nodded. On their faces, disappointment braided with relief. No blood, *for now.*

The punishment of a god was a rare and terrible thing, and talk ran wild through our halls. Prometheus could not be killed, but there were many hellish torments that could take death's place. Would it be knives or swords, or limbs torn off? Red-hot spikes or a wheel of fire? The naiads swooned into each other's laps. The river-lords postured, faces dark with excitement. You cannot know how frightened gods are of pain. There is nothing more foreign to them, and so nothing they ache more deeply to see.

On the appointed day, the doors of my father's receiving hall were thrown open. Huge torches carbuncled with jewels glowed from the walls and by their light gathered nymphs and gods of every variety. The slender dryads flowed out of their forests, and the stony oreads ran down from their crags. My mother was there with her naiad sisters; the horse-shouldered river-gods crowded in beside the fish-white sea-nymphs and their lords of salt. Even the great Titans came: my father, of course, and Oceanos, but also shape-shifting Proteus and Nereus of the Sea; my aunt Selene, who drives her silver horses across the night sky; and the four Winds led by my icy uncle Boreas. A thousand avid eyes. The only ones missing were Zeus and his Olympians. They disdained our underground gatherings. The word was they had already held their own private session of torment in the clouds.

Charge of the punishment had been given to a Fury, one of the infernal goddesses of vengeance who dwell among the dead. My family was in its usual place of preeminence, and I stood at the front of that great throng, my eyes fixed upon the door. Behind me the naiads and river-gods jostled and whispered. *I hear they have serpents for hair. No, they have scorpion tails, and eyes dripping blood.*

The doorway was empty. Then at once it was not. Her face was gray and pitiless, as if cut from living rock, and from her back dark wings lifted, jointed like a vulture's. A forked tongue flicked from her lips. On her head snakes writhed, green and thin as worms, weaving living ribbons through her hair.

"I bring the prisoner."

Her voice echoed off the ceiling, raw and baying, like

a hunting dog calling down its quarry. She strode into the hall. In her right hand was a whip, its tip rasping faintly as it dragged along the floor. In her other hand stretched a length of chain, and at its end followed Prometheus.

He wore a thick white blindfold and the remnants of a tunic around his waist. His hands were bound and his feet too, yet he did not stumble. I heard an aunt beside me whisper that the fetters had been made by the great god of smiths, Hephaestus himself, so not even Zeus could break them. The Fury rose up on her vulture wings and drove the manacles high into the wall. Prometheus dangled from them, his arms drawn taut, his bones showing knobs through the skin. Even I, who knew so little of discomfort, felt the ache of it.

My father would say something, I thought. Or one of the other gods. Surely they would give him some sort of acknowledgment, a word of kindness, they were his family, after all. But Prometheus hung silent and alone.

The Fury did not bother with a lecture. She was a goddess of torment and understood the eloquence of violence. The sound of the whip was a crack like oaken branches breaking. Prometheus' shoulders jerked and a gash opened in his side long as my arm. All around me indrawn breaths hissed like water on hot rocks. The Fury lifted her lash again. *Crack*. A bloodied strip tore from his back. She began to carve in earnest, each blow falling on the next, peeling his flesh away in long lines that crossed and recrossed his skin. The only sound was the snap of the whip and Prometheus' muffled, explosive breaths. The tendons stood out in his neck. Someone pushed at my back, trying for a better view.

The wounds of gods heal fast, but the Fury knew her business and was faster. Blow after blow she struck, until the leather was soaked. I had understood gods could bleed, but I had never seen it. He was one of the greatest of our kind, and the drops that fell from him were golden, smearing his back with a terrible beauty.

Still the Fury whipped on. Hours passed, perhaps days. But even gods cannot watch a whipping for eternity. The blood and agony began to grow tedious. They remembered their comforts, the banquets that were waiting on their pleasure, the soft couches laid with purple, ready to enfold their limbs. One by one they drifted off, and after a final lash, the Fury followed, for she deserved a feast after such work.

The blindfold had slipped from my uncle's face. His eyes were closed, and his chin drooped on his chest. His back hung in gilded shreds. I had heard my uncles say that Zeus had given him the chance to beg on his knees for lesser punishment. He had refused.

I was the only one left. The smell of ichor drenched the air, thick as honey. The rivulets of molten blood were still tracing down his legs. My pulse struck in my veins. Did he know I was there? I took a careful step towards him. His chest rose and fell with a soft rasping sound.

"Lord Prometheus?" My voice was thin in the echoing room.

His head lifted to me. Open, his eyes were handsome, large and dark and long-lashed. His cheeks were smooth and beardless, yet there was something about him that was as ancient as my grandfather.

"I could bring you nectar," I said.

His gaze rested on mine. "I would thank you for that," he said. His voice was resonant as aged wood. It was the first time I had heard it; he had not cried out once in all his torment.

I turned. My breaths came fast as I walked through the corridors to the feasting hall, filled with laughing gods. Across the room, the Fury was toasting with an immense goblet embossed with a gorgon's leering face. She had not forbidden anyone to speak to Prometheus, but that was nothing, her business was offense. I imagined her infernal voice, howling out my name. I imagined manacles rattling on my wrists and the whip striking from the air. But my mind could imagine no further than that. I had never felt a lash. I did not know the color of my blood.

I trembled so much I had to carry the cup in two hands. What would I say if someone stopped me? But the passageways were quiet as I walked back through them.

In the great hall, Prometheus was silent in his chains. His eyes had closed again, and his wounds shone in the torchlight. I hesitated.

"I do not sleep," he said. "Will you lift the cup for me?"

I flushed. Of course he could not hold it himself. I stepped forward, so close that I could feel the heat rising from his shoulders. The ground was wet with his fallen blood. I raised the cup to his lips and he drank. I watched his throat moving gently. His skin was beautiful, the color of polished walnut. It smelled of green moss drenched with rain.

"You are a daughter of Helios, are you not?" he said, when he had finished, and I'd stepped back.

"Yes." The question stung. If I had been a proper daughter, he would not have had to ask. I would have been perfect and gleaming with beauty poured straight from my father's source.

"Thank you for your kindness."

I did not know if I was kind, I felt I did not know anything. He spoke carefully, almost tentatively, yet his treason had been so brazen. My mind struggled with the contradiction. *Bold action and bold manner are not the same.*

"Are you hungry?" I asked. "I could bring you food."

"I do not think I will ever be hungry again."

It was not piteous, as it might have been in a mortal. We gods eat as we sleep: because it is one of life's great pleasures, not because we have to. We may decide one day not to obey our stomachs, if we are strong enough. I did not doubt Prometheus was. After all those hours at my father's feet, I had learned to nose out power where it lay. Some of my uncles had less scent than the chairs they sat on, but my grandfather Oceanos smelled deep as rich river mud, and my father like a searing blaze of just-fed fire. Prometheus' green moss scent filled the room.

I looked down at the empty cup, willing my courage.

"You aided mortals," I said. "That is why you are punished."

"It is."

"Will you tell me, what is a mortal like?"

It was a child's question, but he nodded gravely. "There is no single answer. They are each different. The only thing they share is death. You know the word?"

"I know it," I said. "But I do not understand."

"No god can. Their bodies crumble and pass into earth. Their souls turn to cold smoke and fly to the underworld. There they eat nothing and drink nothing and feel no warmth. Everything they reach for slips from their grasp."

A chill shivered across my skin. "How do they bear it?"

"As best they can."

The torches were fading, and the shadows lapped at us like dark water. "Is it true that you refused to beg for pardon? And that you were not caught, but confessed to Zeus freely what you did?"

"It is."

"Why?"

His eyes were steady on mine. "Perhaps you will tell me. Why would a god do such a thing?"

I had no answer. It seemed to me madness to invite divine punishment, but I could not say that to him, not when I stood in his blood.

"Not every god need be the same," he said.

What I might have said in return, I do not know. A distant shout floated up the corridor.

"It is time for you to go now. Allecto does not like to leave me for long. Her cruelty springs fast as weeds and must any moment be cut again."

It was a strange way to put it, for he was the one who would be cut. But I liked it, as if his words were a secret. A thing that looked like a stone, but inside was a seed.

"I will go then," I said. "You will . . . be well?"

"Well enough," he said. "What is your name?"

"Circe."

Did he smile a little? Perhaps I only flattered myself. I was trembling with all I had done, which was more than I had ever done in my life. I turned and left him, walking back through those obsidian corridors. In the feasting hall, gods still drank and laughed and lay across each other's laps. I watched them. I waited for someone to remark on my absence, but no one did, for no one had noticed. Why would they? I was nothing, a stone. One more nymph child among the thousand thousands.

A strange feeling was rising in me. A sort of humming in my chest, like bees at winter's thaw. I walked to my father's treasury, filled with its glittering riches: golden cups shaped like the heads of bulls, necklaces of lapis and amber, silver tripods, and quartz-chiseled bowls with swan-neck handles.

My favorite had always been a dagger with an ivory haft carved like a lion's face. A king had given it to my father in hopes of gaining his favor.

"And did he?" I once asked my father.

"No," my father had said.

I took the dagger. In my room, the bronze edge shone in the taper's light and the lion showed her teeth. Beneath lay my palm, soft and unlined. It could bear no scar, no festering wound. It would never wear the faintest print of age. I found that I was not afraid of the pain that would come. It was another terror that gripped me: that the blade would not cut at all. That it would pass through me, like falling into smoke.

It did not pass through. My skin leapt apart at the blade's touch, and the pain darted silver and hot as lightning strike. The blood that flowed was red, for I did not have my uncle's power. The wound seeped for a long time before it began to reknit itself. I sat watching it, and as I watched I found a new thought in myself. I am embarrassed to tell it, so rudimentary it seems, like an infant's discovery that her hand is her own. But that is what I was then, an infant.

The thought was this: that all my life had been murk and depths, but I was not a part of that dark water. I was a creature within it.

CHAPTER THREE

WHEN I WOKE, PROMETHEUS was gone. The golden blood had been wiped from the floor. The hole the manacles had made was closed over. I heard the news from a naiad cousin: he had been taken to a great jagged peak in the Caucasus and chained to the rock. An eagle was commanded to come every noon and tear out his liver and eat it steaming from his flesh. Unspeakable punishment, she said, relishing each detail: the bloody beak, the shredded organ regrowing only to be ripped forth again. *Can you imagine?*

I closed my eyes. I should have brought him a spear, I thought, something so he could have fought his way through. But that was foolish. He did not want a weapon. He had given himself up.

Talk of Prometheus' punishment scarcely lasted out the moon. A dryad stabbed one of the Graces with her hairpin. My uncle Boreas and Olympian Apollo had fallen in love with the same mortal youth.

I waited till my uncles paused in their gossip. "Is there any news of Prometheus?"

They frowned, as if I had offered them a plate of something foul. "What news could there be?"

My palm ached where the blade had cut, though of course there was no mark.

"Father," I said, "will Zeus ever let Prometheus go?"

My father squinted at his draughts. "He would have to get something better for it," he said.

"Like what?"

My father did not answer. Someone's daughter was changed into a bird. Boreas and Apollo quarreled over the youth they loved and he died. Boreas smiled slyly from his feasting couch. His gusty voice made the torches flicker. "You think I'd let Apollo have him? He does not deserve such a flower. I blew a discus into the boy's head, that showed the Olympian prig." The sound of my uncles' laughter was a chaos, the squeaks of dolphins, seal barks, water slapping rocks. A group of nereids passed, eel-belly white, on their way home to their salt halls.

Perses flicked an almond at my face. "What's wrong with you these days?"

"Maybe she's in love," Pasiphaë said.

"Hah!" Perses laughed. "Father cannot even give her away. Believe me he's tried."

My mother looked back over her delicate shoulder. "At least we don't have to listen to her voice."

"I can make her talk, watch." Perses took the flesh of my arm between his fingers and squeezed.

"You've been feasting too much," my sister laughed at him.

He flushed. "She's just a freak. She's hiding something." He caught me by the wrist. "What're you always carrying around in your hand? She's got something. Open her fingers."

Pasiphaë peeled them back one by one, her long nails pricking.

They peered down. My sister spat.

"Nothing."

*   *   *

My mother whelped again, a boy. My father blessed him, but spoke no prophecy, so my mother looked around for somewhere to leave him. My aunts were wise by then and kept their hands behind their backs.

"I will take him," I said.

My mother scoffed, but she was eager to show off her new string of amber beads. "Fine. At least you will be of some use. You can squawk at each other."

Aeëtes, my father had named him. *Eagle*. His skin was warm in my arms as a sun-hot stone and soft as petal-velvet. There had never been a sweeter child. He smelled like honey and just-kindled flames. He ate from my fingers and did not flinch at my frail voice. He only wanted to sleep curled against my neck while I told him stories. Every moment he was with me, I felt a rushing in my throat, which was my love for him, so great sometimes I could not speak.

He seemed to love me back, that was the greater wonder. *Circe* was the first word he ever spoke, and the second was *sister*. My mother might have been jealous, if she had noticed. Perses and Pasiphaë eyed us, to see if we would start a war. A war? We did not care for that. Aeëtes got permission from Father to leave the halls and found us a deserted seaside. The beach was small and pale and the trees barely scrub, but to me it seemed a great, lush wilderness.

In a wink he was grown and taller than I was, but still we would walk arm in arm. Pasiphaë jeered that we looked like lovers, would we be those types of gods, who coupled with their siblings? I said if she thought of it, she must have done it first. It was a clumsy insult, but Aeëtes laughed, which made me feel quick as Athena, flashing god of wit.

Later, people would say that Aeëtes was strange because of me. I cannot prove it was not so. But in my memory he was strange already, different from any other god I knew. Even as a child, he seemed to understand what others did not. He could name the monsters who lived in the sea's darkest trenches. He knew that the herbs Zeus had poured down Kronos' throat were called *pharmaka*. They could work wonders upon the world, and many grew from the fallen blood of gods.

I would shake my head. "How do you hear such things?"

"I listen."

I had listened too, but I was not my father's favored heir. Aeëtes was summoned to sit in on all his councils. My uncles had begun inviting him to their halls. I waited in my room for him to come back, so we could go together to that deserted shore and sit on the rocks, the sea spray at our feet. I would lean my cheek upon his shoulder and he would ask me questions that I had never thought of and could barely understand, like: *How does your divinity feel?*

"What do you mean?" I said.

"Here," he said, "let me tell you how mine feels. Like a column of water that pours ceaselessly over itself, and is clear down to its rocks. Now, you."

I tried answers: like breezes on a crag. Like a gull, screaming from its nest.

He shook his head. "No. You are only saying those things because of what I said. What does it really feel like? Close your eyes and think."

I closed my eyes. If I had been a mortal, I would have heard the beating of my heart. But gods have sluggish veins, and the truth is, what I heard was nothing. Yet I hated to disappoint him. I pressed my hand to my chest, and after a little it did seem that I felt something. "A shell," I said.

"Aha!" He shook his finger in the air. "A shell like a clam or like a conch?"

"A conch."

"And what is in that shell? A snail?"

"Nothing," I said. "Air."

"Those are not the same," he said. "Nothing is empty void, while air is what fills all else. It is breath and life and spirit, the words we speak."

My brother, the philosopher. Do you know how many gods are such? Only one other that I had met. The blue sky arched above us, but I was in that old dark hall again, with its manacles and blood.

"I have a secret," I said.

Aeëtes lifted his brows, amused. He thought it was a joke. I had never known anything he did not.

"It was before you were born," I said.

Aeëtes did not look at me while I told him about Prometheus. His mind worked best, he always said, without distractions. His eyes were fixed on the horizon. They were sharp as the eagle he was named for, and could pry into all the cracks of things, like water pricking at a leaky hull.

When I was finished, he was silent a long time. At last he said: "Prometheus was a god of prophecy. He would have known he would be punished, and how. Yet he did it anyway."

I had not thought of that. How even as Prometheus took up the flame for mankind, he would have known he was walking towards the eagle and that desolate, eternal crag.

Well enough, he had answered, when I had asked how he would be.

"Who else knows this?"

"No one."

"You are sure?" His voice had an urgency to it I was not used to. "You did not tell anyone?"

"No," I said. "Who else is there? Who would have believed me?"

"True." He nodded once. "You must tell no one else. You should not talk about it again, even with me. You are lucky Father did not find out."

"You think he would be so angry? Prometheus is his cousin."

He snorted. "We are all cousins, including the Olympians. You would make Father look like a fool who cannot control his offspring. He would throw you to the crows."

I felt my stomach clench with dread, and my brother laughed at the look on my face. "Exactly," he said. "And for what? Prometheus is punished anyway. Let me give you some advice. Next time you're going to defy the gods, do it for a better reason. I'd hate to see my sister turned to cinders for nothing."

Pasiphaë was contracted in marriage. She had been angling for it a long time, sitting in my father's lap and purring of how she longed to bear a good lord children. My brother Perses had been enlisted to help her, lifting goblets to toast her nubility at every meal.

"Minos," my father said from his feasting couch. "A son of Zeus and king of Crete."

"A mortal?" My mother sat up. "You said it would be a god."

"I said he would be an eternal son of Zeus, and so he is."

Perses sneered. "Prophecy talk. Does he die or not?"

A flash in the room, searing as the fire's heart. "Enough! Minos will rule all the other mortal souls in the afterlife. His name will go on through the centuries. It is done."

My brother dared say no more, nor my mother. Aeëtes caught my eye, and I heard his words as if he spoke them. *See? Not a good enough reason.*

I expected my sister to weep over her demotion. But when I looked, she was smiling. What that meant I could not say; my mind was following a different thread. A flush had spread over my skin. If Minos were there, so would his family be, his court, his advisers, his vassals and astronomers, his cupbearers, his servants and underservants. All those creatures Prometheus had given his eternity for. Mortals.

On the wedding day, my father carried us across the sea in his golden chariot. The feast was to be held on Crete, in Minos' great palace at Knossos. The walls were new-plastered and every surface hung with bright flowers; the tapestries glowed with richest saffron. Not only Titans would attend. Minos was a son of Zeus, and all the boot-licking Olympians would also come to pay their homage. The long colonnades filled up quickly with gods in their glory, clattering their adornments, laughing, casting glances to see who else had been invited. The thickest knot was around my father, immortals of every sort pressing in to congratulate him on his brilliant alliance. My uncles were especially pleased: Zeus was unlikely to move against us as long as the marriage held.

From her bridal dais Pasiphaë glowed lush as ripe fruit. Her skin was gold, and her hair the color of sun on polished bronze. Around her crowded a hundred eager nymphs, each more desperate than the last to tell her how beautiful she looked.

I stood back, out of the crush. Titans passed before me: my aunt Selene; my uncle Nereus trailing seaweed; Mnemosyne, mother of memories, and her nine light-footed daughters. My eyes skimmed over, searching.

I found them at last at the hall's edge. A dim huddle of

figures, heads bent together. Prometheus had told me they were each different, but all I could make out was an indistinguished crowd, each with the same dull and sweated skin, the same wrinkled robes. I moved closer. Their hair hung lank, their flesh drooped soft off their bones. I tried to imagine going up to them, touching my hand to that dying skin. The thought sent a shiver through me. I had heard by then the stories whispered among my cousins, of what they might do to nymphs they caught alone. The rapes and ravishments, the abuses. I found it hard to believe. They looked weak as mushroom gills. They kept their faces carefully down, away from all those divinities. Mortals had their own stories, after all, of what happened to those who mixed with gods. An ill-timed glance, a foot set in an impropitious spot, such things could bring down death and woe upon their families for a dozen generations.

It was like a great chain of fear, I thought. Zeus at the top and my father just behind. Then Zeus' siblings and children, then my uncles, and on down through all the ranks of river-gods and brine-lords and Furies and Winds and Graces, until it came to the bottom where we sat, nymphs and mortals both, each eyeing the other.

Aeëtes' hand closed on my arm. "Not much to look at, are they? Come on, I found the Olympians."

I followed, my blood beating within me. I had never seen one before, those deities who rule from their celestial thrones. Aeëtes drew me to a window overlooking a sun-dazzled courtyard. And there they were: Apollo, lord of the lyre and the gleaming bow. His twin, moonlit Artemis, the pitiless huntress. Hephaestus, blacksmith of the gods, who had made the chains that held Prometheus still. Brooding Poseidon, whose trident commands the waves, and Demeter, lady of bounty, whose harvests nourish all the world. I stared at them, gliding sleek in their power. The very air seemed to give way where they walked.

"Do you see Athena?" I whispered. I had always liked the stories of her, gray-eyed warrior, goddess of wisdom, whose mind was swifter than the lightning bolt. But she was not there. Perhaps, Aeëtes said, she was too proud to rub shoulders with earthbound Titans. Perhaps she was too wise to offer compliments as one among a crowd. Or perhaps she was there after all, but concealed even from the eyes of other divinities. She was one of the most powerful of the Olympians, she could do such a thing, and so observe the currents of power, and listen to our secrets.

My neck turned to gooseflesh at the thought. "Do you think she listens to us even now?"

"Don't be foolish. She is here for the great gods. Look, Minos comes."

Minos, king of Crete, son of Zeus and a mortal woman. A demigod, his kind were called, mortal themselves but blessed by their divine parentage. He towered over his advisers, his hair thick as matted brush and his chest broad as the deck of a ship. His eyes reminded me of my father's obsidian halls, shining darkly beneath his golden crown. Yet when he placed his hand on my sister's delicate arm, suddenly he looked like a tree in winter, bare and shriveled-small. He knew it, I think, and glowered, which made my sister glitter all the more. She would be happy here, I thought. Or preeminent, which was the same to her.

"There," Aeëtes said, leaning close to my ear. "Look."

He was pointing to a mortal, a man I had not noticed before, not quite so huddled as the rest. He was young, his head shaved clean in the Egyptian style, the skin of his face fitted comfortably into its lines. I liked him. His clear eyes were not smoked with wine like everybody else's.

"Of course you like him," Aeëtes said. "It is Daedalus. He is one of the wonders of the mortal world, a craftsman almost equal to a god. When I am my own king, I will collect such glories around me too."

"Oh? And when will you be king?"

"Soon," he said. "Father is giving me a kingdom."

I thought he was joking. "And may I live there?"

"No," he said. "It is mine. You will have to get your own."

His arm was through mine as it ever was, yet suddenly all was different, his voice swinging free, as if we were two creatures tied to separate cords, instead of to each other.

"When?" I croaked.

"After this. Father plans to take me straight."

He said it as if it were no more than a point of minor interest. I felt like I was turning to stone. I clung to him. "How could you not tell me?" I began. "You cannot leave me. What will I do? You do not know what it was like before — "

He drew my arms back from his neck. "There is no need for such a scene. You knew this would come. I cannot rot all my life underground, with nothing of my own."

What of me? I wanted to ask. Shall I rot?

But he had turned away to speak to one of my uncles, and as soon as the wedded pair was in their bedchamber, he stepped onto my father's chariot. In a whirl of gold, he was gone.

Perses left a few days later. No one was surprised, those halls of my father were empty for him without my sister. He said he was going east, to live among the Persians. Their name is like mine, he said, fatuously. And I hear they raise creatures called demons, I would like to see one.

My father frowned. He had taken against Perses ever

since he had mocked him over Minos. "Why should they have demons, more than us?"

Perses did not bother to answer. He would go through the ways of water, he did not need my father to ferry him. *At least I will not have to hear that voice of yours anymore*, was the last thing he said to me.

In a handful of days, all my life had been unwound. I was a child again, waiting while my father drove his chariot, while my mother lounged by Oceanos' riverbanks. I lay in our empty halls, my throat scraping with loneliness, and when I could not bear it any longer, I fled to Aeëtes and my old deserted shore. There I found the stones Aeëtes' fingers had touched. I walked the sand his feet had turned. Of course he could not stay. He was a divine son of Helios, bright and shining, true-voiced and clever, with hopes of a throne. And I?

I remembered his eyes as I had pleaded with him. I knew him well, and could read what was in them when he looked at me. *Not a good enough reason.*

I sat on the rocks and thought of the stories I knew of nymphs who wept until they turned into stones and crying birds, into dumb beasts and slender trees, thoughts barked up for eternity. I could not even do that, it seemed. My life closed me in like granite walls. I should have spoken to those mortals, I thought. I could have begged among them for a husband. I was a daughter of Helios, surely one of those ragged men would have had me. Anything would be better than this.

And that is when I saw the boat.

CHAPTER FOUR

I KNEW OF SHIPS from paintings, I had heard of them in stories. They were golden and huge as leviathans, their rails carved from ivory and horn. They were towed by grinning dolphins or else crewed by fifty black-haired nereids, faces silver as moonlight.

This one had a mast thin as a sapling. Its sail hung skewed and fraying, its sides were patched. I remember the jump in my throat when the sailor lifted his face. Burnt it was, and shiny with sun. A mortal.

Mankind was spreading across the world. Years had passed since my brother had first found that deserted land for our games. I stood behind a jut of cliff and watched as the man steered, skirting rocks and hauling at the nets. He looked nothing like the well-groomed nobles of Minos' court. His hair was long and black, draggled from wave-spray. His clothes were worn, and his neck scabbed. Scars showed on his arms where fish scales had cut him. He did not move with unearthly grace, but strongly, cleanly, like a well-built hull in the waves.

I could hear my pulse, loud in my ears. I thought again of those stories of nymphs ravished and abused by mortals.

But this man's face was soft with youth, and the hands that drew up his catch looked only swift, not cruel. Anyway, in the sky above me was my father, called the Watchman. If I was in danger, he would come.

He was close to the shore by then, peering down into the water, tracking some fish I could not see. I took a breath and stepped forward onto the beach.

"Hail, mortal."

He fumbled his nets but did not drop them. "Hail," he said. "What goddess do I address?"

His voice was gentle in my ears, sweet as summer winds.

"Circe," I said.

"Ah." His face was carefully blank. He told me much later it was because he had not heard of me and feared to give offense. He knelt on the rough boards. "Most reverend lady. Do I trespass on your waters?"

"No," I said. "I have no waters. Is that a boat?"

Expressions passed across his face, but I could not read them. "It is," he said.

"I would like to sail upon it," I said.

He hesitated, then began to steer closer to the shore, but I did not know to wait. I waded out through the waves to him and pulled myself aboard. The deck was hot through my sandals, and its motion pleasing, a faint undulation, like I rode upon a snake.

"Proceed," I said.

How stiff I was, dressed in my divine dignity that I did not even know I wore. And he was stiffer still. He trembled when my sleeve brushed his. His eyes darted whenever I addressed him. I realized with a shock that I knew such gestures. I had performed them a thousand times — for my father, and my grandfather, and all those mighty gods who strode through my days. *The great chain of fear.*

"Oh, no," I said to him. "I am not like that. I have scarcely any powers at all and cannot hurt you. Be comfortable, as you were."

"Thank you, kind goddess." But he said it so flinchingly that I had to laugh. It was that laughter, more than my protestation, that seemed to ease him a little. Moment passed into moment, and we began to talk of the things around us: the fish jumping, a bird dipping overhead. I asked him how his nets were made, and he told me, warming to the subject, for he took great care with them. When I told him my father's name, it sent him glancing at the sun and trembling worse than ever, but at day's end no wrath had descended and he knelt to me and said that I must have blessed his nets, for they were the fullest they had ever been.

I looked down at his thick, black hair, shining in the sunset light, his strong shoulders bowing low. This is what all those gods in our halls longed for, such worship. I thought perhaps he had not done it right, or more likely, I had not. All I wanted was to see his face again.

"Rise," I told him. "Please. I have not blessed your nets, I have no powers to do so. I am born from naiads, who govern fresh water only, and even their small gifts I lack."

"Yet," he said, "may I return? Will you be here? For I have never known such a wondrous thing in all my life as you."

I had stood beside my father's light. I had held Aeëtes in my arms, and my bed was heaped with thick-wooled blankets woven by immortal hands. But it was not until that moment that I think I had ever been warm.

"Yes," I told him. "I will be here."

His name was Glaucos, and he came every day. He brought along bread, which I had never tasted, and cheese, which I had, and olives that I liked to see his teeth bite through. I asked him about his family, and he told me that his father was old and bitter, always storming and worrying about food, and his mother used to make herb simples but was broken now from too much labor, and his sister had five children already and was always sick and angry. All of them would be turned out of their cottage if they could not give their lord the tribute he levied.

No one had ever confided so in me. I drank down every story like a whirlpool sucks down waves, though I could hardly understand half of what they meant, poverty and toil and human terror. The only thing that was clear was Glaucos' face, his handsome brow and earnest eyes, wet a little from his griefs but smiling always when he looked at me.

I loved to watch him at his daily tasks, which he did with his hands instead of a blink of power: mending the torn nets, cleaning off the boat's deck, sparking the flint. When he made his fire, he would start painstakingly with small bits of dried moss placed just so, then the smaller twigs, then larger, building upwards and upwards. This art too, I did not know. Wood needed no coaxing for my father to kindle it.

He saw me watching and rubbed self-consciously at his calloused hands. "I know I am ugly to you."

No, I thought. My grandfather's halls are filled with shining nymphs and muscled river-gods, but I would rather gaze on you than any of them.

I shook my head.

He sighed. "It must be wonderful to be a god and never bear a mark."

"My brother once said it feels like water."

He considered. "Yes, I can imagine that. As if you are brimming, like an overfilled cup. What brother is that? You have not spoken of him before."

"He is gone to be a king far away. Aeëtes, he is called."
The name felt strange on my tongue after so long. "I would
have gone with him, but he said no."

"He sounds like a fool," Glaucos said.

"What do you mean?"

He lifted his eyes to mine. "You are a golden goddess,
beautiful and kind. If I had such a sister, I would never let
her go."

Our arms would brush as he worked at the ship's rail.
When we sat, my dress lapped over his feet. His skin was
warm and slightly roughened. Sometimes I would drop
something, so he might pick it up, and our hands would
meet.

That day, he knelt on the beach, kindling a fire to cook
his lunch. It was still one of my favorite things to watch,
that simple, mortal miracle of flint and tinder. His hair
hung sweetly into his eyes, and his cheeks glowed with the
flame's light. I found myself thinking of my uncle who had
given him that gift.

"I met him once," I said.

Glaucos had spitted a fish and was roasting it. "Who?"

"Prometheus," I said. "When Zeus punished him, I
brought him nectar."

He looked up. "Prometheus," he said.

"Yes." He was not usually so slow. "Fire-bearer."

"That is a story from a dozen generations ago."

"More than a dozen," I said. "Watch out, your fish." The
spit had drooped from his hand, and the fish was blacken-
ing on the coals.

He did not rescue it. His eyes were fixed on me. "But
you are my age."

My face had tricked him. It looked as young as his.

I laughed. "No. I am not."

He had been half slouched to one side, knees touching mine. Now he jerked upright, pulling away from me so fast I felt the cold where he had been. It surprised me.

"Those years are nothing," I said. "I made no use of them. You know as much of the world as I do." I reached for his hand.

He yanked it away. "How can you say that? How old are you? A hundred? Two hundred?"

I almost laughed again. But his neck was rigid, and his eyes wide. The fish smoked between us in the fire. I had told him so little of my life. What was there to tell? Only the same cruelties, the same sneers at my back. In those days, my mother was in an especial ill humor. My father had begun to prefer his draughts to her, and her venom over it fell to me. She would curl her lip when she saw me. *Circe is dull as a rock. Circe has less wit than bare ground. Circe's hair is matted like a dog's. If I have to hear that broken voice of hers once more. Of all our children, why must it be she who is left? No one else will have her.* If my father heard, he gave no sign, only moved his game counters here and there. In the old days, I would have crept to my room with tear-stained cheeks, but since Glaucos' coming it was all like bees without a sting.

"I'm sorry," I said. "It was only a stupid joke. I never met him, I only wished to. Never fear, we are the same age."

Slowly, his posture loosened. He blew out a breath. "Hah," he said. "Can you imagine? If you had really been alive then?"

He finished his meal. He threw the scraps to the gulls, then chased them wheeling to the sky. He turned back to grin at me, outlined against the silver waves, his shoulders lifting in his tunic. No matter how many fires I watched him make, I never spoke of my uncle again.

One day, Glaucos' boat came late. He did not anchor it, only stood upon its deck, his face stiff and grim. There was a bruise on his cheek, storm-wave dark. His father had struck him.

"Oh!" My pulse leapt. "You must rest. Sit with me, and I will bring you water."

"No," he said, and his voice was sharp as I had ever heard it. "Not today, not ever again. Father says I loaf and all our hauls are down. We will starve, and it is my fault."

"Yet come sit, and let me help," I said.

"You cannot do anything," he said. "You told me so. You have no powers at all."

I watched him sail off. Then wild I turned and ran to my grandfather's palace. Through its arched passageways I went, to the women's halls, with their clatter of shuttles and goblets and the jangle of bracelets on wrists. Past the na-iads, past the visiting nereids and dryads, to the oaken stool on the dais, where my grandmother ruled.

Tethys, she was called, great nurse of the world's waters, born like her husband at the dawn of ages from Mother Earth herself. Her robes puddled blue at her feet, and around her neck was wrapped a water-serpent like a scarf. Before her was a golden loom that held her weaving. Her face was old but not withered. Countless daughters and sons had been birthed from her flowing womb, and their descendants were still brought to her for blessing. I myself had knelt to her once. She had touched my forehead with the tips of her soft fingers. *Welcome, child.*

I knelt again, now. "I am Circe, Perse's daughter. You

must help me. There is a mortal who needs fish from the sea. I cannot bless him, but you can."

"He is noble?" she asked.

"In nature," I said. "Poor in possessions, yet rich in spirit and courage, and shining like a star."

"And what does this mortal offer you in exchange?"

"Offer me?"

She shook her head. "My dear, they must always offer something, even if it is small, even if only wine poured at your spring, else they will forget to be grateful, after."

"I do not have a spring and I do not need any gratitude. Please. I will never see him again if you do not help me."

She looked at me and sighed. She must have heard such pleas a thousand times. That is one thing gods and mortals share. When we are young, we think ourselves the first to have each feeling in the world.

"I will grant your wish and fill his nets. Yet in return, let me hear you swear you will not lie with him. You know your father thinks to match you better than with some fish-boy."

"I swear," I said.

He came skimming across the waves, shouting for me. His words poured over themselves. He had not even had to work the nets, he said. The fish leapt by themselves onto his deck, big as cows. His father was pacified, and the levy paid, with credit for next year. He knelt before me, head bowed. "Thank you, goddess."

I drew him up. "Do not kneel to me, it was my grandmother's power."

"No." He took my hands. "It was you. You were the one who persuaded her. Circe, miracle, blessing of my life, you have saved me."

He pressed his warm cheeks to my hands. His lips brushed my fingers. "I wish I were a god," he breathed. "Then I could thank you as you deserve."

I let his curls fall around my wrist. I wished I were a real goddess so I could give him whales upon a golden plate, and he would never let me go.

Every day we sat together talking. He was full of dreams, hoping that when he was older he might have his own boat, and his own cottage instead of his father's. "And I will keep a fire," he said, "burning for you always. If you will allow me."

"I would rather you keep a chair," I said. "So I may come to speak with you."

He flushed, and I did too. I knew so little then. I had never lolled with my cousins, those broad-shouldered gods and lissom nymphs, when they talked of love. I had never crept off with a suitor into a private corner. I did not know enough even to say what I wanted. If I touched my hand to his, if I bent down my lips for a kiss, what then?

He was watching me. His face was like the sand, showing a hundred impressions. "Your father — " he said, stumbling a little, for speaking of Helios always unnerved him. "He will choose a husband for you?"

"Yes," I said.

"What sort of husband?"

I thought I would weep. I wanted to press against him and say I wished it could be him, but my oath stood between us. So I made myself speak the truth, that my father sought out princes, or perhaps a king if he were foreign.

He looked down at his hands. "Of course," he said. "Of course. You are very dear to him."

I did not correct him. I went back to my father's halls that night and knelt at his feet and asked him if it was possible to make a mortal a god.

Helios frowned at his draughts in irritation. "You know it is not, unless it is in their stars already. Not even I can change the laws of the Fates."

I said no more. My thoughts were following upon themselves. If Glaucos remained a mortal, then he would grow old, and if he grew old he would die, and there would be a day upon that shore when I would come and he would not. Prometheus had told me, yet I had not understood. What a fool I had been. What a stupid fool. In a panic, I ran back to my grandmother.

"That man," I said, nearly choking. "He will die."

Her stool was oak, draped with softest weavings. The yarn in her fingers was river-stone green. She was winding it on her shuttle. "Oh, granddaughter," she said. "Of course he will. He is mortal, that is their lot."

"It is not fair," I said. "It cannot be."

"Those are two different things," my grandmother said.

All the shining naiads had turned from their talk to listen to us. I pressed on. "You must help me," I said. "Great goddess, will you not take him to your halls and make him eternal?"

"No god can do so much."

"I love him," I said. "There must be a way."

She sighed. "Do you know how many nymphs before you have hoped the same and been disappointed?"

I did not care about those nymphs. They were not Helios' daughter, raised on stories of breaking the world. "Is there not some—I do not know the word. Some device. Some bargain with the Fates, some trick, some *pharmaka*—"

It was the word Aeëtes had used, when he spoke of herbs with wondrous powers, sprung from the fallen blood of gods.

The sea snake at my grandmother's neck uncoiled and flicked a black tongue from its arrow mouth. Her voice was low and angry. "You dare to speak of that?"

The sudden change surprised me. "Speak of what?"

But she was rising, her full height unfurling before me.

"Child, I have done as much for you as may be done, and there is no more. Go from here, and let me never hear you speak of that wickedness again."

My head was churning, my mouth sharp as though I had drunk raw wine. I walked back through the couches, the chairs, past the skirts of whispering, smirking naiads. *She thinks just because she is daughter of the sun, she may uproot the world to please herself.*

I was too wild to feel any shame. It was true. I would not just uproot the world, but tear it, burn it, do any evil I could to keep Glaucos by my side. But what stayed most in my mind was the look on my grandmother's face when I'd said that word, *pharmaka.* It was not a look I knew well, among the gods. But I had seen Glaucos when he spoke of the levy and empty nets and his father. I had begun to know what fear was. What could make a god afraid? I knew that answer too.

A power greater than their own.

I had learned something from my mother after all. I bound my hair in ringlets and put on my best dress, my brightest sandals. I went to my father's feast, where all my uncles gathered, reclining on their purple couches. I poured their wine and smiled into their eyes and wreathed my arms around their necks. Uncle Proteus, I said. He was the one with seal meat in his teeth. You are brave and led valiantly in the war. Will you not tell me about its battles, where they were fought? Uncle Nereus, what about you? You were lord of the sea before Olympian Poseidon robbed you. I long to hear the great deeds of our kind, tell me where the blood fell thickest.

I drew those stories from them. I learned the names of those many places that had been sown with gods' blood, and where those places were. And at last I heard of one not far from Glaucos' shore.

CHAPTER FIVE

"COME," I SAID. IT was midday and hot, the earth crumbling beneath our feet. "It is very close. A perfect sleeping spot to ease your weary bones."

He followed sullenly. He was always ill-tempered when the sun was high. "I do not like to be so far from my boat."

"Your boat will be safe, I promise it. Look! We are here. Are not these flowers worth the walk? They are beautiful, palest yellow and shaped like bells."

I coaxed him down among the crowding blossoms. I had brought water and a basket of food. I was aware of my father's eye above us. A picnic, I meant it to appear, if he should glance our way. I could not be sure what my grandmother might have said to him.

I served Glaucos and watched while he ate. What would he look like as a god? I wondered. A little distance away grew a forest, its shade thick enough to hide us from my father's eyes. When he was changed, I would pull him there, and show him that my oath did not hold us anymore.

I set a cushion on the ground. "Lie back," I said. "Sleep. Won't it be nice to sleep?"

"I have a headache," he complained. "And the sun is in my eyes."

I brushed back his hair and moved so I blocked the sun. He sighed then. He was always tired, and in a moment his eyes were dragging closed.

I stirred the flowers so they lay against him. Now, I thought. *Now.*

He slept on as I had seen him sleep a hundred times. In my fantasies of this moment, the flowers had changed him at a touch. Their immortal blood leapt into his veins and he rose up a god, took my hands and said, *Now I may thank you as you deserve.*

I stirred the flowers again. I plucked some and dropped them on his chest. I blew out my breath, so the scent and pollen would drift over him. "Change," I whispered. "He must be a god. Change."

He slept. The flowers hung lank around us, wan and fragile as moth wings. A line of acid was tracing through my stomach. Maybe I had not found the right ones, I told myself. I should have come to scout ahead, but I had been too eager. I rose and walked the hillside, searching for some crimson clutch of blooms, vivid, leaking obvious power. But all I found were common blossoms that any hill might have.

I crumpled beside Glaucos and wept. The tears of those of naiad blood can flow for eternity, and I thought it might take an eternity to speak all my grief. I had failed. Aeëtes had been wrong, there were no herbs of power, and Glaucos would be lost to me forever, his sweet, perishing beauty withered into earth. Overhead, my father slipped along his track. Those soft, foolish flowers bobbed around us on their stems. I hated them. I seized a handful and ripped it up by the roots. I tore the petals. I broke the stems to pieces. The damp shreds stuck to my hands, and the sap bled across my skin. The scent rose raw and wild, acetic as old wine. I tore up another handful, my hands sticky and hot. In my ears was a dark humming, like a hive.

It is hard to describe what happened next. A knowledge woke in the depths of my blood. It whispered: that the strength of those flowers lay in their sap, which could transform any creature to its truest self.

I did not stop to question. The sun had passed the horizon by then. Glaucos' lips had fallen open as he dreamed, and I lifted a handful of flowers over him, squeezing. The sap leaked and gathered. Drop by milky drop I let it fall into his mouth. A stray bead landed on his lips, and I slid it onto his tongue with my finger. He coughed. Your truest self, I told him. Let it be.

I crouched, another handful ready. I would squeeze the whole field into him if I had to. But even as I thought that, a shadow moved across his skin. It darkened as I watched. Past brown it went, past purple, spreading like a bruise until his whole body was deepest sea-blue. His hands were swelling, his legs, his shoulders. Hairs began to push out from his chin, long and copper-green. Where his tunic gaped, I could see blisters forming on his chest. I stared. They were barnacles.

Glaucos, I whispered. His arm was strange beneath my fingers, hard and thick and slightly cool. I shook it. Wake up.

His eyes opened. For the passing of one breath he did not move. Then he leapt to his feet, towering like a storm-surge, the sea-god he had always been. Circe, he cried, I am changed!

There was no time to go to the forest, no time to draw him to me on the moss. He was wild with his new strength, snorting like a bull in spring air. "Look," he said, holding out his hands. "No scabs. No scars. And I am not tired. For the first time in all my life, I am not tired! I could swim the whole ocean. I want to see myself. How do I look?"

"Like a god," I said.

He seized me by the arms and spun me, white teeth shining in his blue face. Then he stopped, a new thought dawning. "I can go with you now. I can go to the gods' halls. Will you take me?"

I could not tell him no. I brought him to my grandmother. My hands trembled a little, but the lies were ready on my lips. He had fallen asleep in a meadow and woken like this. "Perhaps my wish to turn him immortal was a kind of prophecy. It is not unknown in my father's children."

She scarcely listened. She suspected nothing. No one had ever suspected me.

"Brother," she cried, embracing him. "Newest brother! This is an act of the Fates. You are welcome here until you find a palace of your own."

There was no more walking on the shore. Every day I spent in those halls with Glaucos the God. We sat upon the banks of my grandfather's twilight river, and I introduced him to all my aunts and uncles and cousins, reeling off nymph after nymph, though before that moment I would have said I did not know their names. For their part, they crowded him, clamoring for the story of his miraculous transformation. He spun the tale well: his ill humor, the drowsiness that fell on him like a boulder, and then the power lifting him like cresting waves, granted by the Fates themselves. He would bare his blue chest before them, strapped with god-muscles, and offer his hands, smooth as surf-rolled shells. "See how I am grown into myself!"

I loved his face in those moments, glowing with power and joy. My chest swelled with his. I longed to tell him that it was I who had given him such a gift, but I saw how it pleased him to believe his godhead wholly his own and I did not want to take that from him. I still dreamed of lying with him in those dark woods, but I had begun to think beyond that, to say to myself new words: *marriage, husband*.

"Come," I told him. "You must meet my father and grandfather." I chose his clothes myself, in colors that showed his skin to greatest advantage. I warned him of the courtesies that were expected, and kept to the back, watching, while he offered them. He did well, and they praised him. They took him to Nereus, old Titan god of the sea, who in turn introduced him to Poseidon, his new lord. Together they helped him shape his underwater palace, set with gold and wave-wrack treasures.

I went there every day. The brine stung my skin, and he was often too busy with admiring guests to give me more than the briefest smile, but I did not mind. We had time now, all the time we would ever need. It was a pleasure to sit at those silver tables, watching the nymphs and gods tumble over themselves for his attention. Once they would have sneered at him, called him fish-gutter. Now they begged him for tales of his mortality. The stories grew in the telling: his mother bent-back like a hag, his father beating him every day. They gasped and pressed a hand to their hearts.

"It is well," he said. "I sent a wave to smash my father's boat, and the shock killed him. My mother I blessed. She has a new husband and a slave to help her with the washing. She has built me an altar, and already it smokes. My village hopes I will bring them a good tide."

"And will you?" The nymph who spoke clutched her

hands beneath her chin. She had been one of my sister and Perses' dearest companions, her round face lacquered with malice, but now speaking to Glaucos even she was transformed, open, ripe as a pear.

"We will see," he said, "what they offer me." Sometimes when he was very pleased, his feet turned to a flipping tail, and now it was. I watched it sweep along the marble floor, shining palest gray, its overlapping scales faintly iridescent.

"Is your father truly dead?" I said, when they were gone.

"Of course. He deserved it, for his blasphemy." He was polishing a new trident, a gift from Poseidon himself. During the days, he lounged on couches, drinking from goblets large as his head. He laughed like my uncles did, open-mouthed and roaring. He was not just some scraggled lord of crabs, but one of the greater sea-gods who might call whales to his beck if he wanted, rescue ships from reefs and shoals, lift rafts of sailors from the drowning waves.

"That round-faced nymph," he said, "the beautiful one. What is her name?"

My mind had drifted. I was imagining how he might ask for my hand. On the beach, I thought. That shore where we had first glimpsed each other.

"Do you mean Scylla?"

"Yes, Scylla," he said. "She moves like water, does she not? Silver as a flowing stream." His eyes lifted to hold mine. "Circe, I have never been so happy."

I smiled back at him. I saw nothing but the boy that I loved shining at last. Every honor lavished on him, every altar built in his name, every admirer who crowded him, these felt like gifts to me, for he was mine.

I began to see that nymph Scylla everywhere. Here she was laughing at some jest of Glaucos', here she was touch-

ing her hand to her throat and shaking out her hair. She
was very beautiful, it was true, one of the jewels of our
halls. The river-gods and nymphs sighed over her, and she
liked to raise their hopes with a look and break them with
another. When she moved she clattered faintly from the
thousand presents they pressed on her: bracelets of coral,
pearls about her neck in strings. She sat beside me and
showed them to me, one by one.

"Lovely," I said, scarcely looking. Yet there she was again
at the next feast, her jewels doubled, trebled, enough to
sink a fishing boat. I think now she must have been furious
that it took me so long to understand. By then she was holding her pearls, big as apples, up to my face. "Are they not
the greatest marvel you have ever seen?"

The truth is, I had begun to wonder if she was in love
with me. "They are very fine," I said faintly.

At last she had to set her teeth and say it straight.

"Glaucos says he will empty the sea of them, if it would
please me."

We were in Oceanos' hall, the air sickly with incense. I
started. "Those are from Glaucos?"

Oh, the joy on her face. "All of them are. You mean you
have not heard? I thought you would be first to know, you are
so close. But perhaps you are not the friend that you think
you are to him?" She waited, watching me. I was aware of
other faces too, giddily breathless. Such fights were more
precious than gold in our halls.

She smiled. "Glaucos asked me to marry him. I have not
decided yet what I will say. What is your counsel, Circe?
Should I take him, blue skin, flippers, and all?"

The naiads laughed like a thousand plashing fountains.
I fled so she would not see my tears and wear them as another of her trophies.

*   *   *

My father was with my river-uncle Achelous, and frowned to be interrupted. "What?"

"I want to marry Glaucos. Will you allow it?"

He laughed. "Glaucos? He has his pick. I do not think it will be you."

A shock ran through me. I did not stop to brush my hair or change my dress. Every moment felt like a drop of my blood lost. I ran to Glaucos' palace. He was away at some other god's hall so I waited, trembling, amid his overturned goblets, the wine-soaked cushions from his latest feast.

He came at last. With one flick of his hand, the mess was gone, and the floors gleamed again. "Circe," he said, when he saw me. Just that, as if you might say: foot.

"Do you mean to marry Scylla?"

I watched the light sweep across his face. "Is she not the most perfect creature you have ever seen? Her ankles are so small and delicate, like the sweetest doe in the forest. The river-gods are enraged that she favors me, and I hear even Apollo is jealous."

I was sorry then that I had not used those tricks of hair and eyes and lips that all our kind have. "Glaucos," I said, "she is beautiful, yes, but she does not deserve you. She is cruel, and she does not love you as you might be loved."

"What do you mean?"

He was frowning at me, as if I were a face he could not quite remember. I tried to think of what my sister would do. I stepped to him, trailed my fingers on his arm.

"I mean, I know one who will love you better."

"Who?" he said. But I could see him start to understand. His hands lifted, as though to ward me off. He, who was a towering god. "You have been a sister to me," he said.

"I would be more," I said. "I would be all." I pressed my lips to his.

He pushed me from him. His face was caught, half in anger, half in a sort of fear. He looked almost like his old self.

"I have loved you since that first day I saw you sailing," I said. "Scylla laughs at your fins and green beard, but I cherished you when there were fish guts on your hands and you wept from your father's cruelty. I helped you when — "

"No!" He slashed his hand through the air. "I will not think on those days. Every hour some new bruise upon me, some new ache, always weary, always burdened and weak. I sit at councils with your father now. I do not have to beg for every scrap. Nymphs clamor for me, and I may choose the best among them, which is Scylla."

The words struck like stones, but I would not give him up so easily.

"I can be best for you," I said. "I can please you, I swear it. You will find none more loyal than me. I will do anything."

I do think he loved me a little. For before I could say the thousand humiliating things in my heart, all the proofs of passion I had hoarded, the crawling devotions I would do, I felt his power come around me. And with that same flick he had used upon the cushions, he sent me back to my rooms.

I lay on the dirt, weeping. Those flowers had made him his true being, which was blue, and finned, and not mine. I thought I would die of such pain, which was not like the sinking numbness Aeëtes had left behind, but sharp and fierce as a blade through my chest. But of course I could not die. I would live on, through each scalding moment to the next. This is the grief that makes our kind choose to be stones and trees rather than flesh.

Beautiful Scylla, dainty-doe Scylla, Scylla with her viper heart. Why had she done such a thing? It was not love, I had seen the sneer in her eyes when she spoke of his flippers. Perhaps it was because she loved my sister and brother, who scorned me. Perhaps it was because her father was a nothing river, and her mother a shark-faced sea-nymph, and she liked the thought of taking something from the daughter of the sun.

It did not matter. All I knew was that I hated her. For I was like any dull ass who has ever loved someone who loved another. I thought: if only she were gone, it would change everything.

I left my father's halls. It was the time between the sun's setting and my pale aunt's rise. There was no one to see me. I gathered those flowers of true being and brought them to the cove where it was said Scylla bathed each day. I broke their stems and emptied their white sap drop by drop into the waters. She would not be able to hide her adder malice anymore. All her ugliness would be revealed. Her eyebrows would thicken, her hair would turn dull, and her nose would grow long and snouted. The halls would echo with her furious screams and the great gods would come to whip me, but I would welcome them, for every lash upon my skin would be only further proof to Glaucos of my love.

CHAPTER SIX

NO FURIES CAME FOR me that night. None came the next morning either, or all that afternoon. By dusk I went to find my mother at her mirror.

"Where is Father?"

"Gone straight to Oceanos. The feast is there." She wrinkled her nose, her pink tongue stuck between her teeth. "Your feet are filthy. Can you not at least wash them?"

I did not wash them. I did not want to wait another moment. What if Scylla was at the banquet, lounging in Glaucos' lap? What if they were married already? What if the sap had not worked?

It is strange now, to remember how I worried that.

The halls were even more crowded than usual, stinking of the same rose oil every nymph insisted was her special charm. I could not see my father, but my aunt Selene was there. She stood at the center of a clot of upturned faces, a mother and her baby birds, waiting to be crammed.

"You must understand, I only went to look because the water was so roiled up. I thought perhaps it was some sort of...meeting. You know how Scylla is."

I felt the breath stop in my chest. My cousins were snickering and cutting their eyes at each other. Whatever comes, I thought, do not show a thing.

"But she was flailing very strangely, like some sort of drowning cat. Then — I cannot say it."

She pressed her silvery hand to her mouth. It was a lovely gesture. Everything about my aunt was lovely. Her husband was a beautiful shepherd enchanted with ageless sleep, dreaming of her for eternity.

"A leg," she said. "A hideous leg. Like a squid's, boneless and covered in slime. It burst from her belly, and another burst beside it, and more and more, until there were twelve all dangling from her."

My fingertips stung faintly where the sap had leaked.

"That was only the beginning," Selene said. "She was bucking, her shoulders writhing. Her skin turned gray and her neck began to stretch. From it tore five new heads, each filled with gaping teeth."

My cousins gasped, but the sound was distant, like far-off waves. It felt impossible to picture the horror Selene described. To make myself believe: *I did that.*

"And all the while, she was baying and howling, barking like some wild pack of dogs. It was a relief when she finally dove beneath the waves."

As I had squeezed those flowers into Scylla's cove, I had not wondered how my cousins would take it, those who were Scylla's sisters and aunts and brothers and lovers. If I had thought of it, I would have said that Scylla was their darling, and that when the Furies came for me, they would have shouted loudest of all to see my blood. But now when I looked around me, all I saw were faces bright as whetted blades. They clung to each other, crowing. *I wish I'd seen it! Can you imagine?*

"Tell it again," an uncle shouted, and my cousins cried out their agreement.

My aunt smiled. Her curving lips made a crescent like herself in the sky. She told it again: the legs, the necks, the teeth.

My cousins' voices swarmed up to the ceiling.

You know she's lain with half the halls.

I'm glad I never let her have me. And one of the river-gods' voices, rising over all: *Of course she barks. She always was a bitch!*

Shrieking laughter clawed at my ears. I saw a river-god who had sworn he would fight Glaucos over her crying with mirth. Scylla's sister pretended to howl like a dog. Even my grandparents had come to listen, smiling at the crowd's edge. Oceanos said something in Tethys' ear. I could not hear it, but I had watched him for half an eternity, I knew the movements of his lips. *Good riddance.*

Beside me an uncle was shouting, *Tell it again!* This time my aunt only rolled her pearly eyes. He smelled like squids, and anyway, it was past time for the feast. The gods wafted to their couches. The cups were poured, the ambrosia passed. Their lips grew red with wine, their faces shone like jewels. Their laughter crackled around me.

I knew that electric pleasure, I thought. I had seen it before, in another dark hall.

The doors opened and Glaucos stepped through, his trident in his hand. His hair was greener than ever, fanned out like a lion's mane. I saw the joy leap in my cousins' eyes, heard their hiss of excitement. Here was more sport. They would tell him of his love's transformation, crack his face like an egg and laugh at what ran out.

But before they could say anything, my father was there, striding over to pull him aside.

My cousins sank back on sour elbows. Spoilsport Helios, ruining their fun. No matter, Perse would get it out of him later, or Selene. They lifted their goblets and went back to their pleasures.

I followed after Glaucos. I do not know how I dared, except that all my mind was filled up with a gray wash like churning waves. I stood outside the room where my father had drawn them.

I heard Glaucos' low voice: "Can she not be changed back?"

Every god-born knows that answer from their swaddles. "No," my father said. "No god may undo what is done by the Fates or another god. Yet these halls have a thousand beauties, each ripe as the next. Look to them instead."

I waited. I still hoped Glaucos would think of me. I would have married him in a moment. But I found myself hoping for another thing too, which I would not have believed the day before: that he would weep all the salt in his veins for Scylla's return, holding fast to her as his one, true love.

"I understand," Glaucos said. "It is a shame, but as you say there are others."

A soft metal ping rang out. He was flicking the tines of his trident. "Nereus' youngest is fair," he said. "What is her name? Thetis?"

My father clicked his tongue. "Too salted for my taste."

"Well," Glaucos said. "Thank you for your excellent counsel. I will look to it."

They walked right by me. My father took his golden place beside my grandfather. Glaucos made his way to the purple couches. He looked up at something a river-god said and laughed. It is the last memory I have of his face, his teeth bright as pearls in the torchlight, his skin stained blue.

In years to come, he would take my father's advice indeed. He lay with a thousand nymphs, siring children with green hair and tails, well loved by fishermen, for often they filled their nets. I would see them sometimes, sporting like dolphins in the deepest crests. They never came in to shore.

The black river slid along its banks. The pale flowers nodded on their stems. I was blind to all of it. One by one my hopes were dropping away. I would share no eternity with Glaucos. We would have no marriage. We would never lie in those woods. His love for me was drowned and gone.

Nymphs and gods flowed past, their gossip drifting in the fragrant, torch-lit air. Their faces were the same as always, vivid and glowing, but they seemed suddenly alien. Their strings of jewels clacked loud as bird-bills, their red mouths stretched wide around their laughter. Somewhere Glaucos laughed among them, but I could not pick his voice out from the throng.

Not all gods need be the same.

My face had begun to burn. It was not pain, not exactly, but a stinging that went on and on. I pressed my fingers to my cheeks. How long had it been since I'd thought of Prometheus? A vision of him rose before me now: his torn back and steady face, his dark eyes encompassing everything.

Prometheus had not cried out as the blows fell, though he had grown so covered in blood that he'd looked like a statue dipped in gold. And all the while, the gods had watched, their attention bright as lightning. They would have relished a turn with the Fury's whip, given the chance.

I was not like them.

Are you not? The voice was my uncle's, resonant and deep. *Then you must think, Circe. What would they not do?*

My father's chair was draped with the skins of pure-black lambs. I knelt by their dangling necks.

"Father," I said, "it was I who made Scylla a monster."

All around me, voices dropped. I cannot say if the very furthest couches looked, if Glaucos looked, but all my uncles did, snapped up from their drowsy conversation. I felt a sharp joy. For the first time in my life, I wanted their eyes.

"I used wicked *pharmaka* to make Glaucos a god, and then I changed Scylla. I was jealous of his love for her and wanted to make her ugly. I did it selfishly, in bitter heart, and I would bear the consequence."

"*Pharmaka*," my father said.

"Yes. The yellow flowers that grow from Kronos' spilled blood and turn creatures to their truest selves. I dug up a hundred flowers and dropped them in her pool."

I had expected a whip to be brought forth, a Fury summoned. A place in chains beside my uncle's on the rock. But my father only filled his cup. "It is no matter. Those flowers have no powers in them, not anymore. Zeus and I made sure of that."

I stared at him. "Father, I did it. With my own hands, I broke their stalks and smeared the sap on Glaucos' lips, and he was changed."

"You had a premonition, which is common in my children." His voice was even, firm as a stone wall. "It was Glaucos' fate to be changed at that moment. The herbs did nothing."

"No," I tried to say, but he did not pause. His voice lifted, to cover mine.

"Think, daughter. If mortals could be made into gods so

easily, would not every goddess feed them to her favorite? And would not half the nymphs be changed to monsters? You are not the first jealous girl in these halls."

My uncles were beginning to smile.

"I am the only one who knows where those flowers are."

"Of course you are not," my uncle Proteus said. "You had that knowledge from me. Do you think I would have given it, if I thought you could do any harm?"

"And if there was so much power in those plants," Nereus said, "my fish from Scylla's cove would be changed. Yet they are whole and well."

My face was flushing. "No." I shook off Nereus' seaweed hand. "I changed Scylla, and now I must take the punishment on my head."

"Daughter, you begin to make a spectacle." The words cut across the air. "If the world contained the power you allege, do you think it would fall to such as you to discover it?"

Soft laughter at my back, open amusement on my uncles' faces. But most of all my father's voice, speaking those words like trash he dropped. *Such as you.* Any other day in all my years of life I would have curled upon myself and wept. But that day his scorn was like a spark falling on dry tinder. My mouth opened.

"You are wrong," I said.

He had leaned away to note something to my grandfather. Now his gaze swung back to mine. His face began to glow. "What did you say?"

"I say those plants have power."

His skin flared white. White as the fire's heart, as purest, hottest coals. He stood, yet he kept on rising, as if he would tear a hole in the ceiling, in the earth's crust, as if he would not cease until he scraped the stars. And then the heat came, rolling over me with a sound like roaring waves, blistering my skin, crushing the breath from my chest. I gasped, but there was no air. He had taken it all.

"You dare to contradict me? You who cannot light a single flame, or call one drop of water? Worst of my children, faded and broken, whom I cannot pay a husband to take. Since you were born, I pitied you and allowed you license, yet you grew disobedient and proud. Will you make me hate you more?"

In another moment, the rocks themselves would have melted, and all my watery cousins dried up to their bones. My flesh bubbled and opened like a roasted fruit, my voice shriveled in my throat and was scorched to dust. The pain was such as I had never imagined could exist, a searing agony consuming every thought.

I fell to my father's feet. "Father," I croaked, "forgive me. I was wrong to believe such a thing."

Slowly, the heat receded. I lay where I had fallen upon the mosaic floor, with its fish and purpled fruits. My eyes were half blind. My hands were melted claws. The river-gods shook their heads, making sounds like water over rocks. *Helios, you have the strangest children.*

My father sighed. "It is Perse's fault. All the ones before hers were fine."

I did not move. The hours passed and no one looked at me or spoke my name. They talked of their own affairs, of the fineness of the wine and food. The torches went out and the couches emptied. My father rose and stepped over me. The faint breeze he stirred cut into my skin like a knife. I had thought my grandmother might speak a soft word, bring salve to sooth my burns, but she had gone to her bed.

Perhaps they will send guards for me, I thought. But why should they? I was no danger in the world.

The waves of pain ran cold and then hot and then cold again. I shook and the hours passed. My limbs were raw and blackened, my back bubbled over with sores. I was afraid to touch my face. Dawn would come soon, and my whole family would pour in for their breakfasts, chattering of the day's amusements. They would curl their lips as they passed by where I lay.

Inch by slow inch, I drew myself to my feet. The thought of returning to my father's halls was like a white coal in my throat. I could not go home. There was only one other place in all the world I knew: those woods I had dreamed of so often. The deep shadows would hide me, and the mossy ground would be soft against my ruined skin. I set that image in my eye and limped towards it. The salt air of the beach stabbed like needles in my blasted throat, and each touch of wind set my burns screaming again. At last, I felt the shade close over me, and I curled up on the moss. It had rained a little, and the damp earth was sweet against me. So many times I had imagined lying there with Glaucos, but whatever tears might have been in me for that lost dream had been parched away. I closed my eyes, drifting through the shocks and skirls of pain. Slowly, my relentless divinity began to make headway. My breath eased, my eyes cleared. My arms and legs still ached, but when I brushed them with my fingers I touched skin instead of char.

The sun set, glowing behind the trees. Night came with its stars. It was moondark, when my aunt Selene goes to her dreaming husband. It was that, I think, which gave me heart enough to rise, for I could not have endured the thought of her reporting it: *That fool actually went to look at them! As if she still believed they worked!*

The night air tingled across my skin. The grass was dry,

flattened by high-summer heat. I found the hill and halted up its slope. In the starlight, the flowers looked small, bled gray and faint. I plucked a stalk and held it in my hand. It lay there limp, all its sap dried and gone. What had I thought would happen? That it would leap up and shout, *Your father is wrong. You changed Scylla and Glaucos. You are not poor and patchy, but Zeus come again?*

Yet, as I knelt there, I did hear something. Not a sound, but a sort of silence, a faint hum like the space between note and note in a song. I waited for it to fade into the air, for my mind to right itself. But it went on.

I had a wild thought there, beneath that sky. *I will eat these herbs. Then whatever is truly in me, let it be out, at last.*

I brought them to my mouth. But my courage failed. What was I truly? In the end, I could not bear to know.

It was nearly dawn when my uncle Achelous found me, beard foaming in his haste. "Your brother is here. You are summoned."

I followed him to my father's halls, still stumbling a little. Past the polished tables we went, past the draped bedroom where my mother slept. Aeëtes was standing over our father's draughts board. His face had grown sharp with manhood, his tawny beard was thick as bracken. He was dressed opulently even for a god, robed in indigos and purples, every inch heavy with embroidered gold. But when he turned to me, I felt the shock of that old love between us. It was only my father's presence that kept me from hurtling into his arms.

"Brother," I said, "I have missed you."

He frowned. "What is wrong with your face?"

I touched my hand to it, and the peeling skin flared with pain. I flushed. I did not want to tell him, not here. My father sat in his burning chair, and even his faint, habitual light made me ache anew.

My father spared me from having to answer. "Well? She is come. Speak."

I quivered at the sound of his displeasure, but Aeëtes' face was calm, as if my father's anger were only another thing in the room, a table, a stool.

"I have come," he said, "because I heard of Scylla's transformation, and Glaucos' too, at Circe's hands."

"At the Fates' hands. I tell you, Circe has no such power."

"You are mistaken."

I stared, expecting my father's wrath to fall upon him. But my brother continued.

"In my kingdom of Colchis, I have done such things and more, much more. Called milk out of the earth, bewitched men's senses, shaped warriors from dust. I have summoned dragons to draw my chariot. I have said charms that veil the sky with black, and brewed potions that raise the dead."

From anyone else's mouth these claims would have seemed like wild lies. But my brother's voice carried its old utter conviction.

"*Pharmakeia*, such arts are called, for they deal in *pharmaka*, those herbs with the power to work changes upon the world, both those sprung from the blood of gods, as well as those which grow common upon the earth. It is a gift to be able to draw out their powers, and I am not alone in possessing it. In Crete, Pasiphaë rules with her poisons, and in Babylon Perses conjures souls into flesh again. Circe is the last and makes the proof."

My father's gaze was far away. As if he were looking through sea and earth, all the way to Colchis. It might have been some trick of the hearth-fire, but I thought the light of his face flickered.

"Shall I give you a demonstration?" My brother drew out from his robes a small pot with a wax seal. He broke the seal and touched his finger to the liquid inside. I smelled something sharp and green, with a brackish edge.

He pressed his thumb to my face and spoke a word, too low for me to hear. My skin began to itch, and then, like a taper snuffed out, the pain was gone. When I put my hand to my cheek I felt only smoothness, and a faint sheen as if from oil.

"A good trick, is it not?" Aeëtes said.

My father did not answer. He sat strangely dumb. I felt struck dumb myself. The power of healing another's flesh belonged only to the greatest gods, not to such as us.

My brother smiled, as if he could hear my thoughts. "And that is the least of my powers. They are drawn from the earth itself, and so are not bound by the normal laws of divinity." He let the words hang a moment in the air. "I understand of course that you can make no judgments now. You must take counsel. But you should know that I would be happy to give Zeus a more...impressive demonstration."

A look flashed in his eyes, like teeth in a wolf's mouth.

My father's words came slowly. That same numbness still masked his face. I understood with an odd jolt. *He is afraid.*

"I must take counsel, as you say. This is...new. Until it is decided, you will remain in these halls. Both of you."

"I expected no less," Aeëtes said. He inclined his head and turned to go. I followed, skin prickling with the rush of my thoughts, and a breathless, rearing hope. The myrrh-wood doors shut behind us, and we stood in the hall.

Aeëtes' face was calm, as if he had not just performed a miracle and silenced our father. I had a thousand questions ready to tumble out, but he spoke first.

"What have you been doing all this while? You took forever. I was beginning to think maybe you weren't a *pharmakis* after all."

It was not a word I knew. It was not a word anyone knew, then.

"*Pharmakis*," I said.

Witch.

News ran like spring rivers. At dinner, the children of Oceanos whispered when they saw me and skittered out of my path. If our arms brushed they paled, and when I passed a goblet to a river-god, his eyes dodged away. *Oh no, thank you, I am not thirsty.*

Aeëtes laughed. "You will get used to it. We are ourselves alone now."

He did not seem alone. Every night he sat on my grandfather's dais with my father and our uncles. I watched him, drinking nectar, laughing, showing his teeth. His expressions darted like schools of fish in the water, now light, now dark.

I waited till our father was gone, then went to sit in a chair near him. I longed to take the place beside him on the couch, lean against his shoulder, but he seemed so grim and straight, I did not know how to touch him.

"You like your kingdom? Colchis?"

"It is the finest in the world," he said. "I have done what I said, sister. I have gathered there all the wonders of our lands."

I smiled to hear him call me sister, to speak of those old dreams. "I wish I could see it."

He said nothing. He was a magician who could break the teeth of snakes, tear up oaks by their roots. He did not need me.

"Do you have Daedalus too?"

He made a face. "No, Pasiphaë has him trapped. Perhaps in time. I have a giant fleece made of gold, though, and half a dozen dragons."

I did not have to draw his stories out of him. They burst forth, the spells and charms he cast, the beasts he summoned, the herbs he cut by moonlight and brewed into miracles. Each tale was more outlandish than the last, thunder leaping to his fingertips, lambs cooked and born again from their charred bones.

"What was it you spoke when you healed my skin?"

"A word of power."

"Will you teach it to me?"

"Sorcery cannot be taught. You find it yourself, or you do not."

I thought of the humming I had heard when I touched those flowers, the eerie knowledge that had glided through me.

"How long have you known you could do such things?"

"Since I was born," he said. "But I had to wait until I was out from Father's eye."

All those years beside me, and he had said nothing. I opened my mouth to demand: how could you not tell me? But this new Aeëtes in his vivid robes was too unnerving.

"Were you not afraid," I said, "that Father would be angry?"

"No. I was not fool enough to try to humiliate him in front of everyone." He lifted his eyebrows at me, and I flushed. "Anyway, he is eager to imagine how such strength may be used to his benefit. His worry is over

Zeus. He must paint us just right: that we are threat enough that Zeus should think twice, but not so much that he is forced to act."

My brother, who had always seen into the cracks of the world.

"What if the Olympians try to take your spells from you?"

He smiled. "I think they cannot, whatever they try. As I said, *pharmakeia* is not bound by the usual limits of gods."

I looked down at my hands and tried to imagine them weaving a spell to shake the world. But the certainty I had felt when I dripped the sap into Glaucos' mouth and tainted Scylla's cove, I could not seem to find anymore. Perhaps, I thought, if I could touch those flowers again. But I was not allowed to leave until my father spoke to Zeus.

"And . . . you think I can work such wonders as you do?"

"No," my brother said. "I am the strongest of the four of us. But you do show a taste for transformation."

"That was only the flowers," I said. "They grant creatures their truest forms."

He turned his philosopher's eye on me. "You do not think it convenient that their truest forms should happen to be your desires?"

I stared at him. "I did not desire to make Scylla a monster. I only meant to reveal the ugliness within her."

"And you believe *that's* what was truly in her? A six-headed slavering horror?"

My face was stinging. "Why not? You did not know her. She was very cruel."

He laughed. "Oh, Circe. She was a painted back-hall slattern same as the rest. If you will argue one of the greatest monsters of our age was hiding within her, then you are more of a fool than I thought."

"I do not think anyone can say what is in someone else."

He rolled his eyes and poured himself another cup. "What I think," he said, "is that Scylla has escaped the punishment you intended for her."

"What do you mean?"

"Think. What would an ugly nymph do in our halls? What is the worth of her life?"

It was like the old days, him asking, and me without answers. "I don't know."

"Of course you do. It's why it would have been a good punishment. Even the most beautiful nymph is largely useless, and an ugly one would be nothing, less than nothing. She would never marry or produce children. She would be a burden to her family, a stain upon the face of the world. She would live in the shadows, scorned and reviled. But a monster," he said, "she always has a place. She may have all the glory her teeth can snatch. She will not be loved for it, but she will not be constrained either. So whatever foolish sorrow you harbor, forget it. I think it may be said that you improved her."

For two nights, my father was closeted with my uncles. I lingered outside the mahogany doors but could hear nothing, not even a murmur. When they emerged, their faces were set and grim. My father strode to his chariot. His purple cloak glowed dark as wine, and on his head shone his great crown of golden rays. He did not look back as he leapt into the sky and turned the horses towards Olympus.

We waited in Oceanos' halls for his return. No one lounged on the riverbank or twined with a lover in the shadows. The naiads squabbled with red cheeks. The rivergods shoved each other. From his dais, my grandfather stared out over all of us, his cup empty in his hand. My

mother was boasting among her sisters. "Perses and
Pasiphaë were the ones who knew first, of course. Is it any
wonder Circe was last? I plan to have a hundred more,
and they will make me a silver boat that flies through the
clouds. We will rule upon Olympus."

"Perse!" my grandmother hissed across the room.

Only Aeëtes did not seem to feel the tension. He sat
serene on his couch, drinking from his wrought-gold cup.
I kept to the back, pacing the long passageways, running
my hands over the rock walls, always faintly damp from
the presence of so many water-gods. I scanned the room
to see if Glaucos had come. There was still a piece of me
that longed to look upon him, even then. When I'd asked
Aeëtes if Glaucos feasted with the rest of the gods, he had
grinned. "He's hiding that blue face of his. He's waiting for
everyone to forget the truth of how he came by it."

My stomach twisted. I had not thought how my confession would take Glaucos' greatest pride from him. Too
late, I thought. Too late for all the things I should have
known. I had made so many mistakes that I could not find
my way back through their tangle to the first one. Was it
changing Scylla, changing Glaucos, swearing the oath to
my grandmother? Speaking to Glaucos in the first place? I
felt a sickening unease that it went back further still, back
to the first breath I ever drew.

My father would be standing before Zeus now. My
brother was sure that the Olympians could do nothing to
us. But four Titan witches could not be easily dismissed.
What if war came again? The great hall would crack open
over us. Zeus' head would blot out the light, and his hand
would reach down to crush us one by one. Aeëtes would
call his dragons, at least he could fight. What could I do?
Pick flowers?

My mother was bathing her feet. Two sisters held the silver basin, a third poured the sweet myrrh oil from its flask. I was being a fool, I told myself. There would be no war. My father was an old hand at such maneuvering. He would find a way to appease Zeus.

The room brightened, and my father came. On his face was a look like hammered bronze. Our eyes followed him as he strode to the dais at the room's front. The rays from his crown speared every shadow. He stared out over us. "I have spoken to Zeus," he said. "We have found our way to an agreement."

A soughing relief from my cousins, like wind through wheat.

"He agrees that something new moves in the world. That these powers are unlike any that have come before. He agrees that they grow from my four children with the nymph Perse."

A ripple again, this one tinged with growing excitement. My mother licked her lips, tilting her chin as if there were already a crown on her head. Her sisters glanced at each other, gnawing on their envy.

"We have agreed as well that these powers present no immediate danger. Perses lives beyond our boundaries and is no threat. Pasiphaë's husband is a son of Zeus, and he will be sure she is held to her proper place. Aeëtes will keep his kingdom, as long as he agrees to be watched."

My brother nodded gravely, but I saw the smile in his eyes. *I can veil the sky itself. Just try to watch me.*

"Each of them has sworn besides that their powers came unbidden and unlooked for, from no malice, or attempted revolt. They stumbled upon the magic of herbs by accident."

Surprised, I darted another glance at my brother, but his face was unreadable.

"Each of them, except for Circe. You were all here when she confessed that she sought her powers openly. She had been warned to stay away, yet she disobeyed."

My grandmother's face, cold in her ivory-carved chair.

"She defied my commands and contradicted my authority. She has turned her poisons against her own kind and committed other treacheries as well." The white sear of his gaze landed on me. "She is a disgrace to our name. An ingrate to the care we have shown her. It is agreed with Zeus that for this she must be punished. She is exiled to a deserted island where she can do no more harm. She leaves tomorrow."

A thousand eyes pinned me. I wanted to cry out, to plead, but my breath would not catch. My voice, ever thin, was gone. Aeëtes will speak for me, I thought. But when I cast my gaze to him, he only looked back with all the rest.

"One more thing," my father said. "As I noted, it is clear that the source of this new power comes from my union with Perse."

My mother's face, glossy with triumph, beaming through my haze.

"So it is agreed: I will sire no more children upon her."

My mother screamed, falling backwards on her sisters' laps. Her sobs echoed off the stone walls.

My grandfather got slowly to his feet. He rubbed at his chin. "Well," he said. "It is time for the feast."

The torches burned like stars, and overhead the ceilings stretched high as the sky's vault. For the last time, I watched all the gods and nymphs take their places. I felt dazed. I should say goodbye, I kept thinking. But my cousins flowed away from me like water around a rock. I heard their sneering whispers as they passed. I found myself missing Scylla. At least she would have dared to speak to my face.

My grandmother, I thought, I must try to explain. But she turned away as well, and her sea snake buried its head.

All the while my mother wept in her flock of sisters. When I came close, she raised her face so everyone could see her beautiful, extravagant grief. *Have you not done enough?*

That left only my uncles, with their kelp hair and briny, scraggled beards. Yet when I thought of kneeling at their feet, I could not bring myself to do it.

I went back to my room. Pack, I told myself. Pack, you are leaving tomorrow. But my hands hung numbly at my sides. How should I know what to bring? I had scarcely ever left these halls.

I forced myself to find a bag, to gather clothes and sandals, a brush for my hair. I considered a tapestry on my wall. It was of a wedding and its party, woven by some aunt. Would I even have a house to hang it in? I did not know. I did not know anything. A deserted island, my father had said. Would it be bare rock exposed upon the sea, a pebbled shoal, a tangled wilderness? My bag was an absurdity, full of gilded detritus. The knife, I thought, the lion's-head knife, I will bring that. But when I held it, it looked shrunken, meant to spear up morsels at a feast and no more.

"It could have been much worse, you know." Aeëtes had come to stand in my doorway. He was leaving too, his dragons already summoned. "I heard Zeus wanted to make an example of you. But of course Father can only allow him so much license."

The hairs stirred on my arms. "You did not tell him about Prometheus, did you?"

He smiled. "Why, because he spoke of 'other treacheries'? You know Father. He's only being cautious, in case some further terror of yours comes to light. Anyway, what is there to tell? What did you do after all? Pour a single glass of nectar?"

I looked up. "You said Father would have thrown me to the crows for it."

"Only if you were fool enough to admit it."

My face was hot. "I suppose I should take you as my tutor and deny everything?"

"Yes," he said. "That is how it works, Circe. I tell Father that my sorcery was an accident, he pretends to believe me, and Zeus pretends to believe him, and so the world is balanced. It is your own fault for confessing. Why you did that, I will never understand."

It was true, he would not. He had not been born when Prometheus was whipped.

"I meant to tell you," he said. "I finally met your Glaucos last night. I have never seen such a buffoon." He clicked his tongue. "I hope you will choose better ahead. You have always trusted too easily."

I looked at him leaning in my doorway with his long robes and bright, wolfish eyes. My heart had leapt to see him as it always did. But he was like that column of water he had told me of once, cold and straight, sufficient to himself.

"Thank you for your counsel," I said.

He left and I considered the tapestry again. Its groom was goggle-eyed, the bride buried in her veils, and behind them the family gaped like idiots. I had always hated it. Let it stay and rot.

CHAPTER SEVEN

THE NEXT MORNING, I stepped into my father's char-iot and we lurched into the dark sky without a word. The air blew past us; night receded at every turning of the wheels. I looked over the side, trying to track the rivers and seas, the shadowed valleys, but we were going too fast, and I recognized nothing.

"What island is it?"

My father did not answer. His jaw was set, his lips bled pale with anger. My old burns were aching from standing so close to him. I closed my eyes. The lands streamed by and the wind ran across my skin. I imagined pitching over that golden rail into the open air below. It would feel good, I thought, before I hit.

We landed with a jolt. I opened my eyes to see a high soft hill, thick with grass. My father stared straight ahead. I felt a sudden urge to fall on my knees and beg him to take me back, but instead I forced myself to step down onto the ground. The moment my foot touched, he and his chariot were gone.

I stood alone in that grassy clearing. The breeze blew sharp against my cheeks, and the air had a fresh scent.

I could not savor it. My head felt heavy, and my throat had begun to ache. I swayed. By now, Aeëtes was back on Colchis, drinking his milk and honey. My aunts would be laughing on their riverbanks, my cousins returned to their games. My father, of course, was overhead, shedding his light down on the world. All those years I had spent with them were like a stone tossed in a pool. Already, the ripples were gone.

I had a little pride. If they did not weep, I would not either. I pressed my palms to my eyes until they cleared. I made myself look around.

On the hilltop before me was a house, wide-porched, its walls built from finely fitted stone, its doors carved twice the height of a man. A little below stretched a hem of forests, and beyond that a glimpse of the sea.

It was the forest that drew my eye. It was old growth, gnarled with oaks and lindens and olive groves, shot through with spearing cypress. That's where the green scent came from, drifting up the grassy hillside. The trees shook themselves thickly in the sea-winds, and birds darted through the shadows. Even now I can remember the wonder I felt. All my life had been spent in the same dim halls, or walking the same stunted shore with its threadbare woods. I was not prepared for such profusion and I felt the sudden urge to throw myself in, like a frog into a pond.

I hesitated. I was no wood-nymph. I did not have the knack of feeling my way over roots, of walking through brambles untouched. I could not guess what those shadows might conceal. What if there were sinkholes within? What if there were bears or lions?

I stood there a long time fearing such things and waiting, as if someone would come and reassure me, say yes, you may go, it will be safe. My father's chariot slipped over the sea and began to douse itself in the waves. The shadows of the forest deepened and the trunks seemed to twine against each other. It is too late to go now, I told myself. Tomorrow.

The doors of the house were broad oak, banded with iron. They swung easily at my touch. Inside the air smelled of incense. There was a great-room set with tables and benches as if for a feast. A hearth anchored one end; at the other, a corridor led away to the kitchen and bedrooms. It was large enough to hold a dozen goddesses, and indeed I kept expecting to find nymphs and cousins around every turn. But no, that was part of my exile. To be utterly alone. What worse punishment could there be, my family thought, than to be deprived of their divine presence?

Certainly the house itself was no punishment. Treasures shone on every side: carved chests, soft rugs and golden hangings, beds, stools, intricate tripods, and ivory statues. The windowsills were white marble, the shutters scrolled ash wood. In the kitchen, I ran my thumb across the knives, bronze and iron, but also nacre shell and obsidian. I found bowls of quartz crystal and wrought silver. Though the rooms were deserted, there was no speck of dust, and I would learn that none could cross the marble threshold. However I tracked upon it, the floor was always clean, the tables gleaming. The ashes vanished from the fireplace, the dishes washed themselves, and the firewood regrew overnight. In the pantry there were jars of oil and wine, bowls of cheese and barley-grain, always fresh and full.

Among those empty, perfect rooms, I felt — I could not say. Disappointed. There was a part of me, I think, that had hoped for a crag in the Caucasus after all, and an eagle diving for my liver. But Scylla was no Zeus, and I was no Prometheus. We were nymphs, not worth the trouble.

There was more to it than that, though. My father might have left me in a hovel or a fisherman's shack, on a bare beach with nothing but a tent. I thought back to his face when he spoke of Zeus' decree, his clear, ringing rage. I had assumed it was all for me, but now, after my talks with Aeëtes, I began to understand more. The truce between the gods held only because Titans and Olympians each kept to their sphere. Zeus had demanded the discipline of Helios' blood. Helios could not speak back openly, but he could make an answer of sorts, a message of defiance to rebalance the scales. *Even our exiles live better than kings. You see how deep our strength runs? If you strike us, Olympian, we rise higher than before.*

That was my new home: a monument to my father's pride.

It was past sundown by then. I found the flint and struck it over the waiting tinder as I had seen Glaucos do so often, but never attempted myself. It took me several tries, and when the flames began to catch and spread at last, I felt a novel satisfaction.

I was hungry so I went to the pantry, where the bowls brimmed with enough food to feed a hundred. I spooned some onto a plate and sat at one of the great oak tables in the hall. I could hear the sound of my breath. It struck me that I had never eaten by myself. Even when no one spoke to me or looked at me, there was always some cousin or sibling at my elbow. I rubbed the fine-grained wood. I hummed a little and listened to the sound being swallowed by the air. This is what it will be all my days, I thought. Despite the fire, shadows were gathering in the corners. Outside, birds had begun to scream. At least I thought they were birds. I felt the hairs stir on my neck, thinking again of those dark, thick trunks. I went to the shutters and closed them, I latched the door. I was used to the weight of all the earth's rocks surrounding me, and my father's power on top of that. The house's walls felt to me leaf-thin. Any claw would tear them open. Perhaps that is the secret of this place, I thought. My true punishment is yet to come.

Stop, I told myself. I lit tapers, and made myself carry them down the hall to my room. In the daylight it had seemed large, and I had been pleased, but now I could not watch every corner at once. The feathers of the bed murmured against each other, and the shutter-wood creaked like the ropes of ships in a storm. All around me I felt the wild hollows of the island swelling in their dark.

Until that moment I had not known how many things I feared. Huge, ghostly leviathans slithering up the hillside, nightworms squirming out of their burrows, pressing their blind faces to my door. Goat-footed gods eager to feed their savage appetites, pirates muffling their oars in my harbor, planning how they would take me. And what could I do? *Pharmakis*, Aeëtes named me, *witch*, but all my strength was in those flowers, oceans away. If anyone came, I would only be able to scream, and a thousand nymphs before me knew what good that did.

The fear sloshed over me, each wave colder than the last. The still air crawled across my skin and shadows reached out their hands. I stared into the darkness, straining to hear past the beat of my own blood. Each moment felt the length of a night, but at last the sky took on a deepening texture and began to pale at its edge. The shadows ebbed away and it was morning. I stood up, whole and untouched. When I went outside, there were no prowling footprints, no slithering tail-marks, no gouges clawed in the door. Yet I did not feel foolish. I felt as if I had passed a great ordeal.

I looked again into that forest. Yesterday — was it only yesterday? — I had waited for someone to come and tell me it safe. But who would that be? My father, Aeëtes? That is what exile meant: no one was coming, no one ever would. There was fear in that knowledge, but after my long night of terrors it felt small and inconsequential. The worst of my cowardice had been sweated out. In its place was a giddy spark. I will not be like a bird bred in a cage, I thought, too dull to fly even when the door stands open.

I stepped into those woods and my life began.

I learned to braid my hair back, so it would not catch on every twig, and how to tie my skirts at the knee to keep the burrs off. I learned to recognize the different blooming vines and gaudy roses, to spot the shining dragonflies and coiling snakes. I climbed the peaks where the cypresses speared black into the sky, then clambered down to the orchards and vineyards where purple grapes grew thick as coral. I walked the hills, the buzzing meadows of thyme and lilac, and set my footprints across the yellow beaches. I searched out every cove and grotto, found the gentle bays, the harbor safe for ships. I heard the wolves howl, and the frogs cry from their mud. I stroked the glossy brown scorpions who braved me with their tails. Their poison was barely a pinch. I was drunk, as the wine and nectar in my father's halls had never made me. No wonder I have been so slow, I thought. All this while, I have been a weaver without wool, a ship without the sea. Yet now look where I sail.

At night I went home to my house. I did not mind its shadows anymore, for they meant my father's gaze was gone from the sky and the hours were my own. I did not mind the emptiness either. For a thousand years I had tried to fill the space between myself and my family. Filling the rooms of my house was easy by comparison. I burned cedar in the fireplace, and its dark smoke kept me company. I sang, which had never been allowed before, since my mother said I had the voice of a drowning gull. And when I did get lonely, when I found myself yearning for my brother, or Glaucos as he had been, then there was always the forest. The lizards darted along the branches, the birds flashed their wings. The flowers, when they saw me, seemed to press forward like eager puppies, leaping and clamoring for my touch. I felt almost shy of them, but day by day I grew bolder, and at last I knelt in the damp earth before a clump of hellebore.

The delicate blooms fluttered on their stalks. I did not need a knife to cut them, only the edge of my nail, which grew sticky with flecks of sap. I put the flowers in a basket covered with cloth and only uncovered them when I was home again, my shutters firmly closed. I did not think anyone would try to stop me, but I did not intend to tempt them to it.

I looked at the blossoms lying on my table. They seemed shrunken, etiolated. I did not have the first idea of what I should do to them. Chop? Boil? Roast? There had been oil in my brother's ointment, but I did not know what kind. Would olive from the kitchen work? Surely not. It must be something fantastical, like seed-oil pressed from the fruits of the Hesperides. But I could not get that. I rolled a stalk beneath my finger. It turned over, limp as a drowned worm.

Well, I said to myself, do not just stand there like a stone. Try something. Boil them. Why not?

I had a little pride, as I have said, and that was good. More would have been fatal.

Let me say what sorcery is not: it is not divine power, which comes with a thought and a blink. It must be made and worked, planned and searched out, dug up, dried, chopped and ground, cooked, spoken over, and sung. Even after all that, it can fail, as gods do not. If my herbs are not fresh enough, if my attention falters, if my will is weak, the draughts go stale and rancid in my hands.

By rights, I should never have come to witchcraft. Gods hate all toil, it is their nature. The closest we come is weaving or smithing, but these things are skills, and there is no drudgery to them since all the parts that might be unpleasant are taken away with power. The wool is dyed not with stinking vats and stirring spoons, but with a snap. There is no tedious mining, the ores leap willing from the mountain. No fingers are ever chafed, no muscles strained.

Witchcraft is nothing but such drudgery. Each herb must be found in its den, harvested at its time, grubbed up from the dirt, culled and stripped, washed and prepared. It must be handled this way, then that, to find out where its power lies. Day upon patient day, you must throw out your errors and begin again. So why did I not mind? Why did none of us mind?

I cannot speak for my brothers and sister, but my answer is easy. For a hundred generations, I had walked the world drowsy and dull, idle and at my ease. I left no prints, I did no deeds. Even those who had loved me a little did not care to stay.

Then I learned that I could bend the world to my will, as a bow is bent for an arrow. I would have done that toil a thousand times to keep such power in my hands. I thought: this is how Zeus felt when he first lifted the thunderbolt.

At first, of course, all I brewed were mistakes. Draughts that did nothing, pastes that crumbled and lay dead on the table. I thought that if some rue was good, more was better, that ten herbs mixed were superior to five, that I could let my mind wander and the spell would not wander with it, that I could begin making one draught and halfway through decide to make another. I did not know even the simplest herb-lore that any mortal would learn at her mother's knee: that wort plants boiled made a sort of soap, that yew burnt in the hearth sent up a choking smog, that poppies had sleep in their veins and hellebore death, and yarrow could close over wounds. All these things had to be worked and learned through errors and trials, burnt fingers and fetid clouds that sent me running outside to cough in the garden.

At least, I thought in those early days, once I cast a spell, I would not have to learn it again. But even that was not true. However often I had used an herb before, each cutting had its own character. One rose would give up its secrets if it were ground, another must be pressed, a third steeped. Each spell was a mountain to be climbed anew. All I could carry with me from last time was the knowledge that it could be done.

I pressed on. If my childhood had given me anything, it was endurance. Little by little I began to listen better: to the sap moving in the plants, to the blood in my veins. I learned to understand my own intention, to prune and to add, to feel where the power gathered and speak the right words to draw it to its height. That was the moment I lived for, when it all came clear at last and the spell could sing with its pure note, for me and me alone.

I did not call dragons, or summon serpents. My earliest charms were silly things, whatever came into my head. I started with an acorn, for I had some thought that if the object were green and growing, nourished by water, my na-iad blood might give me some help. For days, months, I rubbed that acorn with oils and salves, speaking words over it to make it sprout. I tried to mimic the sounds I had heard Aeëtes make when he had healed my face. I tried curses, and prayers too, but through it all the acorn kept its seed smugly within. I threw it out the window and got a new one and crouched over that for another half an age. I tried the spell when I was angry, when I was calm, when I was happy, when I was half distracted. One day I told myself that I would rather have no powers than try that spell again. What did I want with an oak seedling anyway? The island was full of them. What I really wanted was a wild strawberry, to slip sweetly down my irritable throat, and so I told that brown hull.

It changed so fast my thumb sank into its soft, red body. I stared, and then I whooped with triumph, startling the birds outside from their trees.

I brought a withered flower back to life. I banished flies from my house. I made the cherries blossom out of season and turned the fire vivid green. If Aeëtes had been there, he would have choked on his beard to see such kitchen-tricks. Yet because I knew nothing, nothing was beneath me.

My powers lapped upon themselves like waves. I found I had a knack for illusion, summoning shadow crumbs for the mice to creep after, making pale minnows leap from the waves beneath a cormorant's beak. I thought larger: a ferret to frighten off the moles, an owl to keep away the rabbits. I learned that the best time to harvest was beneath the moon, when dew and darkness concentrated sap. I learned what grew well in a garden, and what must be left to its place in the woods. I caught snakes and learned how to milk their teeth. I could coax a drop of venom from the tail of a wasp. I healed a dying tree, I killed a poisonous vine with a touch.

But Aeëtes had been right, my greatest gift was transformation, and that was always where my thoughts returned. I stood before a rose, and it became an iris. A draught poured onto the roots of an ash tree changed it to a holm oak. I turned all my firewood to cedar so that its scent would fill my halls each night. I caught a bee and made it into a toad, and a scorpion into a mouse.

There I discovered at last the limits of my power. However potent the mixture, however well woven the spell, the toad kept trying to fly, and the mouse to sting. Transformation touched only bodies, not minds.

I thought of Scylla then. Did her nymph-self live still inside that six-headed monster? Or did plants grown from the blood of gods make the change a true one? I did not know. Into the air I said, *Wherever you are, I hope you are finding your satisfaction.*

Which, of course, now I know she was.

It was one day during that time that I found myself among the thickest brakes of the forest. I loved to walk the island, from its lowest shores to its highest haunts, seeking out the hidden mosses and ferns and vines, collecting their leaves for my charms. It was late afternoon, and my basket overflowed. I stepped around a bush, and the boar was there.

I had known for some time that there were wild pigs on the island. I'd heard them squealing and crashing in the brush, and often I would find some rhododendron trampled, or a stand of saplings rooted up. This was the first one I had seen.

He was huge, even bigger than I had imagined a boar could be. His spine rose steep and black as the ridges of Mount Cynthos, and his shoulders were slashed with the thunderbolt scars of his fights. Only the bravest heroes face such creatures, and then they are armed with spears and dogs, archers and assistants, and usually half a dozen warriors besides. I had only my digging knife and my basket, and not a single spell-draught to hand.

He stamped, and the white foam dripped from his mouth. He lowered his tusks and ground his jaws. His pig-eyes said: *I can break a hundred youths and send their bodies back to wailing mothers. I will tear your entrails and eat them for my lunch.*

I fixed my gaze on his. "Try," I said.

For a long moment he stared at me. Then he turned and twitched off through the brush. I tell you, for all my spells, that was the first time I truly felt myself a witch.

At my hearth that night, I thought of those prancing goddesses who carry birds on their shoulders, or have some fawn always nuzzling their hands, tripping delicately at their heels. I would put them to shame, I thought. I climbed to the highest peaks and found a lonely track: here a flower crushed, here the dirt turned a little and some bark clawed off. I brewed a potion with crocus and yellow jasmine, iris and cypress root dug at the moon's full height. I sprinkled it, singing. *I summon you.*

She came rippling through my door at the next dusk, her shoulder muscles hard as stones. She lay across my hearth, and rasped my ankles with her tongue. During the day, she brought me rabbits and fish. At night she licked honey from my fingers and slept upon my feet. Sometimes we would play, she stalking behind me, then leaping up to grapple me by the neck. I smelled the hot musk of her breath, felt the weight of her forepaws pressing on my shoulders. Look, I said, showing her the knife I had carried with me from my father's halls, the one stamped with a lion's face. "What fool made this? They have never seen your like."

She cracked her great brown mouth in a yawn.

There was a bronze mirror in my bedroom, tall as the ceiling. When I passed it, I scarcely knew myself. My gaze seemed brighter, my face sharper, and there behind me paced my wild lion familiar. I could imagine what my cousins would say if they saw me: my feet dirty from working in the garden, my skirts knotted up around my knees, singing at the height of my frail voice.

I wished that they would come. I wanted to see those goggle eyes of theirs as I walked among the dens of wolves, swam in the sea where the sharks fed. I could change a fish to a bird, I could wrestle with my lion, then lie across her belly, my hair loose around me. I wanted to hear them squeal and gasp, breath-struck. *Oh, she looked at me! Now I will be a frog!*

Had I truly feared such creatures? Had I really spent ten thousand years ducking like a mouse? I understood now Aeëtes' boldness, how he had stood before our father like a towering peak. When I did my magics, I felt that same span and heft. I tracked my father's burning chariot across the sky. Well? What do you have to say to me? You threw me to the crows, but it turns out I prefer them to you.

No answer came, and none from my aunt Moon either, those cowards. My skin was glowing, my teeth set. My lioness lashed her tail.

Does no one have the courage? Will no one dare to face me?

So you see, in my way, I was eager for what came.

CHAPTER EIGHT

IT WAS SUNSET, MY father's face already dipped beneath the trees. I was working in my garden, staking the leggy vines, planting rosemary and aconite. I was singing too, some aimless air. The lion lay in the grass, her mouth bloodied from the wood-grouse she had flushed.

"I admit," the voice said, "I am surprised to see you so plain after such boasting. A flower garden and braids. You might be any country girl."

The young man was leaning against my house, watching me. His hair was loose and tousled, his face bright as a jewel. Though there was no light to catch them, his golden sandals gleamed.

I knew who he was, of course I knew. The power shone from his face, unmistakable, keen as an unsheathed blade. An Olympian, the son of Zeus and his chosen messenger. That laughing gadfly of the gods, Hermes.

I felt myself tremble, but I would not let him see it. Great gods smell fear like sharks smell blood, and they will devour you for it just the same.

I stood. "What did you expect?"

"Oh, you know." A slim wand twirled idly in his fingers.

"Something more lurid. Dragonish. A troupe of dancing sphinxes. Blood dripping from the sky."

I was used to my thick-shouldered uncles with their white beards, not such perfect, careless beauty. When sculptors shape their stone, they shape it after him.

"Is that what they say of me?"

"Of course. Zeus is sure you're brewing poisons against us all, you and your brother both. You know how he frets." He smiled, easy, conspiratorial. As if the anger of Zeus were only a light jest.

"So you come as Zeus' spy then?"

"I prefer the word *envoy*. But no, in this matter, my father can do his own work. I'm here because my brother is angry with me."

"Your brother," I said.

"Yes," he said. "I think you've heard of him?"

From his cloak he drew a lyre, inlaid with gold and ivory, glowing like the dawn.

"I'm afraid I've stolen this," he said. "And I need a place to shelter till the storm passes. I was hoping you might take pity upon me? Somehow I don't think he'll look here."

The hairs stood on the back of my neck. All who were wise feared the god Apollo's wrath, silent as sunlight, deadly as plague. I had the impulse to look over my shoulder, to make sure he was not striding across the sky already, his gilded arrow pointed at my heart. But there was something in me that was sick of fear and awe, of gazing at the heavens and wondering what someone would allow me.

"Come in," I said, and led him through my door.

I had grown up hearing the stories of Hermes' daring: how as an infant he had risen from his cradle and made off with Apollo's cattle, how he had slain the monstrous guardian

Argos after coaxing each of his thousand eyes to sleep, how he could pry secrets out of a stone and charm even rival gods to do his will.

It was all of it true. He could draw you in as if he were winding up a thread. He could spin you out upon a conceit until you were choking with laughter. I had scarcely known true intelligence — I had spoken to Prometheus for only a moment, and in all the rest of Oceanos' halls most of what passed as cleverness was only archness and spite. Hermes' mind was a thousand times sharper and more swift. It shone like light upon the waves, dazzling to blindness. That night he entertained me with tale after tale of the great gods and their foolishness. Lecherous Zeus turning into a bull to lure a pretty maiden. Ares, god of war, bested by two giants, who kept him crammed in a jar for a year. Hephaestus laying a trap for his wife Aphrodite, hoisting her in a golden net, still naked with her lover Ares, for all the gods to see. On and on he went, through the absurd vices, drunken brawls, and petty slapping squabbles, all told in that same slippery, grinning voice. I felt myself flushed and dizzied, as if I had taken my own draughts.

"Will you not be punished for coming here and breaking my exile?"

He smiled. "Father knows I do what I like. And anyway, I break nothing. It is only you who are confined. The rest of the world may come and go as we please."

I was surprised. "But I thought — is it not the greater punishment to force me to be alone?"

"That depends on who visits you, doesn't it? But exile is exile. Zeus wanted you contained, and so you are. They didn't really think about it further."

"How do you know all this?"

"I was there. Watching Zeus and Helios negotiate is

always good entertainment. Like two volcanoes trying to decide if they should blow."

He had fought in the great war, I remembered. He had seen the sky burn, and slain a giant whose head brushed the clouds. For all his lightness, I found I could imagine it.

"Tell me," I said, "can you play that instrument? Or only steal it?"

He touched his fingers to the strings. The notes leapt out into the air, bright and silver-sweet. He gathered them into a melody as effortlessly as if he were a god of music himself, so that the whole room seemed to live inside the sound.

He looked up, the fire caught in his face. "Do you sing?"

That was another thing about him. He made you want to spill your secrets.

"Only for myself," I said. "My voice is not pleasing to others. I am told it sounds like a gull crying."

"Is that what they said? You are no gull. You sound like a mortal."

The confusion must have been plain on my face, for he laughed.

"Most gods have voices of thunder and rocks. We must speak soft to human ears, or they are broken to pieces. To us, mortals sound faint and thin."

I remembered how gentle Glaucos' words had sounded when he had first spoken to me. I had taken it for a sign.

"It is not common," he said, "but sometimes lesser nymphs are born with human voices. Such a one are you."

"Why did no one tell me? And how could it be? There is no mortal in me, I am Titan only."

He shrugged. "Who can ever explain how divine bloodlines work? As for why no one said, I suspect they didn't know. I spend more time with mortals than most gods and have grown accustomed to their sounds. To me it is only another flavor, like season in food. But if you are ever among men, you'll notice it: they won't fear you as they fear the rest of us."

In a minute he had unraveled one of the great mysteries of my life. I raised my fingers to my throat as if I could touch the strangeness that lay there. *A god with a mortal's voice.* It was a shock, and yet there was part of me that felt something almost like recognition.

"Play," I said. I began to sing, and the lyre followed my voice effortlessly, its timbre rising to sweeten my every phrase. When I finished, the flames were down to their coals and the moon veiled. His eyes shone like dark gems held to light. They were black, one of the marks of deep-running power, from the line of the oldest gods. For the first time it struck me how strange it was that we divide Titans from Olympians, when of course Zeus was born from Titan parents, and Hermes' own grandfather was the Titan Atlas. The same blood runs in all our veins.

"Do you know the name of this island?" I said.

"I would be a poor god of travelers if I did not know all the places in the world."

"And will you tell me?"

"It is called Aiaia," he said.

"Aiaia." I tasted the sounds. They were soft, folding quietly as wings in the darkened air.

"You know it," he said. He was watching me closely.

"Of course. It is the place where my father threw his strength to Zeus and proved his loyalty. In the sky above this place, he vanquished a Titan giant, drenching the land with blood."

"It is quite a coincidence," he said, "that your father would send you to this island among all the others."

I could feel his power reaching for my secrets. In the old days I would have rushed forth with a brimming cup of answers, to give him all he wanted. But I was not the same as I had been. I owed him nothing. He would have of me only what I wanted to give.

I rose and stood before him. I could feel my own eyes, yellow as river-stones. "Tell me," I said, "how do you know that your father is not right about my poisons? How do you know I will not drug you where you sit?"

"I do not."

"Yet you would dare to stay?"

"I dare anything," he said.

And that is how we came to be lovers.

Hermes returned often in the years that followed, winging through the dusk. He brought delicacies of the gods — wine stolen from Zeus' own stores, the sweetest honey of Mount Hybla, where the bees drink only thyme and linden blossoms. Our conversations were pleasures, and our couplings were the same.

"Will you bear my child?" he asked me.

I laughed at him. "No, never and never."

He was not hurt. He liked such sharpness, for there was nothing in him that had any blood you might spill. He asked only for curiosity's sake, because it was his nature to seek out answers, to press others for their weaknesses. He wanted to see how moonish I was over him. But all the sop in me was gone. I did not lie dreaming of him during the days, I did not speak his name into my pillow. He was no husband, scarcely even a friend. He was a poison snake, and I was another, and on such terms we pleased ourselves.

He gave me the news that I had missed. In his travels he passed over every quarter of the world, picking up gossip as hems gather mud. He knew whose feasts Glaucos drank at. He knew how high the milk spurted in Colchis' fountains. He told me that Aeëtes was well, arrayed in a cloak of dyed leopard skin. He had taken a mortal to wife, and had a babe in swaddling and another in the belly. Pasiphaë still ruled Crete with her potions, and had in the meantime whelped a ship's crew for her husband, half a dozen heirs and daughters both. Perses kept to the East, raising the dead with pails of cream and blood. My mother had gotten over her tears and added Mother of Witches to her titles, swanning with it among my aunts. We laughed over all of it, and when he left, I knew he told stories of me in turn: my dirt-black fingernails, my musky lion, the pigs that had begun coming to my door, truffling for slops and a scratch on the back. And, of course, how I had thrown myself upon him as a blushing virgin. Well? I had not blushed, but all the rest was true enough.

I questioned him further, where Aiaia was, and how far it was from Egypt and Aethiopia and every other interesting place. I asked how my father's mood waxed, and what the names of my nieces and nephews were, and what empires flourished new in the world. He answered everything, but when I asked him how far to those flowers I had given Glaucos and Scylla, he laughed at me. *Do you think I will sharpen the lioness's claws for her?*

I made my voice as careless as I could. "And what of that old Titan Prometheus on his rock. How fares he?"

"How do you think? He loses a liver a day."

"Still? I have never understood why helping mortals made Zeus so angry."

"Tell me," he said, "who gives better offerings, a miserable man or a happy one?"

"A happy one, of course."

"Wrong," he said. "A happy man is too occupied with his life. He thinks he is beholden to no one. But make him shiver, kill his wife, cripple his child, then you will hear from him. He will starve his family for a month to buy you a pure-white yearling calf. If he can afford it, he will buy you a hundred."

"But surely," I said, "you have to reward him eventually. Otherwise, he will stop offering."

"Oh, you would be surprised how long he will go on. But yes, in the end, it's best to give him something. Then he will be happy again. And you can start over."

"So this is how Olympians spend their days. Thinking of ways to make men miserable."

"There's no cause for righteousness," he said. "Your father is better at it than anyone. He would raze a whole village if he thought it would get him one more cow."

How many times had I gloated inwardly over my father's heaping altars? I lifted my cup and drank, so he would not see the flush on my cheeks.

"I suppose you might go and visit Prometheus," I said. "You and your wings. Bring him something for comfort."

"And why should I do that?"

"For novelty's sake, of course. The first good deed in your dissolute life. Aren't you curious what it would feel like?"

He laughed, but I did not press him further. He was still, always, an Olympian, still Zeus' son. I was allowed license because it amused him, but I never knew when that amusement might end. You can teach a viper to eat from your hands, but you cannot take away how much it likes to bite.

Spring passed into summer. One night, when Hermes and I were lingering over our wine, I finally asked him about Scylla herself.

"Ah." His eyes lit. "I wondered when we would come to her. What would you know?"

Is she unhappy? But he would have laughed at such a mewling question, and he would have been right to. My witchcraft, the island, my lion, all of them sprang from her transformation. There was no honesty in regretting what had given me my life.

"I never heard what happened to her after she dived into the sea. Do you know where she is?"

"Not far from here — less than a day's journey by mortal ship. She has found a strait she likes. On one side is a whirlpool that sucks down ships and fish and whatever else passes. On the other, a cliff face with a cave for her to hide her head. Any ship which would avoid the whirlpool is driven right into her jaws, and so she feeds."

"Feeds," I said.

"Yes. She eats sailors. Six at a time, one for each mouth, and if the oars are too slow, she takes twelve. A few of them try to fight her, but you can imagine how that works out. You can hear them screaming for quite a ways."

I was frozen to my chair. I had always imagined her swimming in the deeps, sucking cold flesh from squids. But no. Scylla had always wanted the light of day. She had always wanted to make others weep. And now she was a ravening monster filled with teeth and armored with immortality.

"Can no one stop her?"

"Zeus could, or your father, if they wished to. But why would they? Monsters are a boon to gods. Imagine all the prayers."

My throat had closed over. Those men she had eaten were sailors as Glaucos had been, ragged, desperate, worn thin with fear. All dead. All of them cold smoke, marked with my name.

Hermes was watching me, his head cocked like a curious bird. He was waiting for my reaction. Would I be skimmed milk for crying, or a harpy with a heart of stone? There was nothing between. Anything else did not fit cleanly in the laughing tale he wanted to spin of it.

I let my hand fall on my lion's head, felt her great, hard skull beneath my fingers. She never slept when Hermes was there. Her eyes were lidded and watchful.

"Scylla never was satisfied with just one," I said.

He smiled. *A bitch with a cliff for a heart.*

"I meant to tell you," he said. "I heard a prophecy of you. I had it from an old seeress who had left her temple and was wandering the fields giving fortunes."

I was used to the swift movements of his mind, and now I was grateful for them. "And you just happened to be passing when she was speaking of me?"

"Of course not. I gave her an embossed gold cup to tell me all she knew of Circe, daughter of Helios, witch of Aiaia."

"Well?"

"She said that a man named Odysseus, born from my blood, will come one day to your island."

"And?"

"That's it," he said.

"That's the worst prophecy I've ever heard," I said.

He sighed. "I know. I think I lost my cup."

I did not dream of him, as I said. I did not braid his name with mine. At night we lay together, and by midnight he was gone, and I could rise and step into my woods. Often my lion would pace beside me. It was the deepest pleasure, walking in the cool air, the damp leaves brushing at our legs. Sometimes I would stop to harvest this flower or that.

But the flower I truly wanted, I waited for. One month I

let go by after Hermes and I first spoke, and then another. I did not want him watching. He had no place in this. It was mine.

I did not bring a torch. My eyes shone in the dark better than any owl's. I walked through the shadowed trees, through the quiet orchards, the groves and brakes, across the sands, and up the cliffs. The birds were still, and the beasts. All the sounds were the air among the leaves and my own breath.

And there it was hidden in the leaf mold, beneath the ferns and mushrooms: a flower small as a fingernail, white as milk. The blood of that giant which my father had spilled in the sky. I plucked a stem out of the tangle. The roots clung hard a moment before yielding. They were black and thick, and smelled of metal and salt. The flower had no name that I knew, so I called it moly, *root*, from the antique language of the gods.

Oh, Father, did you know the gift you gave me? For that flower, so delicate it could dissolve beneath your stepping foot, carried within it the unyielding power of *apotrope*, the turning aside of evil. Curse-breaker. Ward and bulwark against ruin, worshipped like a god, for it was pure. The only thing in all the world you could be certain would not turn against you.

Day by day, the island bloomed. My garden climbed the walls of my house, breathed its scent through my windows. I left the shutters open by then. I did what I liked. If you had asked me, I would have said I was happy. Yet always I remembered.

Cold smoke, marked with my name.

CHAPTER NINE

IT WAS MORNING, THE sun just over the trees, and I was in the garden cutting anemones for my table. The pigs snuffled at their slops. One of the boars grew fractious, shoving and grunting to air his authority. I caught his eye. "Yesterday, I saw you blowing bubbles in the stream, and the day before the spotted sow sent you off with a bitten ear and nothing more. So you may behave."

He huffed at the dirt, then flopped on his belly and subsided.

"Do you always talk to pigs when I am gone?"

Hermes stood in his traveling cloak, his broad-brimmed hat tilted over his eyes.

"I like to think of it the other way around," I said. "What brings you out in the honest daylight?"

"A ship is coming," he said. "I thought you might want to know."

I stood. "Here? What ship?"

He smiled. He always liked seeing me at a loss. "What will you give me if I tell you?"

"Begone," I said. "I prefer you in the dark."

He laughed and vanished.

*   *   *

I made myself go about the morning as I usually would, in case Hermes watched, but I felt the tension in myself, the taut anticipation. I could not keep my eyes from flicking to the horizon. A ship. A ship with visitors that amused Hermes. Who?

They came at mid-afternoon, resolving out of the bright mirror of the waves. The vessel was ten times the size of Glaucos', and even at a distance I could see how fine it was: sleek and brightly painted, with a huge rearing prow-piece. It cut through the sluggish air straight towards me, its oarsmen rowing steadily. As they approached, I felt that old eager jump in my throat. They were mortals.

The sailors dropped the anchor, and a single man leapt over the low side and splashed to shore. He followed the seam of beach and woods until he found a path, a small pig trail that wound upwards through the acanthus spears and laurel groves, past the thorn-bush thicket. I lost sight of him then, but I knew where the trail led. I waited.

He checked when he saw my lion, but only for a moment. With his shoulders straight and unbowed, he knelt to me in the clearing's grass. I realized I knew him. He was older, the skin of his face more lined, but it was the same man, his head still shaved, his eyes clear. Of all the mortals on the earth, there are only a few the gods will ever hear of. Consider the practicalities. By the time we learn their names, they are dead. They must be meteors indeed to catch our attention. The merely good: you are dust to us.

"Lady," he said, "I am sorry to trouble you."

"You have not been trouble yet," I said. "Please stand if you like."

If he noticed my mortal voice, he gave no sign. He stood up — I will not say gracefully, for he was too solidly built for that — but easily, like a door swinging on a well-fitted hinge. His eyes met mine without flinching. He was used to gods, I thought. And witches too.

"What brings the famous Daedalus to my shores?"

"I am honored you would know me." His voice was steady as a west wind, warm and constant. "I come as a messenger from your sister. She is with child, and her time approaches. She asks that you attend her delivery."

I eyed him. "Are you certain you have come to the right place, messenger? There has never been love between my sister and me."

"She does not send to you for love," he said.

The breeze blew, carrying the scent of linden flowers. At its back, the muddy stink of the pigs.

"I'm told my sister has bred half a dozen children each more easily than the last. She cannot die in childbirth and her infants thrive with the strength of her blood. So why does she need me?"

He spread his hands, deft-looking and thickened with muscle. "Pardon, lady, I can say no more, but she bids me tell you that if you do not help her there is no one else who can. It is your art she wants, lady. Yours alone."

So Pasiphaë had heard of my powers and decided they could be of use to her. It was the first compliment I had had from her in my life.

"Your sister instructed me to say besides that she has permission from your father for you to go. Your exile is lifted for this."

I frowned. This was all strange, very strange. What was important enough to make her go to my father? And if she needed more magic, why not summon Perses? It seemed like some sort of trick, but I could not understand why my sister would bother. I was no threat to her.

I could feel myself being tempted. I was curious, of course, but it was more than that. This was a chance to show her what I had become. Whatever trap she might set, she could not catch me in it, not anymore.

"What a relief to hear of my reprieve," I said. "I cannot wait to be freed from my terrible prison." The terraced hills around us glowed with spring.

He did not smile. "There is — one more thing. I am instructed to tell you that our path lies through the straits."

"What straits?"

But I saw the answer in his face: the dark stains under his eyes, the weary grief.

Sickness rose in my throat. "Where Scylla dwells."

He nodded.

"She ordered you to come that way as well?"

"She did."

"How many did you lose?"

"Twelve," he said. "We were not fast enough."

How could I have forgotten who my sister was? She would never just ask a favor, always she must have a whip to drive you to her will. I could see her bragging and laughing to Minos. *Circe's a fool for mortals, I hear.*

I hated her more than I ever had. It was all so cruelly done. I imagined stalking into my house, slamming the door on its great hinge. *Too bad, Pasiphaë. You will have to find some other fool.*

But then six more men, or twelve, would die.

I scoffed at myself. Who said they would live if I went? I knew no spells to ward off monsters. And Scylla would be enraged when she saw me. I would only bring more of her fury upon them.

Daedalus was watching me, his face shadowed. Far beyond his shoulder, my father's chariot was slipping into the sea. In their dusty palace rooms, astronomers were even now tracking its sunset glory, hoping their calculations would hold. Their bony knees trembled, thinking of the headsman's axe.

I gathered up my clothes, my bag of simples. I closed the door behind me. There was nothing else to do. The lion could take care of herself.

"I am ready," I said.

The ship's style was new to me, trim and low in the water. Its hull was beautifully painted with rolling waves and curving dolphins, and by the stern an octopus stretched its snaky arms. As the captain hauled at the anchor, I walked up to the prow to examine the figurehead I had seen.

It was a young girl in a dancing dress. Her face bore a look of happy surprise, eyes wide, lips just parting, her hair loose over her shoulders. Her small hands were clasped to her chest and she was poised on her toes as if music were about to start. Each detail of it, the curls of her hair, the folds of cloth, was so vivid that I thought at any moment she truly would step into the air. Yet that was not even the real miracle. The work showed, I cannot say how, a glimpse of the girl's self. The searching cleverness in her gaze, the determined grace of her brow. Her excitement and innocence, easy and green as grass.

I did not have to ask whose hands had shaped it. A wonder of the mortal world, my brother had called Daedalus, but this was a wonder in any world. I pored over its pleasures, finding a new one every moment: the small dimple in her chin, the knob of her ankle, coltish with youth.

A marvel it was, but also a message. I had been raised

at my father's feet and knew a boast of power when I saw it. Another king, if he had such a treasure, would keep it under guard in his most fortified hall. Minos and Pasiphaë had set it on a ship, exposed to brine and sun, to pirates and sea-wrack and monsters. As if to say: *This is a trifle. We have a thousand more, and better yet the man who makes them.*

The drumbeat drew my attention away. The sailors had taken their benches, and I felt the first judders of motion. The harbor waters began to slide past us. My island dwindled behind.

I turned my eye to the men filling the deck around me. There were thirty-eight in all. At the stern five guards paced in capes and golden armor. Their noses were lumpen, twisted from too many breakings. I remembered Aeëtes sneering at them: *Minos' thugs, dressed up like princes.* The rowers were the pick of Knossos' mighty navy, so large the oars looked dainty in their hands. Around them, the other sailors moved swiftly, raising a canopy to keep off the sun.

At Minos and Pasiphaë's wedding, the huddle of mortals I had glimpsed seemed distant and blurred, as alike as leaves on a tree. But here, beneath the sky, each face was relentlessly distinct. This one was thick, this one smooth, this one bearded with a hooked nose and narrow chin. There were scars and calluses and scrapes, age-lines and cowlicks of hair. One had draped a wet cloth around his neck against the heat. Another wore a bracelet made by childish hands, and a third had a head shaped like a bullfinch's. It made me dizzy to realize that this was but a fraction of a fraction of all the men the world had bred. How could such variation endure, such endless iteration of minds and faces? Did the earth not go mad?

"May I bring you a seat?" Daedalus said.

I turned, glad for the respite of his single face. Daedalus

could not have been called handsome, but his features had a pleasing sturdiness.

"I prefer to stand," I said. I gestured to the prow-piece. "She is beautiful."

He inclined his head, a man used to such compliments. "Thank you."

"Tell me something. Why does my sister have you under watch?" When we had stepped on board, the largest guard, the leader, had roughly searched him.

"Ah." He smiled slightly. "Minos and Pasiphaë fear that I do not fully...appreciate their hospitality."

I remembered Aeëtes saying: *Pasiphaë has him trapped.*

"Surely you might have escaped them on the way."

"I might escape them often. But Pasiphaë has something of mine I will not leave."

I waited for more, but it did not come. His hands rested on the rail. The knuckles were battered, the fingers hatched with white nicks of scars. As though he had plunged them into broken wood or shards of glass.

"In the straits," I said. "You saw Scylla?"

"Not clearly. The cliff was hidden in spray and fog, and she moved too quickly. Six heads, striking twice, with teeth as long as a leg."

I had seen the stains on the deck. They had been scrubbed, yet the blood had soaked deep. All that was left of twelve lives. My stomach twisted with guilt, as Pasiphaë had meant it to.

"You should know I was the one who did it," I said. "The one who made Scylla what she is. That is why I am exiled, and why my sister had you take this route."

I watched his face for surprise or disgust, even terror. But he only nodded. "She told me."

Of course she had. She was a poisoner at heart; she

wanted to be sure I came as villain, not savior. Except this time it was nothing but the truth.

"There is something I do not understand," I said. "For all my sister's cruelty she is not often foolish. Why would she risk you on this errand?"

"I earned my place here myself. I am forbidden to say more, but when we arrive in Crete, I think you will understand." He hesitated. "Do you know if there is anything we can do against her? Scylla?"

Above us, the sun burned away the last shreds of cloud. The men panted, even under the canopy.

"I don't know," I said. "I will try."

We stood in silence beside that leaping girl as the sea fell away.

That night we camped on the shore of a flourishing green land. Around their fires, the men were tense and quiet, muffled by dread. I could hear their whispers, the wine sloshing as they passed it. No man wanted to lie awake imagining tomorrow.

Daedalus had marked out a small space for me with a bedroll, but I left it. I could not bear to be hemmed in by all those breathing, anxious bodies.

It was strange to tread upon earth other than my own. Where I expected a grove, there came a deer thicket. Where I thought there would be pigs, a badger showed its teeth. The terrain was flatter than my island, the forests low, the flowers in different combinations. I saw a bitter almond tree, a flowered cherry. My fingers itched to harvest their fat power. I bent and plucked a poppy, just to hold its color in my hand. I could feel the throb of its black seeds. *Come, make us into magic.*

I did not obey. I was thinking of Scylla, trying to piece

together an image from everything I had heard of her: six mouths, six heads, twelve dangling feet. But the more I tried, the more it slipped away. Instead I saw her face as it had been in our halls, round and laughing. The curve of her wrist had been like a swan's neck. Her chin would tilt delicately to whisper some morsel of gossip in my sister's ear. Beside them, my brother Perses had sat smirking. He used to toy with Scylla's hair, winding it around his finger. She would turn and slap his shoulder, and the sound would echo across the hall. They both laughed, for they loved to be at the center always, and I remembered wondering why my sister did not mind such displays, for she allowed none near Perses but herself. Yet she only watched and smiled.

I thought I had passed those years in my father's halls sightless as a mole, but now more details came back to me. The green robe Scylla used to wear at special feasts, her silver sandals with lapis lazuli on the strap. There was a gold pin with a cat at its end that kept her hair up from her neck. She had it from…Thebes, I thought. Thebes of Egypt, some admirer there, some beast-headed god. What had happened to that bauble? Was it still lying on the grass beside the water, with her discarded clothes?

I had come to a small rise, crowded with black poplars. I walked among their furrowed trunks. One of them had been struck recently by lightning, and the bole bore a charred, oozing wound. I put my finger to the burnt sap. I could feel its force, and was sorry I had not brought an extra bottle to gather it. It made me think of Daedalus, that upright man with fire in his bones.

What was the thing he would not leave behind? His face when he had spoken of it had been careful, his words placed as if they were tiles in a fountain. It must be a lover, I thought. Some pretty handmaid of the palace, or else some handsome groom. My sister could smell such intrigues a year away. Perhaps she had even ordered them to his bed, as the hook to catch the fish. But as I tried to picture their faces, I realized I did not believe in them. Daedalus did not seem like a man newly heart-struck, nor an old lover, with a wife of many years molded to his side. I could not imagine him in a pair, only singular and alone. Gold, then? An invention he had made?

I thought: if I can keep him alive tomorrow, perhaps I will find out.

The moon was passing overhead, and the night with it. Daedalus' voice spoke again in my ears. *Her teeth are long as a leg.* Cold fear ran through me. What had I been thinking, that I could stand against such a creature? Daedalus' throat would be ripped open, my own flesh snatched up in her mouths. What would I become after she was finished with me? Ash, smoke? Immortal bones dragging across the bottom of the sea.

My feet had found the shore. I walked it, cool and gray. I listened to the murmur of the waves, the cries of night birds, but if I am honest I was listening for more than that: the quick rush through the air that I had come to know. Each second, I hoped Hermes would land poised before me, laughing, goading. *So, witch of Aiaia, what will you do tomorrow?*

I thought of begging him for help, the sand beneath my knees, my palms upstretched. Or perhaps I would knock him down to the earth and please him that way, for he loved most of all to be surprised. I could hear the tale he would tell later. *She was so desperate, she was on me like a cat.* He should lie with my sister, I thought. They would like each other. It struck me for the first time that perhaps he had. Perhaps they lay together often and laughed at my dullness. Perhaps all this had been his idea, and that was why he had come this morning, to taunt me and gloat. My mind played over our conversation, sifting it for meaning. See how quickly he made one a fool? That was what he desired most of all: to drive others into doubt, keep them wondering and fretting, stumbling behind his dancing feet. I spoke out to the darkness, to any silent wings that hovered there. "I do not care if you lie with her. Have Perses too, he is the handsomer. You will never be such as I am jealous for."

Perhaps he was listening, perhaps he was not. It did not matter, he would not come. It was the better jest to see what extremes I would try, to see how I would curse and flounder. My father would not help me either. Aeëtes might, if only to feel the flex of his power, but he was a world away. I could no more reach him than I could fly into the air.

I was even more desolate than my sister, I thought. I came for her, but there was no one who would come for me. The thought was steadying. After all, I had been alone my whole life. Aeëtes, Glaucos, these were only pauses in the long stretch of my solitude. Kneeling, I dug my fingers into the sand. I felt the rub of grains beneath my nails. A memory drifted through me. My father speaking our old hopeless law to Glaucos: no god may undo what another has done.

But I was the one who had done it.

The moon passed over us. The waves pressed their cold mouths to my feet. Elecampane, I thought. Ash and olive and silver fir. Henbane with burnt cornel bark and, at the base of all, moly. Moly, to break a curse, to ward off that evil thought of mine that had changed her in the first place.

I brushed away the sand and stood, my bag of simples

hanging from my shoulder. As I walked, the bottles rang softly, like goats shaking their bells. The smells wafted around me, familiar as my own skin: earth and clinging roots, salt and iron blood.

The next morning the men were gray and silent. One oiled the oarlocks to keep them from squeaking, another scrubbed at the stained deck, his face red, though whether from sun or grief I could not tell. In the stern a third with a black beard was praying and pouring wine onto the waves. None looked at me — I was Pasiphaë's sister, after all, and they had long since given up any thought of help from her. But I could feel their tension pressing thickly into the air, the choking terror rising in them moment by moment. Death was coming.

Do not think of it, I told myself. If you hold firm, none will die today.

The guard captain had yellowed eyes set in a swollen face. His name was Polydamas and he was large, but I was a goddess, and we were of a height. "I need your cloak," I said to him, "and your tunic, at once."

His eyes narrowed, and I could see the reflexive *no* in them. I would come to know this type of man, jealous of his little power, to whom I was only a woman.

"Why?" he said.

"Because I do not desire the death of your comrades. Do you feel otherwise?"

The words carried up the deck, and thirty-seven pairs of eyes looked up. He stripped off his clothes and handed them to me. They were the finest on board, extravagant white-combed wool edged with deep purple, sweeping the deck.

Daedalus had come to stand by me. "May I help?"

I gave him the cloak to hold up. Behind it, I disrobed and drew on the tunic. The armholes gaped and the waist billowed. The smell of sour human flesh enveloped me.

"Will you help me with the cloak?"

Daedalus draped it around me, fastening it by its golden octopus pin. The cloth hung heavy as blankets, loose and slipping from my shoulders. "I'm sorry to say, you don't look like much of a man."

"I'm not meant to look like a man," I said. "I'm meant to look like my brother. Scylla loved him once, perhaps she still does."

I touched the paste I had prepared to my lips, hyacinth and honey, ash flowers and aconite crushed with the bark of walnuts. I had cast illusions on animals and plants before, but never upon myself, and I felt a sudden, plunging doubt. I forced the thought away. Fear of failure was the worst thing for any spell. I focused instead on Perses: his lounging, smug face, his puffy muscles and thick neck, his long-fingered, indolent hands. Each of these I summoned in turn, willing them into me.

When I opened my eyes, Daedalus was staring.

"Put the steadiest men at the oars," I said to him. My voice had changed too, it was deep and swollen with divine hauteur. "They must not stop for anything. No matter what."

He nodded. He was holding a sword, and I saw that the other men were similarly armed with spears and daggers and crude cudgels.

"No," I said. I raised my voice for the whole ship. "She is immortal. Weapons are useless, and you will need free hands to keep the ship moving forward."

At once came the rasp of blades being sheathed, the *thunk* of spears set down. Even Polydamas, in his borrowed

tunic, obeyed. I almost wanted to laugh. I had never been
given such deference in my life. Is that what it was like to
be Perses? But already I could make out the faint outline of
the straits on the horizon. I turned to Daedalus. "Listen," I
said. "There is a chance that the spell will not fool her and
she will know me. If she does, be sure you are not standing
near. Be sure none of the men are."

The mist came first. It closed in wet and heavy, obscuring
the cliffs, then the sky itself. We could see little, and the
sound of the sucking whirlpool filled our ears. That
whirlpool was of course the reason Scylla had chosen these
straits. To avoid its pull, ships must steer close to the opposite cliff. It brought them right beneath her teeth.

We pushed on through the thick air. As we entered
the straits, the sound grew hollowed, echoing off the stone
walls. My skin, the deck, the rail: every surface was slick
with spray. The water foamed and an oar scraped the rock-
face. A small sound, but the men flinched as if it were a
thunderclap. Above us, buried in the fog, was the cave, and
Scylla.

We moved, I thought we did, but in such grayness it was
impossible to tell how far, or fast. The oarsmen were trembling with effort and fear, and the oarlocks creaked despite
their oil. I counted the moments. Surely we were beneath
her now. She would be creeping to the cave's opening and
smelling out the plumpest. The sweat was drenching the
men's tunics, their shoulders hunched. Those not rowing
crouched behind coils of rope, the mast base, any cover
they could find.

I strained my eyes upwards, and she came.

She was gray as the air, as the cliff itself. I had always
imagined she would look like something: a snake or an

octopus, a shark. But the truth of her was overwhelming, an immensity that my mind fought to take in. Her necks were longer than ship masts. Her six heads gaped, hideously lumpen, like melted lava stone. Black tongues licked her sword-length teeth.

Her eyes were fixed on the men, oblivious in their sweating fear. She crept closer, slipping over the rocks. A reptilian stench struck me, foul as squirming nests underground. Her necks wove a little in the air, and from one of her mouths I saw a gleaming strand of saliva stretch and fall. Her body was not visible. It was hidden back in the mist with her legs, those hideous, boneless things that Selene had spoken of so long ago. Hermes had told me how they clung inside her cave like the curled ends of hermit crabs when she lowered herself to feed.

Her necks had begun to ripple and bunch back on themselves. She was gathering to strike.

"Scylla!" I cried with my god's voice.

She screamed. The sound was a piercing chaos, like a thousand dogs howling at once. Some of the rowers dropped their oars to cover their ears. At the edge of my vision I saw Daedalus push one to the side and take his place. I could not worry for him now.

"Scylla," I cried again. "It is Perses! I have sailed a year to find you."

She stared at me, her eyes dead holes in gray flesh. From one of her throats came a strangled sound. She had no vocal cords anymore.

"My bitch sister is exiled for what she did to you," I said, "but she deserved worse. What vengeance do you desire? Tell me. Pasiphaë and I will do it."

I was making myself speak slowly. Each moment was another beat of the oars. Those twelve eyes pinned me. I could see the stains of old blood around her mouth, the shreds of flesh still hanging from her teeth. I felt my gorge rise.

"We have been searching out a cure for you. A powerful drug to turn you back. We miss you as you were."

My brother would never have talked so, but it did not seem to matter. She was listening, coiling and uncoiling along the rocks, keeping pace with our ship. How many oar strokes had passed? A dozen? A hundred? I could see her dull mind working. *A god? What does a god do here?*

"Scylla," I said. "Will you have it? Will you have our cure?"

She hissed. The breath from her gullet was rotten and hot as a fire. But already I had lost her attention. Two of her heads had turned to watch the men at their oars. The others were beginning to follow. I saw her necks bunch again. "Look," I cried. "Here it is!"

I lifted the open bottle in the air. Only one neck turned back to see, but that was enough. I hefted the draught and threw it. It hit her in the back of her teeth, and I watched her throat ripple as she swallowed. I spoke the spell to change her back.

For a moment, nothing happened. Then she shrieked, a sound to crack open the world. Her heads whipped, and she dived towards me. I had time only to grab hold of the mast. *Run*, I thought, at Daedalus.

She struck the ship's stern. The deck popped like driftwood, and a length of rail tore away. Splinters flew. Men were tumbling around me, and I would have fallen if I had not been gripping the mast. I heard Daedalus crying orders but could not see him. Already her adder necks were rearing back again and this time, I knew, she would not miss. She would strike the deck itself, crack the ship in half, then pluck us from the water one by one.

But the blow did not come. Her heads smacked into the waves behind us. She jerked, lunging against the water, snapping those huge jaws like a dog fighting its leash. It took my muddy brain a moment to understand: she had reached the end of her tether. Her legs could stretch no farther from their hold in her cave. We were past.

She seemed to realize it at the same time I did. She screamed in rage, slamming our wake with her heads, throwing up huge waves. The boat tipped, gulping sea over its low sides and back. Men grappled at the ropes, their legs trailing in the water, but they held on and each moment we were further away.

She beat the cliff-side, howling her frustration, until the mist closed over her and she was gone.

I leaned my forehead against the mast. The clothes were slipping off my shoulders. The cloak dragged at my neck, and my skin prickled with heat. The spell had ended. I was myself again.

"Goddess."

Daedalus was kneeling. The other men were ranged on their knees behind. Their faces — thick and haggard, scarred and bearded and burnt — were gray and shaken. They bore scrapes and lumps from being thrown across the deck.

I scarcely saw them. Before me was Scylla, her ravening mouths and those dead, empty eyes. She had not known me, I thought. Not as Perses or anything. Only the novelty of my being a god had momentarily checked her. Her mind was gone.

"Lady," Daedalus said. "We will make sacrifice to you every day of our lives for this. You have saved us. You brought us through the straits alive." The men echoed him, murmuring prayers, their great hands lifted like platters. A few pressed their foreheads to the deck, in the Eastern style. Such worship was the payment my kind demanded for services rendered.

The bile rose in my throat.

"You fools," I said. "I am the one who made that creature. I did it for pride and vain delusion. And you thank me? Twelve of your men are dead for it, and how many thousands more to come? That drug I gave her is the strongest I have. Do you understand, mortals?"

The words seared the air. The light from my eyes beat down upon them.

"I will never be free of her. She cannot be changed back, not now, not ever. What she is, she will remain. She will feast on your kind for all eternity. So get up. Get up and get to your oars, and let me not hear you speak again of your imbecile gratitude or I will make you sorry for it."

They cringed and shook like the weak vessels they were, stuttering to their feet and creeping away. Above, the sky was cloudless, and the heat pinned the air to the deck. I yanked off the cloak. I wanted the sun to burn me. I wanted it to scorch me down to bone.

CHAPTER TEN

FOR THREE DAYS I stood at that prow. We did not stay over on an island again. The oarsmen worked in shifts, sleeping on the deck. Daedalus repaired the rail, then took his turn among them. He was unfailingly polite, offering food and wine, a bedroll, but he did not linger. What did I expect? I had loosed my wrath on him as if I were my father. One more thing that I had ruined.

We reached the island of Crete just before noon on the seventh day. The sun threw off great sheets of light from the water, turning the sail incandescent. Around us ships crowded the bay: Mycenaean barges, Phoenician traders, Egyptian galleys, Hittites and Aethiopians and Hesperians. All the merchants who passed through these waters wanted the rich city of Knossos as their customer, and Minos knew it. He welcomed them with wide, safe moorings and agents to collect for the privilege of using them. The inns and brothels belonged to Minos also, and the gold and jewels flowed like a great river to his hands.

The captain aimed us squarely at the first mooring, kept open for royal ships. The noise and motion of the docks clattered around me: men running, shouting, heaving boxes onto decks. Polydamas spoke a word to the harbor-master, then turned to us. "You are to come at once. You and the craftsman both."

Daedalus gestured that I should go first. We followed Polydamas up the docks. Before us, the huge limestone stairs wavered in the heat. Men streamed past us, servants and nobles alike, their shoulders sun-darkened and bare. Above, the palace of mighty Knossos glowed on its hill like a hive. We climbed. I heard Daedalus' breaths behind me and Polydamas' in front. The steps were worn smooth from years of endless hurrying feet.

At last we reached the top and crossed the threshold into the palace. The blinding light vanished. Cool darkness flowed over my skin. Daedalus and Polydamas hesitated, blinking. My eyes were not mortal and needed no time to adjust. I saw at once the beauty of that place, even greater than the last time I had come. The palace was like a hive indeed, each hall leading to an ornate chamber, and each chamber to another hall. Windows were cut in the walls to let in thick squares of golden sun. Intricate murals unrolled themselves on every side: dolphins and laughing women, boys gathering flowers, and deep-chested bulls tossing their horns. Outside in tiled pavilions silver fountains ran, and servants hurried among columns red-dened with hematite. Over every doorway hung a *labrys*, the double-axe of Minos. I remembered that he had given Pasiphaë a necklace with a *labrys* pendant at their wedding. She had held it as if it were a worm, and when the cere-mony came her neck bore only her own onyx and amber.

Polydamas guided us through the twisting passages to-wards the queen's quarters. There it was more lavish still, the paintings rich with ochre and blue copper, but the win-dows had been covered over. Instead there were golden torches and leaping braziers. Cunningly recessed skylights let in light but no glimpse of sky; Daedalus' work, I supposed. Pasiphaë had never liked our father's prying gaze.

Polydamas stopped before a door scrolled with flowers and waves. "The queen is within," he said, and knocked.

We stood in the still and shadowed air. I could hear nothing beyond that heavy wood, but I became aware of Daedalus' ragged breath beside me. His voice was low. "Lady," he said, "I have offended you and I am sorry. But I am sorrier still for what you will find inside. I wish — "

The door opened. A handmaid stood breathless before us, her hair pinned in the Cretan style at the top of her head. "The queen is in her labors — " she began, but my sister's voice cut across her. "Is it them?"

At the room's center, Pasiphaë lay upon a purple couch. Her skin gleamed with sweat, and her belly was shockingly distended, swollen out like a tumor from her slender frame. I had forgotten how vivid she was, how beautiful. Even in her pain, she commanded the room, drawing all the light to herself, leeching the world around her pale as mushrooms. She had always been the most like our father.

I stepped through the door. "Twelve dead," I said. "Twelve men for a joke and your vanity."

She smirked, rising up to meet me. "It seemed only fair to let Scylla have her chance at you, don't you think? Let me guess: you tried to change her back." She laughed at what she saw in my face. "Oh, I knew you would! You made a monster and all you can think of is how sorry you are. *Alas, poor mortals, I have put them in danger!*"

She was as quicksilver cruel as ever. It was a relief of sorts. "It was you who put them in danger," I said.

"But you are the one who failed to save them. Tell me, did you weep as you watched them die?"

I forced my voice to stay even. "You are in error," I said. "I saw no men die. The twelve were lost on the way out."

She did not even pause. "No matter. More will die on every ship that passes." She tapped a finger to her chin. "How many do you think it will be, in a year? A hundred? A thousand?"

She was showing her mink teeth, trying to get me to melt like all those naiads in Oceanos' halls. But there was no wound she could give me that I had not already given myself.

"This is not the way to get my help, Pasiphaë."

"Your help! Please. I am the one who got you off that sand-spit of an island. I hear you sleep with lions and boars for company. But that's an improvement for you, isn't it? After Glaucos the squid."

"If you don't need me," I said, "I will happily go back to my sand-spit."

"Oh, come, sister, don't be so sour, it's only a jest. And look how grown you are, slipping past Scylla! I knew I was right to call you instead of that braggart Aeëtes. You can stop making that face. I've already set aside gold for the families of the men who were lost."

"Gold does not give back a life."

"I can tell you are not a queen. Believe me, most of the families would rather have the gold. Now, are there any other — "

But she did not finish. She grunted and dug her nails into the arm of a handmaiden kneeling at her feet. I had not noticed the girl before, but I saw now that the skin of her arm was purple and smeared with blood.

"Out," I said to her. "Out, all. This is no place for you."

I felt a spurt of satisfaction at how fast the attendants fled.

I faced my sister. "Well?"

Her face was still contorted with pain. "What do you think? It's been days and it hasn't even moved. It needs to be cut out."

She threw back her robes, revealing the swollen skin. A ripple passed across the surface of her belly, from left to right, then back again.

I knew little of childbirth. I had never attended my mother, nor any of my cousins. A few things I remembered hearing. "Have you tried pushing from your knees?"

"Of course I've tried it!" She screamed as the spasm came again. "I've had eight children! Just cut the fucking thing out of me!"

From my bag I drew out a pain draught.

"Are you stupid? I'm not going to be put to sleep like some infant. Give me the willow bark."

"Willow is for headaches, not surgery."

"Give it to me!"

I gave it, and she drained the bottle. "Daedalus," she said, "take up the knife."

I had forgotten he was there. He stood in the doorway, very still.

"Pasiphaë," I said, "do not be perverse. You sent for me, now use me."

She laughed, a savage sound. "You think I trust you with that? You are for after. Anyway, it is fitting that Daedalus should do it, he knows why. Don't you, craftsman? Will you tell my sister now, or shall we let it be a surprise?"

"I will do it," Daedalus said to me. "It is my task." He stepped to the table and took up the knife. The blade was honed to a hair's edge.

She seized his wrist. "Just remember," she said. "Remember what I will do if you think to go astray."

He nodded mildly, though for the first time I saw something like anger in his eyes.

She drew her nail across the lower portion of her belly, leaving a red slice. "There," she said.

The room was hot and close. I felt my hands slicked with sweat. How Daedalus held that knife steady I do not know. The tip bit into my sister's skin, and blood welled, red and gold mixed. His arms were taut with effort, his jaw set. It took a long time, for my sister's immortal flesh fought back, but Daedalus cut on with utmost concentration, and at last the glistening muscles parted, and the flesh beneath gave way. The path lay bare to my sister's womb.

"Now you," she said, looking at me. Her voice was hoarse and torn. "Get it out."

The couch beneath her was sopping. The room was filled with the overripe stink of her ambrosial blood. Her belly had stopped rippling when Daedalus began to cut. It was tensed now. As if it were waiting, I thought.

I looked at my sister. "What is in there?"

Her golden hair was matted. "What do you think? A baby."

I put my hands to that gap in her flesh. The blood pulsed hot against me. Slowly, I pressed through the muscles and the wet. My sister made a strangled croak.

I searched in that slickness, and at last there it was: the soft mass of an arm.

A relief. I could not even say what I had feared. *Just a baby.*

"I have it," I said. My fingers inched upwards for purchase. I remember telling myself that I must be careful to find its head. I did not want it twisted when I began to pull.

Pain burst in my fingers, so shocking I could not cry out. I thought some scrambled thing: that Daedalus must have dropped the scalpel inside of her, that a bone had broken in her labor and stabbed me. But the pain clamped harder, driving deep into my hand, grinding.

Teeth. It was teeth.

I did scream then. I tried to jerk my hand away, but it had me fast in its jaws. In a panic, I yanked. The lips of my sister's wound parted and the thing slid forth. It thrashed like a fish on a hook, and muck flew across our faces.

My sister was shrieking. The thing was like an anchor dragging on my arm, and I felt my finger joints tearing. I screamed again, the agony white-hot, and fell on top of the creature, scrabbling for its throat with my hand. When I found it, I bore down, pinning its body beneath me. Its heels beat on the stone, its head twisted, side to side. At last I saw it clear: the nose broad and flat, shining wetly with birth fluid. The shaggy, thick face crowned with two sharp horns. Below, the froggy baby body bucked with unnatural strength. Its eyes were black and fixed on mine.

Dear gods, I thought, what is it?

The creature made a choking sound and opened its mouth. I snatched my hand away, bloody and mangled. I had lost my last two fingers and part of a third. The thing's jaw worked, swallowing what it had taken. Its chin wrenched in my grip, trying to bite me again.

A shadow beside me. Daedalus, pale and blood-spattered. "I am here."

"The knife," I said.

"What are you doing? Do not hurt him, he must live!" My sister was struggling on her couch, but she could not rise with her muscles cut.

"The cord," I said. It still ran gristle-thick between the creature and my sister's womb. He sawed at it. My knees were wet where I knelt. My hands were a mass of broken pain and blood.

"Now a blanket," I said. "A sack."

He brought a thick wool coverlet, laid it on the floor beside me. With my torn fingers, I dragged the thing into its center. It fought still, moaning angrily, and twice I nearly lost it, for it seemed to have grown stronger even in those moments. But Daedalus gathered up the corners, and when he had them, I jerked my hands away. The creature thrashed in the blanket folds, unable to find purchase. I took the ends from him, lifting it off the floor.

I could hear the rasp of Daedalus' breath. "A cage," he said. "We need a cage."

"Get one," I said. "I will hold it."

He ran. Inside its sack, the creature twisted like a snake. I saw its limbs lined against the fabric, that thick head, the points of horns.

Daedalus returned with a birdcage, the finches still fluttering inside. But it was stout, and large enough. I stuffed the blanket in, and he clanged shut the door. He threw another blanket over it, and the creature was hidden.

I looked at my sister. She was covered in blood, her belly a slaughter-yard. The drips fell wetly to the sodden rug beneath. Her eyes were wild.

"You did not hurt it?"

I stared at her. "Are you mad? It tried to eat my hand! Tell me how such an abomination came to be."

"Stitch me up."

"No," I said. "You will tell me, or I will let you bleed yourself dry."

"Bitch," she said. But she was wheezing. The pain was wearing her away. Even my sister had an end in her, a place she could not go. We stared at each other, yellow eyes to yellow. "Well, Daedalus?" she said at last. "It is your moment. Tell my sister whose fault this creature is."

He looked at me, face weary and streaked with blood. "Mine," he said. "It is mine. I am the reason this beast lives."

From the cage, a wet chewing sound. The finches had gone silent.

"The gods sent a bull, pure white, to bless the kingdom of Minos. The queen admired the creature and desired to see it more closely, yet it ran from any who came near. So I built the hollow likeness of a cow, with a place inside for her to sit. I gave it wheels, so we might roll it to the beach while the creature slept. I thought it would only be...I did not — "

"Oh, please," my sister spat. "The world will be ended before you stammer to your finish. I fucked the sacred bull, all right? Now get the thread."

I stitched my sister up. Soldiers came, their faces carefully blank, and bore the cage to an inner closet. My sister called after them, "No one goes near it without my word. And give it something to eat!" Silent handmaids rolled up the soaked rug and carried off the ruined couch as if they did such work every day. They burned frankincense and sweet violets to mask the stench, then bore my sister to the bath.

"The gods will punish you," I had told her, while I sewed. But she had only laughed with a giddy lushness.

"Don't you know?" she had said. "The gods love their monsters."

The words made me start. "You talked to Hermes?"

"Hermes? What does he have to do with it? I don't need some Olympian to tell me what is plain before my face. Everyone knows it." She smirked. "Except for you, as usual."

A presence at my side brought me back. Daedalus. We

were alone, for the first time since he had come to my island. There were drops of brown spattered across his forehead. His arms were smeared to the elbow. "May I bandage your fingers?"

"No," I said. "Thank you. They will fix themselves."

"Lady." He hesitated. "I am in your debt for all my days. If you had not come, it would have been me."

His shoulders were taut, tensed as if against a blow. The last time he had thanked me, I had stormed at him. But now I understood more: he, too, knew what it was to make monsters.

"I am glad it was not," I said. I nodded at his hands, crusted and stained like everything else. "Yours cannot grow back."

He lowered his voice. "Can the creature be killed?"

I thought of my sister shrieking to be careful. "I don't know. Pasiphaë seems to believe it can. But even so it is the child of the white bull. It may be guarded by a god, or it may bring down a curse upon any who harm it. I need to think."

He rubbed at his scalp, and I saw the hope of an easy solution drain from him. "I must go make another cage then. That one won't hold it long."

He left. The gore was drying stiff upon my cheeks, and my arms were greasy with the creature's stink. I felt clouded and heavy, sick from the pollution of so much blood. If I called the handmaids, they would bring me to a bath, but I knew that would not be enough. Why had my sister made such an abomination? And why summon me? Most naiads would have fled, but one of the nereids might have done it, they were used to monsters. Or Perses. Why had she not called for him?

My mind had no answers. It was limp and dulled, useless

as my missing fingers. One thought came clear: I must do something. I could not stand by while a horror was loosed upon the world. I had the thought that I should find my sister's workroom. Perhaps there would be something there to help me, some antidote, some great drug of reversal.

It was not far, a hall off her bedchamber separated by a curtain. I had never seen another witch's craft room before, and I walked its shelves expecting I do not know what, a hundred grisly things, kraken livers, dragons' teeth, the flayed skin of giants. But all I saw were herbs, and rudimentary ones at that: poisons, poppies, a few healing roots. I had no doubt my sister could work plenty with them, for her will had always been strong. But she was lazy, and here was the proof. Those few simples were old and weak as dead leaves. They had been collected haphazardly, some in bud, some already withered, cut with any knife at any time of day.

I understood something then. My sister might be twice the goddess I was, but I was twice the witch. Her crumbling trash could not help me. And my own herbs from Aiaia would not be enough, strong as they were. The monster was bound to Crete, and whatever would be done, Crete must guide me.

I traced back through the halls and corridors to the palace center. There I had seen stairs that ran not to the harbor but inland, to the wide, bright gardens and pavilions, which in turn opened out to distant fields.

All around, busy men and women swept flagstones, picked fruits, hefted their baskets of barley. They kept their eyes diligently lowered as I went. I suppose living with Minos and Pasiphaë they had grown used to ignoring bloodier things than me. I passed the outlying houses of peasants and shepherds, the groves and grazing herds. The hills were lush and so golden with sun that the light seemed to rise from them, but I did not stop to savor the view. My eyes were fixed upon the black outline that stood against the sky.

Mount Dicte, it is called. No bears or wolves or lions dare to tread there, only the sacred goats, their great horns curling like conch shells. Even in the hottest season, the forests remain dark and cool. At night, the huntress Artemis is said to roam its hills with her shining bow, and in one of its shadowed caves Zeus himself was born and hidden from his devouring father.

There are herbs there that grow nowhere else. They are so rare, few have been given names. I could feel them swelling in their hollows, breathing tendrils of magic into the air. A small yellow flower with a green center. A drooping lily that bloomed orange-brown. And best of all, furred dittany, queen of healing.

I did not walk as a mortal walks, but as a god, and the miles fell away beneath my feet. It was dusk when I reached the foothills and began to climb. The branches laced over me. The shade rose deep as water, tingling across my skin. The whole mountain seemed to hum beneath me. Even bloodied and aching as I was, I felt a spurt of giddiness. I traced the mosses, the hummocks of ground upwards, and, at the base of a white poplar, I found a blooming patch of dittany. Its leaves were threaded with power, and I pressed them to my broken fingers. The spell took hold with a word; my hand would be whole by morning. I gathered some of the roots and seeds for my bag, and kept on. The stink and weight of blood hung still upon me, and at last I found a pool, cold and clear, fed by icy melt. I welcomed the shock of its waters, their clean, scouring pain. I worked those small rites of purification which all gods know. With pebbles from the bank, I scrubbed the filth away.

After, I sat on the bank beneath the silvered leaves and thought of Daedalus' question. *Can the creature be killed?*

Among the gods there are a few who have the gift of prophecy, the ability to peer into the murk and glimpse what fates will come. Not everything may be foreseen. Most gods and mortals have lives that are tied to nothing; they tangle and wend now here, now there, according to no set plan. But then there are those who wear their destinies like nooses, whose lives run straight as planks, however they try to twist. It is these that our prophets may see.

My father has such foreknowledge, and I had heard it said all my life that the trait was passed to his children also. I had never thought to test it. I had been raised to think I had none of his strengths. But now I touched the water and said, *Show me.*

An image formed, delicate and pale, as if made from curls of mist. A smoking torch bobbed in long corridors. A thread unwound through a stone passage. The creature roared, showing its unnatural teeth. It stood tall as a man, dressed in rotting scraps. A mortal, sword in hand, leapt from the shadows to strike it dead.

The mist ebbed, and the pool cleared again. I had my answer, but it was not the one I had hoped for. The creature was mortal, but it could not die as an infant, by my hand or Daedalus'. It had a fate many years in the future, and must live it out. Until then, it could only be contained. That would be Daedalus' work, yet there might be a way for me to help him. I paced among the shadowed trees, thinking of that creature and what weaknesses it might have. I remembered its black eyes fixed ravening on mine. Its sucking hunger as it fought me for my hand. How much would

it take to sate that appetite? If I had not been a god, it would
have crawled up my arm, consuming me inch by inch.

I felt an idea rise in me. I would need all the secret herbs
of Dicte, and with them the strongest binding weeds, ilex
root and withy, fennel and hemlock, aconite, hellebore. I
would need as well the rest of my moly stores. I slipped
through those trees unerring, hunting down each ingredient in its turn. If Artemis walked that night, she kept out of
my way.

I carried the leaves and roots back to the pool and ground
them on its rocks. The paste I gathered in one of my bottles,
and added some of the pool's water. Its waves still bore the
blood it had washed from my hands, mine and my sister's too.
As if it knew, the draught swirled red and dark.

I did not sleep that night. I stayed on Dicte until the sky
went gray and then began walking back to Knossos. By the
time I reached the palace, the sun was bright on the fields.
I passed a courtyard that had caught my eye the day before, and stopped now to examine it more closely. In it was
a great dancing circle, ringed by laurels and oaks for shade
from the beating sun. I had thought its floor was made of
stone, but now I saw it was wood, a thousand tiles of it,
so smoothed and varnished that they seemed like a single
piece. They were painted with a spiral, traveling outwards
from its center like the furling crest of a wave. Daedalus'
work, it could be no other.

A girl was dancing on it. No music played, yet her feet
kept perfect time, each step the beat of a silent drum.
She moved like a wave herself, graceful, but with relentless, driving motion. On her head shone the circlet of a
princess. I would have known her anywhere. The girl from
Daedalus' prow.

Her eyes widened when she saw me, just like her

statue's. She bowed her head. "Aunt Circe," she said. "I am glad to meet you. I am Ariadne."

I could see pieces of Pasiphaë in her, but only if I searched: her chin, the delicacy of her collarbone.

"You are skilled," I said.

She smiled. "Thank you. My parents are looking for you."

"No doubt. But I must find Daedalus."

She nodded, as if I were only one of a thousand who wanted him instead of her parents. "I will take you. But we must be careful. The guards are out looking."

She slipped her fingers into mine, warm and a little damp from her exercise. Through dozens of narrow side-passages she led me, her feet silent on the stones. We came at last to a bronze door. She beat six times in a rhythm.

"I cannot play now, Ariadne," a voice called. "I am busy."

"I am with the lady Circe," she said.

The door swung open, revealing Daedalus, sooty and stained. Behind him was a workroom, half open to the sky. I saw statues with their cloths still on them, gears and instruments I did not recognize. At the back, a foundry smoked, and metal glowed hot in a mold. A fish spine lay on a table, a strange jagged blade beside it.

"I have been to Mount Dicte," I said. "I have glimpsed the creature's fate. It can die, but not now. A mortal will come who is destined to dispatch it. I do not know how long it may be. The creature was full-grown in my vision."

I watched the knowledge settle on him. All the days ahead that he must be on his guard. He drew a breath. "So we contain it then."

"Yes. I have brewed a charm that will help. It craves..." I paused, feeling Ariadne behind me. "It craves that flesh you saw it eat. It is part of its nature. I cannot take away that hunger, but I may set bounds upon it."

"Anything," he said. "I am grateful."

"Do not be grateful yet," I said. "For three seasons of the year, the spell will keep its appetite at bay. But every harvest it will return, and must be fed."

His eyes flicked to Ariadne behind me. "I understand," he said.

"The rest of the time it will still be dangerous, but only as a savage beast might be."

He nodded, but I saw he was thinking of harvest time, and the feeding that must come. He glanced at the molds behind him, tinged red with heat. "I will be finished with the cage tomorrow morning."

"Good," I said. "It cannot come too soon. I will work the spell then."

When the door closed, Ariadne stood waiting. "You were speaking of the baby that was born, were you not? He is the one that must be kept until he's killed?"

"He is."

"The servants say he is a monster, and my father shouted at me when I asked about him. But he is still my brother, is he not?"

I hesitated.

"I know about my mother and the white bull," she said.

No child of Pasiphaë's could remain innocent for long. "I suppose you may say he is your half-brother," I said. "Now come. Take me to the king and queen."

Griffins preened, delicate and regal, on the walls. The windows spilled sun. My sister lay on her silver couch glowing with health. Beside her, on an alabaster chair, Minos looked old and puffed, like something left dead in the waves. His eyes seized on me as snatcher-birds take fish.

"Where have you been? The monster needs tending. That is why you were brought here!"

"I have made a draught," I said. "So we may transfer it to its new cage more safely."

"A draught? I want it killed!"

"Darling, you sound hysterical," Pasiphaë said. "You haven't even heard my sister's idea. Go on, Circe, please." She rested her chin on her hand, theatrically expectant.

"It will bind the creature's hunger for three seasons of each year."

"That's it?"

"Now, Minos, you'll hurt Circe's feelings. I think it's a very fine spell, sister. My son's appetite *is* a bit unwieldy, isn't it? He's gone through most of our prisoners already."

"I want the creature dead, and that is final!"

"It cannot be killed," I told Minos. "Not now. It has a destiny far in the future."

"A destiny!" My sister clapped delightedly. "Oh, tell us what it is! Does it escape and eat someone we know?"

Minos paled, though he tried to hide it. "Be sure," he said to me. "You and the craftsman, be sure it is secure."

"Yes," my sister crooned. "Be sure. I hate to think what would happen if it got out. My husband may be a son of Zeus, but his flesh is thoroughly mortal. The truth is" — she lowered her voice to a whisper — "I think he may be afraid of the creature."

A hundred times I had seen some fool caught between my sister's claws. Minos took it worse than most. He stabbed a finger through the air at me. "You hear? She threatens me openly. This is your fault, you and your whole lying family. Your father gave her to me as if she were a treasure, but if you knew the things she has done to me — "

"Oh, tell her some of them! I think Circe would appreciate the witchcraft. What about the hundred girls who died while you heaved over them?"

I could feel Ariadne, very still, beside me. I wished she were not there.

The hate in Minos' eyes was a living thing. "Foul harpy! It was your spell that caused their deaths! All you breed is evil! I should have ripped that beast from your cursed womb before it could be born!"

"But you did not dare, did you? You know how your dear father Zeus dotes on such creatures. How else can all his bastard heroes win their reputations?" She cocked her head. "In fact, shouldn't you be slavering to take up a sword yourself? Oh, but I forgot. You have no taste for killing unless it is serving girls. Sister, truly, you should learn this spell. You need only — "

Minos had risen from his seat. "I forbid you to speak further!"

My sister laughed, her most silver-fountain sound. It was calculated, like everything she did. Minos raged on, but I was watching her. I had dismissed her coupling with the bull as some perverse whim, but she was not ruled by appetites; she ruled with them instead. When was the last time that I had seen true emotion on her face? I recalled now that moment on her childbed when she had cried out, her face twisted with urgency, that the monster must live. Why? Not love, there was none of that in her. So the creature must somehow serve her ends.

It was my hours with Hermes that helped me to an answer, all the news that he had brought me of the world. When Pasiphaë had married Minos, Crete was the richest and most famous of our kingdoms. Yet since then, every day, more mighty kingdoms were rising up, in Mycenae and Troy, Anatolia and Babylon. Since then too, one of her brothers had learned to raise the dead, the other to tame dragons, and her sister had transformed Scylla. No one spoke of Pasiphaë anymore. Now, at a stroke, she made her fading star shine again. All the world would tell the story of the queen of Crete, maker and mother of the great flesh-eating bull.

And the gods would do nothing. Think of all the prayers they would get.

"It's just so funny," Pasiphaë was saying. "It took you so long to understand! Did you think they were dying from the pleasure of your exertions? From the sheer transported bliss? Believe me — "

I turned to Ariadne, standing beside me silent as air.

"Come," I said. "We are finished here."

We walked back to her dancing circle. Over us, the laurels and oaks spread their green leaves. "When your spell is cast," she said, "my brother will not be so monstrous anymore."

"That is my hope," I said.

A moment passed. She looked up at me, hands clasped to her chest as if she kept a secret there. "Will you stay a little?"

I watched her dance, arms curving like wings, her strong young legs in love with their own motion. This was how mortals found fame, I thought. Through practice and diligence, tending their skills like gardens until they glowed beneath the sun. But gods are born of ichor and nectar, their excellences already bursting from their fingertips. So they find their fame by proving what they can mar: destroying cities, starting wars, breeding plagues and monsters. All that smoke and savor rising so delicately from our altars. It leaves only ash behind.

Ariadne's light feet crossed and recrossed the circle. Every step was perfect, like a gift she gave herself, and she smiled, receiving it. I wanted to seize her by the shoulders. Whatever you do, I wanted to say, do not be too happy. It will bring down fire on your head.

I said nothing, and let her dance.

CHAPTER ELEVEN

WHEN THE SUN TOUCHED the distant fields, guards arrived to collect Ariadne. *The princess is wanted by her parents.* They marched her off, and I was shown to my room. It was small and near the servants' quarters. This was meant, of course, to be an insult, but I liked the respite of the unpainted walls, the narrow window that showed only a sliver of the relentless sun. It was quiet as well, for all the servants crept past, knowing who lay within. *The sister witch.* They left food for me while I was gone and took the tray only when I was out again.

I slept, and the next morning Daedalus came for me. He smiled when I opened my door, and I found myself smiling in return. One thing I could thank the creature for: the ease between us had returned. I followed him down a staircase to the twisting corridors that ran beneath the palace. We passed grain cellars, storage rooms lined with rows of *pithoi*, the great ceramic jars that held the palace's largesse of oil and wine and barley.

"Whatever became of the white bull, do you know?"

"No. It vanished when Pasiphaë began to swell. The priests said it was the bull's final blessing. Today I heard someone say that the monster is a gift from the gods to help us prosper." He shook his head. "They are not naturally fools, it is only that they are caught between two scorpions."

"Ariadne is different," I said.

He nodded. "I have hopes of her. Have you heard what they've decided to name the thing? The Minotaur. Ten ships go out with the announcement at noon, and ten more will go out tomorrow."

"Clever," I said. "Minos claims it, and instead of being a cuckold he shares in my sister's glory. He becomes the great king who begets monsters and names them after himself."

Daedalus made a noise in his throat. "Exactly."

We had come to the large cellar room that held the creature's new cage. It was wide as a ship's deck and half as long, forged of a silver-gray metal. I put my hands to its bars, smooth and thick as saplings. I could smell the iron in it, but what more I could not tell.

"It is a new substance," Daedalus said. "Harder to work, but more durable. Even so, it will not hold the creature forever. He is already freakishly strong, and only just born. But it will give me time to devise something more permanent."

The soldiers followed behind, carrying the old cage on poles to keep their distance. They set it clanging down inside the new and were gone before the echoes had faded.

I went and knelt beside it. The Minotaur was larger than it had been, its flesh plump, pressing at the metal lattice. Clean of birth fluids now and dry, the line between bull and baby was starker than ever, as if some madman had lopped a steer's head and sewed it to a toddler. It stank of old meat, and the cage-bottom rattled with long bones. I felt a wash of nausea. *One of Crete's prisoners.*

The creature was watching me with huge eyes. It rose and snuffled forward, nose working. A moan came from it, sharp and excited. It remembered me. My smell and the taste of my flesh. It opened its squat mouth, like a baby bird begging. *More.*

I took my moment: spoke the words of power and poured the draught through the cage, down its open throat. The creature choked and lunged against the bars, but even as it did its eyes were changing, the fury in them ebbing away. I held its gaze and put out my hand. I heard Daedalus draw in a breath. But the creature did not leap for me. Its rigid limbs had loosened. Another moment I waited, then undid the lock and opened the cage.

It shuffled a little, the bones clattering under its feet. "It is all right," I murmured, whether to myself or Daedalus or the creature, I could not say. Slowly, I moved my hand towards it. Its nostrils flared. I touched its arm, and it made a huff of surprise, but nothing more.

"Come," I whispered, and it did, crouching and stumbling a little as it passed through the cage's small opening. It looked up at me, expectantly, almost sweetly.

My brother, Ariadne had called it. But this creature had not been made for any family. It was my sister's triumph, her ambition made flesh, her whip to use against Minos. In thanks, it would know no comrade, no lover. It would never see the sun, never take a free step. There was nothing it might ever have in the world but hatred and darkness and its teeth.

I picked up the old cage and stepped back. It watched me as I moved away, its head tilted with curiosity. I shut the cage door, and its ear flicked at the metallic sound. When harvest came, it would scream with rage. It would tear at the bars, trying to rip them apart.

Daedalus let out a low breath. "How did you do that?"

"It is half beast," I said. "All the animals on Aiaia are tame."

"Can the spell be undone?"

"Not by another."

We locked the cage. All the while the creature watched us. It made a low noise and rubbed at a hairy cheek with one of its hands. Then we swung the wooden door of the room closed and saw no more.

"And the key?"

"I plan to throw it away. When we have to move it, I will cut the bars."

We walked back through the twisting under-passages and up to the corridors above. In the painted hall, the breeze was blowing, and the air bright. Pretty nobles passed on every side, murmuring their secrets. Did they know what lived beneath them? They would.

"There is a feast this evening," he said.

"I am not going," I said. "I am finished with the court of Crete."

"You are leaving soon, then?"

"I am at the king and queen's mercy for that, they are the ones with the ships. But I imagine it will not be much longer. I think Minos will be glad to have one less witch on Crete. It will be good to be home."

It was true, yet in those ornate corridors, the thought of returning to Aiaia was strange. Its hills and shore, the stone house with my garden, all seemed very distant.

"I must show my face tonight," he said. "Yet I hope to make my excuses before the meal." He hesitated. "Goddess, I know I presume, but will you do me the honor of dining with me?"

He had told me to come when the moon was up. His rooms were at the opposite end of the palace from my sister's. If that was luck or design I could not say. He wore a

finer cloak than I had seen him in before, but his feet were
bare. He drew me to a table, poured a wine dark as mul-
berries. There were platters set out, heaped with fruits and
a salty white cheese.

"How was the feast?"

"I am glad to be gone." His voice was curdled. "They
had a singer in, to tell the tale of the glorious bull-man's
birth. Apparently he fell from a star."

A boy ran out from an inner room. I did not know mortal ages well then, but I think he may have been four. His
black hair curled thick and wild around his ears, and his
limbs were still babyishly round. He had the sweetest face
I had ever seen, gods included.

"My son," Daedalus said.

I stared. I had not even considered that Daedalus' secret
could be a child. The boy knelt, like an infant courtier.

"Noble lady," he piped. "I welcome you to my father's
house."

"Thank you," I said. "And are you a good boy, for your
father?"

He nodded seriously. "Oh, yes."

Daedalus laughed. "Don't believe a word. He looks
sweet as cream, but he does what he wants." The boy
smiled at his father. It was an old joke between them.

He stayed for some time, prattling of his father's work
and how he helped. He brought out the tongs he liked to
use and showed me with a practiced grip how he could
hold them in the fire and not be burnt. I nodded, but it
was his father I watched. Daedalus' face had gone soft as
ripe fruit, his eyes full and shining. I had never thought of
having children, but looking at him, for a moment I could
imagine it. As if I peered into a well and far below glimpsed
a flash of water.

My sister, of course, would have seen such love in an instant.

Daedalus put his hand to his son's shoulder. "Icarus," he said, "it is time for bed. Go find your nurse."

"You will come kiss me goodnight?"

"Of course."

We watched him go, small heels brushing the hem of his too-long tunic.

"He is handsome," I said.

"He has his mother's face." He answered the question before I asked it. "She passed at his birth. A good woman, though I did not know her long. Your sister arranged the marriage."

So I had not been so wrong after all. My sister had baited the hook, but she caught the fish another way.

"I'm sorry," I said.

He bowed his head. "It is difficult, I admit. I have done my best to be father to him and mother too, but I know he feels the lack. Every woman we pass, he asks if I will marry her."

"And will you?"

He was silent a moment. "I think not. Pasiphaë has enough to scourge me with already, and I would never have married in the first place, if she had not insisted. I know what an unfit husband I make, for I am happiest when my hands are busy at my work, and then I come home late and filthy."

"Witchcraft and invention have that in common," I said. "I do not think I would make a fit wife either. Not that my door is battered down. Apparently the market for disgraced sorceresses is thin."

He smiled. "Your sister I think has helped poison that well."

It was easy to speak so openly with him. His face was like a quiet pool that would hold everything safe in its depths.

"Do you know yet how you will keep the creature when it is grown?"

He nodded. "I have been thinking. You see what a honeycomb the palace is beneath. There are a hundred storerooms that go unused, for all the wealth of Crete is in gold these days, not grain. I think I may make them into a sort of maze. Close it at both ends and let the creature roam. It is all dug in the bedrock, so there will be nowhere to break out."

It was a good idea. And at least the creature would have more room than a narrow cage. "It will be a marvel," I said. "A maze that can hold a full-grown monster. You will have to come up with a good name for it."

"I'm sure Minos will have a suggestion, involving himself."

"I'm sorry that I cannot stay to help."

"You have helped more than I deserve." His gaze lifted to touch mine.

A throat cleared. The nurse stood in the doorway. "Your son, sir."

"Ah," Daedalus said. "Excuse me."

I felt too restless to sit patiently. I wandered the room. I had expected it to be filled with more of his wonders, statues and inlay in every corner, but it was simple, the furniture unadorned wood. Yet looking more closely, I saw Daedalus' stamp. The polish glowed and the grain was rubbed soft as flower petals. When I passed my hand over a chair, I could not find its seams.

He came back. "The bedtime kiss," he explained.

"A happy child."

Daedalus sat, drank a swallow of wine. "For now, he is. He

is too young to know himself a prisoner." Those white scars seemed to flare on his hands. "A golden cage is still a cage."

"And where would you go, if you might escape?"

"Wherever would have me. But if I may choose, Egypt. They are building things that make Knossos look like a mudflat. I have been learning the language from some of their traders on the docks. I think they would welcome us."

I looked into his good face. Not good because it was handsome, but because it was itself, like fine metal, tempered and beaten for strength. Two monsters we had fought side by side, and he had not wavered. Come to Aiaia, I wanted to say. But I knew there was nothing for him there.

Instead I told him, "I hope you will get to Egypt one day."

We finished our meal, and I walked the dark corridors back to my room. The evening had been pleasant, but I felt roiled and muddy, my mind like river-silt stirred up from its beds. I could not stop hearing Daedalus talking of his freedom. There had been such yearning in his voice, and bitterness too. At least I had earned my exile, but Daedalus was innocent, kept only as a trophy for my sister and Minos' vanity. I thought of his eyes when he had spoken of Icarus, that pure, shining love. To my sister, it was no more than a tool, a sword to hang over his head and make him her slave. I remembered the pleasure on her face when she had ordered him to cut her open. She had had the same look when I had stepped through her door.

I had been so consumed with the Minotaur that I had not seen what a triumph this had all been for her. Not just the monster and her new fame, but everything that went with it: Daedalus forced into complicity, Minos cringing and humiliated, and all of Crete held hostage to fear.

And me, I was a triumph too. She might have summoned others, but I had always been the dog she liked to whip. She had known how useful I would be, dutifully cleaning her messes, protecting Daedalus, seeing the monster safely contained. And all the while she could laugh from her golden couch. *Do you like my new pet? I give her nothing but blows, yet see how she runs to my whistle!*

My stomach burned. I turned away from my cell. I walked as a god, unseen, past the drowsing guards, past the night servants. I reached the door of my sister's room and stepped through it. I stood over her bed. She was alone. My sister trusted her sleep to none but herself. I had felt the spells when I passed the threshold, but they could not stop me.

"Why did you summon me here?" I demanded. "Let me hear you admit it."

Her eyes opened at once, keen, as if she had been expecting me. "It was a gift, of course. Who else would have enjoyed seeing me bleed so much?"

"I can think of a thousand."

She smiled, as cats smile. It was always more fun to play with a live mouse. "What a shame it is that you can't use your new binding spell on Scylla. But of course you would need her mother's blood. I don't think that shark Krataiis will oblige you."

I had thought of it already. Pasiphaë always knew where to aim the spear.

"You wanted to humiliate me," I said.

She yawned, pink tongue against her white teeth. "I've been thinking," she said, "of naming my son Asterion. Do you like it?"

Starry one, it meant. "The prettiest name for a cannibal I ever heard."

"Don't be so dramatic. He can't be a cannibal, there are

no other Minotaurs to eat." She frowned a little, tilting her chin. "Though, I wonder, do centaurs count? They must have some kinship, don't you think?"

I would not be drawn by her. "You could have sent for Perses."

"Perses." She waved a hand. What that meant, I could not say.

"Or Aeëtes."

She sat up, and the covers fell from her. Her skin was bare, except for a necklace made of squares of beaten gold. Each one was embossed: a sun, a bee, an axe, the great hulk of Dicte. "Oh, I hope we keep talking all night," she said. "I will braid your hair, and we can laugh over our suitors." She lowered her voice. "I think Daedalus would have you in a minute."

My anger spilled its banks. "I am not your dog, Pasiphaë, nor your bear to be baited. I came to your aid, despite all our history, despite the men you sent to their deaths. I helped you with your monster. I have done your work for you, and all you give me is mockery and contempt. For once in your twisting life, speak the truth. You brought me here to make me your fool."

"Oh, that requires no effort from me," she said. "You are a fool on your own." But it was reflexive, not a real answer. I waited.

"It is funny," she said, "that even after all this time, you still believe you should be rewarded, just because you have been obedient. I thought you would have learned that lesson in our father's halls. None shrank and simpered as you did, and yet great Helios stepped on you all the faster, because you were already crouched at his feet."

She was leaning forward, her golden hair loose, embroidering the sheets around her.

"Let me tell you a truth about Helios and all the rest. They do not care if you are good. They barely care if you are wicked. The only thing that makes them listen is power. It is not enough to be an uncle's favorite, to please some god in his bed. It is not enough even to be beautiful, for when you go to them, and kneel and say, 'I have been good, will you help me?' they wrinkle their brows. Oh, sweetheart, it cannot be done. Oh, darling, you must learn to live with it. And have you asked Helios? You know I do nothing without his word."

She spat upon the floor.

"They take what they want, and in return they give you only your own shackles. A thousand times I saw you squashed. I squashed you myself. And every time, I thought, that is it, she is done, she will cry herself into a stone, into some croaking bird, she will leave us and good riddance. Yet always you came back the next day. They were all surprised when you showed yourself a witch, but I knew it long ago. Despite your wet-mouse weeping, I saw how you would not be ground into the earth. You loathed them as I did. I think it is where our power comes from."

Her words were falling on my head like a great cataract. I could scarcely take them in. She hated our family? She had always seemed to me their distillation, a glittering monument to our blood's vain cruelty. Yet it was true what she said: nymphs were allowed to work only through the power of others. They could expect none for themselves.

"If all this is so," I said, "why were you so savage to me? Aeëtes and I were alone, you might have been friends with us."

"Friends," she sneered. Her lips were a perfect blood-red, the color all the other nymphs had to paint on. "There are no friends in those halls. And Aeëtes has never liked a woman in his life."

"That's not true," I said.

"Because you think he liked you?" She laughed. "He tolerated you because you were a tame monkey, clapping after every word he spoke."

"You and Perses were no different," I said.

"You know nothing of Perses. Do you know how I had to keep him happy? The things I had to do?"

I did not want to hear more. Her face was naked as I had ever seen it, and every word sharp as if she had spent years carving it to just that shape.

"Then Father gave me to that ass Minos. Well, I could work with him, and I have. He is fixed now, but it has been a long road, and I will never go back to what I was. So you tell me, sister, whom should I have sent for instead? Some god who could not wait to scorn me and make me beg for crumbs? Or some nymph, to mince uselessly across the sea?" She laughed again. "They would both have run screaming at the first tooth. They cannot bear any pain at all. They are not like us."

The words were a shock, as if all this while her hands had been empty, and now she showed her knife. Sickness flooded my throat. I stepped back.

"I am not like you."

For a moment, I saw the surprise on her face. Then it was gone, like a wave washing clean over sand.

"No," she said. "You are not. You are like Father, stupid and sanctimonious, closing your eyes to everything you do not understand. Tell me, what do you think would happen if I did not make monsters and poisons? Minos does not want a queen, only a simpering jelly he keeps in a jar and breeds to death. He would be happy to have me in chains for eternity, and he need only say the word to his own father to do it. But he does not. He knows what I would do to him first."

I remembered my father saying of Minos, *He will keep her in her place.* "Yet Father will only allow Minos so much license."

Her laughter clawed at my ears. "Father would put me in the chains himself, if it would keep his precious alliance. You are proof of that. Zeus is terrified of witchcraft and wanted a sacrifice. Father picked you because you are worth the least. And now you are shut on that island and will never leave it. I should have known you would be good for nothing to me. Get out. Get out and let me not see you again."

I walked back through those corridors. My mind was bare, my skin bristling as if it would rise off my flesh. Every noise, every touch, the stones beneath my feet, the splash of fountains from a window, crept evilly upon my senses. The air had a stinging weight like ocean waves. I felt myself a stranger to the world.

When the figure separated from the shadows of my door, I was too numb to cry out. My hand fumbled for my bag of draughts, but then the distant torchlight fell upon his hooded face.

He spoke so softly only a god could have heard. "I was waiting for you. Say but one word, and I am gone."

It took me a moment to understand. I had not thought him so bold. But of course he was. Artist, creator, inventor, the greatest the world had known. Timidity creates nothing.

What would I have said, if he had come earlier? I do not know. But his voice then was like a balm upon my raw skin. I yearned for his hands, for all of him, mortal though he was, distant and dying though he would always be.

"Stay," I said.

*   *   *

We lit no tapers. The room was dark and warm from the day's heat. Shadows draped the bed. No frogs sounded, no birds called. It was as if we had found the still heart of the universe. Nothing moved except for us.

After, we lay beside each other, the night breeze trickling over our limbs. I thought of telling him about the quarrel with Pasiphaë, but I did not want her there with us. Outside, the stars were veiled, and a servant passed through the yard with a flickering torch. I thought I imagined it, at first: a faint tremor shaking the room.

"Do you feel that?"

Daedalus nodded. "They're never strong. A few cracks in plaster. They have been coming more often lately."

"It will not damage the cage."

"No," he said. "They would have to get much worse." A moment passed. His voice came quiet through the darkness. "At harvest," he said, "when the creature is grown. How bad will it be?"

"As many as fifteen in a moon."

I heard his indrawn breath. "I feel the weight of it every moment," he said. "All those lives. I helped make that creature, and now I cannot unmake it."

I knew the weight he spoke of. His hand lay beside mine. It was calloused, but not rough. In the darkness, I had run my fingers over it, searching out the faint smooth patches that were his scars.

"How do you bear it?" he said.

My eyes gave off a faint light, and by it I could see his face. It was a surprise to realize that he was waiting for an answer. That he believed I had one. I thought of another dim room, with another prisoner. He had been a craftsman also. On the foundation of his knowledge civilization had been built. Prometheus' words, deep-running as roots, had waited in me all this time.

"We bear it as best we can," I said.

Minos was frugal with his ships, and now that the monster was contained, he made me wait on his convenience. "One of my traders passes near Aiaia. He sails in a few days. You may go then."

I did not see my sister again, except from a distance, carried to her picnics and pleasures. I did not see Ariadne either, though I looked for her at her dancing circle. I asked one of the guards if he might take me to her. I did not think I imagined his smirk. "The queen forbids it."

Pasiphaë and her petty vengeances. My face stung, but I would not give her the satisfaction of knowing her cruelty had hit home. I wandered the palace grounds, its colonnades, its walks and fields. I watched the mortals as they passed with their interesting, untamed faces. Each night Daedalus knocked secretly at my door. It was borrowed time, we knew it, which made it all the sweeter.

The guards came just after dawn on the fourth day. Daedalus had gone already; he liked to be home when Icarus woke. The men stood before me, stiff in their purple capes, looming as if I might try to break past them and escape into the hills. I followed them through the painted halls, down the great steps. Daedalus was waiting amid the chaos of the pier.

"Pasiphaë will punish you for this," I said.

"No more than she does already." He stepped aside as the eight sheep Minos had sent as his thanks were herded onto the ship. "I see the king is as generous as ever." He gestured to two huge crates, already loaded on the deck. "I

remember you like to keep yourself busy. It is my own design."

"Thank you," I said. "You honor me."

"No," he said. "I know what we owe you. What I owe."

The back of my throat burned, but I could feel the eyes
watching us. I did not want to make it worse for him. "Will
you tell Ariadne farewell for me?"

"I will," he said.

I stepped onto the ship and lifted my hand. He lifted his.
I had not fooled myself with false hope. I was a goddess,
and he a mortal, and both of us were imprisoned. But I
pressed his face into my mind, as seals are pressed in wax,
so I could carry it with me.

I did not open those crates until we were out of sight. I
wish I had, so I might have thanked him properly. Inside
one were undyed wools and yarns and flax of every kind. In
the other, the most beautiful loom I had ever seen, made
from polished cedar.

I have it still. It stands near my hearth, and has even
found its way into the songs. Perhaps that is no surprise, poets like such symmetries: Witch Circe skilled at spinning
spells and threads alike, at weaving charms and cloths.
Who am I to spoil an easy hexameter? But any wonder in
my cloth comes from that loom and the mortal who made
it. Even after so many centuries, its joints are strong, and
when the shuttle slides through the warp, the scent of cedar
fills the air.

After I left, Daedalus built his great maze indeed, the
Labyrinth, whose walls confounded the Minotaur's rage.
Harvest piled upon harvest, and the twisting passageways
grew ankle-deep in bones. If you listened, the palace servants said, you could hear the creature clattering up and
down. And all the while, Daedalus was working. He

daubed two wooden frames with yellow wax and onto them he pressed the feathers he had collected from the great seabirds that fed on Crete's shore, long-pinioned, wide and white. Two sets of wings, they made. He tied one to his own arms, and one to his son's. They stood atop the highest cliff of Knossos' shore and leapt.

The ocean draughts caught them, and they were borne aloft. East they went, towards the rising sun and Africa. Icarus whooped, for by then he was a young man, and this was his first freedom. His father laughed to see him diving and wheeling. The boy rose higher still, dazzled by the sky's vastness, the sun's unfettered heat on his shoulders. He did not heed his father's cries of warning. He did not notice the melting wax. The feathers fell, and he fell after, into the drowning waves.

I mourned for that sweet boy's death, but I mourned more for Daedalus, winging doggedly onwards, dragging that desperate grief behind him. It was Hermes who told me, of course, sipping my wine, his feet upon my hearth. I closed my eyes, to find that impression I had made of Daedalus' face. I wished then that we had conceived a child together, to be some comfort to him. But that was a young and silly thought: as if children are sacks of grain, to be substituted one for another.

Daedalus did not long outlive his son. His limbs turned gray and nerveless, and all his strength was transmuted into smoke. I had no right to claim him, I knew it. But in a solitary life, there are rare moments when another soul dips near yours, as stars once a year brush the earth. Such a constellation was he to me.

CHAPTER TWELVE

WE WENT THE LONG way back to Aiaia, avoiding
Scylla. Eleven days it took. The sky bent its arc over us,
clear and bright. I stared into the blinding waves, the
white-flaring sun. No one disturbed me. The men averted
their gazes when I passed, and I saw them cast a rope
I had touched into the waves. I could not blame them.
They lived on Knossos and knew too much of witchery
already.

When we landed on Aiaia, they dutifully carried the
loom up through the woods and set it before my hearth.
They led up the eight sheep. I offered them wine and a
meal, but of course they did not accept. They hurried back
to their ship, strained at their oars, eager to vanish over the
horizon. I watched until the moment they winked out, like
a snuffed flame.

The lion glared from my threshold. She lashed her tail
as if to say, *That had better be the last of that.*

"I think it will be," I said.

After Knossos' sunny, out-flung pavilions, my house was
snug as a burrow. I walked its neat rooms, feeling the silence, the stillness, the scuff of no feet but my own. I put

my hand to every surface, every cupboard and cup. They were all as they had been. As they would ever be.

I went out to my garden. I weeded the same weeds that always grew, and planted the herbs I had gathered on Dicte. They looked strange away from their moonlit hollows, crowded in among my glossy, bright beds. Their hum seemed fainter, their colors faded. I had not considered that perhaps their powers could not survive transplanting.

In the years I had lived on Aiaia, I had never chafed at my constraint. After my father's halls, the island seemed to me the wildest, most giddy freedom. Its shores, its peaks, all of them yawned out to the horizon, filled up with magic. But looking at those fragile blooms, for the first time I felt the true weight of my exile. If they died, I could harvest no more. I would never walk again the humming slopes of Dicte. I could not draw water from its silver pool. All those places Hermes had told me of, Araby, Assur, Egypt, they were lost forever.

You will never leave, my sister had said.

In defiance, I threw myself into my old life. I did what I liked, the moment that I thought of it. I sang upon the beaches, rearranged my garden. I called the pigs and scratched their bristled backs, brushed the sheep, and summoned wolves to lie panting on my floor. The lion rolled her yellow eyes at them, but she behaved herself, for it was my law that all my animals bear each other.

Every night, I went out to dig my herbs and roots. I did whatever spells came to mind, just to feel the pleasure of them knitting in my hands. In the morning I cut flowers for my kitchen. In the evenings after dinner, I set myself before Daedalus' loom. It took me some time to understand it, for it was like no loom I had ever known in the halls of the gods. There was a seat, and the weft was drawn down rather than up. If my grandmother had seen, she would have offered her sea snake for it; the cloth it produced was finer than her best. Daedalus had guessed well: that I would like the whole business of it, the simplicity and skill at once, the smell of the wood, the *shush* of the shuttle, the satisfying way weft stacked upon weft. It was a little like spell-work, I thought, for your hands must be busy, and your mind sharp and free. Yet my favorite part was not the loom at all, but the making of the dyes. I went hunting for the best colors, madder root and saffron, the scarlet kermes bug and the wine-dark murex from the sea, and alum powder to hold them fast in the wool. I squeezed them, pounded, soaked them in great bubbling pots until the stinking liquids foamed up bright as flowers: crimson and crocus yellow and the deep purple that princes wear. If I had had Athena's skill, I could have woven a great tapestry of Iris, goddess of the rainbow, flinging down her colors from the sky.

But I was not Athena. I was happy with simple scarves, with cloaks and blankets that lay like jewels upon my chairs. I draped my lion in one and called her the Queen of Phoenicia. She sat, turning her head this way and that, as if to show off how the purple made her fur shine gold.

You will never see Phoenicia.

I rose from my stool and made myself walk the island, admiring the changes every hour brought: the water-striders skimming over the ponds, the stones rolled green and smooth by river currents, the bees flying low, freighted with pollen. The bays were full of lashing fish, the seeds broke from their pods. My dittany, my lilies from Crete, they thrived after all. *See?* I said to my sister.

It was Daedalus who answered. *A golden cage is still a cage.*

Spring passed into summer, and summer into fragrant autumn. There were mists now in the morning and sometimes storms at night. Winter would come soon with its own beauty, the green hellebore leaves shining amid the brown, and the cypresses tall and black against the metal sky. It was not ever truly cold, not as Mount Dicte's peak, but I was glad for my new cloaks as I climbed the rocks and stood among the winds. Yet, no matter what beauties I sought, what pleasures I found, my sister's words followed me, taunting, worming deep in my bones and blood.

"You are wrong about witchcraft," I told her. "It does not come from hate. I made my first spell for love of Glaucos."

I could hear her mink-voice as if she stood before me. *Yet it was in defiance of our father, in defiance of all those who slighted you and would keep you from your desires.*

I had seen the look in my father's eyes when he knew at last what I was. He was thinking he should have snuffed me in my crib.

Just so. Look how they stopped our mother's womb. Have you not noticed how easily she twists Father and our aunts?

I had noticed it. It seemed to go beyond beauty, beyond whatever bed-tricks she might know. "She is clever."

Clever! Pasiphaë laughed. *You always underestimated her. I would not be surprised if she has witch-blood too. We do not get our charms from Helios.*

I had wondered that myself.

You are sorry now you scorned her. You spent every day licking Father's feet, hoping he would set her aside.

I paced the rocks. I had walked the earth for a hundred generations, yet I was still a child to myself. Rage and grief, thwarted desire, lust, self-pity: these are emotions gods know well. But guilt and shame, remorse, ambivalence, those are foreign countries to our kind, which must be learned stone by stone. I could not stop thinking of my sister's face, that blank shock when I told her I would never be like her. What had she hoped for? That we would send messages back and forth in seabirds' mouths? That we would share spells, fight the gods? That we might be, in our way, sisters at last?

I tried to imagine it: our heads bent together over herbs, her laugh as she devised some cleverness. I wished then — oh, a dozen impossible things. That I had known sooner what she was. That we had grown up somewhere other than those glittering halls. I could have blunted her poisons, drawn her from her abuses, taught her how to gather the best herbs.

Hah! she said. *I will take no lessons from fools like you. You are weak and blind, and it is worse because you choose it. You will be sorry in the end.*

It was always easier when she was hateful. "I am not weak. And I will never be sorry not to be like you. Do you hear?"

There was no answer, of course. Only the air, eating my words.

Hermes returned. I no longer thought that he had conspired with Pasiphaë. It was only his nature to vaunt his knowledge and laugh at what others did not know. He lounged in my silver chair. "So how did you like Crete? I heard you had some excitement."

I gave him food and wine, and took him to my bed that night. He was handsome as ever, keen and playful in our couplings. But a distaste rose in me now when I looked at him. One moment I would be laughing, and the next his jests turned sour in my throat. When his hands reached for me, I felt a strange dislocation. They were perfect and unscarred.

My ambivalence, of course, only encouraged him. Any challenge was a game, and any game a pleasure. If I had loved him, he would have been gone, yet my revulsion brought him back and back. He pressed hard to wrap me up, bringing gifts and news, unfolding the whole tale of the Minotaur to me without my asking.

After I had sailed away, he said, Minos and Pasiphaë's eldest, Androgeos, had visited the mainland and been killed near Athens. By then, the people of Crete were restive at having to lose their sons and daughters every harvest, and were threatening revolt. Minos seized his opportunity. He demanded, as payment for his son, that the Athenian king send seven youths and seven maids to feed the monster, or else Crete's mighty navy would bring war. The frightened king agreed, and one of the youths chosen was his own child, Theseus.

This prince was the mortal I had seen in the mountain pool. But my vision had not told me all: he might have died, if not for the princess Ariadne. She fell in love with him, and to save his life smuggled him a sword and taught him the way through the Labyrinth, which she had learned from Daedalus himself. Yet when he came out from that maze with his hands covered in the monster's blood, she had wept, and not for joy.

"I heard," Hermes said, "that she had an unnatural love for the creature. She would go often to its cage and speak softly to it through the bars, and offer delicacies from her own table. Once, she got too close, and its teeth caught her shoulder. She escaped and Daedalus sewed up the wound, but it left a scar at the base of her neck, in the shape of a crown."

I remembered her face as she said, *my brother.* "Was she punished? For helping Theseus?"

"No. She fled with him after the creature was dead. Theseus would have married her, but my brother decided he wanted her for himself. You know how he loves the ones with light feet. He told Theseus to leave her on an island, and he would come to claim her."

I knew which brother he meant. Dionysus, lord of ivy and the grape. Riotous son of Zeus, whom mortals call Releaser, for he frees them from their cares. At least, I thought, with Dionysus she would dance every night.

Hermes shook his head. "He came too late. She had fallen asleep, and Artemis killed her."

He spoke so casually that for a moment I thought I'd misheard. "What? She is dead?"

"I led her to the underworld myself."

That lithe and hopeful girl. "For what reason?"

"I couldn't get a straight answer out of Artemis. You know how ill-tempered she is. Some incomprehensible slight." He shrugged.

My witchcraft was no match against an Olympian, I knew it. But in that moment, I wanted to try. To summon up all my charms, to throw my will upon the spirits of the earth, the beasts, the birds, and set them after Artemis, until she knew what it was to be truly hunted.

"Come," Hermes said. "If you cry every time some mortal dies, you'll drown in a month."

"Get out," I said.

Icarus, Daedalus, Ariadne. All gone to those dark fields, where hands worked nothing but air, where feet no more touched the earth. If I had been there, I thought. But what would it have changed? It was true what Hermes said. Every moment mortals died, by shipwreck and sword, by wild beasts and wild men, by illness, neglect, and age. It was their fate, as Prometheus had told me, the story that they all shared. No matter how vivid they were in life, no matter how brilliant, no matter the wonders they made, they came to dust and smoke. Meanwhile every petty and useless god would go on sucking down the bright air until the stars went dark.

Hermes came back, as always. I let him. When he glittered in my hall, my shores did not feel so narrow, the knowledge of my exile did not weigh so heavy. "Tell me the news," I said. "Tell me of Crete. How did Pasiphaë take the Minotaur's death?"

"She went mad, is the rumor. She wears nothing but black now in mourning."

"Don't be a fool. She is only mad if it suits her," I said.

"She is said to have cursed Theseus, and he is plagued and plagued since then. Did you hear how his father died?"

I did not care about Theseus, I wanted to hear of my sister. Hermes must have been laughing as he fed me tale after tale. How she had forbidden Minos from her bed, and her only joy was her youngest daughter, Phaedra. How she was haunting the slopes of Mount Dicte, digging up the whole mountain searching out new poisons. I hoarded every tidbit like a dragon guards its treasure. I was looking for something, I realized, though I could not say what.

Like all good storytellers, Hermes knew to save the best for last. One evening, he told me of a trick Pasiphaë had played upon Minos in the early days of their marriage. Minos used to order any girl he liked to his bedchamber in front of her face. So she cursed him with a spell that turned his seed to snakes and scorpions. Whenever he lay with a woman, they stung her to death from the inside.

I remembered the fight I had heard between them. A hundred girls, Pasiphaë had said. They would have been serving maidens, slaves, merchants' daughters, anyone whose fathers would not dare raise a fuss against the king. All extinguished for nothing but petty pleasure and revenge.

I sent Hermes from me, and closed my shutters as I never did. Anyone would have thought I was casting a great spell, but I reached for no herbs. I felt a weightless joy. The story was so ugly, so outlandish and disgusting, that it felt like a fever breaking. If I was trapped on this island, at least I did not have to share the world with her and all her kind. Pacing by my lion, I said, "It is done. I will think of them no more. I cast them out and I am finished."

The cat pressed her cheek upon her folded paws and kept her eyes upon the floor. So perhaps she knew what I did not.

CHAPTER THIRTEEN

IT WAS SPRING AND I was down on the eastern slope, picking early strawberries. The sea-winds blew strongly there, and the sweetness of the fruits was always tinged with salt. The pigs began squealing, and I looked up. A ship was making its way towards us through the slanting afternoon light. There was a headwind against it, yet it did not slow or tack. The oarsmen drove it straight as a well-sent arrow.

My stomach turned over. Hermes had given me no warning, and I could not think what that might mean. The vessel was Mycenaean in style, and bore a figurehead so massive it must have altered the draught of the ship. A pair of black-rimmed eyes smoked on its hull. I caught a strange, faint odor on the wind. I hesitated a moment, then wiped my hands and walked down to the beach.

The ship was close to shore by then, its prow casting a shadow like a needle over the waves. I counted some three dozen men aboard. Later, of course, there would be a thousand who claimed they were there, or who invented genealogies to trace their blood back. The greatest heroes of their generation, that crew was called. Bold and unshakable, masters of a hundred wild adventures. Certainly, they looked the part: princely and tall, big-shouldered, with rich cloaks and thick hair, raised up on the best their kingdoms had to offer. They wore weapons the way most men wear their clothes. No doubt they'd been wrestling boars and slaying giants from their cradles.

Yet their faces at the rail were pinched and tense. That smell was stronger now, and there was a heaviness in the air, a dragging weight that seemed to hang from the mast itself. They saw me, yet they made no sound and gave no signs of greeting.

The anchor dropped with a splash and the plank followed. Above, gulls circled, crying. Two descended, arms touching, heads bowed. A man, broad and muscular, his dark hair lifting in the late breeze. And — it surprised me — a woman, tall and wrapped in black, a long veil flowing down behind her. The pair moved towards me gracefully and without hesitation, as if they were expected guests. They knelt at my feet and the woman held her hands up, long-fingered and bare of any adornment. Her veil was arranged so that not one strand of hair showed beneath it. Her chin stayed resolutely down, concealing her face.

"Goddess," she said, "Witch of Aiaia. We come to you for aid." Her voice was low but clear, with a musicality to it, as if it were used to singing. "We have fled great evil, and to escape it we have done great evil. We are tainted."

I could feel it. That unwholesome air had thickened, coating everything with an oily heaviness. *Miasma*, it was called. Pollution. It rose from unpurified crimes, from deeds done against the gods, and from the unsanctified spilling of blood. It had touched me after the Minotaur's birth, until Dicte's waters washed me clean. But this was stronger: a foul, seeping contagion.

"Will you help us?" she said.

"Help us, great goddess, we are at your mercy," the man echoed.

It was not magic they asked for, but the oldest rite of our kind. *Katharsis*. The cleansing by smoke and prayer, water and blood. It was forbidden for me to question them, to demand their transgressions, if transgressions they were. My part was only yes or no.

The man did not have his partner's discipline. When he had spoken, his chin had lifted a little, and I had glimpsed his face. He was young, even younger than I had thought, his beard still in patches. His skin was raw from wind and sun, but it glowed with health. He was beautiful — like a god, the poets would say. But it was his mortal determination that struck me most, the brave set of his neck, despite the burdens upon him.

"Rise," I said. "And come. I will help you as I can."

I led them up the pig trails. His hand clasped her arm solicitously, as if he would steady her, but she never stumbled. If anything, her feet were surer than his. And still she was careful to keep her face down.

I brought them inside. They stepped past the chairs and knelt silently upon the floor stones. Daedalus might have carved a lovely statue of them: *Humility*.

I went to the back door, and the pigs ran to me. I put my hand on one, a piglet not half a year old, pure and unspotted. If I were a priest I would have drugged him so he would not take fright and struggle, marring the ritual. In my hands, he went limp as a sleeping child. I washed him, tied the sacred fillets, wove a garland for his neck, and all the while he was quiet, as if he knew and agreed.

I set the golden basin on the floor and took up the

great bronze knife. I had no altar, but I did not need one: anywhere I was became my temple. The animal's throat opened easily beneath the blade. He did kick then, but only for a moment. I held him firm until his legs stilled, while the red stream poured into the bowl. I sang the hymns, and bathed their hands and faces in sacred water while fragrant herbs burned. I felt the heaviness lifting. The air grew clean, and the oily scent faded. They prayed while I carried away the blood to pour over a tree's wrinkled roots. I would butcher the body later and cook it for their meal.

"It is done," I told them, when I returned.

He lifted the hem of my cloak to his lips. "Great goddess."

She was the one I was watching. I wanted to see her face, freed at last from its careful custody.

She looked up. Her eyes shone bright as torches. She drew off her veil, revealing hair like the sun on Crete's hills. A demigod, she was, that potent mix of human and divinity. And more than that: she was my kin. None had such a golden look except the direct line of Helios.

"I am sorry for my deception," she said. "But I could not risk you sending me away. Not when I have wished all my life to know you."

There was a quality to her that is hard to describe, a fervency, a heat that went to your head. I had expected her to be beautiful, for she walked like a queen of the gods, but it was an odd beauty, not like my mother's or sister's. Each of her features alone was nothing, her nose too sharp, her chin over-strong. Yet together they made a whole like the heart of a flame. You could not look away.

Her eyes were clinging to me as if they would peel me. "You and my father were close as children. I could not know what messages he might have sent you about his way-ward daughter."

The force in her, the certainty. I should have recognized who she was at first glance, only from the set of her shoulders.

"You are Aeëtes' child," I said. I searched for the name Hermes had told me. "Medea, is it not?"

"And you are my aunt Circe."

She looked like her father, I thought. That high brow and sharp, unyielding gaze. I said no more, but rose and went into the kitchen. I put plates and bread on a tray, added cheese and olives, goblets and wine. It is law that guests must be fed before the host's curiosity.

"Refresh yourselves," I said. "There will be time to make all clear."

She served the man first, offering him the most tender morsels, urging bite upon bite. He ate what she gave him hungrily, and when I refilled the tray, he chewed that as well, his hero's jaw working steadily. She ate little. Her eyes were lowered, a secret again.

At last the man pushed back his plate. "My name is Jason, heir by rights to the kingdom of Iolcos. My father was a virtuous king but soft-hearted, and when I was a child, my uncle seized his throne from him. He said he would return it to me when I was grown, if I gave him proof of my worth: a golden fleece, kept by a sorcerer in his land of Colchis."

I believed that he was a proper prince. He had the trick of speaking like one, rolling words like great boulders, lost in the details of his own legend. I tried to imagine him kneeling before Aeëtes among the milk fountains and coiling dragons. My brother would have thought him dull, and arrogant besides.

"Lady Hera and Lord Zeus blessed my purpose. They

guided me to my ship and helped me gather my comrades. When we arrived in Colchis, I offered King Aeëtes fair treasure in payment for the fleece, but he refused. He said I might have it only if I performed a task for him. The yoking of two bulls, and the plowing and sowing of a great field in a single day. I was willing, of course, and accepted at once. Yet — "

"Yet the task was impossible." Medea's voice slipped between his words easy as water. "A ploy designed to keep him from the fleece. My father had no intention of giving it up, for it is a thing of great story and power. No mortal, however valiant and brave" — at this she turned to Jason, touched her hand to his — "could accomplish those things unaided. The bulls were my father's own magic, crafted of knife-sharp bronze and breathing fire. Even if Jason yoked them, the seeds he had to sow were another trap. They would become warriors springing up to kill him."

Her gaze was fixed passionately on Jason's face. I spoke, more to bring her back than anything else.

"So you contrived a trick," I said.

Jason did not like that. He was a hero of the great golden age. Trickery was for cowards, men not bull-necked enough to show true courage. Medea spoke quickly over his frown.

"My love would have refused all help," she said. "But I insisted, for I could not bear to see him in danger."

It softened him. This was a more pleasing tale: the princess swooning at his feet, forswearing her cruel father to be with him. Coming to him at night, in secret, that face of hers the only light. Who could say no?

But her face was hidden now. Her voice was low, aimed at her own clasped hands.

"I have some small skill in those crafts you and my father know. I made a simple draught that would protect Jason's skin from the bulls' fire."

Now that I knew who she was, such meekness looked absurd on her, like a great eagle trying to hunch down to fit inside a sparrow's nest. Simple, she called that draught? I had never imagined a mortal might perform any magic, let alone such a powerful charm. But Jason was speaking again, rolling out more boulders, yoking the bulls, plowing and seeding the field.

When the warriors sprang up, he said, he knew the secret for subduing them, which Medea had told him. He must throw a rock among them, and in their rage, they would attack each other. So he did, yet Aeëtes still did not yield the fleece. He said Jason must first defeat the deathless dragon that guarded it. Medea mixed another draught and put the worm to sleep. He ran for his ship with the treasure and Medea as well — his honor could never permit him to abandon an innocent girl to such a wicked tyrant.

In his mind, he was already telling the tale to his court, to wide-eyed nobles and fainting maidens. He did not thank Medea for her aid; he scarcely looked at her. As if a demigoddess saving him at every turn was only his due.

She must have sensed my displeasure, for she spoke. "He is honorable indeed, for he married me upon the ship that very night, even with my father's forces in pursuit. When he has his throne again in Iolcos, I will be his queen."

Was it my imagination, or did Jason's light fade a little at that? There was a silence.

"What of the blood I washed from your hands?" I said.

"Yes," she said softly. "I come to it. My father was enraged. He set out after us, his witchcraft drawing the winds to his sail, and by morning he was very close. I knew my spells were no match for his. Our ship, however blessed, could not outrun him. One hope only I had: my younger brother, whom I had taken with us. He was my father's heir, and I had thought to exchange him as a hostage for our safety. But when I saw my father at his prow, shouting curses across the water, I knew it would not work. The killing rage was plain on his face. He would be satisfied with nothing but our ruin. He spoke spells in the air, he lifted his staff to bring them down upon our heads. I felt a great fear run through me. Not for myself, but for blameless Jason and his crew."

She looked at Jason, but his face was turned to the fire.

"At that moment — I cannot describe it. A madness came over me. I seized Jason and commanded him to kill my brother. Then I cut the body into pieces and threw them into the waves. Wild as my father was, I knew he must stop to give him proper burial. When I woke from my fit the seas were empty. I thought it had been a dream until I saw my hands covered in my brother's blood."

She held them out to me, as if in proof. They were clean. I had cleaned them.

Jason's skin had gone gray as raw lead.

"Husband," she said. He started, though she had not spoken loudly. "Your wine cup is dry. May I fill it for you?" She rose, moving with the goblet to the brimming bowl. Jason did not watch, and I would not have noticed if I were not witch myself: the pinch of powder that she dropped into the wine, the whispered word.

"Here, my love," she said.

Her tone was coaxing as a mother's. He took the wine and drank. When his head rolled back, and the cup would have fallen from his hands, she caught it. Carefully, she set it upon the table, and took her seat again.

"You understand," she said. "It is too difficult for him. He blames himself."

"There was no madness," I said.

"No." Her golden eyes pierced mine. "Yet some call lovers mad."

"If I had known I would not have done the rite."

She nodded. "You and most others. Perhaps that is why suppliants may not be questioned. How many of us would be granted pardon if our true hearts were known?"

She took off her black cloak and laid it over the chair beside her. Her dress beneath was lapis blue, bound with a thin silver belt.

"Do you feel no remorse?"

"I suppose I could weep and rub my eyes to please you, but I choose not to live so falsely. My father would have destroyed the whole ship if I had not acted. My brother was a soldier. He sacrificed himself to win the war."

"Except he did not sacrifice himself. You murdered him."

"I gave him a draught so he would not suffer. It is better than most men get."

"He was your blood."

Her eyes burned, bright as a comet in the night's sky. "Is one life worth more than another? I have never thought so."

"He did not have to die. You could have turned yourself in with the fleece. Gone back to your father."

The look that passed over her face. Like a comet indeed, when it veers to earth and turns the fields to ash.

"I would have been made to watch while my father tore Jason and his crew limb from limb, then been tormented myself. You will pardon me if I do not call that a choice."

She saw the look on my face.

"You do not believe me?"

"You have said many things of my brother that I do not recognize."

"Let me introduce you then. Do you know what my father's favorite sport is? Men come often to our isle, looking to prove themselves against a wicked sorcerer. My father likes to set the captains of those ships loose among his dragons and watch them run. The crew he enslaves, stealing away their minds so they have no more will than stones. To entertain his guests, I have seen my father light a brand and hold it to one of those men's arms. The slave will stand there burning until my father releases him. I have wondered if they are merely empty shells, or if they understand what is being done to them and scream inside. If my father catches me, I will find out, for that is what he will do to me."

It was not the voice she had used with Jason, that cloying sweetness. It was not her gleaming self-assurance either. Each word was dark as an axe-head, heavy and unrelenting, and my blood drained at every blow.

"Surely he would not hurt his own child."

She scoffed. "I am no child to him. I was his to dispose of, like his seed-warriors or his fire-breathing bulls. Like my mother, whom he dispatched as soon as she bore him an heir. Perhaps it might have been different if I'd had no witchcraft. But by the time I was ten I could tame the adders from their nests, I could kill lambs with a word and bring them back with another. He punished me for it. He said it made me unmarketable, but in truth, he did not want me taking his secrets to my husband."

I heard Pasiphaë as if she whispered in my ear: *Aeëtes has never liked a woman in his life.*

"His greatest wish was to trade me off to some sorcerer-god like himself who would pay with exotic poisons. None could be found except his brother, Perses, so he offered me to him. I say my prayers every night that that beast did not want me. He has some goddess of Sumeria he keeps in chains for a wife."

I remembered the stories Hermes had told me: Perses and his palace of corpses. Pasiphaë saying, *Do you know how I had to keep him happy?*

"It is strange," I said, the words weak even to my own ears. "Aeëtes always hated Perses."

"Not now. They are closest friends, and when Perses visits they talk of nothing but raising the dead and bringing down Olympus."

I felt numb, barren as a winter field. "Does Jason know all this?"

"Of course he does not, are you mad? Every time he looked at me, he would think of poisons and burning skin. A man wants a wife like new grass, fresh and green."

Had she not seen Jason flinch? Or did she not want to see? *He shrinks from you already.*

She stood, her dress bright as a cresting wave. "My father pursues us still. We must leave at once and drive on to Iolcos. They have an army not even he can stand against, for the goddess Hera fights with them. He will be forced to turn back. Then Jason will be king, and I queen at his side."

Her face was incandescent. She spoke each word as if it were a stone she built her future with. Yet for the first time she seemed to me a creature clinging to a precipice, desperate, its claws already slipping. She was young, younger than Glaucos when I had first met him.

I looked at Jason, drugged, his mouth hanging open. "You are sure of his regard?"

"You suggest he does not love me?" Her voice sharpened in an instant.

"He is still half a child, and full mortal besides. He cannot understand your history, nor your witchcraft."

"He need not understand them. We are married now, and I will give him heirs and he will forget all this like a fever dream. I will be his good wife, and we will prosper."

I touched my fingers to her arm. Her skin was cool, as if she had been walking a long time in the wind.

"Niece, I fear you do not see all clearly. Your welcome in Iolcos may not be what you imagine."

She drew her arm away, frowning. "What do you mean? Why would it not be? I am a princess, worthy of Jason."

"You are a foreigner." I could see it, suddenly, as plain as if it were painted before me. The fractious nobles waiting at home for Jason's return, each jockeying to match their daughter with the new-made hero and claim a piece of his glory. Medea would be the one thing they would agree upon. "They will resent you. Worse, they will suspect you, for you are the daughter of a sorcerer and a witch in your own right. You have lived only in Colchis, you cannot know how *pharmakeia* is feared among mortals. They will seek to undermine you at every turn. It will not matter that you helped Jason. They will push that aside, or else use it against you as proof of your unnaturalness."

She was staring at me, but I did not stop. My words were tumbling out, catching fire as they went. "You will find no safety there, no peace. Yet still you may be free from your father. I cannot undo his cruelties, but I can ensure that they follow you no further. He said once that witchcraft cannot be taught. He was wrong. He kept his knowledge from you, but I will give you all I know. When he comes, we will turn him away together."

She was silent a long moment. "What of Jason?"

"Let him be a hero. You are something else."

"And what is that?"

In my mind I saw us already, our heads bent together over the purple flowers of aconite, the black roots of moly. I would rescue her from her tainted past.

"A witch," I said. "With unbound power. Who need answer to none but herself."

"I see," she said. "Like you? A pathetic exile, who stinks of her loneliness?" She saw the shock on my face. "What, do you think because you surround yourself with cats and pigs, you are deceiving anyone? You do not know me for an afternoon, yet you are scrabbling to keep me. You claim you want to help me, but whom do you really help? 'Oh, niece, dearest niece! We will be the best of friends and do our magics side by side. I will keep you close, and so fill up my childless days.'" She curled her lip. "I will not sentence myself to such a living death."

Restless, I had thought. I was only restless in those days, and a little sad. But she had stripped me to my skin, and now I saw myself in her eyes: a bitter, abandoned crone, a spider, scheming to suck out her life.

Face stinging, I rose to meet her. "It is better than being married to Jason. You are blind not to see what a weak reed he is. He flinches from you already. And you are what, three days married? What will he do in a year? He is led by his love for himself — you were only expedient. In Iolcos your position will rest on his goodwill. How long do you think that will last, when his countrymen come crying that the murder of your brother brings a curse to their land?"

Her fists were clenched. "None will learn of my brother's death. I have sworn the crew to silence."

"Such a secret cannot be kept. If you were not a child you would know it. The moment those men are out of earshot they will start their gossip. In a day, the whole kingdom will know, and they will shake your trembling Jason till he falls. 'Great king, it was not your fault the boy died. It was that villainess, that foreign witch. She carved her own kin, what worse evils does she work even now? Cast her out, cleanse the land, and take a better in her place.'"

"Jason would never listen to such slander! I delivered him the fleece! He loves me!" She stood fixed in her outrage, bright and defiant. All my hammering had only made her harder. Just so must I have seemed to my grandmother when she said to me: *Those are two different things.*

"Medea," I said. "Listen to me. You are young, and Iolcos will make you old. There is no safety for you there."

"Every day makes me old," she said. "I do not have your years to waste. As for that safety, I do not want it. It is only more chains. Let them come at me if they dare. They will never take Jason from me. I have my powers, and I will use them."

Every time she said his name, a fierce eagle love flashed in her eyes. She had him in her grip and would clench him till he died.

"And if you try to keep me," she said, "I will fight you too."

She would, I thought. Though I was a god, and she a mortal. She would fight the whole world.

Jason stirred. The spell was fading.

"Niece," I said, "I will not keep you against your will. But if you ever — "

"No," she said. "I want nothing more from you."

She led Jason to the shore. They did not pause to rest or eat, they did not wait for dawn. They drew up the anchor and sailed into the darkness, their path lit only by the veiled moon and the unwavering gold of Medea's eyes. I kept among the trees, so she would not see me watching and scorn me for that too. But I need not have bothered. She did not look back.

Out on the beach, the sand was cool, and the starlight dappled my skin. The waves were busy washing away their footprints. I closed my eyes and let the breeze move over me, carrying its scents of brine and ocean-weed. Overhead I felt the constellations turning on their distant tracks. I waited there a long time, listening, sending my mind out into the waves. I heard nothing, no sound of oars, no snap of sail, no voices on the wind. But I knew when he came. I opened my eyes.

The curve-beaked hull was splitting the waves of my harbor. He stood on its prow, his golden face outlined against the dawning sky. A pleasure rose in me so old and sharp it felt like pain. My brother.

He lifted his hand and the ship stopped, hanging perfectly still in the waves.

"Circe," he cried over the water between us. His voice rang the air like struck bronze. "My daughter came here."

"Yes," I said. "She did."

The satisfaction shone on his face. When he was an infant, his head had seemed to me delicate as glass. I used to trace its bones with my finger while he slept.

"I knew she would. She is desperate. She sought to bind me, but she has bound herself. Her fratricide will hang upon her all her days."

"I grieve for your son's death," I said.

"She will pay for it," he said. "Send her out."

My woods had gone quiet behind me. All the animals were still, crouching to the ground. As a child, he had liked to lean his head upon my shoulder and watch the seagulls dip to catch their fish. His laugh had been bright as morning sun.

"I met Daedalus," I said.

He frowned. "Daedalus? He has been dead for years. Where is Medea? Give her to me."

"She is not here," I said.

If I had turned the sea to stone I do not think he could have been more shocked. His face bloomed with incredulity and rage.

"You let her go?"

"She did not want to stay."

"Did not *want* to? She is a criminal and a traitor! It was your duty to keep her for me!"

I had never seen him so angry before. I had never seen him angry at all. Even so, his face was beautiful, like the waves when they lift their storm-heads. I could still ask for his forgiveness, it was not too late. I could say she tricked me. I was his foolish sister, who trusted too easily and could not see into the cracks of the world. Then he would come ashore and we might — but my imagination would not finish the thought. Behind him at their oar benches sat his men. They stared straight ahead. They had not stirred, not even to brush off a fly or scratch an itch. Their faces were slack and empty, their arms covered in scars and crusted scabs. Old burns.

I had lost him long ago.

The air whipped around us. "Do you hear?" he shouted. "I should punish you."

"No," I said. "In Colchis you may work your will. But this is Aiaia."

A second moment's true surprise on his face. Then his mouth twisted. "You have done nothing. I will have her in the end."

"That may be true. But I do not think she will make it easy. She is like you, Aeëtes, as oak to oak. She must live with that, and so, it seems, must you."

He sneered, then turned and lifted his arm. His sailors moved their joints as one. The oars beat the water and carried him from me.

CHAPTER FOURTEEN

OUTSIDE THE WINTER RAINS had begun to fall. My lioness whelped, and her cubs tumbled across the hearth on their clumsy, new-made paws. I could not smile at it. The earth seemed to echo where I walked. Above me the sky stretched out its empty hands.

I waited for Hermes so I might ask him what became of Medea and Jason, but he always seemed to know when I wanted him, and stayed away. I tried to weave, but my mind felt needle-pricked. Now that Medea had named my loneliness, it hung from everything, clinging like spiderwebs, unavoidable. I ran along the beach, gasped up and down the forest paths, trying to shake it from me. I sifted and resifted my memories of Aeëtes, all those hours we had leaned against each other. That old sickening feeling returned: that every moment of my life I had been a fool.

I helped Prometheus, I reminded myself. But it sounded pathetic even to my ears. How long would I cling to that handful of minutes, trying to cover myself as if with some threadbare blanket? It did not matter what I had done then. Prometheus was on his crag, and I was here.

The days moved slowly, dropping like petals from a blown rose. I gripped the cedar loom and made myself breathe its scent. I tried to remember the feel of Daedalus' scars beneath my fingers, but the memories were built of air, and blew away. Someone will come, I thought. All the ships in the world, all the men. Someone must. I stared into the horizon until my eyes blurred, hoping for some fishermen, some cargo, even a shipwreck. There was nothing.

I pressed my face into my lion's fur. Surely there was some divine trick to make the hours go faster. To let them slip past unseen, to sleep for years, so that when I woke again the world would be new. I closed my eyes. Through the window I heard the bees singing in the garden. My lion's tail beat against the stones. An eternity later, when I opened my eyes, the shadows had not even moved.

She was standing over me, frowning. Dark-haired, dark-eyed, with round limbs and a head neat as a nightingale's breast. A familiar smell wafted from her skin. Rose oil and my grandfather's river.

"I am come to serve you," she said.

I had been drowsing in my chair. I stared up blearily, thinking she must be an apparition, some hallucination of my solitude. "What?"

She wrinkled her nose. Apparently all her humility had been used up in those words. "I am Alke," she said. "Is this not Aiaia? Are you not the daughter of Helios?"

"I am."

"I am sentenced to be your servant."

I felt as if I dreamed. Slowly, I got to my feet. "Sentenced? By whom? I have not heard of such a thing. Speak, what power sent you?"

Naiads show their feelings as water shows ripples. However she had told herself this would go, it was not like this. "The great gods sent me."

"Zeus?"

"No," she said. "My father."

"And who is he?"

She named some minor river-lord in the Peloponnese. I had heard of him, perhaps met him once, but he had never sat in my father's halls.

"Why send you to me?"

She looked at me as if I were the greatest idiot she had ever met. "You are a daughter of Helios."

How could I have forgotten what it was like among the lesser gods? The desperate clawing for any advantage. Even disgraced, I still had the blood of the sun in my veins, which made me a desirable mistress. Indeed, for such as her father, my disgrace would be encouragement, lowering me enough that he dared to reach up.

"Why were you punished?"

"I fell in love with a mortal," she said. "A noble shepherd. My father disapproved and now I must do a year's penance."

I considered her. Her back was straight, her eyes up. She showed no fear, not of me, not of my wolves and lions. And her father disapproved of her.

"Sit," I said. "Be welcome."

She sat, but her mouth was puckered as if she sucked an unripe olive. She looked around with distaste. When I offered her food, she turned her head aside like a sulky baby. When I tried to speak to her, she folded her arms and pursed her lips. They only opened to voice her complaints: about the smell of the dyes bubbling on the stove, the lion hairs on the rugs, even Daedalus' loom. And for all her protestations about serving, she did not offer to carry a single dish.

There is no need to be surprised, I told myself. She is a nymph, which means a dry well. "Go home, then," I said, "if you are so miserable. I release you from your sentence."

"You cannot. The great gods have commanded me. There is nothing you can do to release me. I am staying a year."

It should have upset her, but she was smirking. Preening as if in victory before a crowd. I watched. When she had spoken of the gods exiling her, she had showed no anger, and no grief either. She took their authority as natural, irresistible, like the movements of the spheres. But I was a nymph like her, and an exile too, a daughter of a greater father, yes, but with no husband and dirty fingers and oddly dressed hair. It put me in her reach, she reasoned. So I was the one she would fight.

You are being foolish. I am not your enemy, and pulling faces is no real power. They have convinced you — But even as the words formed in my mouth, I let them go. It would be like Persian to her. She would not understand it, not in a thousand years. And I was done giving lessons.

I leaned forward and spoke the language she understood. "Here is how it will go, Alke. I will not hear you. I will not smell your rose oil or find your hairs about my house. You will feed yourself, care for yourself, and if you cause me a moment's more trouble, I will turn you into a blindworm and drop you in the sea for the fish."

Her smirks were wiped away. She blanched and pressed her fingers to her mouth and fled. After that she kept to herself as I had ordered. But word had spread among the gods that Aiaia was a good place to send difficult daughters. A dryad arrived who had fled her intended husband. Two stone-faced oreads followed, exiled from their mountains. Now whenever I tried to cast a spell, all I could hear was rattling bracelets. As I worked at the loom, they flashed in and out of the corners of my vision. They whispered and rustled from every corner. There was always someone leaning moon-faced over a pool when I wanted to swim. As I passed, their snickering laughter washed against my heels. I would not live that way again. Not on Aiaia.

I went to the clearing and called Hermes. He came, smiling already. "So? How do you like your new handmaids?"

"I do not," I said. "Go to my father and see how they can be taken away."

I feared he might object to being sent on an errand, but it was too amusing for him to miss. When he came back he said, "What did you expect? Your father is delighted. He says it's only right that his high blood is served by lesser divinities. He will encourage more fathers to send their daughters."

"No," I said. "I will take no more. Tell my father."

"Prisoners don't usually dictate their own conditions."

My face stung, but I knew better than to show it. "Tell my father I will do something awful to them if they do not leave. I will turn them into rats."

"I can't imagine Zeus would like that. Weren't you already exiled for acts against your kin? You should beware further punishment."

"You could speak on my behalf. Try to persuade him."

His black eyes glittered. "I'm afraid I'm only a messenger."

"Please," I said. "I do not want them here, truly. I am not being funny."

"No," he said, "you are not. You are being very dull. Use

your imagination, they must be good for something. Take
them to your bed."

"That is absurd," I said. "They would run screaming."

"Nymphs always do," he said. "But I'll tell you a secret:
they are terrible at getting away."

At a feast on Olympus such a jest would have been followed by a roar of laughter. Hermes waited now, grinning
like a goat. But all I felt was a white, cold rage.

"I am finished with you," I said. "I have been finished a
long time. Let me not see you again."

If anything, his grin deepened. He vanished and did not
return. It was no obedience. He was finished with me too,
for I had committed the unpardonable sin of being dull. I
could imagine the stories he was telling of me, humorless,
prickly, and smelling of pigs. From time to time, I could
sense him just out of sight, finding my nymphs in the hills,
sending them back flushed and laughing, giddy from the
great Olympian who had shown them favor. He seemed
to think I would go mad with jealousy and loneliness, and
turn them into rats indeed. A hundred years he had been
coming to my island, and in all that time he had never
cared for more than his own entertainment.

The nymphs remained. When they finished their terms
of service, others arrived to take their place. Sometimes
there were four, sometimes six or seven. They trembled
when I passed, ducking and calling me mistress, but it
meant nothing. I had been put in my place. At a word and
a whim from my father all my vaunted power blew away.
Not even my father: any river-god had the right to fill my
island, and I could not stop him.

The nymphs wafted around me. Their smothered
laughter drifted down the halls. At least, I told myself, it
was not their brothers, who would have bragged and fought

and hunted down my wolves. But of course that was never a real danger. Sons were not punished.

I sat at my hearth watching the stars turn through the window. Cold, I felt. Cold as a garden in winter, gone deep to ground. I did my spells. I sang and worked at my loom and husbanded my animals, but it all felt shrunk to the size of ants. The island had never needed my hand. It prospered on no matter what I did. The sheep multiplied and wandered freely. They ambled over the grass, nudging aside the wolf pups with their blunt faces. My lioness stayed inside by the fire. White fur stained her mouth. Her grandchildren had their own grandchildren, and her haunches trembled when she walked. A hundred years at least she must have lived with me, pacing at my side, her life extended by the close pulse of my divinity. A decade that time had seemed to me. I assumed there would be many more, but one morning I woke to find her cold beside me on the bed. I stared at her unmoving sides, my brain stupid with disbelief. When I shook her a fly buzzed off. I pried open her stiff jaws and forced herbs down her throat, chanting one spell, then another. Still she lay there, all her golden strength turned dun. Perhaps Aeëtes could have brought her back, or Medea. I could not.

I built the pyre with my own hands. Cedar it was, and yew, and mountain ash that I chopped myself, its white pith spraying where the axe blade struck. I could not lift her, so I made a sledge out of the purple cloth I had used to wind around her neck. I dragged her through my hall, past the stones worn smooth by the pads of her great paws. I pulled her up to the pyre's top and lit the flames. There was no wind that day, and the flames fed slowly. It took the whole afternoon for her fur to blacken, her long yellow body to burn down to ash. For the first time the cold underworld of mortals seemed a mercy. At least some part of them lived on. She was utterly lost.

I watched until the last flame was gone, then went back inside. A pain was gnawing in my chest. I pressed my hands to it, the hollows and hard bones. I sat before my loom and felt at last like the creature Medea had named me: old and abandoned and alone, spiritless and gray as the rocks themselves.

I sang often in those days, for it was the best company I had. That morning it was an old hymn in praise of farming. I liked the shape of it on my lips, the soothing lists of plants and crops, of crofts and cotes, herds and flocks, and the stars that wheeled above them. I let the words float in the air as I stirred the boiling pot of dye. I had seen a fox and wanted to match the color of her coat. The liquid foamed up, saffron mixed with madder. My nymphs had fled the stink, but I liked it: the sharp stinging in my throat, the watering of my eyes.

It was the song that caught their attention, my voice drifting down the trails to the beach. They followed it through the trees and sighted the smoke from my chimney.

A man's voice called out. "Is anyone there?"

I remember my shock. *Visitors.* I turned so quickly the dye splashed, and a burning drop fell on my hand. I smeared it away as I hurried to the door.

There were twenty of them, wind-rough and shiny from sun. Their hands were thickly calloused, their arms puckered with old scars. After so long amid only the smooth sameness of nymphs, each imperfection was a pleasure: the lines around their eyes, the scabs on their legs, the fingers broken off at the knuckle. I drank in their threadbare clothes, their worn faces. These were not heroes, or the crew of a king. They must scrabble for their livelihoods as Glaucos once did: hauling nets, carrying odd cargo, hunting down whatever dinner they could find. I felt a warmth run through me. My fingers itched as if for needle and thread. Here was something torn that I could mend.

A man stepped forward. He was tall and gray, his body lean. Many of the men behind him still had their hands on their sword hilts. It was wise. Islands were dangerous places. You met monsters as often as friends.

"Lady, we are hungry and lost," he said. "And hope such a goddess as yourself will help us in our need."

I smiled. It felt strange on my face after so long. "You are welcome here. You are very welcome. Come in."

I shooed the wolves and lions outside. Not all men were as unshakable as Daedalus, and these sailors looked as though they had known shocks enough already. I led them to my tables, then hurried to the kitchen to bring out heaping platters of stewed figs and roasted fish, brined cheese and bread. The men had eyed my pigs on the way in, elbowing each other and whispering loudly their hope that I might kill one. But when the fish and fruits were before them, they were so eager they did not complain, nor even pause to wash their hands or take off their swords. They bolted and shoveled, the grease and wine darkening their beards. I carried more fish, more cheese. Each time I passed they ducked their heads at me. *Lady. Mistress. Our thanks.*

I could not stop smiling. The fragility of mortals bred kindness and good grace. They knew how to value friendship and an open hand. If only more of them would come, I thought. I would feed a ship a day, and gladly. Two ships. Three. Perhaps I would start to feel like myself again.

The nymphs peeked in from the kitchen, eyes wide. I hurried over, sent them off before they were noticed. These men were mine, my guests to welcome as I pleased, and I enjoyed seeing to all their comforts myself. I set out fresh water in bowls, so they might wash their fingers. A knife fell to the floor, and I picked it up. When the captain's cup was dry, I filled it from the brimming bowl. He lifted it to me. "Thank you, sweet."

Sweet. The word set me back a moment. They had called me goddess before, and so I believed they thought me. But they showed no awe or religious deference, I realized. The title had been only a flattering courtesy for a woman alone. I remembered what Hermes had told me long ago. *You sound like a mortal. They won't fear you as they fear the rest of us.*

And so they did not. In fact, they thought I was the same as they were. I stood there, charmed by the idea. What would my mortal self be? An enterprising herbwoman, an independent widow? No, not a widow, for I did not want some grim history. Perhaps I was a priestess. But not to a god.

"Daedalus once visited this place," I told the man. "I keep the shrine of it."

He nodded. I was disappointed at how unimpressed he was. As if there were shrines to dead heroes all over. Well, perhaps there were. How would I know?

The men's appetites were slowing, and their heads lifted from their plates. I saw them begin to look around, at the silver on the bowls, the golden goblets, the tapestries. My nymphs took such riches as their due, but the men's gazes were bright with wonder, searching out each new marvel. I thought of how I had trunks filled with down pillows, enough to make them beds on the floor. When I handed them over, I would say, *These were meant for gods*, and their eyes would go wide.

"Mistress?" It was the leader again. "When will your husband be home? We would toast such fine hospitality."

I laughed. "Oh, I do not have a husband."

He smiled back. "Of course," he said. "You are too young to be married. Then it is your father we must thank."

It was full dark outside, and the room glowed warm and bright. "My father lives far away," I said. I waited for them to ask who he was. A lamplighter, that would be a good jest. I smiled to myself.

"Then perhaps there is some other host we should thank? An uncle, a brother?"

"If you would thank your host," I said, "thank me. This house is mine alone."

At the word, the air changed in the room.

I plucked up the wine bowl. "It is empty," I said. "Let me bring you more." I could hear my own breath as I turned. I could feel their twenty bodies filling up the space behind me.

In the kitchen, I put a hand to one of my draughts. You are being silly, I thought. They were surprised to find a woman by herself, that is all. But my fingers were already moving. I took the lid off a jar, mixed its contents into the wine, then added honey and whey to cover the taste. I brought the bowl out. Twenty gazes followed me.

"Here," I said. "I have kept back the best for last. You must have some, all of you. It comes from the finest vine-yard on Crete."

They smiled, pleased at such solicitous luxury. I watched every man fill his cup. I watched them drink. By then each of them must have had a cask in his belly.

The platters were empty, licked clean. The men leaned together, speaking low.

My voice felt too loud. "Come, I have fed you well. Will you tell me your names?"

They looked up. Their eyes darted like ferrets to their leader. He rose, the bench scraping on the stone. "Tell us yours first."

There was something in his voice. I almost said it then, the spell-word that would send them to sleep. But even after all the years that had passed, there was a piece of me that still only spoke what I was bid.

"Circe," I answered.

The name meant nothing to them. It dropped onto the floor like a stone. The benches scraped again. All the men were rising now, their eyes fixed on me. And still I said nothing. Still I told myself I was wrong. I must be wrong. I had fed them. They had thanked me. They were my guests.

The captain stepped towards me. He was taller than I was, every sinew taut from labor. I thought — what? That I was being foolish. That something else would happen. That I had drunk too much of my own wine, and this was the fear it conjured. That my father would come. My father! I did not want to be a fool, to make a fuss for nothing. I could hear Hermes telling the tale after. *She always was a hysteric.*

The captain was close now. I could feel the heat of his skin. His face was rutted, cracked like old streambeds. I kept waiting for him to speak some ordinary thing, to offer thanks, ask a question. Somewhere in her palace, my sister was laughing. *You have been tame your whole life, and now you will be sorry. Yes Father, yes Father — see what it gets you.*

My tongue touched my lips. "Is there —" The man

threw me back against the wall. My head hit the uneven stone and the room sparked. I opened my mouth to cry out the spell, but he jammed his arm against my windpipe and the sound was choked off. I could not speak. I could not breathe. I fought him, but he was stronger than I had thought he would be, or maybe I was weaker. The sudden weight of him shocked me, the greasy push of his skin on mine. My mind was still scrambled, disbelieving. With his right hand, he tore my clothes, a practiced gesture. With his left, he kept his weight against my throat. I had said there was no one on the island, but he had learned not to take chances. Or perhaps he just didn't like screaming.

I don't know what his men did. Watched maybe. If my lion had been there, she would have clawed down the door, but she was ash upon the winds. Outside I heard the pigs squealing. I remember what I thought, bare against the grinding stone: I am only a nymph after all, for nothing is more common among us than this.

A mortal would have fainted, but I was awake for every moment. At last, I felt the man tremble, and his arm loosened. My throat was crushed inward like a rotted log. I could not seem to move. A drop of sweat fell from his hair onto my bare chest, and began to slide. I became aware of his men speaking behind him. Is she dead? one of them was saying. She better not be dead, it's my turn. A face loomed over the captain's shoulder. Her eyes are open.

The captain stepped back and spat at the floor. The jellied glob quivered on the stone. The drop of sweat slid onwards, carving its slimy furrow. A sow shrieked in the yard. Convulsively, I swallowed. My throat clicked. I felt a space open in me. The sleep-spell I had been going to say was gone, dried up, I could not have cast it even if I wanted to. But I did not want to. My eyes lifted to his rutted face.

Those herbs had another use, and I knew what it was. I drew breath, and spoke my word.

His eyes were muddy and uncomprehending. "What — "

He did not finish. His rib cage cracked and began to bulge. I heard the sound of flesh rupturing wetly, the pops of breaking bone. His nose ballooned from his face, and his legs shriveled like a fly sucked by a spider. He fell to all fours. He screamed, and his men screamed with him. It went on for a long time.

As it turned out, I did kill pigs that night after all.

CHAPTER FIFTEEN

I PICKED UP THE overturned benches, wiped the soaked floors. I stacked the platters and carried them to the kitchen. I had scrubbed myself in the waves with sand till the blood came through. I'd found the glob of spit on the flagstone and scrubbed that too. It did nothing. With every movement I could feel the prints of his fingers.

The wolves and lions had crept back, shadows in the dark. They lay down, pressing their faces to the floor. At last, when there was nothing else to clean, I sat before the hearth ash. I was not shaking anymore. I did not move at all. My flesh seemed to have congealed around me. My skin stretched over it like a dead thing, rubbery and vile.

It was shading to dawn, when the silver horses of the moon go to their stables. My aunt Selene's chariot had been full all night, her light strong in the sky. By the brightness of her face I had dragged those monstrous carcasses down to the boat, struck flint, and watched the flames leap up. She would have told Helios by now. My father would appear any moment, the patriarch outraged at the insult to his child. My ceiling would creak as his shoulders pressed against it. Poor child, poor exiled daughter. I should never have let Zeus send you here.

The room turned gray, then yellow. A sea breeze stirred, but it was not enough to push away the stink of burnt flesh. My father had never spoken that way in his life, I knew it. But surely, I thought, he would still have to come, if only to reproach me. I was no Zeus, I would not be allowed to strike down twenty men in a moment. I spoke out to the pale edge of my father's rising chariot. Did you hear what I did?

The shadows moved across the floor. The light crept over my feet, touched the hem of my dress. Each moment stretched into the next. No one came.

Maybe the true surprise, I thought, was that it had not happened sooner. My uncles' eyes used to crawl over me as I poured their wine. Their hands found their way to my flesh. A pinch, a stroke, a hand slipping under the sleeve of my dress. They all had wives, it was not marriage they thought of. One of them would have come for me in the end and paid my father well. Honor on all sides.

The light had reached the loom, and its cedar scent was rising in the air. The memory of Daedalus' white-scarred hands, and the pleasure I had taken in them, was like a hot wire pushed through my brain. I dug my nails into my wrist. There are oracles scattered across our lands. Shrines where priestesses breathe sacred fumes and speak the truths they find in them. *Know yourself* is carved above their doors. But I had been a stranger to myself, turned to stone for no reason I could name.

Daedalus had told me a story once about the lords of Crete who used to hire him to enlarge their houses. He would arrive with his tools, begin taking down the walls, pulling up the floors. But whenever he found some problem underneath that must first be fixed, they frowned. *That was not in the agreement!*

Of course not, he said, it has been hidden in the foundation, but look, there it is, plain as day. See the cracked beam? See the beetles eating the floor? See how the stone is sinking into the swamp?

That only made the lords angrier. *It was fine until you dug it up! We will not pay! Close it up, plaster over. It has stood this long, it will stand longer.*

So he would seal that fault up, and the next season the house would fall down. Then they would come to him, demanding back their money.

"I told them," he said to me. "I told them and told them. When there is rot in the walls, there is only one remedy."

The purple bruise at my throat was turning green at its edges. I pressed it, felt the splintered ache.

Tear down, I thought. Tear down and build again.

They came, I cannot say why. Some revolution of the Fates, some change in trade and shipping routes. Some scent upon the air, wafting: *here are nymphs, and they live alone.* The boats flew to my harbor as if yanked on a string. The men splashed to shore and looked around, pleased. Fresh water, game, fish, fruits. *And I thought I saw hearth smoke above the trees. Is that someone singing?*

I could have cast an illusion over the island to keep them away, I had the power to do it. Drape my gentle shores in an image of staving rocks and whirlpools, of jagged, unscaleable cliffs. They would sail on, and I would never need to see them, nor anyone, again.

No, I thought. It is too late for that. I have been found. Let them see what I am. Let them learn the world is not as they think.

They climbed up the trails. They crossed the stones of my garden path. They all had the same desperate story: they were lost, they were weary, they were out of food. They would be so grateful for my help.

A few of these, so few I can count them on my fingers, I let go. They did not see me as their dinner. They were pious men, honestly lost, and I would feed them, and if there was a handsome one among them I might take him to my bed. It was not desire, not even its barest scrapings. It was a sort of rage, a knife I used upon myself. I did it to prove my skin was still my own. And did I like the answer I found?

"Leave," I told them.

They knelt to me on my yellow sands. "Goddess," they said, "at least give us your name so we may send you our thankful prayers."

I did not want their prayers, nor my name in their mouths. I wanted them gone. I wanted to scrub myself in the sea until the blood showed through.

I wanted the next crew to come, so I might see again their tearing flesh.

There was always a leader. He was not the largest, and he need not be the captain, but he was the one they looked to for instruction in their cruelty. He had a cold eye and a coiling tension. Like a snake, the poets might say, but I knew snakes better by then. Give me the honest asp, who strikes me if I trouble him and not before.

I did not send my animals away anymore when men came. I let them loll where they liked, around the garden, under my tables. It pleased me to see the men walk among them, trembling at their teeth and unnatural tameness. I did not pretend to be a mortal. I showed my lambent, yellow eyes at every turn. None of it made a difference. I was alone and a woman, that was all that mattered.

I set my feasts before them, the meats and cheese, the fruits and fish. I set as well my largest bronze mixing bowl, filled to the brim with wine. They gulped and chewed, seized dripping cuts of mutton and dangled them down their throats. They poured and poured again, soaking their lips, slopping the table with red. Bits of barley and herbs stuck to their lips. The bowl is empty, they would say to me. Fill it. Add more honey this time, the vintage has a bitter tang.

Of course, I said.

The edge came off their hunger. They began to look around. I saw them notice the marble floors, the platters, the fine weave of my clothes. They smirked. If this was what I dared to show them, imagine what might be hiding in the back.

"Mistress?" the leader would say. "Do not tell me that such a beauty as yourself dwells all alone?"

"Oh, yes," I would answer. "Quite alone."

He would smile. He could not help it. There was never any fear in him. Why should there be? He had already noted for himself that there was no man's cloak hanging by the door, no hunter's bow, no shepherd's staff. No sign of brothers or fathers or sons, no vengeance that would follow after. If I were valuable to anyone, I would not be allowed to live alone.

"I'm sorry to hear it," he said.

The bench would scrape, and he would stand. The men watched with bright eyes. They wanted the freeze, the flinch, the begging that would come.

It was my favorite moment, seeing them frown and try to understand why I wasn't afraid. In their bodies I could feel my herbs like strings waiting to be plucked. I savored their confusion, their dawning fear. Then I plucked them.

Their backs bent, forcing them onto hands and knees, faces bloating like drowned corpses. They thrashed and the benches turned over, wine splattered the floor. Their screams broke into squeals. I am certain it hurt.

I kept the leader for last, so he could watch. He shrank, pressed against the wall. Please. Spare me, spare me, spare me.

No, I would say. Oh, no.

When it was over it remained only to drive them out to the pen. I raised my staff of ash wood and they ran. The gate closed after them and they pressed back against the posts, their piggy eyes still wet with the last of their human tears.

My nymphs said not a word, though I suspected they watched sometimes through the crack of the door.

"Mistress Circe, another ship. Shall we go back to our room?"

"Please. And pull out the wine for me before you go."

From one task to another I went, weaving, working, slopping my pigs, crossing and recrossing the isle. I moved straight-backed, as if a great brimming bowl rested in my hands. The dark liquid rippled as I walked, always at the point of overflow, yet never flowing. Only if I stopped, if I lay down, did I feel it begin to bleed.

Brides, nymphs were called, but that is not really how the world saw us. We were an endless feast laid out upon a table, beautiful and renewing. And so very bad at getting away.

The rails of my sty cracked with age and use. From time to time the wood buckled and a pig escaped. Most often, he would throw himself from the cliffs. The seabirds were grateful; they seemed to come from half world away to feast on the plump bones. I would stand watching as they stripped the fat and sinew. The small pink scrap of tail-skin dangled from one of their beaks like a worm. If it were a man, I wondered if I would pity him. But it was not a man.

When I passed back by the pen, his friends would stare at me with pleading faces. They moaned and squealed, and pressed their snouts to the earth. *We are sorry, we are sorry.*

Sorry you were caught, I said. Sorry that you thought I was weak, but you were wrong.

On my bed, the lions rested their chins on my stomach. I pushed them off. I rose and walked again.

He asked me once, why pigs. We were seated before my hearth, in our usual chairs. He liked the one draped in cowhide, with silver inlaid in its carvings. Sometimes he would rub the scrolling absently beneath his thumb.

"Why not?" I said.

He gave me a bare smile. "I mean it, I would like to know."

I knew he meant it. He was not a pious man, but the seeking out of things hidden, this was his highest worship.

There were answers in me. I felt them, buried deep as last year's bulbs, growing fat. Their roots tangled with those moments I had spent against the wall, when my lions were gone, and my spells shut up inside me, and my pigs screamed in the yard.

After I changed a crew, I would watch them scrabbling and crying in the sty, falling over each other, stupid with their horror. They hated it all, their newly voluptuous flesh, their delicate split trotters, their swollen bellies dragging in the earth's muck. It was a humiliation, a debasement. They were sick with longing for their hands, those appendages men use to mitigate the world.

Come, I would say to them, it's not that bad. You should appreciate a pig's advantages. Mud-slick and swift, they are hard to catch. Low to the ground, they cannot easily be knocked over. They are not like dogs, they do not need your love. They can thrive anywhere, on anything, scraps and trash. They look witless and dull, which lulls their enemies, but they are clever. They will remember your face.

They never listened. The truth is, men make terrible pigs.

In my chair by the hearth, I lifted my cup. "Sometimes," I told him, "you must be content with ignorance."

He did not like that answer, yet that was the perversity of him: in a way he liked it best of all. I had seen how he could shuck truths from men like oyster shells, how he could pry into a breast with a glance and a well-timed word. So little of the world did not yield to his sounding. In the end, I think the fact that I did not was his favorite thing about me.

But I am ahead of myself now.

A ship, the nymphs said. Very patched, with eyes upon the hull.

That caught my attention. Common pirates did not have the gold to waste on paint. But I did not go look. The anticipation was part of the pleasure. The moment when the knock came, and I would rise from my herbs, swing wide the door. There were no pious men anymore, there had not been for a long time. The spell was polished in my mouth as a river stone.

I added a handful of roots to the draught I was making. There was moly in it, and the liquid gleamed.

The afternoon passed, and the sailors did not appear. My nymphs reported they were camped on the beach with fires burning. Another day went by, and at last on the third day came the knock.

That painted ship of theirs was the finest thing about them. Their faces had lines like grandfathers. Their eyes were bloodshot and dead. They flinched from my animals.

"Let me guess," I said. "You are lost? You are hungry and tired and sad?"

They ate well. They drank more. Their bodies were lumpish here and there with fat, though the muscles beneath were hard as trees. Their scars were long, ridged and slashing. They had had a good season, then met someone who did not like their thieving. They were plunderers, of that I had no doubt. Their eyes never stopped counting up my treasures, and they grinned at the tally they came to.

I did not wait anymore for them to stand and come at me. I raised my staff, I spoke the word. They went crying to their pen like all the rest.

The nymphs were helping me set right the toppled benches and scrub away the wine stains when one of them glanced at the window. "Mistress, another on the path."

I had thought the crew too small to man a full ship. Some of them must have waited on the beach, and now one had been sent to scout after his fellows. The nymphs set out new wine and slipped away.

I opened the door at the man's knock. The late sun fell on him, picking out the red in his neat beard, the faint silver in his hair. He wore a bronze sword at his waist. He was not so tall as some, but strong, I saw, his joints well seasoned.

"Lady," he said, "my crew has taken shelter with you. I hope I may as well?"

I put all my father's brightness into my smile. "You are as welcome as your friends."

I watched him while I filled the cups. Another thief, I thought. But his eyes only grazed my rich trappings. They lingered instead on a stool, still upended on the floor. He bent down and set it upright.

"Thank you," I said. "My cats. They are always tumbling something."

"Of course," he said.

I brought him food and wine, and led him to my hearth. He took the goblet and sat in the silver chair I indicated. I saw him wince a little as he bent, as if at the pull of recent wounds. A jagged scar ran up his muscled calf from heel to thigh, but it was old and faded. He gestured with his cup.

"I have never seen a loom like that," he said. "Is it an Eastern design?"

A thousand of his kind had passed through this room. They had catalogued every inch of gold and silver, but not one had ever noticed the loom.

I hesitated for the briefest moment.

"Egyptian."

"Ah. They make the best things, don't they? Clever to use a second beam instead of loom weights. So much more efficient to draw the weft down. I would love to have a sketch." His voice was resonant, warm, with a pull to it that reminded me of ocean tides. "My wife would be thrilled. Those weights used to drive her mad. She kept saying someone ought to invent something better. Alas, I have not found time to apply myself to it. One of my many husbandly failings."

My wife. The words jarred me. If any of the men in all those crews had had a wife, they never mentioned her. He smiled at me, his dark eyes on mine. His goblet was lifted loosely in his hand, as if any moment he would drink.

"Though the truth is, her favorite thing about weaving is that while she works, everyone around her thinks she can't hear what they're saying. She gathers all the best news that way. She can tell you who's getting married, who's pregnant, and who's about to start a feud."

"Your wife sounds like a clever woman."

"She is. I cannot account for the fact that she married

me, but since it is to my benefit, I try not to bring it to her attention."

It surprised me to a huff of laughter. What man spoke so? None that I had ever met. Yet at the same time there was something in him that felt nearly familiar.

"Where is your wife now? On your ship?"

"At home, thank the gods. I would not make her sail with such a ragged bunch. She runs the house better than any regent."

My attention was sharp on him now. Common sailors did not talk of regents, nor look so at home next to silver inlay. He was leaning on the carved arm of the chair as if it were his bed.

"You call your crew ragged?" I said. "They seem no different from other men to me."

"You are kind to say so, but half the time I'm afraid they behave like beasts." He sighed. "It's my fault. As their captain, I should keep them in better line. But we have been at war, and you know how that can tarnish even the best men. And these, though I love them well, will never be called best."

He spoke confidingly, as if I understood. But all I knew of war came from my father's stories of the Titans. I sipped my wine.

"War has always seemed to me a foolish choice for men. Whatever they win from it, they will have only a handful of years to enjoy before they die. More likely they will perish trying."

"Well, there is the matter of glory. But I wish you could've spoken to our general. You might have saved us all a lot of trouble."

"What was the fight over?"

"Let me see if I can remember the list." He ticked his

fingers. "Vengeance. Lust. Hubris. Greed. Power. What have I forgotten? Ah yes, vanity, and pique."

"Sounds like a usual day among the gods," I said.

He laughed and held up his hand. "It is your divine privilege to say so, my lady. I will only give thanks that many of those gods fought on our side."

Divine privilege. He knew I was a goddess then. But he showed no awe. I might be his neighbor, whose fence he leaned over to discuss the fig harvest.

"Gods fought among mortals? Who?"

"Hera, Poseidon, Aphrodite. Athena, of course."

I frowned. I had heard nothing of this. But then, I had no way to hear anymore. Hermes was long gone, my nymphs did not care for worldly news, and the men who sat at my tables thought only of their appetites. My days had narrowed to the ambit of my eyes and my fingers' ends.

"Fear not," he said, "I will not tax your ear with the whole long tale, but that is why my men are so scraggled. We were ten years fighting on Troy's shores, and now they are desperate to get back to home and hearth."

"Ten years? Troy must be a fortress."

"Oh, she was stout enough, but it was our weakness that drew the war out, not her strength."

This too surprised me. Not that it was true, but that he would admit it. It was disarming, that wry deprecation.

"It is a long time to be away from home."

"And now it is longer still. We sailed from Troy two years ago. Our journey back has been somewhat more difficult than I would have wished."

"So there is no need to worry about the loom," I said. "By now your wife will have given up on you and invented a better one herself."

His expression remained pleasant, but I saw something

shift in it. "Most likely you are right. She will have doubled our lands too, I would not be surprised."

"And where are these lands of yours?"

"Near Argos. Cows and barley, you know."

"My father keeps cows himself," I said. "He favors a pure-white hide."

"They are hard to breed true. He must husband them well."

"Oh, he does," I said. "He cares for nothing else."

I was watching him. His hands were wide and calloused. He gestured with his cup now here, now there, sloshing his wine a little, but never spilling it. And never once touching it to his lips.

"I am sorry," I said, "that my vintage is not to your liking."

He looked down as if surprised to see the cup still in his hand. "My apologies. I've been so much enjoying the hospitality, I forgot." He rapped his knuckles on his temple. "My men say I would forget my head if it weren't on my neck. Where did you say they've gone again?"

I wanted to laugh. I felt giddy, but I kept my voice as even as his. "They're in the back garden. There's an excellent bit of shade to rest in."

"I confess I'm in awe," he said, "they're never so quiet for me. You must have had quite an effect on them."

I heard a humming, like before a spell is cast. His gaze was a honed blade. All this had been prologue. As if we were in a play, we stood.

"You have not drunk," I said. "That is clever. But I am still a witch, and you are in my house."

"I hope we may settle this with reason." He had put the goblet down. He did not draw his sword, but his hand rested on the hilt.

"Weapons do not frighten me, nor the sight of my own blood."

"You are braver than most gods then. I once saw Aphrodite leave her son to die on the field over a scratch."

"Witches are not so delicate," I said.

His sword hilt was hacked from ten years of battles, his scarred body braced and ready. His legs were short but stiff with muscles. My skin prickled. He was handsome, I realized.

"Tell me," I said, "what is in that bag you keep so close at your waist?"

"An herb I found."

"Black roots," I said. "White flowers."

"Just so."

"Mortals cannot pick moly."

"No," he said simply. "They cannot."

"Who was it? No, never mind, I know." I thought of all the times Hermes had watched me harvest, pressed me about my spells. "If you had the moly, why did you not drink? He must have told you that no spell I cast could touch you."

"He did tell me," he said. "But I have a quirk of prudence in me that's hard to break. The Trickster Lord, for all I am grateful to him, is not known for his reliability. Helping you turn me into a swine would be just his sort of jest."

"Are you always so suspicious?"

"What can I say?" He held out his palms. "The world is an ugly place. We must live in it."

"I think you are Odysseus," I said. "Born from that same Trickster's blood."

He did not start at the uncanny knowledge. He was a man used to gods. "And you are the goddess Circe, daughter of the sun."

My name in his mouth. It sparked a feeling in me, sharp and eager. He was like ocean tides indeed, I thought. You could look up, and the shore would be gone.

"Most men do not know me for what I am."

"Most men, in my experience, are fools," he said. "I confess you nearly made me give the game away. Your father, the cowherd?"

He was smiling, inviting me to laugh, as if we were two mischievous children.

"Are you a king? A lord?"

"A prince."

"Then, Prince Odysseus, we are at an impasse. For you have the moly, and I have your men. I cannot harm you, but if you strike at me, they will never be themselves again."

"I feared as much," he said. "And, of course, your father Helios is zealous in his vengeances. I imagine I would not like to see his anger."

Helios would never defend me, but I would not tell Odysseus that. "You should understand your men would have robbed me blind."

"I am sorry for that. They are fools, and young, and I have been too lenient with them."

It was not the first time he had made that apology. I let my eyes rest on him, take him in. He reminded me a little of Daedalus, his evenness and wit. But beneath his ease I could feel a roil that Daedalus never had. I wanted to see it revealed.

"Perhaps we might find a different way."

His hand was still on his hilt, but he spoke as if we were only deciding dinner. "What do you propose?"

"Do you know," I said, "Hermes told me a prophecy about you once."

"Oh? And what was it?"

"That you were fated to come to my halls."

"And?"

"That was all."

He lifted an eyebrow. "I'm afraid that is the dullest prophecy I've ever heard."

I laughed. I felt poised as a hawk on a crag. My talons still held the rock, but my mind was in the air.

"I propose a truce," I said. "A test of sorts."

"What sort of test?" He leaned forward a little. It was a gesture I would come to know. Even he could not hide everything. Any challenge, he would run to meet it. His skin smelled of labor and the sea. He knew ten years of stories. I felt keen and hungry as a bear in spring.

"I have heard," I said, "that many find their trust in love."

It surprised him, and oh, I liked the flash of that, before he covered it over.

"My lady, only a fool would say no to such an honor. But in truth, I think also only a fool would say yes. I am a mortal. The moment I set down the moly to join you in your bed, you may cast your spell." He paused. "Unless, of course, you were to swear an oath you will not hurt me, upon the river of the dead."

An oath by the River Styx would hold even Zeus himself. "You are careful," I said.

"It seems we share that."

No, I thought. I was not careful. I was reckless, headlong. He was another knife, I could feel it. A different sort, but a knife still. I did not care. I thought: give me the blade. Some things are worth spilling blood for.

"I will swear that oath," I said.

CHAPTER SIXTEEN

LATER, YEARS LATER, I would hear a song made of our meeting. The boy who sang it was unskilled, missing notes more often than he hit, yet the sweet music of the verses shone through his mangling. I was not surprised by the portrait of myself: the proud witch undone before the hero's sword, kneeling and begging for mercy. Humbling women seems to me a chief pastime of poets. As if there can be no story unless we crawl and weep.

We lay together in my wide, gold bed. I had wanted to see him loosened with pleasure, passionate, laid bare. He was never laid bare, but the rest I saw. We did find some trust between us.

"I am not really from Argos," he said. The firelight flickered over us, casting long shadows across the sheets. "My island is Ithaca. It's too stony for cows. We run to goats and olive groves."

"And the war? A fiction also?"

"The war was real."

There was no rest in him. He looked as though he could have parried a spear-thrust out of the shadows. Yet the weariness had begun to show through, like rocks when the tide recedes. By the law of guests I should not question him before he had fed and refreshed himself, but we were past such observances.

"You said your journey was difficult."

"I sailed from Troy with twelve ships." His face in the yellow light was like an old shield, battered and lined. "We are all that is left."

In spite of myself I was shocked. Eleven ships was more than five hundred men lost. "How did such disaster strike you?"

He recited the story as if he were giving a recipe for meat. The storms that had blown them half across the world. The lands filled with cannibals and vengeful savages, with sybarites who drugged their wills. They had been ambushed by the cyclops Polyphemus, a savage one-eyed giant who was a son of Poseidon. He had eaten half a dozen men and sucked their bones. Odysseus had had to blind him to escape, and now Poseidon hunted them across the waves in vengeance.

No wonder he limped, no wonder he was gray. *This is a man who has faced monsters.*

"And now Athena, who was ever my guide, has turned her back."

I was not surprised to hear her name. The clever daughter of Zeus honored wiles and invention above all. He was just the sort of man she would cherish.

"What offended her?"

I was not sure he would answer, but he drew in a long breath. "War breeds many sins, and I was not last in committing them. When I asked her pardon, she always gave it. Then the sack of the city came. Temples were razed, blood spilled on altars."

It was the greatest sacrilege, gore upon the holy objects of the gods.

"I was a part of such things with the rest, but when others stayed to offer her prayers, I did not stay with them. I was...impatient."

"Ten years you had fought," I said. "It is understandable."

"You are kind, but I think we both know it is not. As soon as I was on board, the seas around me lifted wrathful heads. The sky darkened to iron. I tried to turn the fleet around, but it was too late. Her storm spun us far off from Troy." He rubbed his knuckles as if they ached. "Now when I speak to her, she does not answer."

Disaster upon disaster. Yet he had walked into a witch's house, even weary as he was, and raw with grief. He had sat at my hearth showing no hint of anything but charm and smiles. What resolve that must have taken, what vigilant will. But no man is infinite. Exhaustion stained his face. His voice was hoarse. A knife I had named him, but I saw that he was sliced down to the bone. I felt an answering ache in my chest. When I had taken him to my bed, it had been a kind of dare, but the feeling that flickered in me now was much older. There he was, his flesh open before me. *This is something torn that I can mend.*

I held the thought in my hand. When that first crew had come, I had been a desperate thing, ready to fawn on anyone who smiled at me. Now I was a fell witch, proving my power with sty after sty. It reminded me suddenly of those old tests Hermes used to set me. Would I be skimmed milk or a harpy? A foolish gull or a villainous monster?

Those could not still be the only choices.

I reached for his hands and drew him up. "Odysseus, son of Laertes, you have been hard-pressed. You are dry as leaves in winter. But there is harbor here."

The relief in his eyes ran warm over my skin. I led him

to my hall and commanded my nymphs to see to his comforts: to fill a silver bath for him and wash his sweated limbs, bring him fresh clothes. After, he stood shining and clean before the tables we had heaped with food. But he did not move to take his seat. "Forgive me," he said, his eyes on mine. "I cannot eat."

I knew what he wanted. He did not storm or beg, only waited for my decision.

The air felt limned in gold around me. "Come," I said. I strode down the hall and out to the sty. Its gate swung wide at my touch. The pigs squealed, but when they saw him behind me their terror eased. I brushed each snout with oil and spoke a charm. Their bristles fell away and they rose to their feet as men. They ran to him, weeping and pressing their hands to his. He wept as well, not loudly but in great streams, until his beard was wet and dark. They looked like a father and his wayward sons. How old had they been when he'd left for Troy? Scarcely more than boys, most of them. I stood a little distant, like a shepherd watching a flock. "Be welcome," I said, when their tears had slowed. "Draw your ship up on the beach and bring your fellows. All of you are welcome."

They ate well that night, laughing, toasting. They looked younger, new-made in their relief. Odysseus' weariness too was gone. I watched him from my loom, interested to see another facet: the commander with his men. He was as good at that as all the rest, amused at their antics, gently reproving, reassuringly untroubled. They circled him like bees their hive.

When the platters were empty and the men drooped on their benches, I gave them blankets and told them to find beds wherever they were comfortable. A few stretched out in empty rooms, but most went outside to sleep beneath the summer stars.

Only Odysseus remained. I led him to the silver chair at the hearth and poured wine. His face was pleasant, and he leaned forward again, as if eager for whatever I might offer.

"The loom you admired," I said. "It was made by the craftsman Daedalus. You know the name?"

I was gratified to see genuine surprise and pleasure. "No wonder it is such a marvel. May I?"

I inclined my head, and he went to it at once. With a hand he ran its beams, base to top. His touch was reverent, like a priest at an altar. "How did you come to have it?"

"A gift."

There was speculation in his eyes, bright curiosity, but he did not press further. Instead, he said, "When I was a boy and everyone played at wrestling monsters like Heracles, I dreamed of being Daedalus instead. It seemed the greater genius to look at raw wood and iron, and imagine marvels. I was disappointed to find out I did not have the talent for it. I was always cutting my fingers open."

I thought of the white scars on Daedalus' hands. But I held back.

His hand rested on the side-beam as if upon the head of a beloved dog. "May I watch you weave with it?"

I was not used to having anyone so close while I worked. The yarn seemed to thicken and tangle in my fingers. His eyes followed every motion. He asked me questions about what each piece did, and how it differed from other looms. I answered him as best I could, though at last I had to confess that I had no comparison. "This is the only loom I have ever used."

"Imagine such a happiness. Like drinking wine your

whole life, instead of water. Like having Achilles to run your errands."

I did not know the name.

His voice rolled like a bard's: Achilles, prince of Phthia, swiftest of all the Greeks, best of the Achaian warriors at Troy. Beautiful, brilliant, born from the dread nereid Thetis, graceful and deadly as the sea itself. The Trojans had fallen before him like grass before the scythe, and the mighty Prince Hector himself perished at his ash-spear's end.

"You did not like him," I said.

Some inward amusement touched his face. "I appreciated him, in his way. But he made a terrible soldier, however many men he could bleed. He had a number of inconvenient ideas about loyalty and honor. Every day was a new struggle to yoke him to our purpose, keep him straight in his furrow. Then the best part of him died, and he was even more difficult after that. But as I said, his mother was a goddess, and prophecies hung on him like ocean-weed. He wrestled with matters larger than I will ever understand."

It was not a lie, but it was not truth either. He had named Athena as his patron. He had walked with those who could crack the world like eggs.

"What was his best part?"

"His lover, Patroclus. He didn't like me much, but then the good ones never do. Achilles went mad when he died; nearly mad, anyway."

I had turned from the loom by then. I wanted to watch his face as he talked. Through the windows the dark sky was ebbing to gray. A wolf sighed on her paws. I saw him hesitate at last. "Lady Circe," he said. "Golden witch of Aiaia. You gave us mercy, and we needed it. Our ship is splintered. The men are close to breaking. I am ashamed

to ask for more, but I think I must. In my dearest hopes we
stay a month. Is it too long?"

A burst of joy, like honey in my throat. I kept my face
steady though.

"I do not think a month should be too long."

He spent his days working on the ship. In the evenings, we
would sit before the hearth while the men ate their sup-
pers, and at night he came to my bed. His shoulders were
thick, carved from his warrior hours. I ran my hands across
his ragged scars. There were pleasures there, but in truth
the greater pleasure was after, when we lay together in the
darkness and he told me stories of Troy, conjuring the war
for me spear by spear. Proud Agamemnon, leader of the
host, brittle as badly tempered iron. Menelaus, his brother,
whose wife Helen's abduction had begun the war. Brave,
dull-brained Ajax, built like a mountainside. Diomedes,
Odysseus' ruthless right hand. And then the Trojans: handsome Paris, laughing thief of Helen's heart. His father,
white-bearded Priam, king of Troy, beloved by the gods for
his gentleness. Hecuba, his queen with a warrior's spirit,
whose womb had borne so many noble fruits. Hector, her
eldest, noble heir and bulwark to his great walled city.

And Odysseus, I thought. The spiral shell. Always another curve out of sight.

I began to see what he'd meant when he had talked of
his army's weakness. It was not their sinews that had wavered, but their discipline. There had never been a parade
of prouder men, more fractious and unyielding, each certain the war would fail without them.

"Do you know who truly wins wars?" he asked me one
night.

We lay on the rugs at the foot of my bed. Moment by

moment, his vitality had returned. His eyes were bright now, storm-lit. When he talked, he was lawyer and bard and crossroads charlatan at once, arguing his case, entertaining, pulling back the veil to show you the secrets of the world. It was not just his words, though they were clever enough. It was everything together: his face, his gestures, the sliding tones of his voice. I would say it was like a spell he cast, but there was no spell I knew that could equal it. The gift was his alone.

"The generals take the credit, of course, and indeed they provide the gold. But they are always calling you into their tent and asking for reports of what you're doing instead of letting you go do it. The songs say it is heroes. They are another piece. When Achilles puts on his helmet and cleaves his red path through the field, the hearts of common men swell in their chests. They think of the stories that will be told, and they long to be in them. *I fought beside Achilles. I stood shield to shield with Ajax. I felt the wind and fan of their great spears.* Those soldiers, of course, are yet another piece, for though they are weak and unsteady, when they are harnessed together they will carry you to victory. But there is a hand that must gather all those pieces and make them whole. A mind to guide the purpose, and not flinch from war's necessities."

"And that is your part," I said. "Which means you are like Daedalus after all. Only instead of wood, you work in men."

The look he gave me. Like purest, unmixed wine. "After Achilles died, Agamemnon named me Best of the Greeks. Other men fought bravely, but they flinched from war's true nature. Only I had the stomach to see what must be done."

His chest was bare and hatched with scars. I tapped it lightly, as if sounding what lay within. "Such as?"

"You promise mercy to spies so they will spill their story, then you kill them after. You beat men who mutiny. You coax heroes from their sulks. You keep spirits high at any cost. When the great hero Philoctetes was crippled with a festering wound, the men lost their courage over it. So I left him behind on an island and claimed he had asked to be left. Ajax and Agamemnon would have battered at Troy's locked gates until they died, but it was I who thought of the trick of the giant horse, and I spun the story that convinced the Trojans to pull it inside. I crouched in the wooden belly with my picked men, and if any shook with terror and strain, I put my knife to his throat. When the Trojans finally slept, we tore through them like foxes among soft-feathered chicks."

These were no songs to sing before a court, no tales from the great golden age. Yet somehow in his mouth they did not seem dishonorable, but just and inspired and wisely pragmatic.

"Why did you go to war in the first place, if you knew what the other kings were like?"

He rubbed at his cheek. "Oh, because of a foolish oath I swore. I tried to get out of it. My son was a year old, and I still felt new-married. There would be other glories, I thought, and when Agamemnon's man came to collect me I pretended to be mad. I went out naked and began plowing a winter field. He put my infant son in the blade's path. I stopped, of course, and so I was collected with the rest."

A bitter paradox, I thought: to keep his son he had to lose him.

"You must have been angry."

He lifted his hands, let them drop. "The world is an unjust place. Look what happened to that counselor of Agamemnon's. Palamedes, his name was. He served the army well, but fell in a pit while on a night watch. Someone had set sharpened stakes in the bottom. Terrible loss."

His eyes glittered. If good Patroclus had been there he might have said, Sir, you are no true hero, no Heracles, no Jason. You speak no honest speeches from pure heart. You do no noble deeds in the gleaming sunlight.

But I had met Jason. And I knew what sort of deeds could be done in the sun's sight. I said nothing.

The days passed, and the nights with them. My house was crowded with some four dozen men, and for the first time in my life, I found myself steeped in mortal flesh. Those frail bodies of theirs took relentless attention, food and drink, sleep and rest, the cleaning of limbs and fluxes. Such patience mortals must have, I thought, to drag themselves through it hour after hour. The fifth day, Odysseus' awl slipped and punctured the pad of his thumb. I gave him salves and worked my charms to drive off infection, but it still took half a moon to heal. I watched the pain passing over his face. Now it hurt, and now still it hurt, and now, and now. And that was only one among his discomforts, stiff neck and acid stomach and the ache of old wounds. I ran my hands over his ribbed scars, easing him as I could. The scars themselves I offered to wipe away. He shook his head. "How would I know myself?"

I was secretly glad. They suited him. Enduring Odysseus, he was, and the name was stitched into his skin. Whoever saw him must salute and say: There is a man who has seen the world. There is a captain with stories to tell.

I might have told him, in those hours, stories of my own. Scylla and Glaucos, Aeëtes, the Minotaur. The stone wall cutting into my back. The floor of my hall wet with blood, reflecting the moon. The bodies I had dragged one by one down the hill, and burned with their ship. The sound flesh makes when it tears and re-forms and how, when you change a man, you may stop the transformation partway through, and then that monstrous, half-beast thing will die.

His face would be intent as he listened, his relentless mind examining, weighing and cataloguing. However I pretended I could conceal my thoughts as well as he, I knew it was not true. He would see down to my bones. He would gather my weaknesses up and set them with the rest of his collection, alongside Achilles' and Ajax's. He kept them on his person as other men keep their knives.

I looked down at my body, bare in the fire's light, and tried to imagine it written over with its history: my palm with its lightning streak, my hand missing its fingers, the thousand cuts from my witch-work, the gristled furrows of my father's fire, the skin of my face like some half-melted taper. And those were only the things that had left marks.

There would be no salutes. What had Aeëtes called an ugly nymph? *A stain upon the face of the world.*

My smooth belly glowed beneath my hand, the color of honey shining in the sun. I drew him down to me. I was a golden witch, who had no past at all.

I began to know his men a little, those unsteady hearts that he had spoken of, those leaky vessels. Polites was better-mannered than the rest, Eurylochos stubborn and sulky. Thin-faced Elpenor had a laugh like a screechy owl. They reminded me of wolf pups, their griefs gone when their bellies were full. They looked down when I passed, as if to be sure their hands were still their own.

Every day they spent at games. They held races through the hills and on the beach. They were always running up to Odysseus, panting. Will you judge our archery contest? Our discus throw? Our spears?

Sometimes he would go off smiling with them, but sometimes he would shout, or strike them. He was not so easy and even as he pretended. Living with him was like standing beside the sea. Each day a different color, a different foam-capped height, but always the same restless intensity pulling towards the horizon. When the rail broke on his ship he kicked it out in fury and threw the pieces into the sea. The next day he went grimly to the forest with his axe, and when Eurylochos offered to help him, he bared his teeth. He could still marshal himself, show the face he must have worn each day to harness Achilles, but it cost him, and after he was prone to moods and tempers. The men would slink away, and I saw the confusion on their faces. Daedalus had said to me once: *Even the best iron grows brittle with too much beating.*

I was smooth as oil, calm as windless water. I drew him out, asked him for stories of his travels among foreign lands and men. He told me of the armies of Memnon, son of the Dawn, king of Aethiopia, and the Amazon horsewomen with their crescent shields. He had heard that in Egypt some of their pharaohs were women dressed in men's clothes. In India, he'd heard, there were ants the size of foxes who dig up gold among the dunes. And to the far north were a people who did not believe that Oceanos' river circled the earth, but instead it was a great girdling serpent, thick around as a boat and always hungry. It could never be still, for its appetite drove it ever onwards, devouring everything bite by bite, and one day when it had eaten all the world, it would devour itself.

But however far afield he traveled, always he came back to Ithaca. His olive groves and his goats, his loyal servants and the excellent hunting dogs he'd raised by hand. His noble parents and his old nurse and his first boar hunt, which had given him the long scar I had seen on his leg. His son, Telemachus, would be bringing the herds down from the mountains by now. *He will be good with them, I always was. Every prince needs to know his lands, and there's no better way to learn than by grazing the goats.* He never said, What if I go home, and all of it is ash? But I saw the thought in him, living like a second body, and feeding in the dark.

It was autumn by then, the light thinning, the grass crackling underfoot. The month was nearly gone. We were lying in my bed. "I think we must leave very soon, or else stay the winter."

The window was open; the breeze passed over us. It was a trick of his, to set a sentence out like a plate on a table and see what you would put on it. But he surprised me by continuing. "I would stay," he said. "If you would have me. It will only be until spring. I will go as soon as the seas are passable. It will be scarcely any delay."

That last was not said to me, but to some person he argued with silently. His men perhaps, his wife, I did not care. I kept my face turned away so he would not see my pleasure.

"I will have you," I said.

Something shifted in him after that, the releasing of a tension I had not realized he held. The next day he went humming down to the shore with his crew. They dragged the ship into a sheltered cave. They staked it, rolled the sail, stowed all the gear to keep it safely through the winter storms till spring.

Sometimes, I would see him watching me. An intentness would come over his face, and he would begin to ask me his casual, sideways questions. About the island, about my father, the loom, my history, witchcraft. I had come to know that look well: it was the same he wore when he spotted a crab with a triple claw, or wondered over the trick tides of Aiaia's east bay. The world was made of mysteries, and I was only another riddle among the millions. I did not answer him, and though he pretended frustration, I began to see that it pleased him in some strange way. A door that did not open at his knock was a novelty in its own right, and a kind of relief as well. All the world confessed to him. He confessed to me.

Some stories he told me by daylight. Others came only when the fire was burnt out, and there was no one to know his face but the shadows.

"It was after the cyclops," he said. "We had a bit of luck at last. We landed on the Island of the Winds. You know it?"

"King Aeolus," I said. One of Zeus' pets, whose job it was to keep track of the gusts that spin ships across the world.

"I pleased him, and he sped us on our way. He gave me besides a great bag holding all of the contrary winds, so they could not trouble us. For nine days and nine nights we skimmed across the waves. I did not sleep, not even an hour, for I was guarding the bag. I had told my men what it was, of course, but — " He shook his head. "They decided it was treasure I did not wish to share. The portions they had received from Troy had been long lost in the waves. They did not want to come home empty-handed. Well." He drew a deep breath. "You may imagine what happened."

I did imagine it. His men were unrulier than ever now, giddy with the prospect of a whole winter's idleness. At night they liked to play a game of throwing wine dregs.

They picked some trencher as the target, but their aim was terrible, for by then they had drunk down bowl after bowl. The table grew stained as if with slaughter, and they looked to my nymphs to clear it up. When I told them they would do it themselves, they eyed each other, and if I had been anyone else, they would have defied me. But they still remembered their snouts.

"At last when I could fight it no longer," Odysseus said, "I fell asleep. I did not feel them take the bag from my hand. It was the howling of the winds that woke me. They whirled out of the bag and blew us back as if we had never left. Every league undone. They think I grieve for their dead comrades, and I do. But sometimes it is all I can do not to kill them myself. They have wrinkles, but no wisdom. I took them to war before they could do any of those things that steady a man. They were unmarried when they left. They had no children. They had no years of lean harvest, when they must scrape the bottom of their stores, and no good years either, that they might learn to save. They have not seen their parents grow old and begin to fail. They have not seen them die. I fear I have robbed them not only of their youth but their age as well."

He rubbed at his knuckles. He had been a bowman when he was young, and the strength it takes to string and nock and shoot taxes hands like nothing else. He had left his bow behind when he went to war, but the pain had followed him. He'd told me once that if he had brought the bow, he would have been the best archer in both armies.

"Then why leave it?"

Politics, he had explained. The bow was Paris' weapon. Paris, the pretty wife-stealer. "Among heroes, he was seen as cowardly. No bowman would ever have been made Best of the Greeks, no matter how skilled he was."

"Heroes are fools," I had said.

He had laughed. "We are agreed."

His eyes were closed. He was silent so long I thought he slept. Then he said: "If you could have seen how close we were to Ithaca. I could smell the fishing fires from the beach."

I began to ask him for small favors. Would he kill a buck for dinner? Would he catch a few fish? My sty was falling to pieces, might he mend some of the posts? It gave me a sharp pleasure to see him come in the door with full nets, with baskets of fruit from my orchards. He joined me in the garden, staking vines. We spoke of what winds were blowing, how Elpenor had taken to sleeping on the roof, and whether we should forbid it.

"That idiot," he said. "He will break his neck."

"I will tell him he only has permission when he's sober."

He snorted. "That will be never."

I knew I was a fool. Even if he stayed past that spring to the next, such a man could never be happy closed up on my narrow shores. And even if somehow I found a way to keep him contented, yet still there were limits, for he was mortal, and not young. Give thanks, I told myself. A winter is more than you had with Daedalus.

I did not give thanks. I learned his favorite foods and smiled to see his pleasure in them. At night we sat together at the hearth and talked over the day. "What do you think," I asked him, "about the great oak, struck by lightning? Do you think there is rot within?"

"I will look," he said. "If there is, it will not be hard to take down. I will do it before dinner tomorrow."

He cut it down, then hacked the rest of the day at my brambles. "They were overrun. What you really need is some goats. A flock of four would have them flat in a month. And they'd keep it flat."

"And where will I find goats?"

That word between us, *Ithaca*, like the breaking of a spell.

"Never mind," I said. "I will transform a few of the sheep, that will fix it."

At dinner, my nymphs had begun to linger near the men, to lead the ones they liked to their beds. This pleased me too. My household mingling with his. I had once told Daedalus that I would never marry, because my hands were dirty, and I liked my work too much. But this was a man with his own dirty hands.

And where, Circe, do you think he learned all these domestic niceties?

My wife, he always said, when he talked of her. *My wife, my wife*. Those words, carried before him like a shield. Like country folk who will not say the god of death's name, for fear he will come and take their dearest heart.

Penelope, she was called. While he slept, I would sometimes speak those syllables to the black air. It was a dare, or maybe a proof. See? She does not come. She does not have the powers you believe.

I held off as long as I could, but in the end she was the scab that I must pick. I waited for the sound of his breath that meant he was awake enough to talk.

"What is she like?"

He told me of her gentle manner, how her mild direction made men jump faster than any shout. She was an excellent swimmer. Her favorite flower was the crocus, and she wore the first bloom of the season in her hair for luck. He had a trick of speaking of her as if she were only in the next room, as if they were not twelve years and distant seas apart.

She was Helen's cousin, he said. A thousand times cleverer and wiser, though Helen was clever in her way, but of course fickle. I had heard his stories of Helen by then, the queen of Sparta, mortal daughter of Zeus, most beautiful woman in the world. Paris, prince of Troy, had spirited her away from her husband, Menelaus, and so started the war.

"Did she leave with Paris by choice, or was she forced?" I asked.

"Who can say? For ten years we were camped outside her gates, and she never tried to run that I heard. But the moment Menelaus stormed the city she threw herself upon him naked, swearing it had been a torment, and all she wanted was her husband back. You will never get the whole truth from her. She has as many coils as a snake, and an eye always to her advantage."

Not unlike you, I thought.

"My wife, though," he said. "She is constant. Constant in all things. Even wise men go astray sometimes, but never her. She is a fixed star, a true-made bow." A silence, in which I felt him moving deep among his memories. "Nothing she says has a single meaning, nor a single intention, yet she is steady. She knows herself."

The words slid into me, smooth as a polished knife. I had known he loved her from the moment he'd spoken of her weaving. Yet he had stayed, month after month, and I had let myself be lulled. Now I saw more clearly: all those nights in my bed had been only his traveler's wisdom. When you are in Egypt, you worship Isis; when in Anatolia, you kill a lamb for Cybele. It does not trespass on your Athena still at home.

But even as I thought that, I knew it was not the whole

answer. I remembered all the hours he had spent at war, managing the fine glass tempers of kings, the sulks of princes, balancing each proud warrior against his fellow. It was a feat equal to taming Aeëtes' fire-breathing bulls, with only his own wiles for aid. But back home in Ithaca, there would be no such fractious heroes, no councils, no midnight raids, no desperate stratagems that he must devise or men would die. And how would such a man go home again, to his fireside and his olives? His domestic harmony with me was closer to a sort of rehearsal, I realized. When he sat by the hearth, when he worked in my garden, he was trying to remember the trick of it. How an axe might feel in wood instead of flesh. How he might fit himself to Penelope again, smooth as one of Daedalus' joints.

He slept beside me. Every now and then his breath caught in the back of his throat. *Tick.*

Pasiphaë would have counseled me to make a love draught and bind him to me. Aeëtes would say I should steal away his wits. I imagined his face empty of all thoughts but what I put into it. He would sit at my knee, gazing up, fatuous and adoring and empty.

The winter rains began, and the whole island smelled of earth. I loved the season, the cold sands, the white hellebore blooming. Odysseus had put on flesh and did not wince so often when he moved. The worst of his tempers had ebbed. I tried to find satisfaction in it. Like seeing a garden well tended, I told myself. Like watching new lambs struggle to their feet.

The men stayed close to the house, drinking themselves warm. For entertainment, Odysseus told them heroic stories of Achilles, Ajax, Diomedes, making them live again in the twilight air and perform their glorious deeds. The men were rapt, their faces struck with wonder. *Remember,* they whispered with awe. *We walked among them. We stood against Hector. Our sons will tell the tale.*

He smiled over them like an indulgent father, but that night he scoffed: "They could no more stand against Hector than fly. Anyone with a brain ran when they saw him."

"Including you?"

"Of course. Ajax could barely hold against him, and only Achilles could have beaten him. I am a fair enough warrior, but I know where I end."

He did, I thought. So many closed their eyes and spun fantasies of their wished-for strength. But he was mapped and surveyed, each stone and hummock noted with clear-eyed precision. He measured his gifts to the scruple.

"I met Hector once," he said. "It was the early days of the war, when we still pretended there might be a truce. He sat beside his father, Priam, on a rickety stool and made it look like a throne. He did not gleam like gold. He was not polished and perfect. But he was the same all the way through, like a block of marble cut whole from a quarry. His wife, Andromache, poured our wine. Later, we heard she bore him a son. Astyanax, *Commander of the city*. But Hector called him Scamandrios, after the river that ran past Troy."

Something in his voice.

"What happened to him?"

"The same that happens to all sons in war. Achilles killed Hector, and after, when Achilles' son, Pyrrhus, stormed the palace, he took the child Astyanax and smashed open his head. It was a horror, like everything Pyrrhus did. But it was necessary. The child would have grown up with a blade in his heart. It is a son's highest duty to avenge his father. If he had lived, he would have rallied men to his side and come after us."

The moon had slivered down to a shard outside the window. He was silent, turning through his thoughts.

"It is strange how comforting the idea is to me. That if I am killed, my son will take to the seas. He will hunt down those men who laid me low. He will stand before them and say, 'You dared to spill the blood of Odysseus, and now yours is spilled in turn.'"

The room was still. It was late, the owls long gone to their trees.

"What was he like? Your son?"

He rubbed at the base of his thumb, where the awl-puncture had been. "We named him Telemachus after my skill with the bow." *Distant fighter*, it meant. "But the joke was that he screamed his whole first day as if he were living in the battlefield's heart. The women tried every trick they knew, rocking, walking, swaddling his arms, a thumb wetted with wine to suck. The midwife said she had never seen such passion. Even my old nurse was covering her ears. My wife had gone gray, for she feared there was something wrong with him. Give him to me, I said. I held him up before me and looked into his screaming face. 'Sweet son,' I said, 'you are right, this world is a wild and terrible place, and worth shouting at. But you are safe now, and all of us need to sleep. Will you let us have a little peace?' And he calmed. Just went quiet in my hands. After that, you could not find an easier child. He was always smiling, laughing for anyone who'd stop to speak to him. The maids would invent excuses to come and pinch his fat cheeks. 'What a king he will be one day!' they would say. 'Mild as the west wind, oh!'"

He went on with his memories. Telemachus' first bite of bread, his first word, how he loved goats and hiding beneath chairs, giggling to be found. He had more stories of his son from a single year, I thought, than my father had of me in all eternity.

"I know his mother will keep me in his mind, but I was leading the hunts by his age. I had killed a boar myself. I only hope there will still be something to teach him when I return. I want to leave some mark upon him."

I said something vague and soothing, I am sure. You will leave a mark. Every boy wants a father, he will wait for you. But I was thinking again of the relentlessness of mortal lives. Even as we spoke, the moments were passing. The sweet baby was vanished. His son was aging, growing, sharpening into a man. Thirteen years Odysseus had lost of him already. How many more?

My thoughts returned often to that quiet-eyed, watchful boy. I wondered if he knew what his father expected, if he felt the weight of those hopes. I imagined him out on the cliffs every day, praying for a ship. I imagined his weariness, his soft, inward grief before he went to sleep each night, curling on his bed as he had once been cradled in his father's hands.

I cupped my own hands in the dark. I did not have a thousand wiles, and I was no fixed star, yet for the first time I felt something in that space. A hope, a living breath, that might yet grow between.

CHAPTER SEVENTEEN

THE TREES WERE JUST beginning to bud. The sea was still foam-capped, but soon its waves would calm, and it would be spring and time for Odysseus to sail. He would race across the sea, tacking between storms and Poseidon's great hand, his eye fixed on home. And my island would fall silent again.

I lay beside him in the moonlight each night. Just one more season, I imagined saying to him. Just till summer's end, that is when the best winds come. It would surprise him. I would catch the faintest flicker of disappointment in his eyes. Golden witches are not supposed to beg. I let the island plead for me instead, speaking with its eloquent beauty. Every day the stones shed more of their icy chill, and the blossoms swelled. We ate picnics on the green grass. We walked on the sun-warm sand and swam in the bright bay. I took him to the shade of an apple tree, so that the scent would waft over him while he slept. I unrolled all Aiaia's wonders like a rug before him, and I saw him begin to waver.

His men saw too. Thirteen years they had lived beside him, and though his twisting thoughts were mostly beyond their ken, they sensed a change, as hounds scent the moods of their master. Day by day, they grew more restless. Ithaca, they said, loudly, every chance they got. Queen Penelope. Telemachus. Eurylochos stalked about my halls, glaring. I saw him whispering in corners with the others. When I passed by, they fell silent, gazes down. In ones and twos, they made their creeping way to Odysseus. I waited for him to send them away, but he only stared over their shoulders into the dusty sunset air. I should have left them pigs, I thought.

Death's Brother is the name that poets give to sleep. For most men those dark hours are a reminder of the stillness that waits at the end of days. But Odysseus' slumber was like his life, tossed and restless, heavy with murmurs that made my wolves prick up their ears. I watched him in the pearl-gray light of dawn: the tremors of his face, the striving tension in his shoulders. He twisted the sheets as if they were opponents he tried to throw in a wrestling match. A year of peaceful days he had stayed with me, and still every night he went to war.

The shutters were open. It must have rained in the night, I thought. The air that drifted in felt washed and very clear. Each sound — bird trills, fluttering leaves, the hush of waves — hung in the air like a chime. I dressed and followed that glory outside. His men still slept. Elpenor was up on the roof, wrapped in one of my best blankets. The wind rippled past me like lyre notes, and my own breath seemed to pipe in harmony. A dewdrop fell from a branch. It struck the earth like the ringing of a bell.

I felt my mouth go dry.

He stepped out from my stand of laurels. Every line of his body was beautiful, perfect with grace. His dark, loose hair was crowned with a wreath. From his shoulder hung a shining, silver-tipped bow carved from olive wood.

"Circe," Apollo said, and it was the greatest chime of all. Every melody in the world belonged to him.

He held up an elegant hand. "My brother warned me about your voice. I think it will be better if you speak as little as possible."

His words carried no malice. Though perhaps that was what malice sounded like in those perfect tones.

"I will not be silenced on my own island."

He winced. "Hermes said that you were difficult. I come with a prophecy for Odysseus."

I felt myself tense. Olympian riddles were always double-edged. "He is inside."

"Yes," he said, "I know."

The wind struck me across the face. I had no time to cry out. It rushed into my throat, battering its way to my belly as if all the sky were being funneled through me. I gagged, but its swelling force poured on and on, choking off my breath, drowning me in its alien power. Apollo watched, his face pleasant.

The island clearing was swept away. Odysseus stood on a shore with cliffs rising around him. In the distance were goats and olive groves. I saw a wide-halled house, its courtyard set with stones, its walls gleaming with ancestral weapons. *Ithaca*.

Then Odysseus stood upon a different shore. Dark sand and a sky that never saw my father's light. Shadowed poplars loomed and willows trailed their leaves in black water. No birds sang, no beast moved. I knew the place at once, though I had never been there. A great cave gaped, and in its mouth stood an old man with unseeing eyes. I heard his name in my mind: *Teiresias*.

I threw myself down into the dirt of my garden bed. Scrabbling, tugging up the moly roots, I stuffed a few into my mouth, brown earth still clinging. At once the wind ceased, dying as quickly as it had come. I coughed, my whole body shaking. My tongue tasted of slime and ash. I fought to my knees.

"You dare," I said. "You dare to misuse me on my own island? I am Titan blood. This will bring war. My father — "

"It was your father who suggested it. My vessels must have prophecy in their blood. You should be honored," he said. "You have borne a vision of Apollo."

His voice was a hymn. His beautiful face showed only the faintest puzzlement. I wanted to tear him with my nails. The gods and their incomprehensible rules. Always there was a reason you must kneel.

"I will not tell Odysseus."

"That is beneath my concern," he said. "The prophecy is delivered."

He was gone. I pressed my forehead to the wrinkled bole of an olive. My chest was heaving. I shook with rage and humiliation. How many times would I have to learn? Every moment of my peace was a lie, for it came only at the gods' pleasure. No matter what I did, how long I lived, at a whim they would be able to reach down and do with me what they wished.

The sky was not yet fully blue. Inside, Odysseus still slept. I woke him and led him to the hall. I did not tell him the prophecy. I watched him eat and fingered my rage as if it were a knife's point. I wanted to keep it sharp as long as I could, for I knew what would come after. In the vision, he had been back again on Ithaca. The last of my little hopes were gone.

I set out my best dishes, broached my oldest wine. But

there was no savor in it. His face was abstracted. All day he kept turning to look out the window as if someone would come. We spoke politely, but I felt him waiting for the men to eat, to go to bed. When the last of their voices had died into sleep, he knelt.

"Goddess," he said.

He never called me that, and so I knew. I truly knew. Perhaps some divinity had come to him as well. Perhaps he had dreamed of Penelope. Our idyll was finished. I looked down at his hair, woven with gray. His shoulders were set, his eyes on the ground. I felt a dull anger. At least he might look me in the face.

"What is it, mortal?" My voice was loud. My lions stirred.

"I must go," he said. "I have stayed too long. My men are impatient."

"Then go. I am a host, not a jailer."

He did look at me then. "I know it, lady. I am grateful to you beyond measure."

His eyes were brown and warm as summer earth. His words were simple. They had no art to them, which of course was also art. He always knew how to show himself to best advantage. It felt a kind of vengeance to say:

"I have a message for you from the gods."

"A message." His face grew wary.

"You will reach home, they say. But first they command you to speak with the prophet Teiresias in the house of death."

No sane man could hear such a thing without quailing. He had gone rigid and pale as stone. "Why?"

"The gods have their own reasons, which they have not seen fit to share."

"Will there never be an end to it?"

His voice was raw. His face was like a wound that had opened again. My anger drained away. He was not my adversary. His road would be hard enough without the hurt we might do each other.

I touched his chest where his great captain's heart beat. "Come," I said. "I do not desert you." I led him to my room and spoke there the knowledge that had been rising in me all day, quick and unceasing, like bubbles from a stream.

"The winds will carry you past lands and seas to the living world's edge. There is a strand there, with a black poplar grove, and still, dark waters hung with willows. The entrance to the underworld. Dig a pit, as big as I will show you. Fill it with the blood of a black ewe and ram, and pour libations all around. The hungry shadows will come swarming. They will be desperate for that steaming life after so long in the dark."

His eyes were closed. Imagining, perhaps, the souls spilling from their gray halls. He would know some of them. Achilles and Patroclus, Ajax, Hector. All the Trojans he had killed, and all the Greeks too, and his crew that had been eaten, still crying out for justice. But this would not be the worst. There would be as well souls there he could not predict: the ones from home who had died in his absence. Perhaps his parents or Telemachus. Perhaps Penelope herself.

"You must hold them off from the blood until Teiresias comes. He will drink his fill and give you his wisdom. Then you will return here, for a single day, as there may be more help I can give you."

He nodded. His lids were gray. I touched his cheek. "Sleep," I said. "You will need it."

"I cannot," he said.

I understood. He was bracing himself, summoning up

his strength to do battle once more. We lay beside each other in silent vigil through the long hours of the night. When it was dawn, I helped him dress with my own hands. I pinned his cloak around his shoulders. I settled his belt and gave him his sword. When we opened the front door, we found Elpenor sprawled upon the flagstones. He had fallen from my roof at last. We gazed down at his bluing lips, the ugly angle of his neck.

"Already it comes." Odysseus' voice was grim with resignation. I knew what he meant. The Fates had him in their yoke again.

"I will keep him for you. You have no time for a funeral now."

We carried the body to one of my beds, wrapped it in a sheet. I brought out stores for their journey, and the sheep he needed for the rite. The ship was already prepared, his men had rigged it days ago. Now they loaded it, and pushed it into the waves. The seas were churning and cold, the air misted with spray. They would have to fight for every league, and by night their shoulders would be knots. I should have given them salves for it, I thought. But it was too late.

I watched the ship struggle over the horizon, then I went back and drew the sheet from Elpenor's body. The only corpses I had ever seen were those that had lain broken on my floor, unrecognizable as men. I touched his chest. It was hard and cool. I had heard that in death faces looked younger than they were, but Elpenor had laughed often, and without the spark of life his face was slack with lines. I washed him and rubbed oils into his skin, as carefully as if he could still feel my fingers. I sang as I worked, a melody to keep his soul company while he waited to cross the great river to the underworld. I wrapped him again in his shroud, spoke a charm to keep away the rot, and closed the door behind me.

In my garden, the green leaves were so new they shone like blades. I ran my fingers through the soil. Humid summer was gathering, and soon I must start staking out the vines. Last year Odysseus had helped me. I touched the thought like a bruise, testing its ache. When he was gone, would I be like Achilles, wailing over his lost lover Patroclus? I tried to picture myself running up and down the beaches, tearing at my hair, cradling some scrap of old tunic he had left behind. Crying out for the loss of half my soul.

I could not see it. That knowledge brought its own sort of pain. But perhaps that is how it was meant to be. In the stories, gods and mortals never joined for long.

That night, I stayed in my kitchen stripping aconite. Already Odysseus would be facing his dead. As he'd left, I had pressed a phial into his hand and asked him to bring me blood from the pit he would make. The shades would infuse it with their chill presence, and I had wanted to feel that power, ashen and unearthly. Now I was sorry I had asked. It was something Perses or Aeëtes might do, someone with only witchcraft in their veins and no warmth.

I moved carefully through my work, my fingers precise, aware of every sensation. From their shelves my herbs watched me. Row upon row of simples whose powers I had harvested with my own hands. I liked to see them there, in their bowls and bottles: sage and rose, horehound, chicory, wild laurel, the moly in its stoppered glass. And last of all, still in its cedar box: silphium ground with wormwood, the draught I had taken each moon since the first time I lay with Hermes. Each moon except the last.

*   *   *

My nymphs and I waited on the sand, watching the ship row in. The men waded to the shore in silence. Their bodies sagged as if borne down by stones, sickly and aged. I searched Odysseus' face. It was ghastly, I could not read it. Even their clothes were faded, the fabric leached and gray. They looked like fish, caught beneath a winter's skim of ice.

I stepped forward, shining my eyes over them. "Welcome!" I cried. "Welcome back, you hearts of gold. You men of oak! You are heroes for the legends. You have done one of Heracles' labors: seen the house of death and lived. Come, there are blankets here, laid for you upon the soft grass. There is wine and food. Rest and be well!"

They moved slowly, like old men, but they sat. The roast platters stood by, and the wine, deep and red. We served and poured until their cheeks took color. The sun beat down, burning off the cold mist of death.

I drew Odysseus aside to a green thicket. "Tell me," I said.

"They live," he said. "That is the best news I have. My son and wife live. My father too."

Not his mother. I waited.

He stared across his scarred knees. "Agamemnon was there. His wife had taken a lover, and when he returned, she slaughtered him in the bath like an ox. I saw Achilles and Patroclus, and Ajax bearing the wound he gave himself. They envied me my life, but at least their battles are done."

"Yours will be done. You will reach Ithaca. I have seen it."

"I will reach it, but Teiresias said that when I do I will find men besieging my home. Eating my stores and usurp-

ing my place. I must find a way to kill them. But then I will
die of the sea, while I still walk on land. The gods love their
riddles."

His voice was more bitter than I had ever heard it.

"You cannot think of it," I said. "It will only torment you.
Think instead of the path before you, which carries you
home to your wife and son."

"My path," he said, darkly. "Teiresias laid it before me. I
must pass Thrinakia."

The word was an arrow striking home. How many years
had it been since I had heard that island's name? The
memory rose before me: my shining sisters, and Darling
and Pretty and all the rest, swaying like lilies in the gilded
dusk.

"If I do not disturb the cattle, then I will reach home
with my men. But if any are harmed, your father will loose
his wrath. It will be years before I see Ithaca again, and all
my men will die."

"Then you will not stop," I said. "You will not even land
on the shore."

"I will not stop."

But it was not so simple, and we knew it. The Fates
lured and tricked. They set obstacles to drive you into their
toils. Anything might serve them: the winds, the waves, the
weak hearts of men.

"If you run aground," I said, "keep to the beach. Do not
go look at the herds. You cannot know how they will tempt
your hunger. They are to cows what gods are to mortals."

"I will hold."

It was not his will I feared. But what good would it do to
say so, to sit over his door like a death-owl? He knew what
his men were. And a new thought was rising in me. I was
remembering the sea-routes Hermes had drawn for me so

long ago. I traced them in my mind. If he went by Thrinakia, then...

I closed my eyes. Another punishment from the gods. For him, and me as well.

"What is it?"

I opened my eyes. "Listen to me," I said. "There are things you must know." I drew the journey for him. One by one, I laid out the dangers he must avoid, the shoals, the barbarous islands, the Sirens, those birds with women's heads who lure men to their death with song. At last I could delay no more. "Your path takes you past Scylla as well. You know her?"

He knew. I watched the blow fall. Six men, or twelve.

"There must be some way to prevent her," he said. "Some weapon I might use."

It was one of my favorite things about him: how he always fought for his chance. I turned away, so I would not have to see his face when I said, "No. There is nothing. Not even for such a mortal as you. I faced her once, long ago, and escaped only through magic and godhead. But the Sirens, there you may use your tricks. Fill your men's ears with wax, and leave your own free. If you tie yourself to the mast, you may be the first man to ever hear their song and tell the tale. Would that not make a good story for your wife and son?"

"It would." But his voice was dull as a ruined blade. There was nothing I could do. He was passing from my hands.

We carried Elpenor to his pyre. We did the rites for him, sang his deeds of war, set his name in the record of men who lived. My nymphs wailed, and the men wept, but he and I stood dry and silent. After, we loaded his ship with all the stores of mine that it could hold. His men stood at the ropes and oars. They were eager now, darting glances at each other, scuffling at the deck with their feet. I felt hollowed, gouged like a beach beneath a keel.

Odysseus, son of Laertes, the great traveler, prince of wiles and tricks and a thousand ways. He showed me his scars, and in return he let me pretend that I had none.

He stepped onto his ship, and when he turned back to look for me, I was gone.

CHAPTER EIGHTEEN

HOW WOULD THE SONGS frame the scene? The goddess on her lonely promontory, her lover dwindling in the distance. Her eyes wet but inscrutable, cast inward to private thoughts. Beasts gather at her hem. The lindens bloom. And at the last, just before he disappears over the horizon, she lifts one hand and touches it to her belly.

My guts began to boil the moment his anchor was up. I, who had never been sick in my life, now was sick every moment. I heaved until my throat was torn, my stomach rattling like an old nut, my mouth cracked at its corners. As if my body would cast up everything it had eaten for a hundred years.

My nymphs wrung their hands and clutched each other. They had never seen such a thing. In pregnancy, our kind glowed and swelled like buds. They thought I was poisoned, or else cursed with some unholy transformation, my body turning itself inside out. When they tried to help me, I pushed them away. The child I carried would be called demigod, but that word was deceiving. From my blood he would have a few special graces, beauty or speed, strength or charm. But all the rest would come from his father, for mortality always bred truer than godhead. His flesh would be subject to the same thousand pricks and fatalities that threaten every man. I trusted such frailty to no god, no family of mine, to none but myself alone.

"Leave now," I said to them in my new, ragged voice. "I do not care how you do it — send to your fathers and go. This is for me."

What they thought of such words, I never knew. I was seized again, my eyes blind and watering. By the time I found my way back to the house, they were gone. I suppose their fathers obliged because they feared pregnancy by a mortal might be catching. The house felt strange without them, but I had no time to think of it, and no time to mourn for Odysseus either. The sickness did not cease. Every hour it rode me. I could not understand why it took me so hard. I wondered if it was the mortal blood fighting with mine, or if I was cursed indeed, if some stray hex of Aeëtes' had circled all this while and found me at last. But the affliction yielded to no counterspell, not even moly. It is no mystery, I said to myself. Have you not always insisted on being difficult in everything you do?

I could not defend myself from sailors in such shape and I knew it. I crawled to my herb-pots and cast the spell I had thought of so long ago: an illusion to make the island look like hostile, wrecking rocks to any ship that passed. I lay on the ground after, breathing with effort. I would be left in peace.

Peace. I would have laughed if I were not so ill. The sour tang of cheese in the kitchen, the salt-stink of seaweed on the breeze, the wormy earth after rain, the sickly roses browning on the bush. All of them brought the bile stinging to my throat. Headaches followed, like urchin spines driven into my eyes. This is how Zeus must have felt before

Athena leapt from his skull, I thought. I crawled to my room and lay in the shuttered dark, dreaming of how sweet it would be to cut through my neck and make an end.

Yet, as strange as it sounds, even in such extremities of misery I was not wholly miserable. I was used to unhappiness, formless and opaque, stretching out to every horizon. But this had shores, depths, a purpose and a shape. There was hope in it, for it would end, and bring me my child. My son. For whether by witchcraft or prophetic blood, that is what I knew he was.

He grew, and his fragility grew with him. I had never been so glad of my immortal flesh, layered like armor around him. I was giddy feeling his first kicks and I spoke to him every moment, as I crushed my herbs, as I cut clothes for his body, wove his cradle out of rushes. I imagined him walking beside me, the child and boy and man that he would be. I would show him all the wonders I had gathered for him, this island and its sky, the fruits and sheep, the waves and lions. The perfect solitude that would never be loneliness again.

I touched my hand to my belly. *Your father said once that he wanted more children, but that is not why you live. You are for me.*

Odysseus had told me that Penelope's pains began so faintly, she thought them a stomachache from too many pears. Mine dropped from the sky like a thunderbolt. I remember crawling to the house from the garden, hunched against the tearing contraction. I had the willow draught ready, and I drank some, then all, and by the end I was licking the bottle's neck.

I knew so little of childbirth, its stages and progression. The shadows changed, but it was all one endless moment,

the pain like stones grinding me to meal. I screamed and
pushed against it for hours, and still the baby did not come.
Midwives had tricks to help the child move, but I did not
know them. One thing I did understand: if it took too long,
my son would die.

On it went. In my agonies, I overturned a table. After,
I would find the room torn apart as if by bears, tapestries
ripped from the walls, stools shattered, platters broken. I do
not remember it. My mind was lurching through a thousand terrors. Was the baby dead already? Or was I like my
sister, growing some monster within me? The unremitting
pain only seemed a confirmation. If the baby were whole
and natural, wouldn't he come?

I closed my eyes. Putting a hand inside myself, I felt
for the smooth curve of the child's head. It had no horns,
no other horrors I could tell. It was only stuck against
the inner opening, squeezed between my muscles and
my bones.

I prayed to Eileithyia, goddess of childbirth. She had the
power to loosen the womb's hold and bring the child into
the world. She was said to watch over the birth of every god
and demigod. Help me, I cried out. But she did not come.
The animals whined in their corners, and I began to remember the whispers of my cousins in Oceanos' halls so
long ago. If a god did not wish your child to be born, they
might hold Eileithyia back.

The thought seized my careering mind. Someone was
keeping her from me. Someone dared to try to harm my
son. It gave me the strength I needed. I bared my teeth
at the dark and crawled to the kitchen. I seized a knife
and dragged a great bronze mirror to face me, for there
was no Daedalus now to help. I leaned against the marble
wall, amid the broken table legs. The coolness of the stone

calmed me. This child was no Minotaur, but a mortal. I must not cut too deep.

I had been afraid the pain would undo me, but I scarcely felt it. There was a rasping sound, like stone upon stone, that I realized was my own breath. The layers of flesh parted, and I saw him at last: limbs curled like a snail in its shell. I stared, afraid to move him. What if he was dead already? What if he was not, and I killed him with my touch? But I drew him forth, and his skin met the air, and he began to wail. I wailed with him, for I had never heard a sweeter sound. I laid him on my chest. The stones beneath us felt like feathers. He was shuddering and shuddering, pressing my skin with his wet, living face. I cut the cord, holding him all the while.

See? I told him. We do not need anyone. In answer, he made a froggy croak and closed his eyes. My son, Telegonus.

I did not go easy to motherhood. I faced it as soldiers face their enemies, girded and braced, sword up against the coming blows. Yet all my preparations were not enough. In those months I had spent with Odysseus, I had thought I'd learned some tricks of mortal living. Three meals a day, the fluxes, the washing and cleaning. Twenty diaper cloths I had cut, and believed myself wise. But what did I know of mortal babies? Aeëtes was in arms less than a month. Twenty cloths got me only through the first day.

Thank the gods I did not have to sleep. Every minute I must wash and boil and clean and scrub and put to soak. Yet how could I do that, when every minute he also needed something, food and change and sleep? That last I had always thought the most natural thing for mortals, easy as breathing, yet he could not seem to do it. However I wrapped him, however I rocked and sang, he screamed, gasping and shaking until the lions fled, until I feared he would do himself harm. I made a sling to carry him, so he might lie against my heart. I gave him soothing herbs, I burned incenses, I called birds to sing at our windows. The only thing that helped was if I walked — walked the halls, walked the hills, walked the shore. Then at last he would wear himself out, close his eyes, and sleep. But if I stopped, if I tried to put him down, he would wake at once. Even when I walked without ceasing, he was soon up, screaming again. Within him was an ocean's worth of grief, which could only be stoppered a moment, never emptied. How often in those days did I think of Odysseus' smiling child? I tried his trick, along with all the rest. Held my son's floppy body up into the air, promised him he was safe. He only screamed louder. Whatever made the prince Telemachus so sweet, I thought, it must have come from Penelope. This was the child I deserved.

We did find some moments of peace. When he finally slept, when he nursed at my breast, when he smiled at a flight of birds scattering from a tree. I would look at him and feel a love so sharp it seemed my flesh lay open. I made a list of all the things I would do for him. Scald off my skin. Tear out my eyes. Walk my feet to bones, if only he would be happy and well.

He was not happy. A moment, I thought, I only need one moment without his damp rage in my arms. But there was none. He hated sun. He hated wind. He hated baths. He hated to be clothed, to be naked, to lie on his belly, and his back. He hated this great world and everything in it, and me, so it seemed, most of all.

I thought of all those hours I had spent working my spells, singing, weaving. I felt their loss like a limb torn

away. I told myself I even missed turning men to pigs, for
at least that I had been good at. I wanted to hurl him from
me, but instead I marched on in that darkness with him,
back and forth before the waves, and at every step I yearned
for my old life. I spoke sourly to the night air as he wailed:
"At least I do not worry he is dead."

I clapped a hand to my mouth, for the god of the underworld comes at much less invitation. I held his fierce
little face against me. The tears were standing in his eyes,
his hair disordered, a small scratch on his cheek. How had
he gotten it? What villain dared to hurt him? Everything
that I had heard of mortal babies flooded back: how they
died for no reason, for any reason, because they grew too
cold, too hungry, because they lay one way, or another. I
felt each breath in his thin chest, how improbable it was,
how unlikely that this frail creature, who could not even lift
his head, could survive in the harsh world. But he would
survive. He would, if I must wrestle the veiled god myself.

I stared into the darkness. I listened like wolves do,
pricked for any danger. I wove again those illusions that
made my island look like savage rocks. But still I feared.
Sometimes men were reckless in their desperation. If they
landed on the rocks anyway, they would hear his screams
and come. What if I had forgotten my tricks and could
not make them drink? I remembered the stories Odysseus
had told me of what soldiers did to children. Astyanax and
all the sons of Troy, smashed and spitted, torn to pieces,
trampled by horses, killed and killed so they would not live
and grow to strength and one day come looking for their
vengeance.

My whole life, I had waited for tragedy to find me. I
never doubted that it would, for I had desires and defiance
and powers more than others thought I deserved, all the

things that draw the thunderstroke. A dozen times grief had
scorched, but its fire had never burned through my skin.
My madness in those days rose from a new certainty: that
at last, I had met the thing the gods could use against me.

I fought on and he grew. That is all I can say. He calmed,
and that calmed me, or maybe it was the opposite. I did not
stare so much, think so often of scalding myself. He smiled
for the first time and began to sleep in his cradle. He went a
whole morning without screaming, and I could work in my
garden. Clever child, I said. You were testing me, weren't
you? He looked up from the grass at the sound of my voice
and smiled again.

His mortality was always with me, constant as a second beating heart. Now that he could sit up, reach and
grasp, all the ordinary objects of my house showed their
hidden teeth. The boiling pots on the fire seemed to
leap for his fingers. The blades slipped from the table a
hairsbreadth from his head. If I set him down, a wasp
would come droning, a scorpion scuttle from some hidden crevice and raise its tail. The sparks from the fire
always seemed to pop in arcs towards his tender flesh.
Each danger I turned aside in time, for I was never more
than a step from him, but it only made me more afraid
to close my eyes, to leave him for an instant. The wood-
pile would topple on him. A wolf who had been gentle
her whole life would snap. I would wake to see a viper
reared over his crib, jaws wide.

It is a sign, I think, of how addled I was with love and
fear and no sleep, that it took me so long to realize: that
stinging insects should not come in battalions, and ten
falling pots in a morning was beyond even my tired clumsiness. To remember how, in the long agony of my labor,

Eileithyia had been kept from me. To wonder if, thwarted, the god that had done it might try again.

I slung Telegonus against me and walked to the pool that lay halfway up the peak. There were frogs in it, silver minnows and water-skimmers. The weeds were thickly tangled. I could not say why it was water that I wanted at that moment. Perhaps some relic of my naiad blood.

I touched my finger to the pool's surface. "Does a god seek to harm my son?"

The pool shivered, and an image of Telegonus formed. He lay wrapped in a wool shroud, gray and lifeless. I started back, gasping, and the vision broke to pieces. For a moment I could do nothing but breathe and press my cheek to Telegonus' head. His faint wisps of hair were worn away at the back with endless fidgeting in his cot.

I put my trembling hand to the water again. "Who is it?"

The water showed only the sky overhead. "Please," I begged. But no answer came, and I felt the panic climbing my throat. I had assumed it was some nymph or river-god who threatened us. Tricks of insects and fire and animals were just at the limits of a lesser divinity's natural power. I had even wondered if it was my mother, in a fit of jealousy that I might bear new children when she could not. But this god had the strength to escape my vision. There were only a handful of such deities in all the world. My father. My grandfather, perhaps. Zeus and a few of the greater Olympians.

I clutched Telegonus against me. Moly could ward off a spell, but not a trident, not a lightning bolt. I would fall to those powers like a stalk of wheat.

I closed my eyes and fought back the strangling fear. I must be clear and clever. I must remember all the tricks that lesser gods have used against greater since the beginning of time. Had not Odysseus once told me a story about Achilles' sea-nymph mother, who had found a way to bargain with Zeus? But he had not said what that way was. And in the end, her son had died.

My breath felt like sawblades in my chest. I must learn who it is, I told myself. That is first. I cannot guard against shadows. Give me something to face and fight.

Back at the house, I made a small fire in the hearth, though we did not need it. The night was warm, summer waxing to autumn, but I wanted the smell of cedar in the air, and the tang of my herbs which I had sprinkled over the flames. I was aware of a tingling on my skin. Any other time I would have taken it for a change in the weather, but now it seemed curdled with malice. My neck bristled. I paced the stone floor, cradling Telegonus against me until at last, exhausted from his wailing, he slept. It was what I had waited for. I laid him in his crib, then drew it close to the fire and set my lions and wolves around it. They could not stop a god, but most divinities are cowards. Claws and teeth might buy me a little time.

I stood before the hearth, my staff in my hand. The air was thick with a listening silence.

"You who would try to kill my child, come forth. Come forth, and speak to my face. Or do you only do your murdering from the shadows?"

The room was utterly still. I heard nothing but Telegonus' breaths and the blood in my veins.

"I need no shadows." The voice sliced the air. "And it is not for such as you to question my purposes."

She struck the room, tall and straight and sudden-white, a talon of lightning in the midnight sky. Her horse-hair helmet brushed the ceiling. Her mirror armor threw off sparks. The spear in her hand was long and thin, its keen edge limned in firelight. She was burning certainty, and before her all the shuffling and stained dross of the world must shrink away. Zeus' bright and favorite child, Athena.

"What I desire will come to pass. There is no mitigation." That voice again, like shearing metal. I had stood in the presence of great gods before: my father and grandfather, Hermes, Apollo. Yet her gaze pierced me as theirs had not. Odysseus had said once she was like a blade honed to a hair's fineness, so delicate you would not even know you had been cut, while beat by beat your blood was emptying on the floor.

She extended one immaculate hand. "Give me the child."

All the warmth in the room had fled. Even the fire popping beside me seemed only a painting on the wall.

"No."

Her eyes were braided silver and stone gray. "You would stand against me?"

The air had thickened. I felt as though I gasped for breath. On her chest shone her famous *aigis*, leather armor fringed with golden threads. It was said to be made from the skin of a Titan that she had flayed and tanned herself. Her flashing eyes promised: just so will I wear you, if you do not submit and beg for mercy. My tongue withered, and I felt myself trembling. But if there was one thing I knew in all the world, it was that there was no mercy among gods. I twisted my skin between my fingers. The sharp pain steadied me.

"I would," I said. "Though it hardly seems a fair battle, you against an unarmed nymph."

"Give him to me willingly, and there need not be a battle. I will make sure it is quick. He will not suffer."

Do not listen to your enemy, Odysseus had once told me. Look at them. It will tell you everything.

I looked. Armed and armored, she was, from head to foot, helmet, spear, *aigis*, greaves. A terrifying vision: the goddess of war, ready for battle. But why had she assembled such a panoply against me, who knew nothing of combat? Unless there was something else she feared, something that made her feel somehow stripped and weak.

Instinct carried me forward, the thousand hours I had spent in my father's halls, and with Odysseus *polymetis*, man of so many wiles.

"Great goddess, all my life I have heard the stories of your power. So I must wonder. You have wanted my child dead for some time, and yet he lives. How can that be?"

She had begun swelling like a snake, but I pressed on.

"I can only think, then, that you are not permitted. That something prevents you. The Fates, for their purposes, do not allow you to kill him outright."

At that word, *Fates*, her eyes flashed. She was a goddess of argument, born from the bright, relentless mind of Zeus. If she was forbidden something, even by the three gray goddesses themselves, she would not simply submit. She would set about parsing the constraint down to its atoms, and try to eke a way through.

"So that is why you have worked as you have. With wasps and falling pots." I regarded her. "How such low means must have galled your warrior spirit."

Her hand glowed white on her spear-shaft. "Nothing is changed. The child must die."

"And so he will, when he is a hundred."

"Tell me, how long do you think your witcheries will stand against me?"

"As long as they need to."

"You are too quick." She took a step towards me. The horse-hair plume hissed against my ceiling. "You have forgotten your place, nymph. I am a daughter of Zeus. Perhaps I cannot strike directly at your son, but the Fates say nothing about what I can do to you."

She set the words in the room precisely as stones in a mosaic. Even among gods, Athena was known for her wrath. Those who defied her were turned to stones and spiders, driven mad, snatched up by whirlwinds, hounded and cursed to the ends of the world. And if I were gone, then Telegonus…

"Yes," she said. Her smile was flat and cold. "You begin to understand your situation."

She lifted her spear from the floor. It did not shine now. It flowed like liquid darkness in her hand. I stepped back against the woven side of the crib, my mind scrambling.

"It is true, you might harm me," I said. "But I have a father too, and a family. They do not take lightly the careless chastising of our blood. They would be angry. They might even be stirred to action."

The spear still hovered off the floor, but she did not heft it. "If there is war, Titan, Olympus will win it."

"If Zeus wanted war, he would have sent his thunderbolt against us long ago. Yet he holds off. What will he think of you destroying his hard-won peace?"

I saw in her eyes the click of counters, stones tallied on this side and that. "Your threats are crude. I had hoped we might discuss this reasonably."

"There can be no reason as long as you seek to murder my child. You are angry with Odysseus, but he does not even know the boy exists. Killing Telegonus will not punish him."

"You presume, witch."

If it were not my son's life at stake, I might have laughed at what I saw in her eyes. For all her cleverness, she had no skill at concealing her emotions. Why would she? Who would dare harm the great Athena for her thoughts? Odysseus had said she was angry with him, but he did not understand the true nature of gods. She was not angry. Her absence was only that old trick Hermes had spoken of: turn your back on a favorite and drive him to despair. Then return in glory, and revel in the groveling you will get.

"If not to hurt Odysseus, why seek my son's death?"

"That knowledge is not for you. I have seen what will come and I tell you that this infant cannot live. If he does, you will be sorry for it all the rest of your days. You are tender to the child and I do not blame you for it. But do not let a mother's doting cloud your sense. Think, daughter of Helios. Is it not wiser to give him to me now, when he is barely set into the world, when his flesh and your affections are still half formed?" Her voice softened. "Imagine how much worse it will be for you in a year, or two, or ten, when your love is full-grown. Better to send him easy to the house of souls now. Better to bear another child and begin to forget with new joys. No mother should have to see her child's death. And yet, if such must come, if there is no other way, still there may be recompense."

"Recompense."

"Of course." Her face shone bright upon me as the forge's heart. "You do not think I ask for sacrifice without offering reward? You will have the favor of Pallas Athena. My goodwill, through eternity. I will set a monument for him upon this isle. In time, I will send another good man to you, to father another son. I will bless the birth, protect the child from all ills. He will be a leader among mortals, feared in battle, wise in counsel, honored by all. He will leave heirs behind him and fulfill your every maternal hope. I will ensure it."

It was the richest prize in all the world, rare as the golden apples of the Hesperides: the sworn friendship of an Olympian. You would have every comfort, every pleasure. You would never fear again.

I looked into that shining gray gaze, her eyes like two hanging jewels, twisting to catch the light. She was smiling, her hand open towards me, as if ready to receive mine. When she had spoken of children, she had nearly crooned, as if to lull her own babe. But Athena had no babe, and she never would. Her only love was reason. And that has never been the same as wisdom.

Children are not sacks of grain, to be substituted one for the other.

"I will pass over the fact that you think me a mare to be bred at your whim. The true mystery is why my son's death is worth so much to you. What will he do that the mighty Athena would pay so dearly to avoid?"

All her softness was gone in an instant. Her hand withdrew, like a door slamming shut. "You set yourself against me then. You with your weeds and your little divinity."

Her power bore down on me, but I had Telegonus, and I would not give him up, not for anything.

"I do," I said.

Her lips curled back, showing the white teeth within. "You cannot watch him all the time. I will take him in the end."

She was gone. But I said it anyway, to that great empty room and my son's dreaming ears: "You do not know what I can do."

CHAPTER NINETEEN

ALL THE REST OF that night I paced, running through Athena's words. My son would grow up to do something she feared, something that touched her deeply. But what? Something that I would be sorry for as well, she had said. I paced, turning it over and over, but I could find no answer. At last I forced myself to set it aside. There was no profit in chasing riddles of the Fates. The point was: she would come and come.

I had boasted that Athena did not know what I could do, but the truth was I did not know either. I could not kill her, and I could not change her. We could not outpace her, and we could not hide. No illusion I cast would cover us from her piercing gaze. Soon Telegonus would walk and run, and how could I keep him safe then? Black terror was rising in my brain. If I did not think of something, the vision in the pool would come to pass, his body ashen and cold in its shroud.

I remember those days only in pieces. My teeth clenched in concentration as I scoured the island, digging up flowers and grinding leaves, searching out every feather and stone and root in the hopes that one of them might help me. They teetered in piles around the house, and the air of the kitchen grew grainy with dust. I chopped and boiled, my eyes wide and staring like an over-ridden horse. I kept Telegonus bound against me while I worked, for I was afraid to put him down. He hated such constraint and screamed, his puffy fists shoving at my chest.

Wherever I walked, I smelled the iron-scorch of Athena's skin. I could not tell if she was taunting me, or if my panic made me imagine it, but it drove me onwards like a goad. In desperation, I tried to remember every story of Olympians brought low that my uncles had told. I thought of calling on my grandmother, the sea-nymphs, my father, throwing myself at their feet. But even if they were disposed to help me, they would not dare to stand against Athena in her wrath. Aeëtes might have dared, but he hated me now. And Pasiphaë? It was not even worth asking.

I do not know what season it was, what time of day. I saw only my hands working ceaselessly before me, my smeared knives, the herbs mashed and crushed on the table, the moly I boiled and boiled again. Telegonus had fallen asleep, head tipped back, the flush of rage still on his cheeks. I paused to breathe and steady myself. My eyelids scratched when I blinked. The walls no longer seemed stone, but soft as cloth, sagging inwards. I had rooted up an idea at last, but I needed something: a token from the house of Hades. The dead have passed where most gods cannot go, and therefore can hold our kind as the quick do not. But there was no way to get such a token. No gods, save those who govern souls, may set foot in the underworld. I spent hours pacing in profitless conjecture: how I might try to suborn an infernal deity to pluck a handful of gray asphodels or scoop some of Styx's waves, or else how I might build a raft and sail it to the underworld's edge, then use Odysseus' trick to lure the ghosts out and catch a bit of their smoke. The thought made me remember the phial Odysseus had filled for me, with blood from his pit. Shades had touched their greedy lips to it, and it might still stink of their breath. I lifted it from its box and held it to the light. The dark liquid swam in its glass. One drop I poured off, and all day I worked with it, distilling, drawing out that weak scent. I added moly to strengthen it, shape it. My heart beat in alternating hope and despair: it will work, it will not.

I waited until Telegonus slept again, for I could not summon the focus I needed while he was fighting against me. Two spells I made that night. One carried the drop of blood and moly; the other had fragments of every part of the island, from its cliffs to its salt flats. I worked in a great frenzy, and when the sun rose I held two stoppered flasks before me.

My chest was heaving with exhaustion, but I would not wait, not another moment. With Telegonus still bound against me, I climbed to the highest peak, a bare strip of rock beneath the hanging sky. I set my feet upon the stone. "Athena would kill my child, and so I defend him," I cried. "Be witness now to the power of Circe, witch of Aiaia."

I poured the blood-draught on the rock. It hissed like molten bronze in water. White smoke billowed into the air, rising, spreading. It massed, forming a great arc over the island, closing us in. A layer of living death. If Athena came, she would be forced to turn aside, like a shark meeting fresh water.

The second spell I cast beneath it. It was an enchantment woven into the island itself, every bird and beast and grain of sand, every leaf and rock and drop of water. I marked them, and all the generations in their bellies, with Telegonus' name. If ever she did break through that smoke, the island would rise up in his defense, the beasts and birds, the branches and rocks, the roots in the earth. Then we would make our stand together.

I stood beneath the sun, waiting for an answer: a sizzling thunderbolt. Athena's gray spear, pinning my heart to the rock. I could hear myself panting a little. The weight of those spells was dragging at my neck like a yoke. They were too great to stand by themselves, and hour after hour I would have to carry them with me, brace them up with my will, and renew them in full each month. Three days it would take me. One to regather all those pieces of the island, beach and grove and meadow, scale and feather and fur. Another day to mix them. A third of utmost concentration to draw out the stink of death from the drops of blood I hoarded. And all the while Telegonus would twist and wail against me, and the spells would grind down upon my shoulders. None of that mattered. I had said I would do anything for him, and now I would prove it and hold up the sky.

I waited all morning, tensed, but no answer came. It was done, I finally realized. We were free. Not just from Athena, but from all of them. The spells hung on me, yet I felt weightless. For the first time, Aiaia was ours alone. Giddily, I knelt and unwrapped my fighting son. I set him down upon the earth, free. "You are safe. We may be happy at last."

What a fool I was. All those days of my fear and his constraint were like a debt that must be paid. He careered across the island, refusing to sit, or even stop for a moment. Athena had been barred, yet there still remained all the ordinary dangers of the island, rocks and cliffs and stinging creatures that I had to pry from his hands. Whenever I tried to reach for him, he would run, darting and defiant, towards some precipice. He seemed angry at the world. The stone he could not throw far enough, his own legs, which did not run fast enough. He wanted to scale the trees like the lions did, in a great leap, and when he could not he would beat at their trunks with his fists.

I would try to take him in my arms, telling him, *Have patience, your strength will come in time.* But he arched away from me screaming, and nothing could console him, for he was not one of those children whom you may wave something shiny at and they will forget. I gave him soothing herbs and possets, even sleeping draughts, but they did nothing. The only thing that calmed him was the sea. The wind that was as restless as he was, the waves filled with their motion. He would stand in the surf, his small hand in mine, and point. The horizon, I named. The open sky. The waves and tides and currents. He would whisper the sounds to himself all the rest of the day, and if I tried to pull him away, show him something else, fruits or flowers, some small spell, he would leap from me, twisting up his face. *No!*

The worst were the days when I had to shape those two spells again. He ran from me whenever I wanted him, but the moment I took up my work, he would drum at the floor with his heels, crying for my attention. Tomorrow I will take you to the sea, I promised. But that was nothing to him, and he would tear apart the house to draw my eye. He was older by then, too big to be slung to my chest, and the disasters he could cause had grown with him. He toppled over a table filled with plates; he climbed up the shelves and smashed my phials. I would set the wolves to watch him, but he was too much for them, and they fled to the garden. I could feel my panic rising. The spell would run out before I could cast it. Athena would arrive in her rage.

I know what I was in those days: unsteady, inconstant,

a badly made bow. Every fault in me his raising laid bare. Every selfishness, every weakness. One day, when the spells were due, he picked up a great glass bowl and broke it in shards on his bare feet. I came running to pluck him away, to sweep and scrub, but he battered at me as if I had taken his dearest friend. At last I had to put him in a bedroom and shut the door between us. He screamed and screamed, and there came a pounding like his head against the wall. I finished my cleaning and tried to work, but my own head was beating at itself by then. I kept thinking that if I let him rage long enough, he must at last wear himself out and sleep. But he only went on, wilder and wilder as the shadows lengthened. The day was passing and the spell not done. It would be easy to say that my hands moved on their own, but that is not how it was. I was angry, burning hot.

I had always sworn to myself that I would not use magic on him. It seemed like something Aeëtes would do, setting my will over his. But in that moment I seized the poppy, sleep-drugs, all the rest, brewed them till they sizzled. I went to the room. He was kicking the pieces of shutter that he had torn from the windows. Come, I said. Drink this.

He drank and went back to his tearing. I did not mind now. It was almost a pleasure to watch. He would learn his lesson. He would understand who his mother was. I spoke the word.

He fell like a toppled stone. His head hit the floor so loudly I gasped. I ran to him. I had thought it would be like sleep, his eyes gently closed. But his whole body was rigid, frozen mid-movement, his fingers curled into claws, his mouth open. His skin was cold beneath my fingers. Medea had said she did not know if those slaves in her father's halls could perceive what happened to them. I knew. Behind his blank eyes, I could feel his confusion and terror.

I cried out in horror, and the spell broke. His body sagged, then he scrambled away, staring wildly back at me like a cornered beast. I wept. My shame was hot as blood. I'm sorry, I told him, again and again. He let me come to him, take him in my arms. Gently, I touched the lump that had risen where he had struck his head. I spoke a word to ease it.

The room was dark by then. Outside, the sun was gone. I held him in my lap as long as I dared, murmuring to him, singing. Then I carried him to the kitchen and gave him dinner. He ate it, clinging to me, and revived. He slid down and began to run again, slamming doors, pulling everything from the shelves that he could reach. I felt a weariness in me so great I thought I would sink into the earth. And every moment that passed, the spell against Athena went undone.

He kept looking at me over his shoulder. As if he were daring me to come at him, to witch him, to hit him, I did not know. Instead I reached up to the highest shelf for the great clay honey jar he was always yearning for. Here, I said. Take it.

He ran to it, rolling it in circles until it broke to pieces. Then he wallowed in the sticky puddles, and raced off, trailing threads for the wolves to lick. And so I finished the spells. It took a long time to bathe him and carry him to bed, but at last he lay beneath the quilts. He held my hand, his small warm fingers curled around mine. Guilt and shame sawed at me. He should hate me, I thought. He should flee. But I was all he had. His breath began to drag, and his limbs slackened. "Why can you not be more peaceful?" I whispered. "Why must it be so hard?"

As if in answer, a vision of my father's halls drifted up: the sterile earth floor, the black gleam of obsidian. The sound of the game pieces moving on their board, and my father's golden legs beside me. I had lain quiet and still, but I remembered the ravening hunger that was in me always: to climb into my father's lap, to rise and run and shout, snatch the draughts from the board and batter them against the walls. To stare at the logs until they burst into flame, to shake him for every secret, as fruits are shaken from a tree. But if I had done even one of those things there would have been no mercy. He would have burnt me down to ash.

The moon lay on my son's forehead. I saw the smudges that water and cloth had not quite scrubbed away. Why should he be peaceful? I never was, nor his father either, when I knew him. The difference was that he was not afraid to be burnt.

In the long days that followed I clutched that thought like a spar that would save me from the waves. And it did help a little. For when he stared at me, furious and defiant, his whole spirit drawn up against me, I could think of it and take one more breath.

A thousand years I had lived, but they did not feel so long as Telegonus' childhood. I had prayed that he would speak early, but then I was sorry for it, since it only gave voice to his storms. No, no, no, he cried, wrenching away from me. And then, a moment later, he would climb over my lap, shouting *Mother* until my ears ached. I am here, I told him, right *here*. Yet it was not close enough. I might walk with him all day, play every game he asked for, but if my attention strayed for even a moment, he would rage and wail, clinging to me. I yearned for my nymphs then, for anyone that I might seize by the arm and say, What is wrong with him? But then in the next moment, I was glad no one could see what I had done to him, letting all those early months of my terror batter at his head. No wonder he stormed.

Come, I coaxed. Let's do something fun. I will show you magic. Shall I change this berry for you? But he flung it away and ran off to the sea again. Every night when he slept, I stood over his bed and told myself: tomorrow I will do better. Sometimes it was even true. Sometimes, we would run laughing down to the beach and he would sit snug in my lap as we watched the waves. His feet still kicked, his hands pulled restlessly at the skin of my arms. Yet his cheek lay on my chest, and I felt the swell and fall of his breath. My patience overflowed. Scream and scream, I thought. I can bear it.

Will it was, every hour, will. Like a spell after all, but one that I had to cast upon myself. He was a great river in flood, and I must have channels ready every moment to safely draw his torrent. I began to tell him stories, easy things of a rabbit who looks for food and finds it, of a baby waiting, whose mother comes. He clamored for more, so I went on. I hoped such gentle tales would soothe his fighting soul, and maybe they did. One day I realized that the moon had come and gone since he had thrown himself to the earth. Another moon passed, and somewhere in those months was the last time he ever screamed. I wish I could remember when it was. No, I wish rather I could have told myself when it would come, so all those hopeless days I could have looked to its horizon.

His mind put forth leaves, thoughts and words that seemed to spring out of the air. Six years old, he was. His brow had cleared, and he would watch me working in the garden, hacking at some root. "Mother," he said, putting his hand to my shoulder, "try cutting here." He took out a little knife he had begun to carry, and the root gave way to him. "See?" he said, gravely. "It is easy."

He still loved the sea. He knew every shell and fish. He made rafts out of logs and floated in the bay. He blew bubbles into the tidal pools and watched the crabs skitter. "Look at this one," he would say, towing me by the hand. "I have never seen a larger, I have never seen a smaller. This is the brightest, this is the blackest. This crab has lost one claw, and here its other is growing larger to take its place. Is that not clever?"

Once again, I wished that someone else were there on the island. Not to commiserate now, but to cherish him with me. I would say, Look, can you believe it? We have come through the rocks and winds. I failed him, yet he is a sweet wonder of this world.

He made a face, for he saw that my eyes were wet. "Mother," he said, "the crab will be fine. I told you, the claw is already growing back. Now come here and look at this one. It has spots like eyes. Can it see from them, do you think?"

At night, he no longer wanted my stories, he made up his own. I think it is where his wildness went, for every tale was filled with outlandish creatures: griffins and leviathans and chimeras who came to feed from his hands, whom he led on adventures or else bested with clever stratagems. Perhaps any child with only his mother for company would have been so imaginative. I cannot say, but his face was rapt as he conjured those visions. He seemed to age with every day, eight and ten and twelve. His gaze grew serious, his limbs tall and strong. He had a habit of tapping one finger on the table as he gave out morals like an old man. He liked best the stories of courage and virtue rewarded. *And that is why you must never, you must always, that is why one should be sure to...*

I loved his certainty, his world that was an easy place of right action divided sharply from wrong, of mistake and consequence, of monsters defeated. It was no world I knew, but I would live in it as long as he would let me.

It was one of those nights, summer, the pigs truffling softly below our window. He was thirteen. I laughed and said, "You have more tales in you than your father."

I saw him hesitate, as if I were a rare bird he feared to put to flight. He had asked about his father before, but I had always said, *Not yet*.

"Go on," I said, and smiled at him. "I will answer you. It is time."

"Who was he?"

"A prince who came to this island. He had a thousand and one tricks in him."

"What did he look like?"

I had thought my memories of Odysseus would taste of salt. But there was a pleasure in conjuring him up. "Dark-haired, dark-eyed, with red in his beard. His hands were large, and his legs short and strong. He was always faster than you expected him to be."

"Why did he leave?"

The question was like an oak seedling, I thought. A simple, green shoot above, but underneath the taproot burrowed, spreading deep. I took a breath.

"When he left, he did not know I carried you. He had a wife at home, and a son as well. But it was more than that. Gods and mortals do not last together happily. He was right to leave when he did."

His face, drawn together in thought. "How old was he?"

"Not far over forty."

I saw him counting. "So not even sixty yet. He still lives?"

It was strange to think of: Odysseus walking on Ithaca's

shore, breathing the air. I had had so little time for dreaming since Telegonus was born. But the image felt solid, wholesome, before me. "I believe he does. He was very strong. In spirit, I mean."

Now that the gates were open he sought all I could remember of Odysseus, his lineage, his kingdom, his wife, his son, his childhood occupations, his honors in the war. The stories were still in me, vivid as when Odysseus had first told them, those thousand wily conspiracies and trials. Yet a strange thing happened when I began to recite them back to Telegonus. I found myself hesitating, omitting, altering. With my son's face before me, their brutalities shone through as they never had before. What I had thought of as adventure now seemed blood-soaked and ugly. Even Odysseus himself seemed changed, callous instead of unflinching. The few times I did leave a story as it was, my son would frown. You did not tell it correctly, he said. My father would never have done such a thing.

You are right, I would say. Your father let that Trojan spy with his weasel-skin cap go, and he returned safely home to his family. Your father always kept his word.

Telegonus would beam. "I knew he was an honorable man. Tell me more of his noble deeds." And so I would spin another lie. Would Odysseus have reproached me for it? I did not know, and I did not care. I would have done worse, much worse, to make my son happy.

From time to time, in those days, I wondered what I would tell Telegonus if he ever asked me for my own stories. How I might polish Aeëtes, Pasiphaë, Scylla, the pigs. In the end, I did not have to try. He never asked.

He began spending long hours away upon the island. When he came back, he would be flushed and spilling over with talk. His limbs were stretching, and I heard the crack in his voice. Tell me more about my father, he said. Where is Ithaca? What is it like? How far from here? And what dangers on the way?

It was autumn, and I was boiling the fruits in syrup for winter. I could have made the trees bloom fresh at any time, but this was something I had come to enjoy, the bubbling sugars, the translucent jewel colors, the storing up of a good season in my jars.

"Mother!" He came shouting into the house. "There is a ship which needs us. They are off our shore, half foundered — they will sink if they do not land!"

It was not the first time he had spotted sailors. They passed often by our isle. But it was the first time he had wanted to help them. I let him pull me out to the cliff. It was true, the ship was tilted over and the hull taking in water.

"See? Just this once, will you drop the spell? I am sure they will be very grateful."

How would you know? I wanted to say. *Often those men in most need hate most to be grateful, and will strike at you just to feel whole again.*

"Please," he said. "What if it is someone like my father?"

"There is no one like your father."

"They will sink, Mother. They will drown! We cannot just stand here and watch, we must do something!"

His face was stricken. His eyes were sheened with tears.

"Please, Mother! I cannot bear to watch them die."

"This once," I said. "Once only."

We could hear their shouts carried on the wind. *Shore, a shore!* They turned their boat, lurching towards us. I made him promise to stay hidden while they climbed the trail up to the house. He was to remain in his room until the

wine was drunk, and to leave again at my slightest signal.
He agreed to all of it, he would have agreed to anything. I
went to the kitchen and brewed my old potion. I felt as if
I stood in two rooms at once. Here I was mixing the herbs
I had mixed a hundred times, my fingers finding their old
shapes. And here was my son, leaping and wild. *Where are
they from, can you tell? What rocks do you think they staved
on? Can we help them fix the hull?*

I do not know how I answered. My blood had gone solid
in my veins. I was trying to remember that trick of command I used to have. *Come in, of course I will help you.
Will you not have more wine?*

Though I expected it, I started when the knock came. I
opened the door and there they were: ragged, hungry, desperate as always. The captain, did he look like a coiled
snake? I could not tell. I felt a sudden, gagging nausea. I
wanted to slam the door shut on them, but it was too late
for that. They had seen me now, and my son was pressed
to the wall, listening to everything. I had warned him that
I might need to use magic on them. He had nodded. *Of
course, Mother, I understand.* But he had no idea. He had
never heard the crack of ribs remaking themselves, the wet
tearing of flesh from its shape.

They sat at my benches. They ate, and the wine went
down their throats. Still, I watched the captain. His eyes
were keen. They lingered on the room, on me. He rose.
"Lady," he said. "Your name? Whom should we honor for
our meal?"

I would have done it then, ripped them from themselves. But Telegonus was already stepping out into the
hall. He wore a cape and a sword at his waist. He stood tall
and straight as a man. He was fifteen.

"You are in the house of the goddess Circe, daughter of

Helios, and her son, called Telegonus. We saw your ship founder and allowed you to come to our island, though usually it is closed to mortals. We will be glad to help you all we can while you are here."

His voice was crackless, firm as seasoned planks. His eyes were dark as his father's, but there were flecks of yellow that shone in them. The men stared. I stared. I thought of Odysseus, separated from Telemachus for years, the shock it must have been to see him suddenly grown.

The captain knelt. "Goddess, great lord. The blessed Fates themselves must have brought us here."

Telegonus gestured for the man to rise. He took the head of the table and served out food from the platters. The men scarcely ate. They were growing towards him like vines to sun, their faces awestruck, competing to tell him their stories. I watched, wondering at where such a gift had hidden in him all this while. But then I had done no magic till I had plants to work upon.

I let him go down to the shore with them, help them with their repairs. I did not worry, or at least, not much. My spell over the island's beasts would protect him, but more than that his own spell would, for those men were like creatures enchanted. He was younger than all of them, but they nodded at every word from his lips. He showed them where the best groves were, what trees they could chop down. He showed them the streams and shade. Three days they stayed while they patched the hole in their ship and fed themselves upon our stores. In all that time, he left them only when they slept. Lord, they called him, when they spoke of him, and solicited his opinion earnestly, as if he were some master carpenter of ninety instead of a boy seeing his first hull. *Lord Telegonus, sir, what do you think, will this do?*

He examined the patch. "Nicely, I think. Well constructed."

They beamed, and when they sailed, they hung off the side, shouting their thanks and prayers. His face stayed bright as long as he could see the ship. Then his joy bled away.

For many years, I confess, I had hoped he might be a witch. I had tried to teach him about my herbs, their names and properties. I used to do small spells in his presence, hoping one might catch his eye. But he never showed even the faintest interest. Now I saw why. Witchcraft transforms the world. He wanted only to join it.

I tried to say something, I do not know what. But he was already turning from me, heading for the woods.

He kept outside all that winter, and all that spring and summer too. From the sun's first light in the sky until its setting, I did not see him. A few times I asked him where he went, and he waved his hand vaguely at the beach. I did not press. He was preoccupied, always running somewhere breathlessly, coming home flushed with burrs all over his tunic. I saw the strength rising in his shoulders, his jaw widening. "That cave down by the beach," he said. "The one where my father kept his ship. Can I have it?"

"Everything here is yours," I said.

"But can it be mine alone? You promise not to go in?"

I remembered how much my young privacies had meant to me. "I promise," I said.

I have wondered since if he used those same charms on me that he had worked on the sailors. For I was like a well-fed cow in those days, placid, unquestioning. Let him go, I told myself. He is happy, he is growing. What harm can find him here?

"Mother," he said. It was just after dawn, the pale light warming the leaves. I was kneeling in the garden, weeding. He was not usually up so early, but it was his birthday. Sixteen, he was.

"I made you honeyed pears," I said.

He held up his hand, showing a half-eaten fruit, shining with juice. "I found them, thank you." He paused. "I have something to show you."

I wiped off the dirt and followed him down the forest path to the cave. Inside was a small boat, near the size Glaucos' had been.

"Whose is this?" I demanded. "Where are they?"

He shook his head. His cheeks were flushed, his eyes bright. "No, Mother, it is mine. I had the idea before the men came but seeing them made it go much faster. They gave me some of their tools and showed me how to make the others. What do you think?"

Now that I looked I could see that its sail was stitched from my sheets, its boards roughly planed, still full of splinters. I was angry, but a wondering pride glowed in me as well. My son had built it alone, with nothing but crude tools and his will.

"It is very trim," I said.

He grinned. "It is, isn't it? He said I should not say anything. But I did not want to keep it from you. I thought — "

He stopped at the look on my face.

"Who said?"

"It is all right, Mother, he means me no harm. He has been helping me. He said he used to visit often. That you are old friends."

Old friends. How had I not seen this danger? I remembered now Telegonus' giddiness when he would come home at night. My nymphs used to come back with that same face. Athena could not cross my spell, no, she had no powers in the underworld. But he walked everywhere. When he was not rolling his dice, he led the spirits to the doors of Hades himself. God of meddling, god of change.

"Hermes is no friend of mine. Tell me everything he said to you. At once."

His face was mottled with embarrassment. "He said he could help me, and he did. He said that it must be sudden. If a scab is to come off, he said, the best way is quickly. It will not even take me half a month, and I will be back by spring. We have tried it in the bay, and it is sound."

His words tumbled out so fast I struggled to parse them. "What do you mean? What will not take you half a month?"

"The journey," he said. "To Ithaca. Hermes says he can lead me around the monsters, so you do not have to fear about that. If I sail at the noon tide, I will make the next island before dark."

I felt speechless, as if he had torn my tongue from my mouth.

He put a hand to my arm. "You do not have to worry. I will be safe. Hermes is my ancestor through my father, he tells me. He would not betray me. Mother, do you hear?" He was peering at me anxiously from beneath his hair.

My blood ran cold to see his greenness. Had I ever been so young?

"He is a god of lies," I said. "Only fools put their faith in him."

He flushed, but a defiance had come into his face. "I know what he is. I do not just rely on him. I have packed my bow. And he has been teaching me a little spear-work besides." He gestured to a stick leaning in the corner, one of my old kitchen knives laced to its end. He must have

seen my horror, for he added, "Not that I will have to use
it. It is just a few days to Ithaca, and then I will be safe with
my father."

He was leaning forward, earnestly. He thought he had
answered all my objections. He was proud of himself,
bright in his new-forged plans. How easily those words tumbled from him, *safe*, *my father*. I felt myself running with
swift, clear rage.

"What makes you think you will be welcome on Ithaca?
All you know of your father is stories. And he already has
a son. How do you think Telemachus will like his bastard
brother appearing?"

He flinched a little at *bastard*, but answered bravely. "I
don't think he would mind. I don't come for his kingdom,
or his inheritance, and so I will explain to him. I will stay
the whole winter, and there will be time for us to know
each other."

"So that is it. It is settled. You and Hermes have the plan,
and now you think all that is needed is for me to wish you
fair wind."

He looked at me, uncertain.

"Tell me," I said. "What does all-knowing Hermes say
about his sister who wants you dead? About the fact that
you will be killed the moment you step away from the island?"

He nearly sighed. "Mother, it was so long ago. Surely
she has forgotten."

"Forgotten?" My voice clawed the cave walls. "Are you
an idiot? Athena does not forget. She will eat you in one
gulp, like an owl takes a stupid mouse."

His face paled, but he pressed on like the valiant heart
he was. "I will take my chances."

"You will not. I forbid it."

He stared at me. I had never forbidden him anything before. "But I must go to Ithaca. I have built the ship. I'm ready."

I stepped towards him. "Let me explain more clearly. If you leave, you will die. So you will not sail. And if you try, I will burn that boat of yours to cinders."

His face was blank with shock. I turned and walked away.

He did not sail that day. I stalked back and forth in my kitchen, and he kept to his woods. It was dusk when he returned to the house. He banged through the trunks, loudly gathered up bedding. He had come only to show me that he would not stay beneath my roof.

When he passed me I said, "You want me to treat you like a man, but you act like a child. You have been protected here your whole life. You do not understand the dangers that wait for you in the world. You cannot simply pretend that Athena does not exist."

He was ready for me, like tinder for the spark. "You are right. I don't know the world. How could I? You don't let me out of your sight."

"Athena stood upon that very hearth and demanded I give you to her so she could kill you."

"I know," he said. "You've told me a hundred times. Yet she has not tried since, has she? I'm alive, aren't I?"

"Because of the spells I cast and carry!" I rose to face him. "Do you know what I have had to do to keep them strong, the hours I have spent fretting over them, testing them to be sure she cannot break through?"

"You like doing that."

"Like it?" The laugh scraped from me. "I like doing my own work, which I have scarcely had time for since you were born!"

"Then go do your spells! Go do them and let me leave! Be honest, you do not even know if Athena is still angry. Have you tried to speak with her? It has been sixteen years!"

He said it as if it were sixteen centuries. He could not imagine the scope of gods, the mercilessness that comes of seeing generations rise and fall around you. He was mortal and young. A slow afternoon felt like a year to him.

I could feel my face kindling, gathering heat. "You think all gods are like me. That you may ignore them as you please, treat them as your servants, that their wishes are only flies to be brushed aside. But they will crush you for pleasure, for spite."

"Fear and the gods, fear and the gods! That is all you talk about. It is all you have ever talked about. Yet a thousand thousand men and women walk this world and live to be old. Some of them are even happy, Mother. They do not just cling to safe harbors with desperate faces. I want to be one of them. I mean to be. Why can't you understand that?"

The air around me had begun to crackle. "You are the one who does not understand. I have said you will not leave, and that is the end of it."

"So that's it then? I just stay here my whole life? Until I die? I never even try to leave?"

"If need be."

"No!" He slammed the table between us. "I will not do it! There is nothing for me here. Even if another ship comes and I beg you to let it land, what then? A few days' respite, then they will leave, and I will still be trapped. If this is life, then I would rather die. I would rather Athena kills me, do you hear? At least then I will have seen one thing in my life that was not this island!"

My vision went white.

"I do not care what you would *rather*. If you are too stupid to save your own life, then I will do it for you. My spells will do it."

For the first time, he faltered. "What do you mean?"

"I mean you would not even know what you missed. You would never think of leaving again."

He took a step backwards. "No. I will not drink your wine. I will not touch anything you give me."

I could taste the venom in my mouth. It was a pleasure to see him frightened at last. "You think that will stop me? You have never understood how strong I am."

His look I will remember all my life. A man who has seen the veil lifted and beholds the true face of the world.

He wrenched open the door and fled into the dark.

I stood there a long time, a bolt-struck tree scorched to its roots. Then I walked down to the shore. The air was cool but the sand still held the day's heat. I thought of all the hours I had carried him there, his skin against mine. I had wanted him to walk freely in the world, unburnt and unafraid, and now I had gotten my wish. He could not conceive of a relentless goddess with her spear aimed at his heart.

I had not told him of his infancy, how angry and difficult it was. I had not told him the stories of the gods' cruelty, of his own father's cruelty. I should have, I thought. For sixteen years, I had been holding up the sky, and he had not noticed. I should have forced him to go with me to pick those plants that saved his life. I should have made him stand over the stove while I spoke the words of power. He should understand all I had carried in silence, all that I had done for his safekeeping.

But then what? He was somewhere in the trees, hiding

from me. So easily those spells had risen in my mind, the ones that would let me cut his desires from him, like paring rot from fruit.

I ground my jaw. I wanted to rage and tear myself and weep. I wanted to curse Hermes for his half-truths and temptations — but Hermes was nothing. I had seen Telegonus' face when he used to look into the sea and whisper, *horizon*.

I closed my eyes. I knew the shore so well, I did not have to see to walk. When he was a child I used to make lists of all the things I would do to keep him safe. It was not much of a game, because the answer was always the same. Anything.

Odysseus had told me a story once about a king who had a wound that could not be healed, not by any doctor, not by any amount of time. He went to an oracle and heard its answer: only the man who had given the wound could fix it, with the same spear he had used to make it. So the king had limped across the world until he found his enemy, who mended him.

I wished Odysseus were there so I could ask him: but how did the king get that man to help him, the one who had struck him so deep?

The answer that came to me was from a different tale. Long ago, in my wide bed, I had asked Odysseus: "What did you do? When you could not make Achilles and Agamemnon listen?"

He'd smiled in the firelight. "That is easy. You make a plan in which they do not."

CHAPTER TWENTY

I FOUND HIM IN the olive grove. The blankets were tangled around him, as if he had fought on against me in his dreams.

"My son," I said. The words were loud in the still air. It was not dawn yet, but I felt it coming, the great rolling wheels of my father's chariot. "Telegonus."

His eyes opened, and his hands flew up, to ward me off. The pain was like a dagger's point.

"I come to say that you may go, and I will help you. But there must be conditions."

Did he know how much those words cost me? I do not think he could. It is youth's gift not to feel its debts. The joy was already washing over him. He threw himself upon me, pressed his face to my neck. I closed my eyes. He smelled like green leaves and running sap. We had breathed only each other for sixteen years.

"Two days' delay," I said. "And three things within them."

He nodded eagerly. "Anything." Now that I had lost, he was pliant. At least he was gracious in victory. I led him to the house and filled his arms with herbs and bottles. Together we carried them clinking down to his ship. There upon his deck I began chopping, grinding, mixing my pastes. He surprised me by watching. Usually he drifted away when I did spells.

"What will it do?"

"It is a protection."

"Against what?"

"Whatever I can think of. Whatever Athena can summon — storms, leviathans, a split hull."

"Leviathans?"

I was glad to see him pale a little.

"This will keep it at bay. If Athena wants to strike at you by sea, she will have to do it herself, directly, and I think she cannot, for she is bound by the Fates. You must keep to the boat, and as soon as you land on Ithaca, go to your father, and ask him to intercede with Athena for you. She is his patron and may listen. Swear to me."

"I will." His face was solemn in the shadows.

I poured those draughts over each rough board, every inch of sail, speaking my charms.

"May I try?" he said.

I gave him what was left of a draught. He drenched a bit of the deck, spoke the words he had heard me say.

He poked at the wood. "Did it work?"

"No," I said.

"How do you know what words to use?"

"I speak what has meaning for me."

His face worked with effort, as if he pushed a boulder up a hill. He stared at the boards and spoke different words, then different words still. The deck was unchanged. He looked at me, accusing. "It is hard."

In spite of everything, I laughed. "Did you not think it was? Listen. When you set out to build this ship, you didn't lift an axe once and expect it to be finished. It was work, day after day of it. Witchcraft is the same. I have labored for centuries and still I have not mastered it."

"But it is more than that," he said. "It is also that I am not a witch like you."

It was my father I thought of. All those years ago when he had turned the log in our hearth to ash, and said, *And that is the least of my powers.*

"It is likely you are not a witch," I said. "But you are something else. Something you have not found yet. And that is why you go."

His smile reminded me of Ariadne's, warm as summer grass. "Yes," he said.

I led him to a shaded part of the beach. While he ate the last of the pears, I marked out his route with stones, tracing the stops and dangers. He would not go past Scylla. There were other ways to Ithaca. That Odysseus had not been able to take them had been a piece of Poseidon's vengeance.

"If Hermes helps you, that is well, but you must never depend on him. Anything he says is written on the wind. And always, you must be careful of Athena. She may come to you in other forms. A beautiful maiden, perhaps. You must not be taken in, not by any temptations she would offer."

"Mother." His face was red. "I'm looking for my father. That's all I think of."

I said no more. We were gentler with each other in those days than we had been, even before our fight. In the evenings, we sat together at the hearth. He had a foot stuck under one of the lions. It was only autumn, but the nights were cool already. I served his favorite meal, fish stuffed with roasted herbs and cheeses. He ate and let me lecture him. "Penelope," I said. "Show her every honor. Kneel before her, offer her praises and gifts — I will give you suitable ones. She is reasonable, but no woman is happy with her husband's by-blow at her feet.

"And Telemachus. Be wary of him above all. He is the one with the most to lose from you. Many bastards have become kings in their day, and he will know it. Do not trust him. Do not turn your back on him. He will be clever and quick, trained by your father himself."

"I am good with a bow."

"Against oak boles and pheasants. You are not a warrior."

He took a breath. "Anyway, whatever he tries, your powers will guard me."

I stared at him in horror. "Do not be a fool. I have no powers that can serve you away from this place. To rely on that is death."

He touched my arm. "Mother, I only mean that he is a mortal. I am half your blood and have the tricks that come with that."

What tricks? I wanted to shake him. A little glamour? A way of charming mortals? His face, so full of its bold hopes, made me feel old. His youth had swelled in him, ripening. The dark curls hung into his eyes, and his voice had deepened. Girls and boys would sigh over him, but all I saw were the thousand soft places of his body where his life might be ended. The bareness of his neck looked obscene in the firelight.

He leaned his head against mine. "I will be fine, I promise you."

You cannot make that promise, I wanted to shout. You know nothing. But whose fault was that? I had kept the face of the world veiled from him. I had painted his history in bright, bold colors, and he had fallen in love with my art. And now it was too late to go back and change it. If I was so old, I should be wise. I should know better than to howl when the bird was already flown.

Three things, I had told him we must do. But the last was for me alone. He did not question me about it. Some spell, he thought. Some herb she wants to grub up. I waited until he went to bed, then I walked by starlight to the ocean's edge.

The waves slid across my feet, twisted at the hem of my dress. I was near the cave where Telegonus' boat waited. In a few hours he would board it, heave up the square rock anchor, unfurl the sail with its ragged stitches. He was a sweet boy and would wave to me as long as he knew I could see. Then he would turn, straining his eyes for the small, rocky island that lay at the end of his hopes.

I was remembering my grandfather's halls, the black currents of Oceanos, that great river that girdles all the earth. If a god had naiad blood, they could slip inside its waves and be borne onwards through tunnels of rock, through a thousand tributaries until they were brought to the place where its stream ran beneath the very bottom of the sea itself.

We used to go there, Aeëtes and I. Where the two waters met they did not mingle, but made a sort of membrane, viscous as a jellyfish. Through it, you could watch the glimmers of phosphorescence in the ocean's dark, and if you pressed your hand to it, you could feel the deep water on the other side, shockingly cold. Our fingers would come back tingling and tasting of salt.

"Behold," Aeëtes had said.

He pointed to something moving in that endless murk. A pale gray shadow gliding forward, huge as a ship. It bore down on us, ghostly wings silent in the black. The only sound was the scrape of its spine tail, dragging on the sand floor.

Trygon, my brother named it. The greatest of its kind, a god itself. Father Ouranos, maker of the world, was said to have placed it there for safety, for the poison in the creature's tail was the most potent in the universe. A single touch would kill a mortal instantly, condemn a great god to an eternity of torment. And a lesser god? What would it do to us?

We stared at its eerie, alien face, its flat slashing mouth. We watched its white-gilled stomach pass over us. Aeëtes' eyes had been wide and bright. "Think of the weapon it would make."

I was about to break my exile, I knew it. It was why I had waited for night and the drifting clouds across my aunt's eyes. If I succeeded, I would return by morning, before my absence was noticed. And if I did not, well. I would likely be past punishments.

I stepped into the waves. They rose over my legs, my belly. They rose over my face. I did not have to weight myself with rocks as a mortal would have, fighting against my own buoyancy. I walked steadily down the ocean's shelves. Above me the tides kept up their relentless motion, but I was too deep to feel them. My eyes lit the way. The sand stirred around me, and a flounder darted from my feet. No other creatures came near. They could smell my naiad blood, or perhaps the lingering poisons on my hands from so many years of witcheries. I wondered if I should have tried to speak to the sea-nymphs, seek their aid. But I did not think they would like what I had come to do.

Deeper I went, falling into the fathoms of blackness. That water was not my element and it knew it. The chill dug at my bones, the salt scoured my face. The ocean's weight piled like mountains on my shoulders. But endurance had always been my virtue and I kept on. In the distance, I glimpsed the floating hulks of whales and giant squids. I gripped my knife, its edge sharp as the bronze could hold, but they too stayed away.

At last, I landed upon the sea's lowest floor. The sand was so cold it burned my feet. All was silent there, the water utterly still. The only light came from drifting strands of luminescence. He was wise, this god. To make his visitors travel to such a hostile place, where nothing lived but him.

I cried out: "Great lord of the deep, I am come from the world to challenge you."

I heard no sound. Around me stretched the blind expanse of salt. Then the darkness parted, and he came. Huge he was, white and gray, burned onto the depths like an afterimage of the sun. His silent wings rippled, rills of current flowing off their tips. His eyes were thin and slitted like a cat's, his mouth a bloodless slash. I stared. When I had stepped into the water, I had told myself that this would be only another Minotaur to wrestle, another Olympian I might outwit. But now, with his ghastly immensity before me, I quailed. This creature was older than all the lands of the world, old as the first drop of salt. Even my father would be like a child before him. You could no more stand against such a thing than stem the sea. Cold terror sluiced through me. My whole life I had feared a great horror was coming for me. I did not have to wait anymore. It was here.

For what purpose do you challenge me?

All the great gods have the power to speak in thoughts, but hearing that creature in my mind turned my belly to water.

"I come to win your poison tail."

And why would you desire such strength?

"Athena, daughter of Zeus, seeks my son's life. My power cannot protect him, but yours can."

His unblinking eyes rested on mine. *I know who you are, daughter of the sun. All that the sea touches comes to me at last in the depths. I have tasted you. I have tasted all your family. Your brother came once also seeking my power. He went away empty-handed, like all the rest. I am not such a one as you may fight.*

The despair rolled through me, for I knew he spoke truth. All the monsters of the depths were covered in scars from battles with their brother leviathans. Not him. He was smooth all over, for none dared to cross his ancient power. Even Aeëtes had recognized his limit.

"Still," I said, "I must try. For my son."

It is impossible.

The words were flat as the rest of him. Moment by moment, I could feel my will leaching from me, bled away by the relentless chill of those waves and his unblinking gaze. I forced myself to speak.

"I cannot accept that," I said. "My son must live."

There is no must to the life of a mortal, except death.

"If I cannot challenge you, perhaps I can give you something in exchange. Some gift. Perform a task."

The slit of his mouth opened in silent laughter. *What could you have that I want?*

Nothing, I knew it. He regarded me with his pale cat eyes.

My law is as it has ever been. If you would take my tail you must first submit to its poison. That is the price. Eternal pain in exchange for a few more mortal years for your son. Is it worth the cost?

I thought of childbirth, which had nearly ended me. I thought of it going on and on with no cure, no salve, no relief.

"You offered the same to my brother?"

The offer stands for all. He refused. They always do.

It gave me a sort of strength to know it. "What other conditions?"

When you have no more need of its power, cast it into the waves, so it may return to me.

"That is all? You swear it?"

You would seek to bind me, child?

"I would know you will honor your bargain."

I will honor it.

The currents moved around us. If I did this thing, Telegonus would live. That was all that mattered. "I am ready," I said. "Strike."

No. You must put your hand to the venom yourself.

The water sucked at me. The darkness shriveled my courage. The sand was not smooth but jumbled with pieces of bone. All that died in the sea came to rest there at last. My skin rose, prickling and prickling, as if it would tear away and leave me. There was no mercy among the gods, I had known it all my life. I made myself walk forward. Something caught at my foot. A rib cage. I pulled free. If I stopped, I would never move again.

I came to the seam where his tail joined gray skin. The flesh above looked unwholesomely soft, like something rotted. The spine rasped faintly against the ocean floor. Up close I could see its sawtooth edge, and I smelled its power, thick and gagging-sweet. Would I be able to climb out of the deep again, once the venom was in me? Or would I only lie there, clutching the tail, while my son died in the world above?

Do not draw it out, I told myself. But I could not move

another inch. My body, with its simple good sense, balked at self-destruction. My legs tensed to flee, to scramble back to the safety of the dry world. Just as Aeëtes had before me, and all the others who had come for Trygon's power.

Around me was murk and dark currents. I set Telegonus' bright face before me. I reached.

My hand passed through empty water, touching nothing. The creature was floating in front of me again, its flat gaze on mine.

It is finished.

My mind was black as that water. It was as if time had skipped. "I do not understand."

You would have touched the poison. That is enough.

I felt as though I were mad. "How can this be?"

I am old as the world, and make the conditions that please me. You are the first to meet them.

He rose from the sand. The beat of his wing brushed my hair, and when he stopped, the seam where his tail met his body was before me again.

Cut. Begin in the flesh above, else the venom will leak.

His voice was calm, as if he told me to slice a fruit. I felt dizzied, still reeling. I looked at that skin, unmarked and delicate as the inside of a wrist. I could no more imagine cutting it than an infant's throat.

"You cannot allow this," I said. "It must be a trick. I could blight the world with such power. I could threaten Zeus."

The world you speak of is nothing to me. You have won, now take the prize. Cut.

His voice was neither harsh nor gentle, yet I felt it like a lash. The water pressed upon me, vast depths stretching out into their endless night. His soft flesh waited before me, smooth and gray. And still I did not move.

You were ready to fight me to have it. Not if I am willing?

My stomach churned against itself. "Please. Do not make me do this."

Make you? Child, you have come to me.

I could not feel the knife handle in my hand. I could not feel anything. My son seemed distant as the sky. I lifted the blade, touched its tip to the creature's skin. It tore as flowers tear, ragged and easy. The golden ichor welled up, drifting over my hands. I remember what I thought: surely, I am condemned for this. I can craft all the spells I want, all the magic spears. Yet I will spend the rest of my days watching this creature bleed.

The last shred of skin parted. The tail came free in my hand. It was nearly weightless, and up close there was a quality to it almost like iridescence. "Thank you," I said, but my voice was air.

I felt the currents move. The grains of sand whispered against each other. His wings were lifting. The darkness around us shimmered with clouds of his gilded blood. Beneath my feet were the bones of a thousand years. I thought: I cannot bear this world a moment longer.

Then, child, make another.

He glided off into the dark, trailing a ribbon of gold behind him.

It was a long way back up with that death in my hand. I saw no creature, not even in the distance. They had disliked me before; now they fled. When I emerged onto the beach it was nearly dawn and there was no time to rest. I went to the cave and found the old stick Telegonus had been using as a spear. Still trembling a little, my hands unwound the cord that bound the knife to its end. I stood a moment looking at its crooked length, wondering if I should find a new haft.

But this was what he had practiced with, and I thought it safer to keep it as he was used to, crooks and all.

I held the spine gently by its base. It had filmed over with a clear fluid. I bound it to the stick's end with twine and magic, then fitted over it a sheath of leather, enchanted with moly, to keep the poison at bay.

He was sleeping, his face smooth, his cheeks faintly flushed. I stood watching him until he woke. He started up, then squinted. "What is that?"

"Protection. Do not touch anything but the shaft. A scratch is death to men and torment to gods. Always keep it sheathed. It is only for Athena, or utmost danger. It must return to me after."

He was fearless, he had always been. Without hesitation, he reached and took the haft against his palm. "This is lighter than bronze. What is it?"

"The tail of Trygon."

The stories of monsters had always been his favorite. He stared at me. "Trygon?" His voice was filled with wonder. "You took his tail from him?"

"No," I said. "He gave it to me, for a price." I thought of that gold blood, staining the ocean depths. "Carry it now, and live."

He knelt before me, his eyes on the ground. "Mother," he began. "Goddess — "

I put my fingers to his mouth. "No." I drew him up. He was as tall as I was. "Do not start now. It does not suit you, nor me either."

He smiled at me. We sat together at the table, eating the breakfast I had made, then we readied the ship, loading it with stores and guest-gifts, dragging it to the water's edge. His face grew brighter by the minute, his feet skimmed the earth. He let me embrace him a last time.

"I will give Odysseus your greetings," he said. "I will bring you back so many stories, Mother, you will not believe them all. I will get you so many presents, you won't be able to see the deck."

I nodded. I touched my fingers to his face, and he sailed away, waving indeed, until he vanished from my sight.

CHAPTER TWENTY-ONE

THE WINTER STORMS CAME early that year. It rained in stinging drops that scarcely seemed to wet the ground. A stripping wind followed, tearing the leaves from the trees in a day.

I had not been alone on my island in…I could not count. A century? Two? I had told myself that when he was away I would do all the things I had set aside for sixteen years. I would work at my spells from dawn until dusk, dig up roots and forget to eat, harvest the withy stems and weave baskets till they piled to the ceiling. It would be peaceful, the days drifting by. A time of rest.

Instead, I paced the shore, gazing out, as if I could make my eyes stretch all the way to Ithaca. I counted the moments, measuring each one against his journey. He would be stopping for fresh water now. Now he would be sighting the island. He would have made his way to the palace and knelt. Odysseus would — what? I had not told him I was pregnant before he left. I had told him so little. What would he make of a child come from us?

It will be well, I assured myself. He is a boy to be proud of. Odysseus would see his qualities clearly, just as he had

picked out Daedalus' loom. He would take him into his
confidence and teach him all those arts of mortal men,
swordplay, archery, hunting, speaking in council. Telegonus would sit at feasts and charm the Ithacans while his
father looked on proudly. Even Penelope would be won
over, and Telemachus. Perhaps he might find a place in
their court, going back and forth between us, and so make
a good life.

And what else, Circe? Will they ride griffins and all become immortal?

The air smelled of frost, and one or two flakes trickled
from the sky. A thousand thousand times, I had crossed
Aiaia's slopes. The poplars, black and white, lacing their
bare arms. The cornels and apple trees with fallen fruits
still shriveling on the ground. The fennel tall as my waist,
the sea rocks white with drying salt. Overhead, the skimming cormorants called to the waves. Mortals like to name
such natural wonders changeless, eternal, but the island
was always changing, that was the truth, flowing endlessly
through its generations. Three hundred years and more
had passed since I had come. The oak that creaked over
my head I had known as a sapling. The beach ebbed and
flowed, its curves changing with every winter season. Even
the cliffs were different, carved by the rain and wind, by the
claws of countless scrabbling lizards, by the seeds that stuck
and sprouted in their cracks. Everything was united by the
steady rise and fall of nature's breath. Everything except for
me.

For sixteen years, I had pushed the thought aside. Telegonus made it easy, his wild babyhood filled with Athena's
threats, then the tantrums, his blooming youth and all the
messy details of life that he trailed behind him every day:
the tunics that must be washed, the meals served, the sheets

changed. But now that he was gone, I could feel the truth lifting its head. Even if Telegonus survived Athena, even if he made it all the way to Ithaca and back, still I would lose him. To shipwreck or to sickness, to raids or wars. The best that I could hope for would be to watch his body fail, limb by limb. To see his shoulders droop, his legs tremble, his belly sink into itself. And at the last, I would have to stand over his white-haired corpse and watch it fed to the flames. The hills and trees before me, the worms and lions, stones and tender buds, Daedalus' loom, all wavered as if they were a fraying dream. Beneath them was the place I truly dwelt, a cold eternity of endless grief.

One of my wolves had begun howling. "Quiet," I said. But she kept it up, her voice rattling off the walls, grating at my ears. I had fallen asleep before the fire, my head on the hearthstones. I sat up, bleary, skin printed with the weave of my blanket. Through the windows streamed winter light, harsh and pale. It darted into my eyes and left shadows knee-deep on the ground. I wanted to sleep again. But she whined and howled, and at last I made myself get up. I went to the door and yanked it open. There!

The wolf shoved past me and went racing across the clearing. I watched her go. Arcturos, we called her. Most of the animals did not have names, but she had been Telegonus' favorite. She angled upwards, to the cliff that overlooked the shore. I left the door hanging and went after. I had not put on a cloak, and the rising storm-winds buffeted me as I climbed the peak to where Arcturos stood. The seas were at their winter worst, dragging and gusting, white-topped, savage. Only utmost necessity would take a sailor out. I stared, sure that I was wrong. But there it was: a ship. Telegonus'.

I ran back down through the trees and the bare thorn thickets. Terror and joy jostled together in my throat. He is back. He is back too soon. There must have been some disaster. He is dead. He is changed.

He collided with me among the laurels. I seized him, pulled him into my arms, pressing my face to his shoulder. He smelled of salt and felt broader than before. I clung to him, nerveless in my relief.

"You are back already."

He did not answer. I lifted my head and took in his face. It was haggard, bruised and unslept. Thick with misery. I felt alarm flash through me. "What is it? What is the matter?"

"Mother. I have to tell you."

He sounded as if he were choking. Arcturos pressed to his knee, but he did not touch her. All his body was cold and stiff. Mine had gone cold with it.

"Tell me," I said.

But he was at a loss. He had spun so many stories in his life, but this one stuck in him, like ore to its rock. I took his hand. "Whatever it is, I will help."

"No!" He jerked away from me. "Do not say that! You must let me speak."

His face was gray, as if he had swallowed poison. The winds still blew, twisting at our clothes. I felt nothing but those bare inches between us.

"He was gone when I arrived. My father." He swallowed. "I went to the palace and they said it was some hunting trip. I did not stay there. I stayed on the boat as you told me to."

I nodded. I was afraid he would break if I said a word.

"In the evenings I would walk the beach a little. I took the spear always. I did not like to leave it in the boat. I did not want — "

A spasm passed over his face.

"It was sunset when the boat came driving in. A small craft, like mine, but piled with treasures. They flashed as the boat rocked in the waves. Armor, I think, and some weapons, bowls. Its captain threw down the anchor and jumped from the prow."

He met my eyes.

"I knew. Even from that distance. He was shorter than I had thought he would be. His shoulders were broad as a bear's. His hair was all gray. He could have been any sailor. I cannot say how I knew. It was as if...as if all this while, my eyes had been waiting for just that shape."

I knew the feeling. It is how I had felt first looking down at him in my arms.

"I called out to him, but he was already moving towards me. I knelt. I thought..."

His fist was pressing against his chest, as if he could press it through the skin. He mastered himself.

"I thought he knew me too. But he was shouting. He said I could not steal from him and raid his lands. He would teach me a lesson."

I could imagine Telegonus' shock. He who had never been accused of anything in his life.

"He was running towards me. I said that he misunderstood. I had the permission of his son, the prince. It only made him angrier. I am ruler here, he said."

The winds were scouring us, and his skin was rough with gooseflesh. I tried to put my arms around him, but I might as well have embraced an oak.

"He stood over me. His face was lined and salt-stained. There was a bandage on his arm, with the blood soaking through. He wore a knife at his belt."

His eyes were distant, as if he knelt on that beach again.

I remembered those scarred arms of Odysseus', marked from a hundred such shallow cuts. He liked fighting at close quarters. Taking blows on your arms, he said, was better than taking them in your guts. His smile in the dark of my room. *Those heroes. You should see the look on their faces when I run straight for them.*

"He told me to put down my spear. I told him I could not, but he just kept shouting that I must set it down, set it down. Then he grabbed for me."

The scene bloomed in my mind: Odysseus with his bear shoulders, his corded legs, lunging at my son whose beard was not yet grown. All those stories I had hidden from him leapt into my mind. Of Odysseus beating the mutinous Thersites into unconsciousness. Of all the times contrary Eurylochos bore black eyes and a lumpen nose. Odysseus had endless patience for Agamemnon's caprice, but with those beneath him he could be harsh as winter storms. It made him weary, all the ignorance in the world. So many stubborn wills that must be harnessed again and again to his purpose, so many foolish hearts that had to be led daily away from their hopes to his. No mouth could carry all that persuasion. There must be shortcuts, and so he found them. It might even have been a pleasure of sorts, to squash some little complaining soul who dared to stand in the way of the Best of the Greeks.

And what would the Best of the Greeks have seen, looking at my son? A sweet temper, without fear. A young man who had never bent to another's will in his life.

I felt like an overdrawn rope, unbearably tight. "What happened?"

"I ran. For the palace. They could tell him I meant no harm. But he was so fast, Mother."

Odysseus' short legs were deceptive. His speed was sec-

ond only to Achilles'. At Troy, he had won all the footraces.
At wrestling once he had tripped up Ajax.

"He grabbed the spear and yanked me back. The leather
sheath flew off. I was afraid to let go. I was afraid that..."

Telegonus stood before me living, but I felt the belated
wash of panic. How close it had been. If the spear had
twisted in his grip, had grazed him...

And then I knew. I knew then. His face like a burnt-out
field. His voice, cracked with grief.

"I shouted that he must be careful. I told him, Mother.
I said, don't let it touch you. But he wrenched it away
from me. It was just the barest scratch. The tip against his
cheek."

Trygon's tail. The death I had put into his hand.

"His face just...stopped. He fell. I tried to wipe the poison away, but there was not even a wound. I will take you
to my mother, I said, and she will help. His lips were white.
I held him. I am your son, Telegonus, born from the goddess Circe. He heard. I think he heard. He looked at me
before...he was gone."

My mouth was empty. All was coming clear at last.
Athena's armored desperation, her stiff face saying we
would be sorry if Telegonus lived. She feared he would hurt
someone that she loved. And who did Athena love most?

I pressed my hand to my mouth. "Odysseus."

He shrank from the word like a curse. "I tried to warn
him. I tried — " He choked off.

The man I had lain with so many nights, dead from the
weapon I had sent, dead in my son's arms. The Fates were
laughing at me, at Athena, at all of us. It was their favorite
bitter joke: those who fight against prophecy only draw it
more tightly around their throats. The shining snare had
closed, and my poor son, who had never harmed any man,

was caught. He had sailed home all those empty hours with this crushing guilt on his heart.

My hands were numb, but I made them move. I took him by the shoulders. "Listen," I said. "Listen to me. You cannot blame yourself. It was fated long ago, fated a hundred different ways. Odysseus told me once he was destined to be killed by the sea. I thought it meant shipwreck, I did not even consider anything else. I was blind."

"You should have let Athena kill me." His shoulders were fallen, his voice dull.

"No!" I shook him, as if I could throw off that evil thought. "I never would have. Never. Even if I knew then. Are you listening to me?" The desperation scraped in my voice. "You know the stories. Oedipus, Paris. Their parents tried to murder them, yet still they lived to bear their fates. This was always the path you walked. You must take comfort in that."

"Comfort?" He looked up. "He is dead, Mother. My father is dead."

My old mistake, running so quickly to help him that I did not stop to think. "Oh, son," I said. "It is agony. I feel it too."

He wept. My shoulder grew wet against his face. Beneath the bare branches we grieved together, for the man I had known, and the man he had not. Odysseus' wide, plowman's hands. His dry voice, drawing with precision the follies of gods and mortals. His eyes which saw everything and gave away so little. All perished. We had not been easy, but we had been good to each other. He had trusted me, and I him, when there was no one else. He was half of my son.

After a little time, he drew back. His tears had slowed, though I knew they would come again.

"I had hoped..." He trailed off, but the rest was clear. What do children always hope? To make their parents shine with pride. I knew how painful the death of that hope could be.

I put my hand to his cheek. "The shades in the underworld learn the deeds of the living. He will not hold a grudge. He will hear of you. He will be proud."

Around us, the trees shook. The wind had changed directions. My uncle Boreas, breathing his chill over the world.

"The underworld," he said. "I did not think of that. He will be there. When I die, I will be able to see him. I will be able to beg forgiveness then. We will have all the rest of time together. Will we not?"

His voice was vivid with hope. I saw the picture of it in his eyes: the great captain walking to him across the fields of asphodel. He would kneel on smoky knees, and Odysseus would gesture him up. They would dwell side by side in the house of the dead. Side by side, where I could never go.

The grief of it was climbing my throat, threatening to swallow me. But I would have touched crippling poison for him. Could I not say those simple words, to give him a crumb of comfort?

"So you will," I said.

His chest heaved, but he was calming. He rubbed the stains from his cheeks. "You understand why I had to bring them. I could not leave them, after what I did. Not when they asked to come. They are so weary, and mourning too."

I was weary myself, overwatched, buffeted by wave upon wave. "Who?"

"The queen," he said. "And Telemachus. They are waiting in the boat."

The branches tilted around me. "You brought them here?"

He blinked at the sharpness of my voice. "Of course. They asked me to. There was nothing left for them on Ithaca."

"Nothing left? Telemachus is king now, and Penelope dowager queen. Why would they leave?"

He was frowning. "That is what they said. They said they needed help. How could I question them?"

"How could you not?" My pulse was beating in my throat. I heard Odysseus as if he stood beside me. *My son will hunt down those men who laid me low. He will say, "You dared to spill the blood of Odysseus, and now yours is spilled in turn."*

"Telemachus is sworn to kill you!"

He stared at me. All the stories he had heard of avenging sons, and it was still a surprise to him. "No," he said, slowly. "If he wanted to, he could have done it on the way."

"That is proof of nothing," I said. My voice was jagged. "His father had a thousand wiles, and the first of them was to pretend friendship. Perhaps he means to try to harm us both. Perhaps he wants me to watch you fall."

A moment ago we had held each other. But now he stepped back.

"That is my brother you speak of," he said.

That word, *brother*, on his lips. I thought of Ariadne reaching out her hands to the Minotaur, and the scar on her neck.

"I have brothers too," I said. "Do you know what they would do if I were in their power?"

We stood on his father's tomb, yet still we fought that same old fight. Gods and fear, gods and fear.

"He is the only blood of my father's left in the world. I will not turn him away." His breaths were harsh upon the air. "I cannot undo what I have done, but at least I can do this. If you will not have us, I will go. I will take them somewhere else."

He would do it, I had no doubt. Take them far away. I felt that old rage rising in me, the one that swore it would burn down the world before I let any harm come to him. With it, I had faced Athena and held up the sky. I had walked into the lightless deeps. There was a pleasure to it, that great hot rush through me. My mind leapt with images of destruction: the earth sent spiraling into darkness, islands drowned in the sea, my enemies transformed and crawling at my feet. But now when I sought those fantasies, my son's face would not let them take root. If I burned down the world, he would burn with it.

I breathed, letting the salt air fill me. I did not need such powers, not yet. Penelope and Telemachus might be clever, but they were not Athena, and I had held her off for sixteen years. They overreached if they thought to harm him here. The spells were still in place that protected him on the island. His wolf never left his side. My lions watched from their rocks. And here I stood, his witch mother.

"Come then," I said. "Let us show them Aiaia."

They waited on the deck. Behind them, the pale circle of sun glowed against the cold sky, casting their faces in shadow. I wondered if they had planned that. Odysseus had told me once that half of a duel is maneuvering around the sun, trying to get the light to stab at your enemy's eyes. But I was the blood of Helios, and no light could blind me. I saw them clear. Penelope and Telemachus. What would they do, I wondered, half-giddy. Kneel? What is the proper greeting for the goddess who bore a child with your husband? And if that child then brings about his death?

Penelope inclined her head. "You honor us, goddess. We thank you for your shelter." Her voice was smooth as cream, her face calm as still water. Very well, I thought. That is how we will do it. I know the tune.

"You are my honored guest," I said. "Be welcome here."

Telemachus wore a knife at his waist. It was the kind men used for gutting animals. I felt my pulse leap. Clever. A sword, a spear, these are articles of war. But an old hunting blade, with its grip unraveling, passes without suspicion.

"And you, Telemachus," I said.

His head jerked a little at his name. I thought he would have looked like my son, brimming with youth and flashing grace. But he was narrow, his face serious. Thirty years, he would have been. He looked older.

He said, "Has your son told you of my father's death?"

My father. The words hung in the air like a challenge. His boldness surprised me. I had not expected it from such a look.

"He has," I said. "I grieve for it. Your father was a man about whom songs are made."

A stiffening across Telemachus' face. Anger, I thought, that I would dare to speak his father's epitaph. Good. I wanted him angry. He would make mistakes that way.

"Come," I said.

The wolves flowed, silent and gray, around us. I strode ahead. A breathing space, I wanted, before they occupied my house and hearth. A moment to plan. Telegonus was carrying the bags, he had insisted. They had not brought much, scarcely the wardrobe of a royal family, but then, Ithaca was not Knossos. I could hear Telegonus behind me, pointing out the treacherous places, the slippery roots and rocks. His guilt was thick in the air as winter mists. At least their presence seemed to distract him, pull him out of despair. He had touched my arm at the beach, whispering, *She is very weak, I think she has not been eating. You see how thin she is? You should keep the animals back. And simple food. Can you make broth?*

I felt as if I were untethered from the earth. Odysseus was gone, and Penelope was here, and I must make her broth. After all those times I had spoken her name, at last she was summoned. Vengeance, I thought. It must be. What other purpose would bring them?

They reached my door. Our words were cream still, *come in, thank you, will you eat, you are too kind.* I served the meal: broth indeed, platters of cheese and bread, wine. Telegonus heaped their plates, kept an eye on their cups. His face was still taut with that guilty attendance. My boy who had presided so skillfully over a boatload of sailors now hovered, watching like a dog, hoping for any morsel of forgiveness. It was dark by then, the tapers lit. The flames shook with our breaths. "Lady Penelope," he said, "do you see that loom I told you of? I am sorry you had to leave yours behind, but you may use this one any time you like. If my mother agrees."

Under other circumstances, I would have laughed. It was an old saying: weaving at another woman's loom is like lying with her husband. I watched to see if Penelope would flinch.

"I am glad to see such a wonder. Odysseus told me of it often."

Odysseus. The name naked in the room. I would not quail if she did not.

"Then perhaps," I said, "Odysseus told you also that Daedalus himself made it? I have never been a weaver wor-

thy of such a gift, but you are famed for your skill. I hope
you will try it."

"You are too kind," she said. "I'm afraid whatever you
have heard is much exaggerated."

And so it went. There were no tears, no recriminations,
and Telemachus did not lunge across the table. I watched
his knife, but he wore it like he did not know it was there.
He did not speak, and his mother spoke only rarely. My son
labored on, filling up the silence, but with every moment,
I saw his grief rising. He grew dull-eyed. A faint convulsive
tremor had begun passing over him.

"You are overtaxed," I said. "I will take you to your
beds."

It was not a question. They rose, Telegonus swaying
a little. I showed Penelope and Telemachus their rooms,
brought them water to wash with and saw their doors shut.
I followed my son and sat beside him on the bed.

"I can give you a draught to sleep," I said.

He shook his head. "I will sleep."

In his despair and fatigue, he was pliant. He let me
hold his hand and draw his head down onto my shoulder. I
could not help finding a little pleasure in it, he so rarely allowed me such closeness. I stroked his hair, a shade lighter
than his father's. I felt the shiver run through him again.
"Sleep," I murmured, but he already did. I lowered him
gently onto the pillow, pulling up the blanket and spinning
a spell over the room to dull noise, to douse light. Arcturos
panted at the bed's end.

"Where are the rest of your fellows?" I said to her. "I
would have them here too."

She looked at me with pale eyes. *I am enough.*

I closed the door behind me and walked through the
night shadows of my house. I had not sent my lions away

after all. It was always instructive to see how people would take them. Penelope and Telemachus had not faltered. My son had warned them, perhaps. Or was it something Odysseus had mentioned? The thought sent an eerie chill through me. I listened, as if I might hear an answer from their rooms. The house was still. They slept, or else kept to their thoughts in silence.

When I stepped into my dining hall, Telemachus was there. He stood in the room's center, poised as an arrow nocked to its string. The knife gleamed at his waist.

So, I thought. It comes. Well, it would be on my terms. I walked past him to the hearth. I poured a cup of wine and took my chair. All the while, his eyes followed me. *Good.* My skin felt shot through with power, like the sky before a storm.

"I know you plan to kill my son."

Nothing moved but the flames in the hearth. He said, "How do you know it?"

"Because you are a prince, and the son of Odysseus. Because you respect the laws of gods and men. Because your father is dead, and my son the cause. Perhaps you think to try your hand at me as well. Or did you just want me to watch?"

My eyes shone and made their own shadows.

He said, "Lady, I bear neither you nor your son ill will."

"How kind," I said. "I am completely reassured."

His muscles were not a warrior's, bunched and hardened. He had no scars or calluses I could see. But he was a Mycenaean prince, honed and supple, trained to combat from his cradle. Penelope would have been scrupulous in his rearing.

"How may I prove myself to you?" His voice was grave. He mocked me, I thought.

"You cannot. I know a son is bound to avenge his father's murder."

"I do not deny that." His gaze did not waver. "But that only holds if he was murdered."

I lifted an eyebrow. "You say he was not? Yet you bring a blade into my house."

He looked down as if surprised to see it. "It is for carving," he said.

"Yes," I said. "I imagine so."

He drew the knife from his belt and slid it down the table. It made a raw, juddering sound.

"I was on the beach when my father died," he said. "I had heard the shouts and feared a confrontation. Odysseus was not...welcoming in recent years. I came too late, but I saw the end. He had wrested away the spear. It was not by Telegonus' hand that he died."

"Most men do not look for reasons to forgive their father's death."

"I cannot speak for those men," he said. "To insist upon your son's fault would be unjust."

It was a strange word to hear on his lips. It had been one of his father's favorites. That wry smile, his hands uplifted. *What can I say? The world is an unjust place.* I considered the man before me. In spite of my anger, there was something in him that compelled. He showed no courtly polish. His gestures were simple, even awkward. He had the grim purpose of a ship, battened against a storm.

"You should understand," I said, "that any attempt to harm my son would fail."

He cast an eye to the lions in their heaps. "I think I can understand that."

I had not expected it of him, that dryness, but I did not laugh. "You told my son there was nothing left for you on

Ithaca. We both know a throne waits there. Why are you not in it?"

"I am not welcome on Ithaca now."

"Why?"

He did not hesitate. "Because I watched while my father fell. Because I did not kill your son where he stood. And after, when the pyre burned, I did not weep."

The words were calm but they had a heat to them like fresh coals. I remembered the look that had passed over his face when I'd spoken of honoring Odysseus.

"You do not grieve for your father?"

"I do. I grieve that I never met the father everyone told me I had."

I narrowed my eyes. "Explain."

"I am no storyteller."

"I am not asking for a story. You have come to my island. You owe me truth."

A moment passed, and then he nodded. "You will have it."

I had taken the wooden chair, so he took the silver. His father's old seat. It had been one of the first things that had caught my eye about Odysseus, how he'd lounged there like it was a bed. Telemachus sat up straight like a pupil called to recitation. I offered him wine. He declined.

When Odysseus had not come home after the war, he said, suitors had begun to arrive seeking Penelope's hand. Scions of Ithaca's most prosperous families and ambitious sons from the neighboring islands, looking for a wife, and a throne if they could get it. "She refused them, but they lingered in the palace year after year, eating up our stores, demanding my mother choose one of them. She asked them to leave again and again, but they would not." The old anger still burned in his voice. "They saw we could do nothing to them, a young man and a woman alone. When I reproached them, they only laughed."

I had known such men myself. I had sent them to my sty.

But then Odysseus had returned. Ten years after he sailed from Troy, seven after he left Aiaia.

"He came in disguise as a beggar and revealed himself only to a few of us. We devised an opportunity: a test of the suitors' mettle. Whoever could string the great Odysseus' bow would win my mother's hand. One by one the suitors tried and failed. At last my father stepped forward. In a single motion he strung the bow and put an arrow through the throat of the worst among them. I had been frightened of those men for so long, but they fell to him like grass before the scythe. He killed them all."

The man of war, honed by twenty years of strife. The Best of the Greeks after Achilles, wielding his bow once more. Of course they had not stood a chance. They were green boys, overfed and spoiled. It made a good tale: the suitors, lazy and cruel, besieging the faithful wife, threatening the loyal heir. They had earned their punishment by all the laws of gods and men, and Odysseus came like Death himself to deal it, the wronged hero making the world right. Even Telegonus would have approved of such a moral. Yet somehow, it was a queasy vision for me: Odysseus, wading heart-deep in the halls he had dreamed of so long.

"The next day the suitors' fathers came. They were all men of the island. Nicanor, who kept the largest herds of goats. Agathon, with his carved-pine staff. Eupeithes, who used to let me pick pears from his orchard. He was the one who spoke. He said: *Our sons were guests in your home, and you killed them. We seek reparation.*

"'Your sons were thieves and villains,' my father said. He

gestured, and my grandfather threw his spear. Eupeithes' face burst open, scattering the dust with his brains. My father ordered us to kill the rest, but Athena descended."

So Athena had come back to him at last.

"She declared the feud finished. The suitors had paid fair price and there would be no more bloodshed. But the next day, the fathers of his soldiers began to come. 'Where are our sons?' they wanted to know. 'We have waited twenty years to welcome them home from Troy.'"

I knew the stories Odysseus would have had to tell them. Your son was eaten by a cyclops. Your son was eaten by Scylla. Your son was torn to pieces by cannibals. Your son got drunk and fell from a roof. His ship was sunk by giants while I fled.

"Your father still had crew when he sailed from my island. Did none of them survive?"

He hesitated. "You do not know?"

"Know what?" But as I spoke, my mouth went dry as Aiaia's yellow sands. In the wildness of Telegonus' childhood, I had had no time to fret for what was out of my hands. But I remembered now Teiresias' prophecy as clearly as if Odysseus had just spoken it. "The cattle," I said. "They ate the cattle."

He nodded. "Yes."

A year those eager, reckless men had lived with me. I had fed them, cared for their illnesses and scars, taken pleasure in watching them mend. And now they were wiped from the earth as if they had never lived.

"Tell me how it happened."

"As their ship was passing Thrinakia, a storm blew in and forced them to land. My father kept watch for days but the storm went on and on, stranding them, and at last my father had to sleep."

That same old story.

"While he slept, his men killed some of the cows. The two nymphs who guard the island witnessed them and went to..." He hesitated again. I saw him consider those words: *your father*. "Lord Helios. When my father set sail again, the ship was blasted to pieces. All the men were drowned."

I could imagine my half-sisters with their long golden hair and painted eyes, bent on pretty knees. *Oh, Father, it was not our fault. Punish them.* As if he had ever needed urging. Helios and his endless wrath.

I felt Telemachus' eyes on me. I made myself lift my cup and drink. "Go on. Their fathers came."

"Their fathers came, and when they learned their sons were dead, they began demanding their sons' shares of the treasure won fighting at Troy. Odysseus said it was all at the bottom of the sea, but the men did not give up. They came again and again, and each time my father's rage grew. He beat Nicanor about the shoulders with a stick. Kleitos he knocked down. 'You want the true story of your son? He was a fool and a braggart. He was greedy and stupid and disobeyed the gods.'"

It was a shock to hear such blunt words put into Odysseus' mouth. There was a piece of me that wanted to object, say that it didn't sound like him. But how many times had I heard him praise such tactics? The only difference was how plainly Telemachus told it. I could imagine Odysseus sighing and holding out his empty hands. *Such is the commander's lot. Such is the folly of humanity. Is it not our human tragedy that some men must be beaten like donkeys before they will see reason?*

"They stayed away after that, but still my father brooded. He was sure they were plotting against him. He wanted sentries posted all around the palace, day and night. He talked of training dogs and digging trenches to catch villains in the dark. He drew up plans for a great palisade to be built. As if we were some war camp. I should have said something then. But I...still hoped it would pass."

"And your mother? What did she think?"

"I do not claim to know what my mother thinks." His voice had stiffened. They had not spoken to each other all night, I remembered.

"She brought you up herself. You must have some idea."

"There is no one who can guess what my mother is doing until it is done." There was not just stiffness in his voice now, but bitterness. I waited. I had begun to see that silence prompted him better than words.

"There was a time we shared every confidence," he said. "We plotted each night's strategy against the suitors together, if she should come down or not, speak haughtily or conciliate, if I should bring out the good wine, if we should stage for them some confrontation. When I was a child we were together every day. She would take me swimming, and afterwards we would sit beneath a tree and watch the people of Ithaca go about their business. Each man or woman who passed, she knew their history and would tell it to me, for she said that you must understand people if you would rule them."

Telemachus' gaze was fixed upon the air. The firelight picked out a crook in his nose I had not noticed before. An old break.

"Whenever I fretted for my father's safety, she would shake her head. 'Never fear for him. He is too clever to be killed, for he knows all the tricks of men's hearts, and how to turn them to his advantage. He will survive the war and return home again.' And I was comforted, for what my mother said always came to pass."

A true-made bow, Odysseus had called her. A fixed star. A woman who knew herself.

"I asked her how she did it once, how she understood the world so clearly. She told me that it was a matter of keeping very still and showing no emotions, leaving room for others to reveal themselves. She tried to practice with me, but I made her laugh. 'You are as secret as a bull hiding on a beach!' she said."

It was true Telemachus was not secret. The pain was drawn clear and precise across his face. I pitied him, but if I were honest, I envied him as well. Telegonus and I had never had such closeness to lose.

"Then my father came home and all of that was wiped away. He was like a summer storm, lightning bright across a pale sky. When he was there, everything else faded."

I knew that trick of Odysseus'. I had seen it each day for a year.

"I went to her the day he beat Nicanor. 'I fear he goes too far,' I said. She would not even look away from her loom. All she would answer was that we must give him time."

"And did time help?"

"No. When my grandfather died, my father blamed Nicanor, the gods know why. He shot him with his great bow and threw the body on the beach for the birds to eat. The only thing he talked of by then was conspiracy, how the men of the island were gathering arms against him, how the servants were colluding in treacheries. At night, he paced the hearth, and every word from his mouth was guards and spies, measures and countermeasures."

"Were there such treacheries?"

"A revolt in Ithaca?" He shook his head. "We don't have time for that. Rebellion is for prosperous islands, or else those so ground down they have no other choice. I was angry by then. I told him that there was no conspiracy, there never had been, and he would do better saying three kind words to our men than plotting how to kill them. He smiled at me. 'Do you know,' he said, 'that Achilles went to war at seventeen? And he was not the youngest man at Troy. Boys of thirteen, fourteen, all did themselves proud in the field. I've found that courage is not a matter of age, but true-made spirits.'"

He did not imitate his father, not exactly. Yet the rhythm of the speech caught Odysseus' confidential, luring mildness.

"He meant I was a disgrace, of course. A coward. I should have fought off the suitors single-handedly. Was I not fifteen when they first came? I should have been able to shoot his great bow, not just string it. At Troy I would not have lived a day."

I could see it: the smoky fire and the tang of old bronze, the must of pressed olives. And Odysseus, expertly wrapping his son with shame.

"I told him we were on Ithaca now. The war was finished and everyone knew it but him. It enraged him. He dropped his smile. He said, 'You are a traitor. You wish for me to die so you can take my throne. Perhaps you even think to speed me along?'"

Telemachus' voice was steady, nearly expressionless, but his knuckles showed white on the chair's arm.

"I told him that he was the one who shamed our house. He could boast all he liked of the war, but all he had brought home was death. His hands would never be clean again and mine would not be either, for I had followed him into his lake of blood and I would be sorry for it all my days. It was finished after that. I was shut from his councils. I was barred from the hall. I heard him shouting at my mother that she had nursed a viper."

The room was silent. I could feel the place where the fire's warmth faded and died against the winter air.

"The truth is, I think he would have preferred me as a traitor. At least then I would have been a son he could understand."

I had been watching him, as he talked, for his father's mannerisms, those tricks that were as indivisible from Odysseus as tides from the ocean. The pauses and smiles, the dry voice and deprecating gestures, all wielded against the listener, to convince, to tease, and most of all, to mitigate. I had seen none. Telemachus took his blows straight on.

"I went to my mother after that, but he had set guards to keep me out, and when I shouted past them she said I must be patient and not provoke him. The only person who would speak to me was my old nurse, Eurycleia, who had been his nurse as well. We sat by the fire, chewing our fish to paste. He was not always like this, she kept telling me. As if that changed anything. This man of rage was all the father I had. She died not long after, but my father did not stay to watch her pyre burn. He was tired of living among ashes, he said. He set out on a skiff and came back a month later with gold belts and cups and a new breastplate, and splashes of dried blood on his clothes. It was the happiest I had ever seen him. But it did not last. By the next morning he was railing about the smoky hall and the clumsiness of the servants."

I had seen him in such moods. Every petty defect of the world enraged him, all the waste and stupidity and slowness of men, and all the irritants of nature too, biting flies and warping wood and the briars that ripped his cloak. When

he had lived with me, I'd smoothed all those things away,
wrapping him in my magic and divinity. Perhaps it was why
he had been so happy. An idyll, I had called our time. *Illusion* might have been a better word.

"After that, he went on some raid every month. Reports
came back, scarcely believable. He had taken a new wife,
the queen of some inland kingdom. He ruled there happily
among the cows and barley. He wore a golden circlet and
feasted till dawn and ate boars whole and roared with
laughter. He had fathered another son."

His eyes were Odysseus'. The shape and color, even the
intensity. But the expression: Odysseus' gaze was always
reaching out, cajoling. Telemachus' held fast to itself.

"Was any of it true?"

He lifted his shoulders, let them drop. "Who can say?
Perhaps he started the rumors himself to wound us. I sent a
message to my mother that the goats needed extra tending
and went to live in an empty hut on the hillside. My father
could plot and rage, but I did not have to see it. My mother
could eat one piece of cheese all day and let her eyes turn
gray on her loom, but I did not have to see that either."

In the fire, the logs had burnt down. Their remains
glowed white, scaled with ash.

"Into such miseries, your son came. Bright as a sunrise, sweet as ripe fruit. He carried that silly-looking
spear, and gifts for us all, silver bowls and cloaks and
gold. His face was handsome and his hopes crackled
loud as a fire. I wanted to shake him. I thought: when
my father returns, this boy will learn that life is not a
bard's song. And so he did."

The moon had lifted away from the window, and the
room was draped in shadows. Telemachus' hands rested on
his knees.

"You were trying to help him," I said. "That is why you went down to the beach."

His eyes were on the fire's ashes. "He did not need me, as it turned out."

I had used to imagine Telemachus so often. As a quiet boy keeping watch for Odysseus, as a burning youth bearing vengeance across land and sea. But now he was a man, and his voice was dull and drained. He was like those messengers who run great distances with news for kings. They gasp out their words, then fall to the ground and do not rise.

Without thinking, I reached across and laid my hand on his arm. "You are not your blood. Do not let him take you with him."

He looked down at my fingers a moment, then up into my face. "You pity me. Do not. My father lied about many things, but he was right when he called me a coward. I let him be what he was for year after year, raging and beating the servants, shouting at my mother, and turning our house to ash. He told me to help him kill the suitors and I did it. Then he told me to kill all the men who had aided them, and I did that too. Then he commanded me to gather up all the slave girls who had ever lain with one of them and make them clean the blood-soaked floor, and when they were finished, I was to kill them as well."

The words jolted me. "The girls would have had no choice. Odysseus would have known it."

"Odysseus told me to carve them into joints like animals." His eyes held mine. "Do you disbelieve it?"

It was not one story that I thought of, but a dozen. He had always loved his vengeances. He had always hated those he thought betrayed him.

"Did you do as he said?"

"No," he said. "I hanged them instead. I found twelve

lengths of rope and tied twelve knots." Each word was like a blade he thrust into himself. "I had never seen it done, but I remembered how in all the stories of my childhood the women were always hanging themselves. I had some thought that it must be more proper. I should have used the sword instead. I have never known such ugly, drawn-out deaths. I will see their feet twisting the rest of my days. Goodnight, Lady Circe."

He picked his knife up from my table and was gone.

The storm had passed, and the night sky was clear again. I walked, wanting to feel the new-washed breeze on my skin, the earth crumbling softly beneath my feet, to shake off that ugly image of twitching bodies. Overhead, my aunt sailed, but I did not trouble with her anymore. She liked to watch lovers, and I had not been one of those for a long time. Perhaps I had never been.

I could imagine Odysseus' face as he killed those suitors, man by man by man. I had seen him chop wood. He did it in one swift motion, clean through. They would have died at his feet, their blood staining him to the knees. He would note it coolly, distantly, like the click of a counter: *done*.

The heat would have come after. When he had stood over the motionless slaughter-yard, and felt his rage still brimming and unspent. So he would have fed more into it, like logs, to keep a fire going. The men who had aided the suitors, the slaves who had lain with them, the fathers who dared to speak against him. On and on he would have gone, if Athena had not intervened.

And what of me? How long would I have gone on filling my sty, if Odysseus had not come? I remembered the night he had asked me about the pigs. "Tell me," he had said, "how do you decide which man deserves punishment and which does not? How can you judge for certain, this heart is rotted and this one good? What if you make a mistake?"

I had been warmed that night by wine and fire, lured by the flush of his regard. "Let us consider," I said, "a boatload of sailors. Among them, some are undoubtedly worse than others. Some exult in rape and piracy, but others are newly come to it and scarcely have their beards. Some would never imagine robbery, except that their families are starving. Some feel shame after, some do it only because their captain commands it, and because they have the crowd of other men there, to hide among."

"And so," he said, "which you change, and which do you let go?"

"I change them all," I said. "They have come to my house. Why should I care what is in their hearts?"

He had smiled and lifted his cup to me. "Lady, you and I are in accord."

An owl passed its wings over my head. I heard the sound of scuffling brush, the beak snap. A mouse had died for its carelessness. I was glad Telemachus would not know of those words between me and his father. At the time I had been boasting, showing off my ruthlessness. I had felt untouchable, filled with teeth and power. I scarcely remembered what that was like.

Odysseus' favorite pose had been to pretend that he was a man like other men, but there were none like him, and now that he was dead, there were none at all. All heroes are fools, he liked to say. What he meant was, all heroes but me. So who could correct him when he erred? He had stood on the beach looking at Telegonus and believing him a pirate. He had stood in his hall and accused Telemachus of conspiracy. Two children he had had, and he had not seen either clearly. But perhaps no parent can truly see their child. When we look we see only the mirror of our own faults.

I was in the cypress grove by then. Their branches showed black in the darkness, and as I passed the needles brushed my face, and I felt the faint sticky catch of their sap. He had liked this place. I remember him running his hand along a trunk. It was one of my favorite things about him, how he admired the world like a jewel, turning its facets to catch the light. A well-made boat, a well-grown tree, a well-told story, these were all pleasures to him.

There were none like him, yet there was one who had matched him and now she slept in my house. Telemachus was no danger, but what of her? Was she plotting to open my son's throat even now, to carry out her vengeance? Whatever she tried, my spells would hold. Not even Odysseus could talk his way past witchcraft. He had talked his way past the witch instead.

The dew was gathering on the grass. My feet were cool and silver with its touch. Telemachus would be in his bed, watching this same dark, seeing the faint tattering at its eastern edge. I thought of his face when he had spoken of hanging the slave girls, how he had held the memory to his skin like a burning brand. I should have said more to him, I thought. I could have told him that he was not the first man led to kill for Odysseus' sake. There had once been a whole army who bent their spears to that task. I scarcely knew Telemachus, but I somehow did not think that would be a comfort. I could see the acid on his face. *You will pardon me if I do not rejoice at being one in a long line of villains.*

Of all the sons in the world, he was not the one I would have guessed for Odysseus. He was stiff as a herald, blunt to the point of rudeness. He carried his wounds openly in his hands. When I'd reached for him, there had been an emotion on his face I could not quite name. Surprise, tinged with something like distaste. Well, he did not have to fear. I would not do it again.

That was the thought that carried me home.

I watched the sun rise at my loom. I set out bread and cheese and fruit, and when I heard my son stir, I went to his door. I was relieved to see his face was not so dull, but the grief was still there, the heavy knowledge: my father is dead.

He would wake up with that thought for a long time, I knew.

"I spoke with Telemachus," I said. "You are right about him."

He lifted his eyebrows. Did he think me incapable of seeing what was before my eyes? Or only of admitting it?

"I am glad you think so," he said.

"Come. I have put breakfast out. And I think Telemachus is waking. Will you leave him alone with the lions?"

"You're not coming?"

"I have spells to cast."

I did not really. I went back to my room and listened to them talking about the boat, the food, the most recent storm. The tonic of ordinary things. Telegonus suggested they go out and drag the boat back to the cave. Telemachus agreed. Two sets of feet upon the stone, and the door swung closed. Yesterday I would have thought myself mad to send them off together. Today it seemed like a gift to my son. I felt a pang of embarrassment: Telemachus and Telegonus. I knew how it looked to have named my son that, like a dog who scratches outside a door when it cannot come in. I wanted to explain that I had never thought they would know each other, that his name had been intended for me alone. *Born far away*, it meant. From his father, yes, but also from mine. From my mother and Oceanos, from the Minotaur and Pasiphaë and Aeëtes. Born for me, on my island of Aiaia.

I would make no excuses for it.

I had retrieved the spear yesterday and now it leaned against the wall of my room. I lifted the leather sheath. The ray's tail looked even stranger on land, spectral and ragged. I turned it, catching the light on the infinitesimal beads of venom that crowned each feathered tooth. I must return it, I thought. *Not yet.*

From down the hall, another stirring. I thought of all those men and women over the years, spilling their secrets while Penelope carefully gathered them up. I pulled the leather sheath back over the spear and opened my shutters. Outside was a beautiful morning, and on the wind were the first hints of what would soon ripen into spring.

The knock upon my door came, as I had guessed it would.

"Open," I said.

She was framed in my doorway, wearing a pale cloak over a gray dress, as if she were wrapped in spider-silk.

"I come to say I am ashamed. I did not speak of my gratitude yesterday as I should have. I do not mean only for your hospitality now. I mean also for your hospitality to my husband."

It was impossible to tell, in that mild voice of hers, if the comment was pointed. If it were, I supposed she was entitled.

She said, "He told me how you helped him on his way. He would not have survived without your advice."

"You give me too much credit. He was wise."

"Sometimes," she said. Her eyes were the color of mountain ash. "Do you know that after he left you, he landed with another nymph? Calypso. She fell in love with him and hoped to make him her immortal husband. Seven years, she stayed him on her isle, draping him in divine fabrics, feeding him delicacies."

"He did not thank her for it."

"No. He refused her and prayed to the gods to free him. At last they forced her to let him go."

I did not think I imagined the trace of satisfaction in her voice.

"When your son came, I thought perhaps he was hers. But then I saw the weave of his cloak. I remembered Daedalus' loom."

It was strange, how much she knew of me. But then, I knew about her too.

"Calypso fawned over him, and you turned his men to pigs. Yet you were the one he preferred. Do you think that strange?"

"No," I said.

It was nearly a smile. "Just so."

"He did not know about the child."

"I know," she said. "He would never have kept that from me." That *was* pointed.

"I spoke with your son last night," I said.

"Did you?" I thought I heard a flicker of something in her voice.

"He explained to me why you had to leave Ithaca. I was sorry to hear it."

"Your son was kind to bring us away." Her eyes had found Trygon's tail. "Is it like a bee's venom, that stings only once? Or like a snake?"

"It could poison a thousand times and more. There is no end to it. It was meant to stop a god."

"Telegonus told us that you faced the great lord of stingrays himself."

"I did."

She nodded, a private gesture, as if in confirmation. "He told us that you took further precautions for him as well. That you have cast a spell over the island, and no god, not even Olympians, can pass."

"Gods of the dead may pass," I said. "No others."

"You are fortunate," she said, "to be able to summon such protections." From the beach came faint shouts: our sons moving the boat.

"I am embarrassed to ask this of you, but I did not bring a black cloak with me when we left. Do you have one I might wear? I would mourn for him."

I looked at her, as vivid in my doorway as the moon in the autumn sky. Her eyes held mine, gray and steady. It is a common saying that women are delicate creatures, flowers, eggs, anything that may be crushed in a moment's carelessness. If I had ever believed it, I no longer did.

"No," I said. "But I have yarn, and a loom. Come."

CHAPTER TWENTY-TWO

HER FINGERS RAN LIGHTLY over the beams, stroked the threads of the weft like a stable master greeting a prize horse. She asked no questions; she seemed to absorb the loom's workings by touch alone. The light from the window glowed on her hands, as if it wished to illuminate her work. Carefully, she took off my half-finished tapestry and strung the black yarn. Her motions were precise, nothing wasted. She was a swimmer, Odysseus had told me, long limbs cutting effortlessly to her destination.

Outside the sky had turned. The clouds hung so low they seemed to graze the windows, and I could hear the first fat drops begin to fall. Telemachus and Telegonus gusted through the door, wet from hauling the boat. When Telegonus saw Penelope at the loom he hurried forward, already exclaiming over the fineness of her work. I watched Telemachus instead. His face went hard and he turned away abruptly to the window.

I set out lunch, and we ate in near silence. The rain tapered off. I could not bear the thought of being shut up all afternoon and drew my son out for a walk along the shore. The sand was hard and wet, and our footprints looked as though they had been cut with a knife. I linked my arm through his and was surprised when he let it stay. His tremor from yesterday was gone, but I knew it would return.

It was only a little after midday, yet something in the air felt dusky and obscuring, like a veil across my eyes. My conversation with Penelope was tugging at me. At the time, I had felt clever and swift, but now that I ran it back through my mind, I realized how little she had said. I had meant to question her, and instead I found myself showing her my loom.

He had talked his way past the witch instead.

"Whose idea was it to come here?" I said.

He frowned at the suddenness of my question. "Does it matter?"

"I am curious."

"I can't remember." But he did not meet my eyes.

"Not yours."

He hesitated. "No. I suggested Sparta."

It was the natural thought. Penelope's father lived in Sparta. Her cousin was a queen there. A widow would find welcome.

"So you said nothing of Aiaia."

"No. I thought it would be . . ." He trailed off. Indelicate, of course.

"So who first mentioned it?"

"It may have been the queen. I remember she said that she would prefer not to go to Sparta. That she would have a little time."

He was choosing his words carefully. I felt a humming beneath my skin.

"Time for what?"

"She did not say."

Penelope the weaver, who could lead you over and under, into her design. We were passing through thickets, angling upwards beneath the dark, wet branches.

"It is strange. Did she think her family would not have wanted her? Was there a rift with Helen? Did she speak of any enemies?"

"I don't know. No. Of course she did not speak of enemies."

"What did Telemachus say?"

"He was not there."

"But when he learned you would come here, was he surprised?"

"Mother."

"Just tell me her words. Say them exactly as you remember."

He had stopped on the path. "I thought you did not suspect them anymore."

"Not of vengeance. But there are other questions."

He took a deep breath. "I cannot remember exactly. Not her words, nor anything at all. It is gray like a fog. It is still gray."

The pain had risen in his face. I said no more, but as we walked my mind kept picking at the thought, like fingers at a knot. There was a secret beneath that spider-silk. She had not wanted to go to Sparta. Instead she had gone to her husband's lover's island. And she wanted time. For what?

We had reached the house by then. Inside, she was working at the loom. Telemachus stood by the window. His hands were tight at his sides and the air was stark. Had they quarreled? I looked at her face, but it was bent to her threads and showed nothing. No one shouted, no one wept, but I thought I would have preferred it to this quiet strain.

Telegonus cleared his throat. "I'm thirsty. Who else would like a cup?"

I watched him broach the cask and pour. My son with his valiant heart. Even in grief, he sought to bear us all up, to carry us through one moment to the next. But there was only so much he could do. The afternoon wore on in silence. Dinner was the same. The moment the food was gone, Penelope rose. "I'm tired," she said. Telegonus stayed a little later, but by moonrise he was yawning into his hands. I sent him off with Arcturos. I expected Telemachus to follow, but when I turned he was still at his place.

"I think you have stories of my father," he said. "I would like to hear them."

His boldness kept taking me by surprise. All day he had hung back, avoiding my gaze, diffident and nearly invisible. Then suddenly he planted himself before me as if he had grown there fifty years. It was a trick even Odysseus would have admired.

"You likely know all I have to tell already," I said.

"No." The word rang a little in the room. "He told my mother his stories, but whenever I asked, he said I should talk to a bard."

A cruel answer. I wondered at Odysseus' reasoning. Had it been merely spite? If there was some other purpose, we would never know it. All the things he had done in life must stand now as they were.

I brought my goblet to the hearth. Outside, the storm had returned. It blew in earnest, muffling the house in wind and wet. Penelope and Telegonus were only down the hall, but the shadows had gathered around us, and they felt a world away. This time I took the silver chair. The inlay was cool against my wrists; the cowhides slipped a little beneath me. "What do you want to hear?"

"Everything," he said. "Whatever you know."

I did not even consider telling him the versions I had told Telegonus, with their happy endings and non-fatal wounds. He was not my child; he was not a child at all, but a man full-grown, who wanted his inheritance.

I gave it. Murdered Palamades and abandoned Philoctetes. Odysseus tricking Achilles out of hiding and bringing him to war, Odysseus creeping at moondark into the camp of King Rhesus, one of Troy's allies, and cutting the men's throats while they slept. How he had devised the horse and taken Troy and seen Astyanax shattered. Then his savage journey home, with its cannibals and piracy and monsters. The stories were even bloodier than I had remembered, and a few times I hesitated. But Telemachus took his blows straight on. He sat silent, his eyes never leaving mine.

I saved the cyclops for last, I cannot say why. Perhaps because I could remember Odysseus telling it so clearly. As I spoke, his words seemed to whisper beneath mine. They had landed exhausted on an island and spied a great cave, heaped with rich stores. Odysseus thought it might be good for plunder, or else they might beg hospitality from its inhabitants. They began feasting on the food within. The giant it belonged to, the one-eyed shepherd Polyphemus, returned with his flock and caught them at it. He rolled a great stone over the entrance to trap them, then seized one of the men and bit him in half. Man after man he gobbled down, until he was so full he belched up pieces of limbs. Despite such horrors, Odysseus plied the monster with wine and friendly words. His name he gave as *Outis* — *No one*. When the creature fell at last into a stupor, he sharpened a great stake, heated it over the fire, and plunged it into his eye. The cyclops roared and thrashed but could not see to catch Odysseus and the rest of the crew. They were able to escape when he let his sheep out to graze, each man clinging to the underside of a woolly beast. The enraged monster called for help from his fellow one-eyes, but they did not come, for he cried, "No one has blinded me! No one is escaping!" Odysseus and his crew reached the ships, and when they were safely distant, Odysseus turned back to shout across the waves, "If you would know the man who tricked you, it is Odysseus, son of Laertes and prince of Ithaca."

The words seemed to echo in the quiet air. Telemachus was silent, as if waiting for the sound to fade. At last he said, "It was a bad life."

"There are many who are unhappier."

"No." His vehemence startled me. "I do not mean a bad life for him. I mean that he made life for others a misery. Why did his men go to that cave in the first place? Because he wanted more treasure. And Poseidon's wrath that everyone pitied him for? He brought it on himself. Because he could not bear to leave the cyclops without taking credit for the trick."

His words were running forward like an undammed flood.

"All those years of pain and wandering. Why? For a moment's pride. He would rather be cursed by the gods than be No one. If he had returned home after the war, the suitors would never have come. My mother's life would not have been blighted. My life. He talked so often of longing for us and home. But it was lies. When he was back on Ithaca he was never content, always looking to the horizon. Once we were his again, he wanted something else. What is that if not a bad life? Luring others to you, then turning from them?"

I opened my mouth to say it was not true. But how often had I lain beside him, aching because I knew he thought of Penelope? That had been my choice. Telemachus had had no such luxury.

"There is one more story I should tell you," I said. "Before he returned to you, the gods demanded that your father journey to the underworld to speak to the prophet Teiresias. There he saw many of the souls he had known in life, Ajax, Agamemnon, and with them Achilles, once Best of the Greeks, who chose an early death as payment for eternal fame. Your father spoke to the hero warmly, praising him and assuring him of his reputation among men. But Achilles reproached him. He said he regretted his proud life, and wished he had lived more quietly, and happily."

"So that is what I must hope for then? That one day I will see my father in the underworld and he will be sorry?"

It is better than some of us get. But I held my peace. He had a right to his anger, and it was not my place to try to take it. Outside, the garden rustled faintly as the lions prowled through the leaves. The sky had cleared. After so long among clouds the stars seemed very bright, hung in the darkness like lamps. If we listened, we would hear the faint twisting of their chains in the breeze.

"Do you think it was true, what my father said? That the good ones never liked him?"

"I think it was the sort of thing your father liked to say, and truth had nothing to do with it. After all, your mother liked him."

His eyes had found mine. "And so did you."

"I do not claim to be good."

"You liked him, though. Despite all of it."

There was a challenge in his voice. I found myself

choosing my words carefully. "I did not see the worst of him. Even at his best he was not an easy man. But he was a friend to me in a time when I needed one."

"It is strange to think of a goddess needing friends."

"All creatures that are not mad need them."

"I think he got the better bargain."

"I did turn his men to pigs."

He did not smile. He was like an arrow shooting to the end of its arc. "All these gods, all these mortals who aided him. Men talk of his wiles. His true talent was in how well he could take from others."

"There are many who would be glad for such a gift," I said.

"I am not one." He set down his cup. "I will tax you no further, Lady Circe. I am grateful for the truth of these stories. There are few who have taken such pains with me."

I did not answer him. Something had begun prickling at me, lifting the hairs on my neck.

"Why are you here?" I said.

He blinked. "I told you, we had to leave Ithaca."

"Yes," I said. "But why come here?"

He spoke slowly, like a man coming back from a dream. "I think it was my mother's idea."

"Why?"

A flush rose on his cheek. "As I have said, she does not share confidences with me."

No one can guess what my mother is doing until it is done.

He turned and passed into the hall's darkness. A moment later, I heard the soft sound of his door closing.

The cold air seemed to rush through the cracks of the walls and pin me to my seat. I had been a fool. I should have held her over the cliff that first day and shaken the truth out of her. I remembered now how carefully she had asked after my spell, the one that could stop gods. *Even Olympians.*

I did not go to her room, rip the door from its hinge. I burned at my window. The sill creaked under my fingers. There were hours till dawn, but hours were nothing to me. I watched the stars outside dim and the island emerge, blade by blade, into the light. The air had changed again and the sky had veiled itself. Another storm. The cypress boughs hissed in the air.

I heard them wake. My son first, then Penelope, and last Telemachus, who had gone to bed so late. One by one they came into the hall, and I felt them pause as they saw me at the window, like rabbits checking at the hawk's shadow. The table was bare, no breakfast laid. My son hurried to the kitchen to clatter plates. I liked feeling their silent glances at my back. My son urged them to eat, his words heavy with apology. I could imagine the speaking looks he was giving them: I'm sorry about my mother. Sometimes she is like this.

"Telegonus," I said, "the sty needs fixing and a storm comes. You will attend to it."

He cleared his throat. "I will, Mother."

"Your brother can help you."

Another silence, while they exchanged their glances.

"I do not mind," Telemachus said, mildly.

A few more sounds of plates and benches. At last, the door closed behind them.

I turned. "You take me for a fool. A dupe to be led by the nose. Asking so sweetly about my spell. Tell me which of the gods pursues you. Whose wrath have you brought upon my head?"

She was seated at my loom. Her lap was full of raw,

black wool. On the floor beside her lay a spindle and an ivory distaff, tipped with silver.

"My son does not know," she said. "He is not to blame."

"That is obvious. I can spot the spider in her web."

She nodded. "I confess that I have done what you say. I did it knowingly. I could claim that I thought because you are a goddess and a witch that the trouble to you would not be much. But it would be a lie. I know more of the gods than that."

Her calmness enraged me. "Is that all? I know what I have done and will brazen it out? Last night your son talked of his father as one who takes from others and brings only misery. I wonder what he would say of you."

The blow landed. I saw the blankness she used to cover it over.

"You think me some tame witch, but you were not listening to your husband's stories of me. Two days you have stayed on my isle. How many meals have you eaten, Penelope? How many cups of my wine have you drunk?"

She paled. A faint graying along her hairline, like the creeping edge of dawn.

"Speak, or I will use my power."

"I believe you have used it already." The words were hard and cool as stones. "I brought danger to your isle. But you brought it to mine first."

"My son came of his own accord."

"I do not speak of your son, and I think you know it. I speak of the spear you sent, whose venom killed my husband."

And there it was between us.

"I grieve that he is dead."

"So you have said."

"If you are waiting for my apology, you will not get it.

Even if I had such powers as could turn back the sun, I would not. If Odysseus had not died on the beach, I think my son would have. And there is nothing I would not trade for his life."

A look passed across her face. I might have called it rage, if it were not pointed so inward. "Well then. You have made your trade and this is what you have: your son lives, and we are here."

"You see it as a sort of vengeance then. Bringing a god down on my head."

"I see it as payment in kind."

She would have made an archer, I thought. That cold-eyed precision.

"You have no ground to make bargains, Lady Penelope. This is Aiaia."

"Then let me not bargain. What would you prefer, begging? Of course, you are a goddess."

She knelt at the foot of my loom and lifted her hands, lowering her eyes to the floor. "Daughter of Helios, Bright-eyed Circe, Mistress of Beasts and Witch of Aiaia, grant me sanctuary on your dread isle, for I have no husband and no home, and nowhere else in the world is safe for me and my son. I will give you blood every year, if you will hear me."

"Get up."

She did not move. The posture looked obscene on her. "My husband spoke warmly of you. More warmly, I confess, than I liked. He said of all the gods and monsters he had met, you were the only one he would wish to meet again."

"I said, get up."

She rose.

"You will tell me everything, and then I will decide."

We faced each other across the shadowed room. The air

tasted of lightning. She said, "You have been talking to my son. He will have implied that his father was lost in the war. That he came home changed, too soaked in death and grief to live as an ordinary man. The curse of soldiers. Is it so?"

"Something like that."

"My son is better than I am, and better than his father too. Yet he does not see all things."

"And you do?"

"I am from Sparta. We know about old soldiers there. The trembling hands, the startling from sleep. The man who spills his wine every time the trumpets blow. My husband's hands were steady as a blacksmith's, and when the trumpets sounded, he was first to the harbor scanning the horizon. The war did not break him; it made him more himself. At Troy he found at last a scope to equal his abilities. Always a new scheme, a new plot, a new disaster to avert."

"He tried to get out of the war."

"Ah, that old story. The madness, the plow. That too was a plot. He had sworn an oath to the gods — he knew there was no getting out. He expected to be caught. Then the Greeks would laugh at his failure and think that all his tricks would be so easily seen through."

I was frowning. "He gave no sign of that when he told me."

"I'm sure he didn't. My husband lied with every breath, and that includes to you, and to himself. He never did anything for a single purpose."

"He said the same of you once."

I meant it to wound her, but she only nodded. "We thought ourselves great minds of the world. When we were first married, we made a thousand plans together, of how we would turn everything we touched to our advantage. Then the war came. He said Agamemnon was the worst commander he had ever seen, but he thought he could use him to make a name for himself. And so he did. His contrivances defeated Troy and reshaped half the world. I contrived too. Which goats to breed with which, how to increase the harvest, where the fishermen could best cast their nets. Such were our pressing concerns on Ithaca. You should have seen his face when he came home. He killed the suitors, but then what was left? Fish and goats. A graying wife who was no goddess and a son he could not understand."

Her voice filled the air, sharp as crushed cypress.

"There were no war councils, no armies to conquer or command. What men there had once been were dead, since half were his crew and the other half my suitors. And every day there seemed to come some fresh report of distant glory. Menelaus had built a brand-new golden palace. Diomedes had conquered a kingdom in Italy. Even Aeneas, that Trojan refugee, had founded a city. My husband sent to Orestes, Agamemnon's son, offering himself as counselor. Orestes sent back that he had all the counselors he needed, and anyway he would never want to disturb the rest of such a hero.

"He sent to more sons after that, Nestor's and Idomeneus' and others', but they all said the same. They did not want him. And do you know what I told myself? That he only needed time. That any moment he would remember the pleasures of modest home and hearth. The pleasures of my presence. We would plot together again." Her mouth twisted in self-mockery. "But he did not want that life. He would go down to the beach and pace. I watched him from my window and remembered a story he'd told me once about a great serpent that the men of the north believe in, which yearns to devour all the world."

I remembered that story too. In the end, the serpent ate itself.

"And as he paced, he would talk to the air, which gathered all around him, glowing brightest silver on his skin."

Silver. "Athena."

"Who else?" She smiled, bitter and cold. "Every time he would calm she came again. Whispering in his ear, darting down from the clouds to fill him up with dreams of all the adventures he was missing."

Athena, that restless goddess whose schemes spun on and on. She had fought to bring her hero home, to see him lifted among his people, for her honor and his. To hear him tell the tales of his victories, of the deaths they had dealt to the Trojans together. But I remembered the greed in her eyes when she spoke of him: an owl with a kill in its claws. Her favorite could never be allowed to grow dull and domestic. He must live in action's eye, bright and polished, always striving and seeking, always delighting her with some new twist of cleverness, some brilliance he summoned out of the air.

Outside, trees struggled in the dark sky. In that eerie light, the bones of Penelope's face showed fine as one of Daedalus' statues. I had wondered why she was not more jealous of me. I understood now. I was not the goddess who had taken her husband.

"Gods pretend to be parents," I said, "but they are children, clapping their hands and shouting for more."

"And now that her Odysseus is dead," she said, "where will she find more?"

The final tiles were set in their place, and at last the picture showed whole. Gods never give up a treasure. She would come for the next best thing after Odysseus. She would come for his blood.

"Telemachus."

"Yes."

The tightness in my throat took me by surprise. "Does he know?"

"I do not think so. It is hard to say."

She still held the wool, matted and stinking in her hands. I was angry, I could feel it searing my belly. She had put my son in danger. It was likely that Athena plotted vengeance against Telegonus already; this would add fuel to fire. Yet if I were honest, my rage was not so hot as it had been. Of all the gods she might have led to my door, this was the one I could bear best. How much more could Athena hate us?

"You truly think you can keep him hidden from her?"

"I know I cannot."

"Then what is it you seek?"

She had drawn her cloak around herself, like a bird wrapped in its wings. "When I was young, I overheard our palace surgeon talking. He said that the medicines he sold were only for show. Most hurts heal by themselves, he said, if you give them enough time. It was the sort of secret I loved to discover, for it made me feel cynical and wise. I took it for a philosophy. I have always been good at waiting, you see. I outlasted the war and the suitors. I outlasted Odysseus' travels. I told myself that if I were patient enough, I could outlast his restlessness and Athena too. Surely, I thought, there must be some other mortal in the world for her to love. But it seems there was not. And while I sat, Telemachus bore his father's rage year after year. He suffered while I turned my eyes away."

I remembered what Odysseus had said about her once. That she never went astray, never made an error. I had been jealous then. Now I thought: what a burden. What an ugly weight upon your back.

"But this world does have true medicines. You are proof of that. You walked into the depths for your son. You defied the gods. I think of all the years of my life I wasted on that little man's boast. I have paid for it, that is only justice, but I have made Telemachus pay as well. He is a good son, he has always been. I seek a little time before I lose him, before we are thrust into the tide again. Will you grant it, Circe of Aiaia?"

She did not use those gray eyes on me. If she had, I would have refused her. She waited only. It was true that it looked well on her. She seemed to fit into the air like a jewel in its crown.

"It is winter," I said. "No ships sail now. Aiaia will bear you a little longer."

CHAPTER TWENTY-THREE

OUR SONS HAD RETURNED from their work windswept but dry. The thunder and rain had stayed out at sea. While the others ate their meal, I went up to the highest peak and felt the spell above me. From bay to bay it reached, from yellow sands to ragged stones. I felt it in my blood as well, that iron weight I had borne so long. Athena tested it surely. She prowled the edges, looking for a crack. But it would hold.

When I returned, Penelope was at the loom again. She looked over her shoulder. "It seems we have a break in the weather. The seas should be calm enough now. Telegonus, would you learn to swim?"

Of all the things I had expected after our conversation, that was not one. But I had no time to think of objecting. Telegonus nearly knocked over his cup in his eagerness. As they left through the garden, I heard him explaining my plants. Since when did he know what hornbeam was, or hemlock? But he pointed to them both and named their properties.

Telemachus had come up silent beside me. "They look like mother and son," he said.

It had been my thought exactly, but I felt a spurt of anger to hear him voice it. I went out to the garden without answering. I knelt in my beds and yanked up weeds.

He surprised me by following. "I do not mind helping your son, but let us be honest, that sty you told us to fix has not been used in years. Will you give me something to do that is actually useful?"

I sat back on my heels, regarding him. "Royalty does not usually beg for chores."

"My subjects seem to have left me with some spare time. Your island is very beautiful, but I will go mad if I have to keep idle on it day after day."

"What can you do then?"

"The usual. Fish and shoot. Tend the goats you do not have. Carve and build. I could fix your son's boat."

"Is something wrong with it?"

"The rudder is slow and unreliable, the sail too short and the mast too long. It wallows like a cow in any surge."

"It did not look so bad to me."

"I do not mean it was not impressive for a first try. Just that I am shocked we did not sink on the way over."

"It is charmed against sinking," I said. "How did you become such a shipwright?"

"I am from Ithaca," he said simply.

"And? Is there anything else I should know about?"

His face was serious, as if giving a diagnosis. "The sheep are matted enough to ruin the spring shearing. Three tables in your hall are unbalanced, and the garden path flagstones wobble. There are at least two birds' nests in your eaves."

I was half amused, half offended. "Is that all?"

"I have not made a complete survey."

"In the morning you may fix the boat with Telegonus. As for now, we will start with the sheep."

He was right, they were matted and, after the wet winter, muddied past their shoulders. I brought out the brush and a large bowl filled with one of my draughts.

He examined it. "What does it do?"

"It cleans the mud without stripping the fleece."

He knew his business and went to it efficiently. My sheep were tame, but he had his own tricks of coaxing and soothing. His hand on their backs guided them effortlessly here and there.

I said, "You have done this before."

"Of course. This wash is excellent, what is it?"

"Thistle, artemisia, celery, sulfur. Magic."

"Ah."

I had the trimming knife by then and set to cutting out burrs. He asked about the animals' pedigree and my breeding methods. He wanted to know if it was a spell that kept them tame or my influence. When his hands were occupied he lost his awkward stiffness. Soon enough he was telling me stories of his follies at goat herding and I was laughing. I did not notice the sun drop into the sea, and I startled when Penelope and Telegonus appeared beside us. I could feel Penelope's gaze on us as we rose and wiped the mud from our hands.

"Come," I said. "You must be hungry."

That night Penelope left dinner early again. I wondered if she meant to make a point, but her weariness seemed real enough. She was still grieving, I reminded myself. We all were. But the swimming had done my son good, or maybe it was Penelope's attention. He was red-cheeked from wind and wanted to talk. Not about his father, which was still too much a wound, but his old, first love: heroic stories. There had apparently been a bard on Ithaca who was skilled at such tales, and he wanted to hear from Telemachus the versions that he'd told. Telemachus began: Bellerophon and Perseus, Tantalus, Atalanta. He had taken the wooden chair again, and I the silver. Telegonus leaned against a wolf on the floor. Looking between them I felt a strange, almost drunken sense of unreality. Had it really only been two days since they had come? It felt much longer. I was not used to so much company, so many conversations. My son begged for another story, and another, and Telemachus obliged. His hair was windblown from our work outside, and the firelight lay along his cheek. So much of him looked older than he was, but there was a sweetly made curve there that might almost be called boyish. He was no storyteller, as he had said, but that made it more enjoyable somehow, watching his serious face as he described flying horses and golden apples. The room was warm and the vintage good. My skin had begun to feel soft as wax. I leaned forward.

"Tell me, did that bard ever speak of Pasiphaë, queen of Crete?"

"The mother of the Minotaur," Telemachus said. "Of course. She is always in the tale of Theseus."

"Did anyone say what happened to her when Minos died? She is immortal, does she still rule there?"

Telemachus was frowning. It was not displeasure but the same face he had made when he examined my sheep wash. I saw him following the threads of genealogies through their tangle. A daughter of the sun, Pasiphaë was said to be. I saw when he understood.

"No," he said. "Her and Minos' line no longer rules. A man named Leukos is king, who usurped from Idomeneus, who was her grandchild. In the story I heard, she went back to the halls of the gods after Minos died and lives in honor there."

CIRCE   351

"Whose halls?"

"The bard did not say."

A giddy recklessness had seized me. "Oceanos' most likely. Our grandfather. She will be terrorizing the nymphs as she used to. I was there when the Minotaur was born. I helped cage it."

Telegonus gaped. "You are related to Queen Pasiphaë? And you saw the Minotaur? Why did you not mention this?"

"You did not ask me."

"Mother! You must tell me everything. Did you meet Minos? And Daedalus?"

"How do you think I came by his loom?"

"I don't know! I thought it was, you know..." He waved his hand in the air.

Telemachus was watching me.

"No," I said. "I knew the man."

"What else have you kept from me?" Telegonus demanded. "The Minotaur and Trygon, and how many others? The Chimera? The Nemean lion? Cerberus and Scylla?"

I had been smiling at his wide-eyed outrage and did not see the blow coming. Where had my son heard her name? Hermes? Ithaca? It did not matter. A cold spear-point was twisting in my guts. What had I been thinking? My past was not some game, some adventure tale. It was the ugly wrack that storms left rotten on the shore. It was as bad as Odysseus'.

"I have said all I will say. Do not ask me again." I stood and walked away from their startled faces. In my room, I lay on my bed. There were no wolves or lions, they had stayed with my son. Over us somewhere was Athena, watching with her flashing eyes. Waiting with her spear to dart at my weakness. I spoke into the shadows. "Keep waiting."

And though I was sure I would not sleep, I did.

﹡   ﹡   ﹡

I woke clearheaded, determined. I had been tired the night before and drunk more than I was used to, but now I was firm again. I laid out breakfast. When Telegonus came, I saw him eyeing me, waiting for another outburst. But I was pleasant. He should not be so surprised, I thought. I could be pleasant.

Telemachus kept his own counsel, but when the meal was finished he took his brother out to begin fixing the ship.

"May I use your loom again?"

Penelope wore a different dress. This one was finer, it had been bleached to a pale cream. It showed off well the dark tones of her skin.

"You may." I thought of going to the kitchen, but I often cut herbs at the long table near the hearth, and I did not see why I should relegate myself. I brought out the knives and bowls and all the rest. The spells that protected Telegonus did not need to be renewed for another half a moon, so what I did was only for my own pleasure, drying and grinding, distilling tinctures for later use.

I thought we would not speak. In our place, Odysseus might have gone on concealing and jockeying, just for the pleasure of it. But after so long alone, I think we had both come to appreciate the value of open conversation.

The light slanted through the window, pooling on our bare feet. I asked her about Helen, and she told me stories of when they were children together, swimming in Sparta's rivers and playing at her uncle Tyndareos' court. We talked of weaving and the best breeds of sheep. I thanked her for offering to teach Telegonus how to swim. She was glad to do it, she said. He reminded her of her cousin Castor,

with his eagerness and good humor, his way of easing those
around him. "Odysseus drew the world to him," she said.
"Telegonus runs after, shaping as he goes, like a river carving a channel."

It pleased me more than I could say to hear her praise
him. "You should have known him as a baby. There was
never such a wild creature. Though if I am honest, I was
the wilder of the two of us. Motherhood seemed easy to
me, before I had a child."

"Helen's baby was like that," she said. "Hermione. She
screamed for half a decade but grew up sweet as anything.
I worried that Telemachus did not scream enough. That
he was well behaved too soon. I was always curious how
a second child might have been different. But by the time
Odysseus came home it seemed that was finished for me."
Her voice was matter-of-fact. Loyal, songs called her later.
Faithful and true and prudent. Such passive, pale words
for what she was. She could have taken another husband,
borne another child while Odysseus was gone, her life
would have been easier for it. But she had loved him
fiercely and would accept no other.

I took down a bunch of yarrow that had been hanging
from a roof beam.

"What is that used for?"

"Healing salves. Yarrow stops bleeding."

"May I watch? I have never seen witchcraft."

It pleased me as much as her praise of Telegonus. I
made room at the table. She was a flattering audience,
asking careful questions as I named each ingredient and explained its purpose. She wanted to see the herbs I had used
to turn men into pigs. I dropped the dried leaves into her
hand.

"I am not about to turn myself into a sow, am I?"

"You would have to ingest it and speak the words of power. Only those plants fallen from divine blood need no spell to summon their magic. And, I think, you would have to be a witch."

"A goddess."

"No," I said. "My niece was mortal, and she cast spells as strong as mine."

"Your niece," she said. "You do not mean Medea?"

It was strange to hear the name aloud after so long. "You know her?"

"I know what is sung by bards and played in courtyards for kings."

"I would hear it," I said.

The trees outside clattered in the wind as she talked. Medea had indeed escaped Aeëtes. She had traveled on to Iolcos with Jason and borne him two sons, but he recoiled from her sorceries, and his people despised her. In time he sought a new marriage with a sweet, well-loved princess from home. Medea praised his wisdom and sent the bride gifts, a crown and cloak that she had made herself. When the girl put them on, she was burnt alive. Then Medea dragged her children to an altar and, swearing that Jason would never have them, slit their throats. She was last seen summoning a chariot drawn by dragons to take her back to Colchis.

The bards had been at the story, no doubt, but I could still see Medea's bright, piercing face. I believed that she would rather set the world on fire than lose.

"I warned her once that grief would come of her marriage. There is no pleasure in hearing I was right."

"There seldom is." Penelope's voice was soft. She was thinking of those slaughtered children, perhaps. I was thinking of them too. And the dragon chariot that was of

course my brother's. It seemed incredible that she would go
back to him, after all that had passed between them. Yet it
also made a sort of sense to me. Aeëtes wanted an heir, and
there was none more like him than Medea. She had grown
up trained around his cruelty, and in the end it seemed she
had not learned how to hold another shape.

I poured honey onto the yarrow, added beeswax to bind
the salve. The air was musky-sweet and sharp with herbs.

Penelope said, "What makes a witch, then? If it is not divinity?"

"I do not know for certain," I said. "I once thought it was
passed through blood, but Telegonus has no spells in him.
I have come to believe it is mostly will."

She nodded. I did not have to explain. We knew what
will was.

That afternoon Penelope and Telegonus went off again to
the bay. I had assumed after my abruptness last night that
Telemachus would keep his distance. But he found me at
my herbs. "I thought I would work on the tables."

I watched him while I ground the hellebore leaves. He
had a measuring string, and a cup he had marked and filled
to the line with water.

"What are you doing?"

"Testing if the floor is level. Your problem is actually the
legs — they are slightly different sizes. It will be easy to adjust."

I watched him using the rasp, checking and rechecking
the legs with his length of string. I asked him how he had
broken his nose. "Swimming with my eyes closed," he said.
"I learned my lesson there." When he was finished, he
went out to do the flagstones. I followed, weeding, though
the garden scarcely needed it. We discussed bees, how I always wished there were more on the island. He asked if I

could tame them like other creatures. "No," I said. "I use smoke like everyone else."

"I saw a hive that looks overfull," he said. "I can split it in the spring, if you like."

I said I would and watched him scrape away the uneven soil. "The roof drains there," I said. "Those flagstones will only wobble again after the next rain."

"That is how things go. You fix them, and they go awry, and then you fix them again."

"You have a patient temper."

"My father called it dullness. Shearing, cleaning out the hearths, pitting olives. He wanted to know how to do such things for curiosity's sake, but he did not want to actually have to do them."

It was true. Odysseus' favorite task was the sort that only had to be performed once: raiding a town, defeating a monster, finding a way inside an impenetrable city.

"Perhaps you get it from your mother."

He did not look up, but I thought I saw him tense. "How is she? I know you speak to her."

"She misses you."

"She knows where I am."

The anger stood out plain and clean on his face. There was a sort of innocence to him, I thought. I do not mean this as the poets mean it: a virtue to be broken by the story's end, or else upheld at greatest cost. Nor do I mean that he was foolish or guileless. I mean that he was made only of himself, without the dregs that clog the rest of us. He thought and felt and acted, and all these things made a straight line. No wonder his father had been so baffled by him. He would have been always looking for the hidden meaning, the knife in the dark. But Telemachus carried his blade in the open.

*   *   *

They were strange days. Athena hung over our heads like an axe, yet so she had hung for sixteen years, I would hardly faint at it now. Every morning Telegonus took his brother out upon the island. Penelope spun or wove while I shaped my herbs. I had drawn my son aside by then and told him some of what I had learned of Odysseus' worsening temper on Ithaca, his suspicions and angers, and day by day I saw the knowledge work upon him. He still grieved, but the guilt began to ease, and the brightness came back to his face. Penelope and Telemachus' presence helped still more. He basked in their attention like my lions in a patch of sun. It panged me to realize how much he had wanted family all these years.

Penelope and Telemachus still did not speak to each other. Hour after hour, meal after meal, the air between them was brittle. It seemed absurd to me that they did not just confess their faults and sorrows and be done. But they were like eggs, each afraid to crack the other.

In the afternoons, Telemachus always seemed to find some task that brought him near, and we would talk until the sun touched the sea. When I went inside to set out the plates for dinner, he followed. If there was work enough for two, he helped. If there was not, he sat at the hearth carving small pieces of wood: a bull, a bird, a whale breaching the waves. His hands had a precise, careful economy that I admired. He was no witch, but he had the temperament for it. I told him that the floor would clean itself, but he always swept the sawdust and wood-curls after.

It was strange to have such constant company. Telegonus and I had mostly kept out of each other's way, and my nymphs had been more like shadows flitting at the corner of my eye. Usually even that much presence wore on me, nagging at my attention until I had to leave and walk the island alone. But there was a contained quality to Telemachus, a quiet assurance that made him companionable without being intrusive. The creature he most reminded me of, I realized, was my lion. They had the same upright dignity, the same steady gaze with deep-set humor. Even the same earthbound grace, which pursued their own ends while I pursued mine.

"What's so funny?" he asked me.

I shook my head.

It was perhaps the sixth day since they had come. He was making an olive tree, shaping the twisting trunk, picking out each knot and hole with his knife's point.

"Do you miss Ithaca?" I asked him.

He considered. "I miss those I knew. And I am sorry not to see my goats breed." He paused. "I think I would not have been a bad king."

"Telemachus the Just," I said.

He smiled. "That's what they call you if you're so boring they can't think of something better."

"I think you would be a good king also," I said. "Perhaps you still can be. The memories of men are short. You could return in glory as the long-awaited heir, bringing prosperity with the rightness of your blood."

"It sounds like a good story," he said. "But what would I do in those rooms that my father and the suitors filled up? Every step would be a memory I wished I did not have."

"It must be difficult for you to be near Telegonus."

His brow creased. "Why would it be?"

"Because he looks so much like your father."

He laughed. "What are you talking about? Telegonus is

stamped from you. I do not just mean your face. It is your gestures, your walk. Your way of speaking, even your voice."

"You make it sound like a curse," I said.

"It is no curse," he said.

Our eyes met across the air. Far away, my hands were peeling pomegranates for dinner. Methodically, I scored the rind, revealed the white lattice. Within, the red juice pips glowed through their waxy cells. My mouth stung a little with thirst. I had been watching myself with him. It was a novelty to me, noticing the expressions shaping themselves on my face, the movement of the words across my tongue. So much of my life had been spent plunged up to the elbows, tacking now here, now there, spattered and impulsive. This new feeling crept over me like a sort of distant sleepiness, almost a languor. This was not the first speaking look that he had given me. But what did it matter? My son was his brother. His father had been in my bed. He was owed to Athena. I knew it, even if he did not.

Outside, the seasons had turned. The sky opened its hands, and the earth swelled to meet it. The light poured thickly down, coating us in gold. The sea lagged only a little behind. At breakfast Telegonus clapped his brother on the back. "In another few days, we can take the boat out in the bay."

I felt Penelope's glance. *How far does the spell extend?*

I did not know. Somewhere beyond the breakers, but I could not name the exact wave. I said, "Don't forget, Telegonus, there's always one last bad storm. Wait till then."

As if in answer, a knock sounded on the door.

In the silence that followed Telegonus whispered, "The wolves did not howl."

"No." I did not look at Penelope in warning; if she did

360 MADELINE MILLER

not guess, she was a fool. I drew my divinity up, cold and bracing around me, and went to open the door.

Those same black eyes, that same perfect and handsome face. I heard my son gasp, felt the frozen stillness behind me.

"Daughter of Helios. May I come in?"

"No."

He lifted an eyebrow. "I have a message that concerns one of your guests."

I felt a grating fear along my ribs, but I kept my voice flat. "They can hear you where you stand."

"Very well." His skin glowed. His drawling, smirking manner vanished. This was the divine messenger of the gods, potent and inevitable.

"Telemachus, prince of Ithaca, I come on behalf of the great goddess Athena, who would speak with you. She requires that the witch Circe lower the spell that bars her from the isle."

"*Requires*," I said. "That is an interesting word for one who tried to kill my son. Who is to say she does not plan to try again?"

"She is not interested in your son in the least." He dropped his glory. His voice was casual once more. "If you will be a fool about it — these are her words, of course — she offers an oath of protection for him. It is Telemachus alone she wants. It is time for him to take his inheritance." He looked past me to the table. "Do you hear, prince?"

Telemachus' eyes were lowered. "I hear. I am humbled by messenger and message both. But I am a guest on this island. I must await my hostess' word."

Hermes cocked his head a little, his eyes intent. "Well, hostess?"

I felt Penelope at my back, risen like an autumn moon. She had asked for time to mend things with Telemachus, and she had not done it yet. I could imagine her bitter thoughts.

"I will do it," I said. "But it will take some effort to unwind the spell's working. She may expect to come in three days."

"You want me to tell the daughter of Zeus she has to wait three days?"

"They have been here half a month. If she was in a hurry, she should have sent you earlier. And you may tell her those are my words."

Amusement flashed in his eyes. I had fed off that look once, when I had been starving and thought such crumbs a feast. "Be sure I will."

We breathed into the empty space he left behind. Penelope met my eye. "Thank you," she said. Then she turned to Telemachus. "Son." It was the first time I had heard her speak to him directly. "I have made you wait too long. Will you walk with me?"

CHAPTER TWENTY-FOUR

WE WATCHED THEM GO down the path to the shore. Telemachus looked half stunned, but that was only natural. He had learned he was Athena's chosen and would make peace with his mother in the same moment. I had wanted to say something to him before he left, but no words had come.

Telegonus bumped at my elbow. "What did Hermes mean, 'Telemachus' inheritance'?"

I shook my head. Just that morning, I had seen the first green buds of spring. Athena had timed it well. She came as soon as she could make Telemachus sail.

"I am surprised the spell takes three days to undo. Can't you use that — what's it called? Moly?"

I turned to him. "You know my spells are governed by my will. If I let go, they will fall in a second. So no, it does not take three days."

He frowned. "You lied to Hermes? Won't Athena be angry when she finds out?"

His innocence could still frighten me. "I do not plan to tell her. Telegonus, these are gods. You must keep your tricks close or you will lose everything."

"You did it so they would have time to talk," he said. "Penelope and Telemachus."

Young he was, but not a fool. "Something like that."

He tapped his finger on the shutters. The lions did not stir; they knew the noise of his restlessness well. "Will we see them again? If they leave?"

"I think you will," I said. If he heard the change I made, he said nothing. I could feel my chest heaving a little. It had been so long since I had spoken to Hermes, I'd forgotten the effort it took to face down that shrewd, all-seeing gaze.

He said, "Do you think Athena will try to kill me?"

"She must swear an oath before she comes, she will be bound by it. But I will have the spear, in case."

I made my hands work through their chores, plates and washing and weeding. When it began to grow dark, I packed a basket of food and sent Telegonus to find Penelope and Telemachus.

"Don't linger," I said. "They should be alone."

He reddened. "I'm not an idiot child."

I drew in a breath. "I know you are not."

I paced while he was gone. I could not explain the stinging tension I felt. I had known he would be leaving. I had known all along.

Penelope returned when the moon rose. "I am grateful to you," she said. "Life is not so simple as a loom. What you weave, you cannot unravel with a tug. But I think I have made a start. Is it wrong of me to confess that I enjoyed watching you set Hermes back?"

"I have a confession of my own. I am not sorry to let Athena twist for three days."

She smiled. "Thank you. Again."

Telegonus sat at the hearth fletching arrows, but he had

scarcely managed a handful. He was as restless as I was, scuffing at the stones, staring out of the window at the empty garden path as if Hermes might appear again. I cleaned the tables that did not need cleaning. I set my pots of herbs now here, now there. Penelope's black mourning cloak hung from the loom, nearly finished. I could have sat and worked awhile, but the change of hands would show in the cloth. "I am going out," I told Telegonus. And before he could speak, I left.

My feet carried me to a small hollow I knew among the oaks and olives. The branches made good shade, and the grass grew soft. You could listen to the night birds overhead.

He was sitting on a fallen tree, outlined against the dark.

"Do I disturb you?"

"No," he said.

I sat beside him. Beneath my feet the grass was cool and faintly damp. The owls cried in the distance, still hungry from winter's scarcity.

"My mother told me what you did for us. Both now and before. Thank you."

"I am glad if it helped."

He nodded, faintly. "She has been three leagues ahead, as always."

Over us the branches stirred, carving the moon into slivers.

"Are you ready to face the gray-eyed goddess?"

"Is anyone?"

"You have seen her before, at least. When she stopped the war between your father and the suitors' kin."

"I have seen her many times," he said. "She used to come to me when I was a child. Never in her own form. I would notice a quality to certain people around me. You know. The stranger with overly detailed advice. The old family friend whose eyes shine in the dark. The air would smell like buttery olives and iron. I would speak her name and the sky would glow bright as polished silver. The dull things of my life, the hangnail on my thumb, the suitors' taunts, would fade. She made me feel like one of the heroes from songs, ready to tame fire-breathing bulls and sow dragons' teeth."

An owl circled on its silent wings. In the quiet, the yearning in his voice rang like a bell.

"After my father returned, I never saw her again. For a long time I waited. I killed ewes in her name. I scrutinized everyone who passed. Did that goatherd linger strangely? Was not that sailor too interested in my thoughts?"

He made a sound in the dark, a half laugh. "You can imagine people didn't love me for it, always staring at them, then turning away in disappointment."

"Do you know what she intends for you?"

"Who can say, with a god?"

I felt it like a rebuke. That old uncrossable gulf, between mortal and divinity.

"You will have power certainly, and wealth. You will likely have your chance to be Telemachus the Just."

His eyes rested on the shadows of the forest. He had scarcely glanced at me since I came. Whatever had been between us was dispersed like smoke on the wind. His mind was with Athena, pointed at his future. I had known it would be so, but it surprised me how much it ached to see it happen so quickly.

I spoke briskly. "You should take the boat, of course. It's charmed against sea-disaster, as you know. With her help, you shouldn't need that, but it will let you leave as soon as you are ready. Telegonus will not mind."

He was quiet so long I thought he had not heard. But at

last he said, "That is a kind offer, thank you. Then you will have your island back."

I heard the crackles in the brush. I heard the sea distant on the shore, the sound of our breaths vanishing into its ceaseless wash.

"Yes," I said. "I will."

In the days that followed, I passed him as if he were a table in my hall. Penelope eyed me, but I did not speak to her either. The two of them were often together now, mending what had been broken. I did not care to see it. I took Telegonus down to the sea to show me his swimming. His shoulders, hard with muscle, cut unerring through the sea. He looked older than sixteen, a man grown. Children of gods always came to their strength faster than mortals. He would miss them when they were gone, I knew. But I would find something else for him. I would help him forget. I would say, some people are like constellations that only touch the earth for a season.

I set out their evening meals, then took my cloak and walked into the darkness. I sought the highest peaks, the brakes where mortals could not follow me. Even as I did it, I laughed at myself. Which of them do you think is going to chase after you? My mind turned through all those stories I had kept from Odysseus, Aeëtes and Scylla and the rest. I had not wanted my history to be only an amusement, grist for his relentless intelligence. But who else would have tolerated it, with all its ugliness and errors? I had missed my chance to speak, and now it was too late.

I went to bed. I dreamed till dawn of the spear tipped with Trygon's tail.

*   *   *

The morning of the third day Penelope touched me on the sleeve. She had finished the black cloak. It made her face look thinner, her skin dulled. She said, "I know I ask much, but will you be there when we speak to her?"

"I will. And Telegonus too. I want it finished and clear. I am tired of games."

All my words felt like that, hard in my teeth. I strode up to the peak. The rocks there were darkened from sixteen years of my draughts. I reached down, rubbed my finger against the pitted stains. So many times I had come here. So many hours spent. I closed my eyes, and felt the spell above me, fragile as glass. I let it fall.

There was the faintest *ping*, like the snap of an over-drawn bowstring. I waited for the old weight to drop from my shoulders, but instead a gray fatigue rolled through me. I put out my hand for balance and found only air. I staggered, knees wavering. But there was no time for such weakness. We were exposed. Athena was coming, arrowing down upon my island like an eagle in her dive. I made my-self start down the mountain. My feet caught on every root, the rocks turned my ankles. My breath came thin and shallow. I opened the door. Three faces startled up to mine. Telegonus rose. "Mother?"

I pushed past him. My sky lay open, and each moment was a danger. The spear, that is what I needed. I seized its crooked shaft from the corner where I kept it and breathed the sweet poison scent. My mind seemed to clear a little. Even Athena would not risk this.

I carried it into the hall and set myself at the hearth. Uncertainly, they followed. There was no time for a warn-ing. Her lightning-bolt limbs struck the room, and the air turned silver. Her breastplate glowed as if it were still half molten. The crest of her helmet bristled over us.

Her eyes fixed on me. Her voice was dark as ore. "I told you that you would be sorry if he lived."

"You were wrong," I said.

"You have always been insolent, Titan." Sharply, as if to wound me with her precision, she turned her gaze to Telemachus. He was kneeling, Penelope beside him. "Son of Odysseus," she said. Her voice changed, gilding itself. "Zeus has foretold that a new empire will rise in the West. Aeneas is fled there with his remnant Trojans, and I would have Greeks to balance and hold them at bay. The land is fertile and rich, thick with beasts of field and forest, overhung with fruits of every kind. You will found a prosperous city there, you will build stout walls and set down laws to hold back the tide of savagery. You will seed a great people who will rule in ages to come. I have gathered good men from across our lands and set them on a ship. They arrive this day to bear you to your future."

The room burned with the aureate sparks of her vision. Telemachus burned too. His shoulders seemed broader, his limbs swollen with strength. Even his voice had deepened. "Goddess," he said, "gray-eyed and wise. I am honored among mortals. No man can deserve such grace."

She smiled like a temple snake over its bowl of cream. "The ship will come for you at dusk. Be ready."

It was his cue to stand. To show off that glory she had bestowed on him, lift it like a glittering standard. But he knelt, unmoving. "I fear I am not worthy of your gifts."

I frowned. Why was he groveling so much? It was not wise. He should thank her and be done, before she found some reason for offense.

Her voice had a tinge of impatience. "I know your weaknesses," she said. "They will not matter, when I am there to steady your spear-arm. I guided you once to victory against the suitors. I will guide you again."

"You have watched over me," he said. "I thank you for it. Yet I cannot accept."

The air in the room hung utterly still.

"What do you mean?" The words sizzled.

"I have considered," he said. "For three days I have considered. And I find in myself no taste for fighting Trojans or building empires. I seek different days."

My throat had gone dry. What was the fool doing? The last man who refused Athena was Paris, prince of Troy. He had preferred the goddess Aphrodite, and now he was dead and his city ash.

Her eyes were augers, boring through the air. "No taste? What is this? Has some other god offered you something better?"

"No."

"What then?"

He did not flinch from her gaze. "I do not desire such a life."

"Penelope." The word was a lash. "Speak to your son."

Penelope's face was bent to the floor. "I have, goddess. He is set in his course. You know his father's blood was always stubborn."

"Stubborn in achievement." Athena snapped each word like a dove's neck. "In ingenuity. What is this degeneracy?" She swung back to Telemachus. "I do not make this offer again. If you persist in this foolishness, if you refuse me, all my glory will leave you. Even if you beg, I will not come."

"I understand," he said.

His calmness seemed to enrage her. "There will be no songs made of you. No stories. Do you understand? You will live a life of obscurity. You will be without a name in history. You will be no one."

Each word was like the blow of a hammer in a forge. He would give in, I thought. Of course he would. The fame she had described was what all mortals yearn for. It is their only hope of immortality.

"I choose that fate," he said.

Disbelief shone naked on her cold, beautiful face. How many times in her eternity had she been told no? She could not parse it. She looked like an eagle who had been diving upon a rabbit, and the next moment found itself in the mud.

"You are a fool," she spat. "You are lucky I do not kill you where you stand. I spare you out of love for your father, but I am patron to you no more."

The glory that had shone upon him vanished. He looked shriveled without it, gray and gnarled as olive bark. I was as shocked as Athena. What had he done? And so wrapped was I in these thoughts that I could not see the path we walked until it was too late.

"Telegonus," Athena said. Her silver gaze darted to him. Her voice changed again; its iron grew filigree. "You have heard what I offered your brother. I offer it now to you. Will you sail and be my bulwark in Italy?"

I felt as though I had slipped from a cliff. I was in the air, falling, with nothing to hold me.

"Son," I cried. "Say nothing."

Fast as arrow-shot, she turned on me. "You dare to obstruct me again? What more do you want from me, witch? I have sworn an oath I will not harm him. I offer him a gift that men would trade their souls for. Will you keep him hobbled all his life, like a broken horse?"

"You do not want him," I said. "He killed Odysseus."

"Odysseus killed himself," she said. The words hissed through the room like a scythe's blade. "He lost his way."

"It was you who made him lose it."

Anger smoked in her eyes. I saw the thought in them, how her spearhead would look tearing the blood from my throat.

"I would have made him a god," she said. "An equal. But in the end, he was too weak."

It was all the apology you would ever get from a god. I bared my teeth and slashed the spear-tip through the air. "You will not have my son. I will fight you before I let you take him."

"Mother." The voice was soft at my side. "May I speak?"

I was breaking to pieces. I knew what I would see when I looked at him, his eager, pleading hope. He wanted to go. He had always wanted to go, from the moment he was born into my arms. I had let Penelope stay on my island so she would not lose her son. I would lose mine instead.

"I have dreamed of this," he said. "Of golden fields that stretch out, unbroken, to the horizon. Orchards, gleaming rivers, thriving flocks. I used to think it was Ithaca I saw."

He was trying to speak gently, to rein in the excitement that rose in him like a flood. I thought of Icarus, who had died when he was free. Telegonus would die if he were not. Not in flesh and years. But all that was sweet in him would wither and fall away.

He took my hand. The gesture was like a bard's. But were we not in a sort of song? This was the refrain we had practiced so often.

"There is risk, I know it, but you have taught me to be careful. I can do this, Mother. I want to."

I was a gray space filled up with nothing. What could I say? One of us must grieve. I would not let it be him.

"My son," I said, "it is yours to decide."

Joy broke from him like a wave. I turned away so I would not have to see it. Athena would be glad, I thought. Here was her vengeance at last.

"Be ready for the ship," she said. "It comes this afternoon. I do not send another."

The light faded back to simple sun. Penelope and Telemachus eased away. Telegonus embraced me as he had not since he was a child. As maybe he never had. Remember this, I told myself. His wide shoulders, the curve of the bones in his back, the warmth of his breath. But my mind felt parched and windswept.

"Mother? Can you not be happy for me?"

No, I wanted to shout at him. No, I cannot. Why must I be happy? Is it not enough that I let you go? But I did not want for that to be the last he saw of me, his mother shrieking and keening as if he were dead, though he was still filled with so many hopeful years.

"I am happy for you," I made myself say. I led him to his room. I helped him pack, filling trunks with medicines of every sort, for wounds and headaches, for pox and sleeplessness and even childbirth, which he blushed at.

"You are founding a dynasty," I said. "Heirs are usually necessary."

I gave him all the warmest clothes I had, though it was spring and would be summer soon. I said he should take Arcturos, who had loved him since she was a puppy. I pressed amulets on him, wrapped him in enchantments. I piled on treasure after treasure, gold and silver and finest embroidery, for new kings fare best when they have wonders to give.

He had sobered by then. "What if I fail?"

I thought of the land Athena had described. The rolling hills, crowded with their heavy fruits and fields of grain, the bright citadel he would build. He would hand down judgments from a lofted chair in its sunniest hall, and men and women would come from far and wide to kneel to him. He will be a good ruler, I thought. Fair-minded and warm. He will not be consumed like his father was. He had never been hungry for glory, only for life.

"You will not fail," I said.

"You do not think she means some harm to me?"

Now he was worried; now that it was too late. He was only sixteen, so new in the world.

"No," I said. "I do not. She values you for your blood, and in time she will value you for yourself as well. She is more reliable than Hermes, though no god can be called steady. You must remember to be your own man."

"I will." He met my eyes. "You are not angry?"

"No," I said. It had never truly been anger, only fear and sorrow. He was what the gods could use against me.

A knock on the door. Telemachus, carrying a long wool parcel. "I am sorry to intrude." His eyes kept away from mine. He held out the package to my son. "This is for you."

Telegonus unwrapped the cloth. A smooth length of wood, tapered at its ends and notched. The bowstrings were coiled neatly around it. Telegonus stroked the leather grip. "It is beautiful."

"It was our father's," Telemachus said.

Telegonus looked up, stricken. I saw a shadow of the old grief pass across his face. "Brother, I cannot. I have already taken your city."

"That city was never mine," he said. "Nor was this. You will do better with them both, I think."

I felt as though I stood a long way distant. I had never

seen the age between them so clearly before. My keen son, and this man who chose to be no one.

We carried Telegonus' bags down to the shore. Telemachus and Penelope said their farewells, then stood back. I waited beside my son, but he scarcely knew it. His eyes had found the horizon, that seam of waves and sky.

The ship came into the harbor. It was large, its sides fresh with resin and paint, its new sail shining. Its men worked cleanly, efficiently. Their beards were trimmed, their bodies honed with strength. When the gangplank was dropped, they gathered eagerly at the rail.

Telegonus stepped forward to meet them. He stood broad and bright with sun. Arcturos heeled, panting at his side. His father's bow was strung and hanging from his shoulder.

"I am Telegonus of Aiaia," he cried out, "son of a great hero, and a greater goddess. Welcome, for you have been led here by gray-eyed Athena herself."

The sailors dropped to their knees. I would not be able to bear it, I thought. I would seize him, hold him to me. But I only embraced him a final time, pressing hard as if to set him into my skin. Then I watched him take his place among them, stand upon the prow, outlined against the sky. The light darted silver from the waves. I lifted my hand in blessing and gave my son to the world.

In the days that followed, Penelope and Telemachus treated me as if I were Egyptian glass. They spoke softly and walked on light feet past my chair. Penelope offered me the place at the loom. Telemachus kept my cup filled. The fire was always freshly stoked. All of it slid away. They were kind, but they were nothing to me. The syrups in my pantry had been my companions longer. I went to my herbs, but they seemed to shrivel in my fingers. The air felt naked without my spell. Gods might come and go as they wished now. They might do anything. I had no power to stop them.

The days grew warmer. The sky softened, opening over us like the ripe flesh of a fruit. The spear still leaned in my room. I went to it, took off the sheath to breathe over its pale, envenomed ridges, but what I wanted from it, I could not say. I rubbed at my chest as if it were bread I kneaded. Telemachus said, "Are you well?"

"Of course I am well. What could be wrong with me? Immortals do not take sick."

I went to the beach. I walked carefully, as if I held an infant in my arms. The sun beat upon the horizon. It beat everywhere, upon my back and arms and face. I wore no shawl. I would not burn. I never did.

My island lay around me. My herbs, my house, my animals. And so it would go, I thought, on and on, forever the same. It did not matter if Penelope and Telemachus were kind. It did not matter even if they stayed for their whole lives, if she were the friend I had yearned for and he were something else, it would only be a blink. They would wither, and I would burn their bodies and watch my memories of them yellow and fade as everything faded in the endless wash of centuries, even Daedalus, even the blood-spatter of the Minotaur, even Scylla's appetites. Even Telegonus. Sixty, seventy years, a mortal might have. Then he would leave for the underworld, where I could never go, for gods are the opposite of death. I tried to imagine those dusky hills and gray meadows, the shades moving slow and white among them. Some walked hand in hand with those they had loved in life; some waited, secure that one day their beloved would come. And for those who had not loved, whose lives had been filled with pain and horror, there was the black river Lethe, where one might drink and forget. Some consolation.

For me, there was nothing. I would go on through the countless millennia, while everyone I met ran through my fingers and I was left with only those who were like me. The Olympians and Titans. My sister and brothers. My father.

I felt something in me then. It was like the old, early days of my spells, when the path would open, sudden and clear before my feet. All those years I had wrestled and fought, yet there was a part of me that had stood still, just as my sister said. I seemed to hear that pale creature in his black depths.

Then, child, make another.

I did nothing to prepare. If I was not ready now, when would I be? I did not even walk up to the peak. He could come here, upon my yellow sands, and face me where I stood.

"Father," I said, into the air, "I would speak with you."

CHAPTER TWENTY-FIVE

HELIOS WAS NOT A god to be summoned, but I was the wayward daughter who had won Trygon's tail. Gods love novelty, as I have said. They are curious as cats.

He stepped from the air. He was wearing his crown, and its rays turned my beach to gold. The purple of his clothes was rich as deep-pooled blood. Hundreds of years and not a thread had changed. He was still that same image that had been seared upon me from my birth.

"I am come," he said. His voice rolled like heat from a bonfire.

"I seek an end to my exile," I said.

"There is none. You are punished for eternity."

"I ask you to go to Zeus and speak on my behalf. Tell him you would take it as a favor to release me."

His face was more incredulous than angry. "Why would I do such a thing?"

There were many answers I might have given. Because I have been your bargaining piece all along. Because you would have seen those men and known what they were and still you let them land on my island. Because after, when I was a broken thing, you did not come.

"Because I am your daughter and would be free."

He did not even pause. "Disobedient as ever, and overbold. Calling me here for foolishness and nothing."

I looked at his face, blazing with its righteous power. The Great Watchman of the Sky. The Savior, he is called. All-Seeing, Bringer of Light, Delight of Men. I had given him his chance. It was more than he had ever given me.

"Do you remember," I said, "when Prometheus was whipped in your hall?"

His eyes narrowed. "Of course."

"I stayed behind, when all the rest of you left. I brought him comfort, and we spoke together."

His gaze burned into mine. "You would not have dared."

"If you doubt me, you may ask Prometheus himself. Or Aeëtes. Though if you get any truth from him it is a miracle."

My skin had begun to ache at his heat; my eyes watered.

"If you did such a thing, it is deepest treason. You are more owed to exile than ever. You deserve greater punishment still, all I can give you. You have exposed us to Zeus' wrath for some foolish whim."

"Yes," I said. "And if you do not see my exile ended, I will expose you again. I will tell Zeus what I did."

His face contracted. For the first time in my life, I had truly shocked him. "You would not. Zeus will destroy you."

"Perhaps he will," I said. "But I think he will listen first. And you are the one he will truly blame, for you should have kept better check on your daughter. Of course, I will tell him other things as well. All those tiptoeing treasons I heard you whisper with my uncles. I think Zeus would be glad to know how deep the Titan mutiny goes, don't you?"

"You dare to threaten me?"

These gods, I thought. They always say the same thing. "I do."

My father's skin flared blinding bright. His voice seared at my bones. "You would start a war."

"I hope so. For I will see you torn down, Father, before I will be jailed for your convenience any longer."

His rage was so hot the air bent and wavered around him. "I can end you with a thought."

It was my oldest fear, that white annihilation. I felt it shiver through me. But enough. At last, enough.

"You can," I said. "But you have always been cautious, Father. You know I have stood against Athena. I have walked in the blackest deeps. You cannot guess what spells I have cast, what poisons I have gathered to protect myself against you, how your power may rebound upon your head. Who knows what is in me? Will you find out?"

The words hung in the air. His eyes were discs of ignited gold, but I did not look away.

"If I do this thing," he said, "it is the last I will ever do for you. Do not come begging again."

"Father," I said, "I never will. I leave this place tomorrow."

He would not ask where, he would not even wonder. So many years I had spent as a child sifting his bright features for his thoughts, trying to glimpse among them one that bore my name. But he was a harp with only one string, and the note it played was himself.

"You have always been the worst of my children," he said. "Be sure you do not dishonor me."

"I have a better idea. I will do as I please, and when you count your children, leave me out."

His body was rigid with wrath. He looked as though he had swallowed a stone, and it choked him.

"Give Mother my greetings," I said.

His jaw bit down and he was gone.

The yellow sands faded to their usual color. The shadows returned. For a moment I stood breathing, unmoving, my chest filled with a wild battering. But then it was gone. My thoughts were loosed forward, skimming the earth, flying up the hill to my room where the spear waited with its pale poison. It should have been returned to Trygon long ago, yet I had kept it for protection and something else I could not name. At last, I knew what it was.

I went up to the house and found Penelope, sitting at my loom.

"It is time for a decision. There are things I must do. I leave tomorrow, I cannot say for how long. I will take you first to Sparta if you would go there."

She looked up from the tapestry she was making. A wild sea, with a swimmer striking out into darkness. "And if I would not?"

"Then you may stay here."

She held the shuttle lightly, as if it were a bird with its hollow bones. She said, "Would that not...intrude? I know what I have cost you."

Telegonus, she meant. There was grief, and so there would always be. But the gray fog was gone. I felt distant and very clear, like a hawk borne upon the highest aether. I said, "He would never have been happy here."

"But because of us, he went with Athena."

It had hurt once, but that was only pride. "She is far from the worst of them."

Them, I heard myself say.

"I give you the choice, Penelope. What would you do?"

A wolf stretched, her mouth squeaking a little with

her yawn. "I find I am in no rush for Sparta," Penelope said.

"Then come, there are things you must know." I led her to the kitchen with its rows of jars and bottles. "There is an illusion upon the island to make it appear inhospitable to ships. That will remain while I am gone. But sailors are reckless sometimes, and the ones that are most reckless are often the most desperate. These are my drugs that do not need witchcraft. There are poisons among them, and salves for healing. This one causes sleep." I handed her a bottle. "It does not work immediately, so you cannot leave it till the last moment. You will need to get it in their wine. Ten drops will be enough. Do you think you can do it?"

She tipped the contents, felt their weight. A faint smile touched her lips. "You may remember I have some experience in handling unwelcome guests."

Wherever Telemachus was, he did not return for dinner. No matter, I told myself. The time when I had softened like wax was past. My path was laid before me. I packed my things. There were a few changes of clothing and a cloak, but the rest was herbs and bottles. I picked up the spear and carried it out into the warm night air. There was spell-work to do, but I wanted to go to the boat first. I had not seen it since Telemachus began his repairs, and I had to be sure it was ready to sail. Streaks of lightning flashed over the sea, and the breeze brought a distant smell of fire. It was that last storm I had told Telegonus to wait for, but I did not fear it. By morning it would blow itself out.

I stepped into the cave, and stared. It was hard to believe I viewed the same boat. It was longer now, and its bow had been rebuilt and narrowed. The mast was better rigged, and the rudder more trim. I walked around it.

At the front a small prow-piece had been added, a seated lioness with her jaws open. The fur was in the Eastern style, each lock separate, curled like the shell of a snail. I reached to touch one.

"The wax is not set." He stepped out from the darkness. "I have always thought every ship needs a prow spirit."

"It is beautiful," I said.

"I was fishing in the cove when Helios came. All the shadows disappeared. I heard you speak to him."

I felt a flare of embarrassment. How baleful and outlandish and cruel we must have seemed. I rested my eyes on the boat so I would not have to look at him. "Then you know my exile is ended and I sail tomorrow. I asked your mother if she would go to Sparta or stay. She said she wished to stay. I offer the same choice to you."

Outside, the sea made a sound like a shuttle weaving. The stars were yellow as pears, low and ripe on the branch.

"I have been angry with you," he said.

It surprised me. The blood rose stinging to my cheeks. "Angry."

"Yes," he said. "You thought I would go with Athena. Even after all I have said to you. I am not your son and I am not my father. You should have known I do not want anything Athena has."

His voice was even, but I felt the sharp edge of his reproach. "I am sorry," I said. "I could not believe that any in this world would refuse her divinity."

"That is amusing coming from you."

"I am not a promising young prince of whom great things are expected."

"It is overrated."

I ran my hand across the lion's clawed foot, felt the sticky sheen of the wax.

"Do you always make beautiful things for those you are angry with?"

"No," he said. "Only you."

Outside, the lightning flickered. "I was angry as well," I said. "I thought you could not wait to leave."

"I do not know how you could think that. You know I cannot hide my face."

I could smell the beeswax, sweet and thick.

"The way you spoke of Athena coming to you. I thought it was longing. Something you kept close, like a secret heart."

"I kept it close because I was ashamed. I did not want you to hear how she had preferred my father all along."

She is a fool. But I did not say it.

"I do not want to go to Sparta," he said. "Nor do I want to stay here. I think you know where I would like to be."

"You cannot come," I said. "It is not safe for mortals."

"I suspect it is not safe at all. You should see your face. You cannot hide either."

What is my face like? I wanted to ask. Instead I said, "You would leave your mother?"

"She will be well here. And content, I think."

Wood dust floated past, fragrant in the air. It was the same smell that rose from his skin when he carved. I felt reckless suddenly. Sick of all my fretting and convincing, my careful plotting. It came to some by nature, but not to me.

"If you want to join me, I will not stop you," I said. "We leave at dawn."

I made my preparations and he made his. We worked until the sky began to pale. The ship was filled with all the stores it could hold: cheese and toasted barley, fruits dried and

fresh. Telemachus added fishing nets and oars, extra rope
and knives, all of it carefully stowed and strapped in its
place. With rollers we pushed the boat down to the sea,
its hull effortlessly slipping through the breakers. Penelope
stood on the shore to wave us off. Telemachus had gone
alone to tell her he was leaving. Whatever she thought of it
she kept from her face.

Telemachus lifted the sail. The storm was past. The
winds were fresh and blowing well. They caught us, and
we glided through the bay. I looked back at Aiaia. Twice in
all my days I had seen her dwindling behind me. The water grew between us, and her cliffs shrank. I could taste the
salt spray on my lips. All around were those silver-scrolling
waves. No thunderbolt came. I was free.

No, I thought. Not yet.

"Where do we go?" Telemachus' hand waited on the
rudder.

The last time I had spoken her name aloud had been to
his father. "To the straits," I said. "To Scylla."

I watched the words register. He maneuvered the prow
with competent hands.

"You are not frightened?"

"You warned me it was not safe," he said. "I do not think
being frightened will help."

The sea flowed by. We passed the island where I had
stopped with Daedalus on the way to Crete. The beach
was still there, and I glimpsed a grove of almond trees. The
storm-blasted poplar would be long gone by now, crumbled
to earth.

A pale smudge appeared on the horizon. With each
hour it grew, belling like smoke. I knew what it was. "Pull
down the sail," I said. "We have business here first."

Over the rail we caught twelve fish, large as we could

find. They thrashed, spraying cold drops of salt across the deck. I pinched my herbs into their gasping mouths and spoke the word. The old cracking sound, the tearing of flesh, and then they were fish no more, but twelve rams, fat and addled. They jostled, eyes rolling, packed against each other in the small space. It was a blessing — they would not have been able to stand otherwise. They were not used to having feet.

Telemachus had to climb over them to get to the oars. "It may be a little hard to row."

"They will not be here long."

He frowned at one. "Do they taste like mutton?"

"I don't know." I lifted from my herb bag the small clay pot that I had filled the night before. It was stoppered with wax and had a looped handle. With a length of leather cord, I tied it around the largest ram's neck.

We unfurled the sail. I had warned Telemachus about the mist and spray, and he had a pair of oars ready in makeshift locks. They were awkward, for the boat was meant for sails, but they would help us through if the wind died completely. "We must keep moving," I told him. "No matter what."

He nodded, as if it would be that easy. I knew better. The spear was in my hand, tipped with its poisonous spine, but I had seen how fast she was. I had told Odysseus once that there was no withstanding her. Yet here I was again.

Lightly, I touched Telemachus' shoulder and whispered a charm. I felt the illusion gather over him: he was gone, bare deck, empty air. It would not hold up to scrutiny, but it would hide him from her passing glance. He watched, asking no questions. He trusted me. I turned away, abrupt, to face the prow.

The mist drifted over us. My hair grew damp, and the

sucking sound of the whirlpool reached us across the waves. Charybdis, men had named that vortex. It had claimed its share of sailors, all those who tried to avoid Scylla's appetite. The rams pressed against me, swaying. They made no sound, as real sheep would have. They did not know how to use their throats. I pitied them, in their trembling, monstrous forms.

The straits loomed, and we slipped into their mouth. I glanced at Telemachus. He held the oars ready, his eyes alert. Hairs lifted on my neck. What had I done? I should never have brought him.

The smell struck me, familiar even after so long: rot and hate. And then she came, slithering out of the gray fog. Those old lumpen heads of hers crept along the cliff, rasping as they went. Her bloodshot gaze was fixed on the rams, reeking of fat and fear.

"Come!" I cried.

She struck. Six rams were snatched up in six wide-split jaws. She darted back with them into the mist. I heard bones crunching, the wet gulping of her throats. Blood drizzled down the cliff face.

I had time for a single glance at Telemachus. The wind was nearly dead, and he was rowing now, intent. The sweat stood out on his arms.

Scylla returned, heads weaving with malevolence. Tufts of fleece showed between her teeth.

"Now the rest," I said.

She took the other six so fast there was no time to count the beat between my words and their vanishing. The ram with the pot had been among them. I tried to listen for its clay shattering in her teeth, but I could make out nothing above the sounds of bones and flesh.

Last night, beneath the cold moon, I had milked the

spear's poison. It had trickled, clear and thin, into my polished bronze bowl. I had added dittany, gathered so long ago from Crete, cypress root, shards of my cliffs and soil from my garden, and last of all my own red blood. The liquid had foamed and turned yellow. All this I had put into that pot, then sealed it with wax. The draught would be slipping down her throat by now, pooling in her guts.

I thought twelve sheep would have dulled the edge of her hunger, but when she returned her eyes looked the same as ever, greedy and ravening. As if it were not her belly she fed, but an undying rage.

"Scylla!" I lifted the spear. "It is I, Circe, daughter of Helios, witch of Aiaia."

She shrieked, that old baying cacophony, clawing at my ears, but there was no recognition in it.

"Long ago I changed you to this form from the nymph you were. I come now with Trygon's power to make an end to what I began."

And into the mist-soaked air, I spoke the word of my will.

She hissed. Her gaze held not the slightest hint of curiosity. Her heads wove on, searching over the deck as if there might be sheep she had overlooked. Behind me, I could hear Telemachus straining at the oars. Our sail hung limp; he was all that kept us moving forward.

I saw the instant her eyes pierced my illusion and spotted him. She moaned, low and eager.

"No!" I brandished the spear. "This mortal is under my protection. You will suffer eternal agony if you try to take him. You see I have Trygon's tail."

She screamed again. Her breath washed over me, stink and searing heat. The heads were weaving faster in her excitement. They snapped the air, long strands of drool swinging from their jaws. She was afraid of the spear, but that would not hold her for long. She had come to like the taste of mortal flesh. She craved it. Stark, black terror rolled through me. I would have sworn I had felt the spell take hold. Had I been wrong? Panic drenched my shoulders. I would have to fight her six ravening heads at once. I was no trained warrior. One of them would get by me and then Telemachus — I would not let myself finish the thought. My mind spat through ideas, all useless: spells that could not touch her, poisons I did not have, gods who would not come to my aid. I could tell Telemachus to jump and swim, but there was nowhere to go. The only path safe from her reach would take him into the devouring whirlpool of Charybdis.

I set myself between her and Telemachus, spear outthrust, nerves drawn up. I must wound her before she gets by me, I told myself. I must at least get Trygon's poison in her blood. I braced for the blow.

It did not come. One of her mouths was working strangely, jaws hinging and unhinging. A choking noise came from deep within her chest. She gagged, and a yellow foam ran over her teeth.

"What is it?" I heard Telemachus say. "What's happening?"

There was no time for an answer. Her body sagged out of the mist. I had never seen it before, gelatinous and huge. As we watched, it scraped down the cliffside above us. Her heads squealed and bucked, as if trying to haul it back up again. But it only sank further, as inexorably as if it were weighted with stones. I could see now the beginnings of her legs, those twelve monstrous tentacles stretching away from her body into the mist. She kept them hidden always, Hermes had told me, coiled in the cave among the bones and bits of old flesh, gripping the cave's stone so that the rest of her might dart down for her meals and return.

Scylla's heads were snapping and whining, rearing back to bite their own necks. Her gray skin was streaked with yellow foam and her own red blood. A noise began like a boulder drawn across the earth, and suddenly a gray blur tumbled past us, smashing the waves beside our boat. The deck dipped wildly, and I nearly lost my balance. When I was steady again I found myself staring at one of her huge legs. It hung limp off her body, thick as the oldest oak on Aiaia, its end disappearing into the waves.

It had let go its hold.

"We must leave," I said. "Now. There will be more." Before the words were out, the dragging sound had begun again.

Telemachus cried out a warning. The leg smashed so close to our stern it sucked the rail half beneath the waves. I was knocked to my knees, and Telemachus thrown from his seat. He managed to cling to the oars, and with effort wrested them back to their places. The waters around us seethed with wash, the boat pitched up and down. In the air over our heads, Scylla cried and thrashed. The weight of the fallen legs had pulled her further down the cliff. The heads were within range now, but she paid no attention to us. She was biting at the limp flesh of her legs, savaging it. I hesitated a moment, then wedged the spear-haft against our supplies so it would not roll in the chaos. I seized one of Telemachus' oars. "Go."

We bent ourselves to rowing. The dragging sound came again and another leg fell, its great surge soaking the deck, slewing the prow towards Charybdis. I caught a glimpse of its whirling chaos that ate ships whole. Telemachus grappled at the rudder, trying to turn us. "A rope," he shouted.

I scrabbled one out from our stores. He looped it around the rudder, yanking at it, fighting to point us back out of the straits. Scylla's body swayed two mast-lengths above us. The legs were still falling, and each impact pulled the dangling trunk further down.

Ten, I counted. Eleven. "We have to go!"

Telemachus had righted the prow. He tied off the rudder, and we scrambled back to the oars. Beneath the cliff the boat tossed back and forth in the chopped waters like a fallen leaf. The waves around us were stained yellow. Her remaining leg stretched back up the cliff face. It was all that held her, pulled grotesquely taut.

She let go. Her massive body struck the water. The wave ripped the oars from our hands, and my head was buffeted by cold salt. I caught a glimpse of our stores washing into the sea, and vanishing with them into the white, Trygon's spear. I felt the loss like a blow to my chest but there was no time to think of it. I seized Telemachus' arm, expecting any moment the deck to crack beneath us. But the stout planks held, and the rope on the rudder too. The wash of that last great wave shoved us forward, out of the straits.

The sound of Charybdis had faded, and the sea lay open around us. I got to my feet and looked back. At the base of the cliff, where Scylla had been, was a hulking shoal. The outline of six snaky necks was still visible upon it, but they did not move. They would never move again. She had turned to stone.

It was a long way to land. My arms and back ached as if they had been whipped, and Telemachus must have been worse, yet our sail was miraculously intact and it bore us on. The sun seemed to drop into the sea like a falling plate, and night rose over the water. I sighted land through the star-pricked black, and we dragged the boat onto its beach. We had lost all our fresh water stores, and Telemachus was dull-eyed, nearly speechless. I went to find a river and carried back a brimming bowl I'd transformed from a rock. He drained it, and afterwards he lay still so long I began to be afraid, but at last he cleared his throat and asked what food there was. I had gathered a few berries by then, and caught a fish which was spitted over the fire. "I am sorry I put you in such danger," I said. "If you had not been there, we would have been smashed to pieces."

He nodded wearily as he chewed. His face was still drawn and pale. "I confess I am glad we will not have to do it again." He leaned back upon the sand, and his eyes drooped closed.

He was safe, for our camp was backed into the corner of a cliff, so I left him to walk the shore. I thought we were on an island, but I could not tell for certain. There was no smoke rising above the trees, and when I listened, I heard nothing but night birds and brush and the hiss of the waves. There were flowers and forests growing thickly inland, but I did not go look. I was seeing before me again that rocky mass that had been Scylla. She was gone, truly gone. For the first time in centuries, I was not lashed to that flood of misery and grief. No more souls would walk to the underworld written with my name.

I faced the sea. It felt strange to have nothing in my hands, no spear-haft to carry. I could feel the air moving across my palms, salt mingling with the green scent of spring. I imagined the gray length of the tail, sinking through the darkness to find its master. *Trygon*, I said, *your tail comes home to you. I kept it too long, but I made good use of it at last.*

The soft waves washed across the sand.

The darkness felt clean against my skin. I walked through the cool air as if it were a pool I bathed in. We had lost everything but the pouch of tools he had worn at his waist, and my spell bag, which had been tied to me. We would have to make oars, I thought, and lay in new stores of food. But those thoughts were for tomorrow.

I passed a pear tree drifted with white blossoms. A fish splashed in the moonlit river. With every step I felt lighter. An emotion was swelling in my throat. It took me a moment to recognize what it was. I had been old and stern for so long, carved with regrets and years like a monolith. But that was only a shape I had been poured into. I did not have to keep it.

Telemachus slept on. His hands were clasped like a child's under his chin. They had been bloodied at the oars, and I had salved them, their warm weight resting in my lap. His fingers had been more calloused than I imagined, but his palms were smooth. So often on Aiaia, I had wondered how it would feel to touch him.

His eyes opened as if I had spoken the words aloud. They were clear as they always were.

I said, "Scylla was not born a monster. I made her."

His face was in the fire's shadows. "How did it happen?"

There was a piece of me that shouted its alarm: *if you speak he will turn gray and hate you*. But I pushed past it. If he turned gray, then he did. I would not go on anymore weaving my cloths by day and unraveling them again at night, making nothing. I told him the whole tale of it, each jealousy and folly and all the lives that had been lost because of me.

"Her name," he said. "Scylla. It means *the Render*. Perhaps it was always her destiny to be a monster, and you were only the instrument."

"Do you use the same excuse for the maids you hanged?"

It was as if I had struck him. "I make no excuse for that. I will wear that shame all my life. I cannot undo it, but I will spend my days wishing I could."

"It is how you know you are different from your father," I said.

"Yes." His voice was sharp.

"It is the same for me," I said. "Do not try to take my regret from me."

He was quiet a long time. "You are wise," he said.

"If it is so," I said, "it is only because I have been fool enough for a hundred lifetimes."

"Yet at least what you loved, you fought for."

"That is not always a blessing. I must tell you, all my past is like today, monsters and horrors no one wants to hear."

He held my gaze. Something about him then reminded me strangely of Trygon. An unearthly, quiet patience.

"I want to hear," he said.

I had kept away from him for so many reasons: his mother and my son, his father and Athena. Because I was a god, and he a man. But it struck me then that at the root of all those reasons was a sort of fear. And I have never been a coward.

I reached across that breathing air between us and found him.

CHAPTER TWENTY-SIX

THREE DAYS WE STAYED upon that shore. We made
no oars and patched no sails. We caught fish and picked
fruit, and looked for nothing but what we found at our
fingers' ends. I laid my palm on his stomach, feeling it
rise and fall with his breath. His shoulders were wiry with
muscle, the back of his neck roughened with sunburn.

I did tell him those stories. By the fire, or the morning's
light, when our pleasures were set aside. Some of it was
easier than I thought it would be. There was a kind of joy
in drawing Prometheus for him, in making Ariadne and
Daedalus live again. But other parts were not so easy, and
sometimes as I spoke an anger would come over me, and the
words would curdle in my mouth. Who was he to be so patient, while I spilled my blood? I was a woman grown. I was
a goddess, and his elder by a thousand generations. I did not
need his pity, his attention, anything.

"Well?" I would demand. "Why don't you say something?"

"I am listening," he would answer.

"You see?" I said, when I was finished with the tale.
"Gods are ugly things."

"We are not our blood," he answered. "A witch once told me that."

On the third day he cut new oars, and I transformed water-skins and filled them, then gathered up fruit. I watched him rig the sail with easy competence, check the hull for any leaks. I said, "I don't know what I was thinking. I cannot sail a boat. What would I have done if you hadn't come?"

He laughed. "You would have gotten there eventually, it just would have taken some of your eternity. Where do we go next?"

"A shore, east of Crete. There is a small cove, half sand, half rocks, and a scrub forest in sight, and hills. Overhead, at this time of the year, the Dragon seems to point the way."

He raised his eyebrows.

"If you get me close enough, I think I will be able to find it." I watched him. "Are you going to ask what is there?"

"I do not think you want me to."

Less than a month we had spent together, yet he seemed to know me better than anyone who had ever walked the world.

It was a smooth voyage, the wind fresh and the sun still shy of its blistering summer heat. At night, we made our camp on whatever shores we could find. He was used to living like a herder, and I found I did not miss my gold and silver bowls, my tapestries. We roasted our fish on stick-ends, I carried fruits in my dress. If there was a house, we might offer services in return for bread and wine and cheese. He carved toys for children, patched skiffs. I had my salves, and if I kept my head covered, I could pass for an herbwoman coming to ease their aches and fevers. Their gratitude was simple and plain, and ours was the same. No one knelt.

While the boat sailed beneath the blue-arched sky, we would sit together on the boards talking of the people we had met, the coastlines we passed, the dolphins that followed us for half the morning, grinning and splashing at our rails.

"Do you know," he said, "that before coming to Aiaia, I only left Ithaca once?"

I nodded. "I have seen Crete and some islands on the way, and that is all. I have always wished to go to Egypt."

"Yes," he said. "And Troy, and the great cities of Sumeria."

"Assur," I said. "And I want to see Aethiopia. And the North as well, the ice-ribbed lands. And Telegonus' new kingdom in the West."

We looked out over the waves, and a silence hung between us. The next sentence should be: let us go together. But I could not speak that, not now and perhaps not ever. And he would keep silent, for he did know me well.

"Your mother," I said. "Do you think she'll be angry at us?"

He snorted. "No," he said. "She likely knew before we did."

"I would not be surprised if we come back and find her a witch."

It always made me happy to startle him, to see his evenness blown wide. "What?"

"Oh, yes," I said. "She has eyed my herbs from the beginning. I would have taught her, if there had been time. I will wager with you."

"If you are so sure, I do not think I will take your odds."

At night we crossed the hollows of each other's skin, and when he slept I would lay beside him, feeling the warmth where our limbs touched, watching the soft pulse at his throat. His eyes had creases, and his neck had more. When people saw us, they thought I was younger. But though I

looked and sounded like a mortal, I was a bloodless fish.
From my water I could see him, and all the sky behind, but
I could not cross over.

Between the Dragon and Telemachus, we did at last find
my old shore. It was morning when we reached the narrow
bay, my father's chariot halfway to its peak. Telemachus
held the anchor stone. "Drop, or draw onto the sand?"

"Drop," I said.

Hundreds of years of tides and storms had changed the
shoreline's shape, but my feet remembered the sand's fineness, the rough grass with its burrs. In the distance drifted
faint gray smoke and the sound of goat bells. I passed the
jutting rocks where Aeëtes and I used to sit. I passed the forest where I had lain after my father burned me, now only a
stand of straggling pines. The hills I had dragged Glaucos
up were crowded with spring: strawflowers and hyacinths,
lilies, violets, and sweet rock roses. And at their center, the
small clutch of yellow flowers, sprung from Kronos' blood.

The old humming note rose up as if in greeting. "Do
not touch them," I said to Telemachus, but even as the
words were out, I realized how foolish they were. The flowers could do nothing to him. He was himself already. I
would not see a hair changed.

Using my knife, I dug up each stalk by its roots. I
wrapped them with soil in strips of cloth and settled them
in the darkness of my bag. There was no more reason to
linger. We hauled up the anchor and pointed the prow towards home. The waves and islands passed but I scarcely
saw them. I was drawn taut as an archer sighting against the
sky, waiting for the bird to flush. On the last evening, when
Aiaia was so close I thought I could smell her blooms drifting on the sea air, I told him the story that I had kept back,

of the first men who had come to my island, and what I had done to them in return.

The stars were very bright, and Vesper shone like a flame overhead. "I did not tell you before because I did not want it to lie between us."

"And now you do not mind if it does?"

From the darkness of my bag, the flowers sang their yellow note. "Now I want you to have the truth, whatever comes."

The light salt breeze rifled in the shore-grass. He was holding my hand against his chest. I could feel the steady beat of his blood.

"I have not pressed you," he said. "And still I will not. I know there are reasons you cannot answer me. But if — " He stopped. "I want you to know, if you go to Egypt, if you go anywhere, I want to go with you."

Pulse by pulse, his life passed under my fingers. "Thank you," I said.

Penelope met us on Aiaia's shore. The sun was high, and the island bloomed wildly, fruits swelling on their branches, new green growth leaping from every crook and crevice. She looked at ease amid that profusion, waving to us, calling her greetings.

If she noticed a change between us, she said nothing. She embraced us both. It had been quiet, she said, no visitors, yet not quiet at all. More lion cubs had been born. A mist had covered the east bay for three days, and there had been such a torrent of rain that the stream burst its banks. Her cheeks showed her blood as she talked. We wound past the glossy laurels, the rhododendrons, through my garden and the great oak doors. I breathed my house's air, thick with the clean smell of herbs. I felt that pleasure the bards sing of so often: homecoming.

In my room the sheets of my wide, gold bed were fresh as they ever were. I could hear Telemachus telling his mother the story of Scylla. I left and went barefoot to walk the island. The earth was warm beneath my feet. The flowers tossed their bright heads. A lion followed at my heels. Was I saying farewell? I was pointed up into the sky's wide arch. Tonight, I thought. Tonight, beneath the moon, alone.

I came back when the sun was setting. Telemachus had gone to catch fish for dinner, and Penelope and I sat at the table. Her fingertips were stained green, and I could smell the spells in the air.

"I have long wondered something," I said. "When we fought over Athena, how did you know to kneel to me? That it would shame me?"

"Ah. It was a guess. Something Odysseus said about you once."

"Which was?"

"That he had never met a god who enjoyed their divinity less."

I smiled. Even dead he could surprise me. "I suppose that is true. You said that he shaped kingdoms, but he also shaped the thoughts of men. Before him, all the heroes were Heracles and Jason. Now children will play at voyaging, conquering hostile lands with wits and words."

"He would like that," she said.

I thought he would too. A moment passed, and I looked at her stained hands on the table before me.

"And? Are you going to tell me? How goes your witchery?"

She smiled her inward smile. "You were right. It is mostly will. Will and work."

"I am finished here," I said, "one way or another. Would you like to be witch of Aiaia in my place?"

"I think I would. I think I truly would. My hair, though, it is not right. It looks nothing like yours."

"You could dye it."

She made a face. "I will say instead it has gone gray from my haggish sorceries."

We laughed. She had finished the tapestry, and it hung behind her on the wall. That swimmer, striking out into the stormy deep.

"If you find yourself in want of company," I said, "tell the gods you will take their bad daughters. I think you will have the right touch for them."

"I will consider that a compliment." She rubbed at a smudge on the table. "And what about my son? Will he be going with you?"

I realized I felt almost nervous. "If he wants to."

"And what do you want?"

"I want him to come," I said. "If it is possible. But there is a thing which still lies before me to be done. I do not know what will come of it."

Her calm gray eyes held mine. Her brow was arched like a temple, I thought. Graceful and enduring. "Telemachus has been a good son, longer than he should have been. Now he must be his own." She touched my hand. "Nothing is sure, we know that. But if I had to trust that a thing would be done, I would trust it to you."

I carried our dishes away, washed them carefully until they shone. My knives I whetted and laid each in its place. I wiped down the tables, I swept the floor. When I came back to my hearth, only Telemachus was there. We walked to the small clearing we both loved, the one where a lifetime ago we had spoken of Athena.

"The spell I mean to do," I said. "I do not know what

will happen when I cast it. It may not even work. Perhaps Kronos' power cannot be carried from its soil."

He said, "Then we will go back. We will go back until you are satisfied."

It was so simple. If you want it, I will do it. If it would make you happy, I will go with you. Is there a moment that a heart cracks? But a cracked heart was not enough, and I had grown wise enough to know it. I kissed him and left him there.

CHAPTER TWENTY-SEVEN

THE FROGS HAD GONE to their wallows; the salamanders slept in brown holes. The pool showed the moon's half-face, the pinpoints of stars, and all around, bending near, the wavering trees.

I knelt on the bank, thick with grass. Before me was the old bronze bowl I had used for my magics since the very first. The flowers rested beside me in their pale root swaddles. Stem by stem, I cut them and squeezed out the drops of running sap. The bottom of the bowl grew dark. It too began to show the moon. The last flower I did not squeeze but planted there on the shore, where the sun fell every morning. Perhaps it would grow.

I could feel the fear in myself, gleaming like water. These flowers had made Scylla a monster, though all she had done was sneer. Glaucos had become a monster of sorts too, everything that was kind in him driven out by godhead. I remembered my old terror, from Telegonus' birth: *what creature waits within me?* My imagination conjured up horrors. I would sprout slimy heads and yellow teeth. I would stalk down to the hollow and savage Telemachus to pieces.

But perhaps, I told myself, it would not be like that. Perhaps all I hoped would come to pass, and Telemachus and I would go to Egypt indeed, and all those other places. We would cross and recross the seas, living on my witchcraft and his carpentry, and when we came to a town a second time, the people would step out of their houses to greet us. He would patch their ships, and I would cast charms against biting flies and fevers, and we would take pleasure in the simple mending of the world.

The vision blossomed, vivid as the cool grass beneath me, as the black sky over my head. We would visit the Lion Gate of Mycenae, where Agamemnon's heirs ruled, and the walls of Troy, their stones chilled by winds from ice-peaked Ida. We would ride elephants and walk in the desert night beneath the eyes of gods who had never heard of Titans or Olympians, who took no more notice of us than they did of the sand beetles toiling at our feet. He would say to me that he wanted children, and I would say, "You do not know what you are asking of me," and he would say, "This time you are not alone."

We have a daughter, and then another. Penelope attends my birthing bed. There is pain, but it passes. We live on the island when the children are young and visit often after. She weaves and casts spells while nymphs glide around her. However gray she gets she never seems to tire, but sometimes I see her eyes turn to the horizon where the house of the dead and its souls wait.

The daughters I dream to life are different from Telegonus, and different from each other. One chases the lions in circles, while the other sits in a corner, watching and remembering everything. We are wild with our love for them, standing over their sleeping faces, whispering about what she said today, what she did. We bring them to meet

Telegonus, throned among his golden orchards. He leaps from his couch to embrace us all and introduces us to his captain of the guard, a tall, dark-haired youth who never leaves his side. He is not married yet, he may not ever be, he says. I smile, imagining Athena's frustration. So polite he is, yet firm and immovable as one of his own city walls. I do not worry for him.

I have aged. When I look in my polished bronze mirror there are lines upon my face. I am thickened too, and my skin has begun growing loose. I cut myself at my herbs and the scars stay. Sometimes I like it. Sometimes I am vain and dissatisfied. But I do not wish myself back. Of course my flesh reaches for the earth. That is where it belongs. One day, Hermes will lead me down to the halls of the dead. We will scarcely recognize each other, for I will be white-haired, and he will be wrapped in his mystery as Leader of Souls, the only time he is solemn. I think I will enjoy seeing that.

I know how lucky I am, stupid with luck, crammed with it, stumbling drunk. I wake sometimes in the dark terrified by my life's precariousness, its thready breath. Beside me, my husband's pulse beats at his throat; in their beds, my children's skin shows every faintest scratch. A breeze would blow them over, and the world is filled with more than breezes: diseases and disasters, monsters and pain in a thousand variations. I do not forget either my father and his kind hanging over us, bright and sharp as swords, aimed at our tearing flesh. If they do not fall on us in spite and malice, then they will fall by accident or whim. My breath fights in my throat. How can I live on beneath such a burden of doom?

I rise then and go to my herbs. I create something, I transform something. My witchcraft is as strong as ever, stronger. This too is good fortune. How many have such power and leisure and defense as I do? Telemachus comes from our bed to find me. He sits with me in the green-smelling darkness, holding my hand. Our faces are both lined now, marked with our years.

Circe, he says, it will be all right.

It is not the saying of an oracle or a prophet. They are words you might speak to a child. I have heard him say them to our daughters, when he rocked them back to sleep from a nightmare, when he dressed their small cuts, soothed whatever stung. His skin is familiar as my own beneath my fingers. I listen to his breath, warm upon the night air, and somehow I am comforted. He does not mean that it does not hurt. He does not mean that we are not frightened. Only that: we are here. This is what it means to swim in the tide, to walk the earth and feel it touch your feet. This is what it means to be alive.

Overhead the constellations dip and wheel. My divinity shines in me like the last rays of the sun before they drown in the sea. I thought once that gods are the opposite of death, but I see now they are more dead than anything, for they are unchanging, and can hold nothing in their hands.

All my life I have been moving forward, and now I am here. I have a mortal's voice, let me have the rest. I lift the brimming bowl to my lips and drink.

CAST OF CHARACTERS

TITAN DIVINITIES

Aeëtes: Brother of Circe and the sorcerer-king of Colchis, a kingdom on the eastern edge of the Black Sea. Aeëtes was also the father of the mortal witch Medea, and the keeper of the Golden Fleece, until it was stolen by Jason and the Argonauts with Medea's help.

Boreas: The north wind personified. He is responsible, in some myths, for the death of the beautiful youth Hyacinthos. His brothers were Zephyros (the west wind), Notos (the south wind), and Euros (the east wind).

Calypso: A daughter of the Titan Atlas who dwells on the island of Ogygia. In the *Odyssey*, she takes in the shipwrecked Odysseus. Having fallen in love with him, she keeps him on her island for seven years, until the gods command her to release him.

Circe: A witch who lived on the island of Aiaia, daughter of Helios and the nymph Perse. Her name is likely derived from the word for *hawk* or *falcon*. In the *Odyssey*, she turns Odysseus' men into pigs, but after he challenges her, she takes him as a lover, allowing him and his men to stay with her and aiding them when they depart again. Circe has had a long literary life, inspiring writers such as Ovid, James Joyce, Eudora Welty, and Margaret Atwood.

Helios: Titan god of the sun. Father of many children, including Circe, Aeëtes, Pasiphaë, and Perses, as well as their half-sisters, the nymphs Phaethousa and Lampetia. He was most often depicted in his chariot of golden horses, which he drove across the sky each day. In the *Odyssey*, he asks Zeus to destroy Odysseus' men after they kill his sacred cows.

Mnemosyne: A goddess of memory, and mother of the nine muses.

Nereus: An early god of the sea, overshadowed by the Olympian Poseidon. Father of many divine children, including the sea-nymph Thetis.

Oceanos: In the poetry of Homer, Oceanos is the Titan god of the great fresh-water river Oceanos, which the ancients imagined encircled the world. In later times, he became associated with the sea and salt-water. He is Circe's maternal grandfather, and the father of numerous nymphs and gods.

Pasiphaë: Circe's sister, a powerful witch who marries Zeus' mortal son Minos and becomes queen of Crete. She has several children with him, including Ariadne and Phaedra, and also contrives to become pregnant by a sacred white bull, giving birth to the Minotaur.

Perse: An Oceanid, one of the nymph daughters of Oceanos. The mother of Circe and wife to Helios. In later stories, she was associated with witchcraft herself.

Perses: Circe's brother, associated in some stories with ancient Persia.

Prometheus: A Titan god who disobeyed Zeus to help mortals, giving them fire and, in some stories, teaching them the arts of civilization as well. Zeus punished him by chaining him to a crag in the Caucasus Mountains, where an eagle came every day to tear out and eat his liver, which then regenerated overnight.

Proteus: A shape-shifting god of the sea, guardian of Poseidon's flocks of seals.

Selene: The goddess of the moon, Circe's aunt and Helios' sister. She drove a chariot of silvery horses across the night sky, and her husband was the beautiful shepherd Endymion, a mortal enchanted to eternal, ageless sleep.

Tethys: Titan wife to Oceanos, and Circe's grandmother. Like her husband, she was initially associated with fresh-water but was later depicted as a goddess of the sea.

OLYMPIAN DIVINITIES

Apollo: God of light, music, prophecy, and medicine. Apollo was the son of Zeus and the twin brother of Artemis, and a champion of the Trojans in the Trojan War.

Artemis: Goddess of the hunt, a daughter of Zeus and sister to Apollo. In the *Odyssey*, she is named as the killer of the princess Ariadne.

Athena: The powerful goddess of wisdom, weaving, and war arts. She was a fierce supporter of Greeks in the Trojan War, and a particular guardian of the wily Odysseus. She appears often in both the *Iliad* and *Odyssey*. Said to be Zeus' favorite child, she was born from his head fully formed and armored.

Dionysus: A son of Zeus, the god of wine, revelry, and ecstasy. He commanded Theseus to abandon the princess Ariadne, wanting her for his own wife.

Eileithyia: Goddess of childbearing who helped mothers in their labors, and also had the power to prevent a child from being born.

Hermes: Son of Zeus and the nymph Maia, messenger of the gods as well as god of travelers and trickery, commerce, and boundaries. He also led the souls of the dead to the underworld. In some stories Hermes was the ancestor of Odysseus, and in the *Odyssey*, he counsels Odysseus on how to counteract Circe's magic.

Zeus: King of gods and men, ruler of all the world from his throne on Mount Olympus. He initiated the war against the Titans to take vengeance on his father, Kronos, and eventually to overthrow him. Father of many gods and mortals both, including Athena, Apollo, Dionysus, Heracles, Helen, and Minos.

MORTALS

Achilles: Son of the sea-nymph Thetis and King Peleus of Phthia, Achilles was the greatest warrior of his generation, as well as the swiftest and most beautiful. As a teenager, Achilles was offered a choice: long life and obscurity, or short life and fame. He chose fame, and sailed with the other Greeks to

Troy. However, in the ninth year of the war he quarreled with Agamemnon and refused to fight any longer, returning to battle only when his beloved Patroclus was killed by Hector. In a rage, he slew the great Trojan warrior and was eventually killed himself by Hector's brother Paris, assisted by the god Apollo.

Agamemnon: Ruler of Mycenae, the largest kingdom in Greece. He served as the over-general of the Greek expedition to retrieve his brother Menelaus' wife, Helen, from Troy. Quarrelsome and proud during the ten years of war, he was murdered by his wife, Clytemnestra, upon returning home to Mycenae. In the *Odyssey*, Odysseus speaks to his shade in the underworld.

Ariadne: A princess of Crete, daughter of the goddess Pasiphaë and the demigod Minos. When the hero Theseus came to slay the Minotaur, she aided him, giving him a sword and a ball of string to unravel behind him so he could find his way out of the Labyrinth once the creature was dead. Afterwards, she fled with him, and the two planned to marry before the god Dionysus intervened.

Daedalus: A master craftsman, credited with several famous ancient inventions and works of art, including a dancing circle used by Ariadne and the great Labyrinth which jailed the Minotaur. Held captive with his son, Icarus, on Crete, Daedalus devised a plan to free himself, building two sets of wings with wax and feathers. He and Icarus successfully escaped, but Icarus flew too close to the sun, and the wax holding the feathers melted. The boy fell into the sea and drowned.

Elpenor: A member of Odysseus' crew. In the *Odyssey*, he dies from falling off the roof of Circe's house.

Eurycleia: Odysseus' old nurse, and Telemachus' as well. In the *Odyssey*, she washes the feet of Odysseus when he returns in disguise, and recognizes him because of the scar on his leg, which he earned in a boar hunt in his youth.

Eurylochos: A member of Odysseus' crew, and cousin to Odysseus. In the *Odyssey*, he and Odysseus are often at odds, and he is the one who convinces the other men to kill and eat Helios' sacred cows.

Glaucos: A fisherman who undergoes a transformation after falling asleep in a patch of magical herbs. A version of his story is told in Ovid's *Metamorphoses*.

Hector: Oldest son of Priam and crown prince of Troy, Hector was known for his strength, nobility, and love of family. In the *Iliad*, Homer shows us a touching scene between Hector; his wife, Andromache; and their young son, Astyanax. Hector is killed by Achilles in vengeance for killing Achilles' lover Patroclus.

Helen: Legendarily the most beautiful woman in the ancient world, Helen was a queen of Sparta, daughter of queen Leda and the god Zeus in the form of a swan. Many men sought her hand in marriage, each swearing an oath (devised by Odysseus) to uphold her union with whatever man prevailed. She was given to Menelaus, but later ran away with the Trojan prince Paris, setting in motion the Trojan War. After the war, she returned home with Menelaus to Sparta, where, Homer tells us, Odysseus' son Telemachus met her looking for information about his father.

Heracles: Son of Zeus and the most famous of the golden-age heroes. Known for his tremendous strength, Heracles was forced to perform twelve labors in penance to the goddess Hera, who hated him for being the product of one of Zeus' affairs.

Icarus: Son of the master craftsman Daedalus. He and his father escaped Crete on sets of wings made from feathers and wax. Icarus ignored his father's warning not to fly too close to the sun, and his wax melted. The wings fell to pieces, dropping Icarus into the sea.

Jason: Prince of Iolcos. Deprived of his throne by his uncle, Pelias, he set out on a quest to prove his worth, bringing home the Golden Fleece, kept by the sorcerer-king of Colchis, Aeëtes. With the help of his patron goddess Hera, Jason secured a ship, the famous *Argo*, and a crew of heroic comrades called the Argonauts. When he arrived on Colchis, King Aeëtes gave him a series of impossible challenges, including yoking two fire-breathing bulls. Aeëtes' daughter, the witch Medea, fell in love with Jason and aided him in his tasks, and they fled together with the fleece.

Laertes: Odysseus' father and king of Ithaca. Though he is still alive in the *Odyssey*, he has retired from the palace to his estates. He stands with Odysseus against the families of the suitors.

Medea: The daughter of King Aeëtes of Colchis, and niece of Circe. She was a witch like her father and aunt, and when Jason came to claim the Golden Fleece, she used her powers to help him seize it on the condition that he would marry her and take her back with him. The two fled, but Aeëtes pursued them, and only through a bloody trick could Medea keep her father at bay. Her story is told in a number of ancient and modern works, including Euripides' famous tragedy *Medea*.

Minos: A son of Zeus, and the king of powerful Crete. His wife, Pasiphaë, was a goddess and the mother of the Minotaur. Minos demanded that Athens send a tribute of its children in order to feed the monster. After Minos' death, he was given pride of place in the underworld as a judge of the other souls.

Odysseus: The wily prince of Ithaca, favorite of the goddess Athena, husband to Penelope, and father of Telemachus. During the Trojan War, he was one of Agamemnon's chief advisers, and devised the trick of the Trojan horse which won the Greeks the war. His voyage home, which lasted ten years, is the subject of Homer's *Odyssey*, and includes his famous encounters with the cyclops Polyphemus, the witch Circe, the monsters Scylla and Charybdis, and the Sirens. Homer gives him a number of epic epithets, including *polymetis* (man of many wiles), *polytropos* (man of many turnings), and *polytlas* (much-enduring).

Patroclus: Most beloved companion of the hero Achilles, and in many retellings also his lover. In the *Iliad* his fateful decision to try to save the Greeks by dressing in Achilles' armor sets in motion the final act of the story. When Patroclus is killed by Hector, Achilles is devastated and takes brutal vengeance upon the Trojans, which also brings about Achilles' own death. In the *Odyssey*, Odysseus sees Patroclus by Achilles' side when he visits the underworld.

Penelope: Cousin to Helen of Sparta, wife of Odysseus, mother of Telemachus, celebrated for her cleverness and faithfulness. When Odysseus failed to come home after the war, she was besieged by suitors who took over her house, trying to pressure her into marrying one of them. She famously promised to choose from among them when a shroud she was weaving was finished. She stalled them this way for years, unweaving every night what she had woven during the day.

Pyrrhus: The son of Achilles, who was instrumental in the sack of Troy. He killed Priam, king of Troy, and in some retellings also Astyanax, Hector's baby, to prevent him from growing up and exacting vengeance.

Telegonus: The son of Odysseus and Circe, credited as the mythical founder of the cities of Tusculum and Praeneste in Italy.

Telemachus: Odysseus and Penelope's only child, the prince of Ithaca. In the *Odyssey*, Homer shows him helping his father plot and enact his vengeance against the suitors besieging their home.

Theseus: Prince of Athens, sent to Crete as part of Athens' promised tribute of fourteen youths to feed the Minotaur's savage appetite. Instead, Theseus killed the Minotaur with the princess Ariadne's help.

MONSTERS

Charybdis: A powerful whirlpool set on one side of narrow straits, across from the monster Scylla. Ships seeking to avoid Scylla's teeth were swallowed whole.

Minotaur: Named after Minos, the king of Crete, the Minotaur was actually the child of the queen Pasiphaë and a sacred white bull. Daedalus built the Labyrinth to contain the flesh-eating monster, and Minos demanded that Athens send fourteen boys and girls as sacrifices to feed it. One of these was the Athenian prince Theseus, who slew the beast.

Polyphemus: A cyclops (one-eyed giant), and a son of Poseidon. In the *Odyssey*, Odysseus and his men land upon Polyphemus' island, enter his cave, and begin eating his stores. When Polyphemus catches them, he traps them in the cave, devouring several of Odysseus' men. Odysseus tricks the monster with friendly words, giving his name as *Outis, No one*. He blinds the monster to escape, and as he sails off, he reveals his true name. Polyphemus calls on his father, Poseidon, to punish Odysseus.

Scylla: According to Homer, a ferocious monster with six heads and twelve dangling legs who hid in a cave on one side of narrow straits, across from the whirlpool Charybdis. When boats passed she would dart down, snatch up a sailor in each of her mouths, and devour them. In later depictions she was given the head of a woman, a sea-monster tail, and savage dogs erupting from her belly. In Ovid's *Metamorphoses*, Scylla was originally a nymph who was transformed into a monster.

Sirens: Often depicted with women's heads and birds' bodies, the Sirens perched atop craggy rocks, singing. Their voices were so sweet that men would forget their reason when hearing them. In the *Odyssey*, Circe advises Odysseus to put beeswax in his men's ears so as to pass safely, and further suggests that he tie himself to the mast with his own ears free, so he may be the first to hear their enchanting song and live.

ACKNOWLEDGMENTS

So many people were supportive of this book's journey that I cannot possibly list them all. I must settle instead for a heartfelt Thank You: to my friends, family, students, readers, and all those who engage passionately with these ancient stories and stop to tell me about it.

Thanks to Dan Burfoot for his time and keen literary insight on an early draft. Huge thanks to Jonah Ramu Cohen for always being enthusiastic about my work, willing to read multiple drafts and to talk storytelling, myths, and feminism.

I continue to be grateful to and inspired by my classics mentors, most especially David Rich, Joseph Pucci, and Michael C. J. Putnam. I am grateful as well to the gracious David Elmer, who let me pick his brain on a few key matters. They all bear no responsibility for my distortions.

Many thanks to Margo Rabb, Adam Rosenblatt, and Amanda Levinson for cheering me on through the writing process, and likewise to Sarah Yardney and Michelle Wofsey Rowe. Much love to my brother, Tull, and his wife, Beverly, for their continued support.

Deepest gratitude to Gatewood West for insight, crucial wisdom, and great warmth that was with me throughout this journey.

I offer eternal devotions to my amazing editor, Lee Boudreaux, for brilliant and patient feedback, for all her faith in my work, and for being generally sublime. Thank you as well to the fabulous team: Pamela Brown, Carina Guiterman, Gregg Kulick, Karen Landry, Carrie Neill, Craig Young, and everyone else at Little, Brown. Very special thanks also to the wonderful Judy Clain and Reagan Arthur for their enthusiasm and support.

I am so grateful as well to the divine Alexandra Pringle, and to the whole Bloomsbury UK family: Ros Ellis, Madeleine Feeny, David Mann, Angelique Tran Van Sang, Amanda Shipp, Rachel Wilkie, and many more.

And, as always, a million thank-yous to Julie Barer, who continues to be Best of All Agents, loving, brilliant, and a fierce advocate for my work, always willing to read another draft, and a great friend to boot. Big thanks to the whole team at The Book Group, especially Nicole Cunningham and Jenny Meyer. And of course to the terrific Caspian Dennis, and Sandy Violette as well.

There are not enough words in the world to adequately express my adoration of and gratitude to Jonathan and Cathy Drake for their love, support, and supreme grandparenting. Thank you! Thanks also to Tina, BJ, and Julia.

Love and hugest appreciation to my lovely stepfather, Gordon, and to my mother, Madeline, who introduced the classics to me, read to me every day of my childhood, and supported this book getting written in ways large and small, not least by being my first example of *dux femina facti*.

Much love to the radiant and potent V. and F., whose magic transformed my life, and who were patient with me disappearing for hours at a time. Finally, unending thanks and love to Nathaniel, my *sine quo non*, who was there for every page.

ABOUT THE AUTHOR

Madeline Miller was born in Boston and grew up in New York City and Philadelphia. She attended Brown University, where she earned her BA and MA in classics. For the last fifteen years she has been teaching and tutoring Latin, Greek, and Shakespeare. *The Song of Achilles*, her first novel, was awarded the 2012 Orange Prize for Fiction and was a *New York Times* bestseller. It has been translated into twenty-five languages. Miller's essays have appeared in a number of publications, including *The Guardian*, the *Wall Street Journal*, *Lapham's Quarterly*, and NPR.org. She currently lives near Philadelphia, Pennsylvania.